A Course in Butterflies

A Novel

Christine Mary McGinley

Gleam of Light Press
U.S.A.

A Course in Butterflies
A Novel

By Christine Mary McGinley

Copyright © 2018 by Christine Mary McGinley

Book design by Joanne Morgan

All rights reserved. No part of this book may be reproduced or transmitted in any form or by any means, electronic or mechanical, including photocopying, recording, or by any information storage and retrieval system, without permission in writing from the publisher.

ISBN: 978-0-9972204-2-1

Library of Congress Control Number: 2017915619

Published by:
Gleam of Light Press LLC
P.O. Box 42
Lakeland, Michigan 48143 U.S.A.

www.GleamofLightPress.com
info@gleamoflightpress.com

Printed in the United States of America

GLEAM
of
LIGHT

This is a work of fiction.

Though the story takes place at a popular public university, the setting could be any American institution of higher learning during the academic year concurrent with the turn of the millennium, September 1999 to September 2000.

Any likeness to real-life persons, programs or institutions, except where the reader finds them heroic, should be considered purely coincidental.

A Course in Butterflies

"So, why study butterflies?"

Katherine Ayers was comfortably perched on the edge of the desk in front of the class, a tall willowy woman with delicate features and full chestnut hair. Her plain silk blouse and long skirt covered her from her throat to her ankles, though everything about her whispered of an allure which understatement can only underscore. This was not the physics professor anyone in her presence had expected. Yet the bold current that radiated from her eyes told her observers to listen carefully. The room was filled with an atmospheric silence like the moment after a deafening sound. Everyone knew what everyone else was thinking. Who was this woman? And what was this course in butterflies?

"What is there of value in understanding butterflies?"

She looked around the room at its new inhabitants and waited for a response.

It was a long still moment before one reluctant hand went up.

"To understand another living species?"

The student was quickly rewarded as her words resounded in the teacher's voice. "To understand another living species." Katherine continued her penetrating scan of the eyes in the room. "And what might be of value to us in understanding another living species?"

The young woman tried again. "To learn something about ourselves?"

Her words were again in even measure delivered back to the class. Katherine asked the student her name. "Well, very interesting," she said as she looked around the room. "Cynthia has given us some direction, don't you think?"

Cynthia tried to conceal her pleasure at the professor's recognition. "So," Katherine continued, "if we're going to study butterflies and learn about another living species and seize the opportunity to learn something about ourselves, how do we want to go about this? How does one learn about butterflies?"

A young man's hand went up. "We would study their biology," he said, "their metamorphosis from the caterpillar to the butterfly."

The students all waited as they watched the teacher's face. It was clear she was waiting for more response.

"We would study their behaviors and how they interact," another student called out.

"We would learn to appreciate their beauty," ventured another.

"Perhaps all of these things and more, yes?" Katherine said. "If we are going to really learn about butterflies?" She continued perusing their faces. "Let's look for a moment at the idea of studying the biology of butterflies." She looked at the student from whom the idea had come. "Biology is a good fundamental discipline. Certainly a good place to begin in the study of a living creature. What other disciplines might we employ? If we have as our goal a comprehensive understanding of butterflies?"

"Chemistry," came from another voice in the room. "Its chemical interactions with other butterflies and with the things it eats and with other things in the environment."

The teacher smiled.

"Physics," came from another student who sensed the momentum.

"Physics," Katherine responded. "We have flapping little wings, don't we — kinetic energy or energy of motion. What about mathematics?"

Katherine looked around at the students' perplexed faces.

"Might a creature that exhibits a physical response to light be of interest to someone measuring the speed of light as it strikes a moving object?" She paused. "Is the butterfly mathematizing as it darts and maneuvers its way into clusters of camouflage with the precise timing to avoid the predator's attack? Or is that psychology? Do butterflies think? How do we know?" She watched the students as they processed her questions. "How about philosophy? Is there philosophy involved in our relationship to butterflies? Do butterflies have a philosophy of life? Is philosophy inherent in all of life?"

The students watched her.

"Let's go back to biology again. Let's imagine that rather than a course in butterflies this was a biology class. What would be the difference in the way we would approach butterflies?" She looked again at the student who was now associated with biology and asked him his name.

"We wouldn't talk about them much probably," Jason answered. "And we'd only talk about them in terms of biology."

Katherine quickly responded. "We would not discuss them in terms of aesthetics, would we? — these beautiful winged creatures. And if we studied them in an aesthetics class, would we learn about their biology?"

Several students responded "no."

"And in an aesthetics or a biology class would we do an in-depth study of their social systems? Or their adaptive and co-evolutionary behaviors?"

A few more lent their voices to the response.

"Would we assess the butterfly's value? Or perhaps contemplate what the butterfly values? How about its ancient archetypal significance?"

The students were shaking their heads.

"So." She continued examining their faces. "If we study butterflies from the perspective of a particular discipline, what are we missing?"

It was only a moment before Cynthia responded, "Everything."

"Everything," Katherine echoed. "Cynthia thinks we would be missing everything. Well, from a biologist's perspective we might ask why in the world we would want to know everything about butterflies. The biologist is interested in understanding biology, right? The chemist and the physicist and the mathematician — they're not interested in butterflies either, are they? — except as they might provide some insight for their study of, say, pheromones, or Fibonacci, or aerodynamics. And is an understanding of these things a prerequisite to an understanding of butterflies?"

The students watched her.

"What in the world is the value of a thorough knowledge of butterflies?" she asked. She glanced at a flickering overhead light. "Let's imagine for a moment that we were all to leave here at the end of this course knowing everything there is to know about butterflies. Imagine first that it is possible and then that we have achieved it. What would be the value of this for each of us?" She looked at a young man in the front row and asked his name. "Isaiah, how would this make you feel?"

"If I knew everything about butterflies?"

"Everything there is to know."

"I guess it would be nice to know everything there is to know about something. To be an expert on something."

Katherine was up off the desk. "Ah, Isaiah would like to be an 'expert.' Anyone else want to be an expert?" She quickly shifted. "Do we have any experts in the room?"

The students looked around at one another. There were a few smirks. They were beginning to sense their togetherness in the room.

"On any subject," Katherine added. She was looking around as though she expected to find at least one respondent.

"Jack's an expert golfer," a student called out as he gestured toward the fellow sitting next to him, obviously a friend of his.

"Jack, are you an expert at golf?" Katherine asked.

Jack was ambivalent about being put on the spot. "No, I just play it a lot," he said sheepishly.

"He's state champion!" his friend declared.

"Ah. Then he has achieved a high level of excellence, yes? Is this the same as being an expert? Jack, do you know everything there is to know about golf?"

"Wish I did," Jack said bluntly. The students around him giggled.

"Okay, I think what we've touched upon here is the difference between having comprehensive knowledge of a subject and excelling at something one does. Jack is very accomplished at golf. He's worked hard to excel at the sport. He will probably always wish to be a better golfer." She elicited an affirmative nod from Jack. "Even after he's overtaken the world champion he'll still be pushing himself, right?"

Jack was now relishing the attention.

"Jack will probably never feel that he knows everything there is to know about golf. But he doesn't aspire to be an expert, does he? He aspires to be the best."

A light went on in a few facial expressions.

"So, who in the room is an expert?" she asked again.

Heads turned to see if anyone would respond and then Isaiah answered for the class. "You're the only one," he said to Katherine. "Ah, but I don't play golf at all," she said. She smiled in response to the students' laughter. Then she continued thoughtfully, "Perhaps because I am teaching a course in butterflies you thought me an expert on the subject." Her eyes indicated her statement was a question.

"Professor Ayers?" asked a young woman with her hand up. "I thought you were an expert in physics."

Katherine responded with gentle precision. "I am trained as a physicist," she said. "But this is a course in butterflies." She observed the students' faces. "Pretty strange, huh?" She waited another moment. "And if I told you I am an expert on butterflies, would you believe me?"

Some students responded quickly with a "yes." Others were not sure what to say. They could see that her message was not yet clear. "If I told you that I know everything there is to know about butterflies, would you believe I was telling the truth?"

This time most of the students responded that they would.

"Then you think it is possible to know everything there is to know about butterflies." Her interrogative tone evoked another silence.

Then "No" was hurled in a decided tone from the back of the lecture hall.

"It's the voice in the back of the room!" Katherine said with obvious frivolity. "There is always a voice in the back of the room, have you noticed that? Every class has one. And it's always there, it never moves, all semester."

There was giggling and stirring as heads turned to see the young man in the last row of the lecture hall.

Katherine raised her voice slightly. "In spite of my teasing, I am very interested in your response. You say it is not possible, and why not?"

"Because it's not possible to know everything there is to know about anything," the young man replied.

"Really?" Katherine exclaimed, clearly stimulated by this remark. "Is there nothing about which we can know everything?" She searched the students' eyes as they groped for the right answer. "How about Mozart? Is it possible to know everything there is to know about Mozart?" She gave them a moment to think. "Or

French literature?" She measured another moment. "Or wild flowers of the Rocky Mountain region?" She reached across the desk and held up one large paper clip in front of the class. "How about paper clips? Is it possible to know everything there is to know about paper clips?"

The students remained fixed on her.

"Let's look at the word 'expert' for a moment. What is an 'expert'?" She signaled in response to a student's hand.

"Someone who is thoroughly educated on a particular subject," he said.

Another student responded to her gesture. "Someone who is known as an authority."

"A thoroughly educated authority on a particular subject," Katherine summarized. "And can someone give us an example?" She fired her next words into the air: "In the last twenty-four hours. Newspapers, radio, television, any media. What 'expert' have you heard quoted? On any subject," she added.

The students were silent for a moment and then a young woman's hand went up. "This morning on television there was an expert on vitamins."

"An expert on vitamins. And who identified this person as an expert?" Katherine asked.

"The morning show lady, uh . . . "

"And what did this expert say?" Katherine asked.

"He said it doesn't make any difference if vitamins are called 'natural,' that it's just a rip-off if you spend your money on natural vitamins, that the generic brands in drug stores are all just as good."

"And after this expert gave his opinion, did the morning show present another expert with a different point of view?" Katherine asked.

The student looked at her blankly.

"Say, someone who believes the human body is ideally kept in the habit of deriving the vitamins and minerals it needs from natural food sources? — that it is the processing of the nutrients from foods that is essential to wellbeing?" She saw minds at work in the eyes in front of her.

Isaiah spoke up. "So are you saying there are no experts?"

"I'm saying that when we hear the word 'expert' we are well served to remember that it is simply a word. One that is used with great frequency and often by people who benefit from the identification of their source as an expert source. In almost any case of an expert opinion we may find a completely contradictory opinion from someone who is also declared to be an expert. If we're relying on the accuracy of the information we need to access as many opinions as possible and examine them closely."

"Is that true even in physics?" a student asked.

"It is true especially in physics," Katherine responded. "In physics, theories are put forward for the very purpose of rigorous testing and proving by other scientists."

"Professor Ayers?"

Katherine looked at the young woman with her hand up. She was the most easily identifiable freshman in the room.

"Professor Ayers, you are an astrophysicist, aren't you?" The young woman's demeanor was as innocent and forthright as her question. She was trying to make the connection between astrophysics and butterflies.

"I am indeed," Katherine replied. "More specifically, I am a cosmologist, which means I study the universe as a whole — its origin and structure, the laws that govern it, and its continuing evolution." She looked around at the students' faces. "And for those of you who are wondering if I got lost on my way to the physics department, let me assure you I am both where I belong and precisely where I wish to be." Her smile became slightly mischievous. "As I'm sure is true for each of you, right? I know you were all intrigued by this class not because it looked like an easy few credits but because you felt it was sure to be stimulating and enriching." Her smile persisted as she continued to survey their faces. "So, for now, putting aside the question of whether or not such a thing exists, there appears to be no one in the room who identifies with the term 'expert.' " She glanced at the young man in the back row of the lecture hall. "And whether it is possible or not," she said, "*I* do not know everything there is to know about anything. Like most people, I know a little about some things, and very little about other things, and there are many things about which I know nothing at all."

"I read your book," announced the young man in the back of the room. "You know a lot about a lot of things."

"*Well.*" Katherine's enthusiasm smacked of amusement. "In every class there is one voice in the back of the room and one person who has read my book." The students laughed. "Today they are one and the same." Another hand was flailing as its owner proclaimed that she too had read *The Relevance of Nature*. Katherine remained focused on the student in the back row. "I think it's time for us to know your name, sir voice."

"Sir Robert Pritchett" was the response from the rear of the room. Everyone was enjoying this interplay.

"Well, thank you, Sir Robert Pritchett, but the truth is I know just enough about butterflies to find them fascinating." She perused the group again. "And why do you suppose I would propose spending an entire semester getting to know everything we can possibly know about butterflies?" Her expression made it clear she was hopeful of a response.

"I think you want us to learn about something in a new way," said one of the students.

Then another spoke up. "I think you want us to *think* in new ways." Katherine continued to smile as she again posed her question. "And how do we want to go about this — learning about something in a new way? How do we want to *learn* about butterflies?" She became obvious about having some fun. "Shall we explore the Internet? Shall we talk to scientists? Shall we all go to Peru and sit on the banks of the Amazon and watch hundreds of species swirl around us? Should we all do the same thing? What do we want to do?"

After a moment a young woman spoke up. "I think we should all do different things," she said. The bodies around her turned in their seats. "We should all look at butterflies from a different angle, for different things, and then put it all together so we'll have the whole picture."

"But we'll have to decide in advance what angles we're each going to take," another student said. Several more students chimed in. There was a growing sense of community in the room.

"Well," Katherine rolled the word as she went to the desk and picked up a stack of papers. "I just happen to have something to get us started. Imagine that," she added with a grin as she handed the materials to two students for distribution.

Several students exchanged smirks. They still had no idea what this course was about but so far they were enjoying the ride. They accepted the handouts, however, with some trepidation. The real meat of course requirements was generally spelled out in just such documents — five pages of ten-point type with the staple neatly planted in the upper-left. To their surprise, the atmosphere remained buoyant.

"There are all kinds of fascinating things for us to learn about butterflies," Katherine declared. "For instance," she said, referring to the handouts the students now had in front of them. She was encouraging an open forum.

A young woman read aloud one of the statements on the pages in front of her. "The butterfly's range of vision is among the largest known of any animal," she said, her tone conveying her surprise.

"They see wavelengths well beyond those visible to the human eye." Cynthia spoke up as she read another. "The butterfly's development from a tiny egg to a fully formed winged creature is the most dramatic metamorphosis in nature. It involves the complete dissolution of one animal and the reconstitution of another."

Another student jumped in with one she found interesting. "Butterflies are sun worshipers! They flock in large numbers to the sunniest areas of tropical regions where their most popular activity is basking in the sun."

"Spring break!" a young man called out. Students around the room laughed.

Another student exclaimed in disbelief, "Butterflies have been known to fly across entire oceans?!"

After the moment it took for this image to penetrate there were a number of looks of astonishment among her colleagues.

Then another student read, "Butterflies are heavily studied by scientists involved in environmental research because of their extraordinary sensitivity to minute atmospheric fluctuations."

Another young man began to laugh with enjoyment as he read, "Butterflies have been known to become intoxicated from drinking fermented nectars, to exhibit wild erratic flight patterns, and to remain at the source of the fermented nectar for inordinate periods of time."

"Spring break!" was again heralded by one of the students, arousing the predictable eruption of laughter.

 The students continued reading aloud the interesting bits of information they found on the pages in front of them. It was clear that these were all brand new insights about a creature they had all encountered during their lives and about which they knew very little. Katherine sat quietly and observed the faces filled with the freshness of youth. She listened to the laughter that rippled through the room and took pleasure in the budding camaraderie.

"Now, on the top of your hand-out you will see a number that coincides with the number of one of those statements," she said. "That statement is now yours. Unless you decide to trade with someone – which is entirely up to you."

The students looked to identify their assignments.

"The idea, of course, is that each of you will be working with a different one," she explained. "You may approach the statement in whatever way you feel will best benefit our understanding of butterflies. And you have as much liberty as you wish in deciding what you will do."

The students were now carefully observing her.

"Our objective is to learn about butterflies," she said. "You may even wish to exercise some liberty in determining what that means — to learn about butterflies."

A number of smiling faces indicated a keen sense of pleasure and admiration. Other students were looking insecure. A few appeared completely baffled. She knew that at any moment there would be a question. And there it was, a hand going up as the student spoke.

"So, my statement is, 'The final fully formed state of the butterfly is called 'imago.' "

"Ah, you have a good one, don't you," Katherine said. She asked the young man his name. She could see he was looking for some direction. "And what are some of the ways Tim might approach 'imago'?" she said. "Anyone want to offer a suggestion?"

A young woman spoke up. "He could examine the word — what it means, and why it applies to the adult butterfly."

"He could examine the word 'imago,' " Katherine said, "its origin and meaning. What else?"

"He could talk about what constitutes a fully formed state, you know, like what it is about it that means it's fully formed," said another student.

Katherine raised her eyebrows as if to acknowledge a good idea.

"Tim, are these ideas helpful?"

"Yeah, I guess," Tim said.

"The important thing is to explore whatever has the greatest interest for you," Katherine said. "And in a way that interests you." A number of students were talking with one another; others had their hands in the air. Katherine acknowledged a young woman whose demeanor conveyed some urgency. She immediately blurted, "Yeah, my name is Melodee. Mine says that butterflies only live for two weeks. Is that true?!"

"I believe it reads, 'The average life span of the adult butterfly is approximately two weeks,' " Katherine said.

"Two weeks?" another student exclaimed. "They only live for two weeks?"

"Jeez, what's the point?" another student followed.

Melodee needed some clarification. "So it's my job to talk about why they live for such a short time?"

Katherine took a moment and savored the thought Melodee's question had evoked. "Or perhaps you want to look at what they achieve in the short time they are here?"

Melodee sat very still and thoughtfully studied Katherine's face.

In the next moment, "When is this due?" was cast into the atmosphere with the confidence of someone who knew he represented everyone in the room.

"Ah yes, when is it due?" Katherine said. "Let's get right down to it, eh?" She smiled at the student who had asked the question and then at the group. "What do you say we use these statements as a beginning point for discovering all of the interesting things there are to learn about butterflies?"

The students looked at her with blank expressions.

"We'll start with these simple statements and see where they take us. And throughout the course we'll share what we're learning with one another. That should make for a pretty rich experience, don't you think?"

The class was silent. Katherine looked at the young man who had asked the question. He was looking at her as though she had hurled a sharp instrument into the lecture hall. He did indeed represent everyone in the room. What did she mean? What were the course requirements? Exactly what would be acceptable for the next class? Katherine continued resolutely on the same course. "Our knowledge and understanding of things is a constantly evolving process, is it not?"

Some students appeared to be absorbing her meaning. Others were still looking at one another in bewilderment.

Katherine remained poised, her tone steadfast. "Let's just see how interesting we can make our next meeting together, shall we?"

As she glanced at the clock, a number of students started for their belongings.

"And one last thing before you leave," she said.

They stopped and looked at Katherine.

"While you're deciding what you will do," she said, "consider the butterfly's perspective."

The students looked at one another as they grabbed their things.

Two

"Beautiful day!"
"Isn't it great!"

Katherine often saw her colleague John Karner this time of day as they passed one another between the Randall Building and West Hall. Their smiles were knowing ones. They both preferred the outdoor route between the two buildings rather than the indoor walkway. September was the month that made sense out of Michigan for Katherine. It was days like this, she thought, that could make up for the dreariest winters.

Students scrambled across the Diag in all directions, the dazed searching freshmen, too green to conceal the uneasiness in which the others basked with pretentious glee. Styles changed over the years, but what Katherine saw in that parade of eyes along the sidewalks was always the same – the fragile, fleeting dreams of youth. To be rich, to make some mark on their father's turf, to get this girl, to be accepted by that sorority – they all had their eye on a prize. At the same time, there was one self-assurance that was shared by all. The flurry of bodies around them could not dampen their sense of themselves as members of a select group – They were at *Michigan*.

Katherine observed the institution around her with almost as much interest as she studied the ever-expanding cosmos. It was a multifarious living system, filled with the dynamics of generations of self-organization. All component parts functioned in accordance with fundamental laws, all designed to support the system as a whole. As an organism the university provides the attentive observer with a complete microcosm of both humanity and society. For Katherine, its most striking reflection of the human condition was its proclivity for perceiving itself as the center of the universe.

New President Meets with Students was spread in bold letters across the stack of newspapers at the entrance to Randall Hall. President Delcourt was now the man on top of the center of the universe, the world reported by *The Michigan Daily*. The shift in energy that came with this new administration was being felt at every level and by every component part of the system. The new vibration was a positive one. Attitudes were hopeful. Commitments were being renewed. In some places, complacency was even rustling with adjustment.

In the physics department there was one thing that year after year was always the same — the vigor with which her new star students approached their work. This year's luminary, Brad Jenkins, was darting toward her the moment she entered the building.

"Professor Ayers!"

"We need to walk and talk, Bradley."

"Yes, I know. Karen told me you have a meeting." He eagerly kept pace with her as she walked up the stairs.

"What's the problem?" she said.

"I'm trying to reproduce your results for quantum fluctuations after the tunneling but I'm having some problems with the ultraviolet divergences."

"You need to revisit Nicholas Smuclovsky's book. I believe it's chapter two, the one on renormalization. Then come talk to me. I can see you tomorrow."

"Oh, good. Thanks, Professor Ayers," he called to her as she passed through the stairwell door.

She had barely put down her things when her friend and colleague, Charles Lewis appeared, his head and one shoulder inside her office.

"See you in a few minutes?"

"Yeah, I'm going to check my email real quick," she said. She was rolling her chair to the front of her computer.

"Me too," Charles said, with a rap of his hand on her office door. "Pick you up in a few."

She quickly scanned the long list of names and subjects displayed in her email in-box. The one from Karen Rodzik, the department secretary, with the subject "Physics Department Executive Committee Meeting Agenda" referenced the meeting she was about to attend. Harold Thurman, the department head, was true to form in delivering the agenda with as little advance notice as possible without being thoroughly obvious. As the printer hummed she looked out her office window and surveyed her predicament. Her enthusiasm for this beautiful day and for a new era at Michigan was about to undergo a – "root canal," she uttered under her breath as she pulled the agenda from the printer. Quickly, she pulled up her friend Mary Claire's message, the subject of which read, "READ THIS ONE NOW!" Katherine cherished Mary Claire's insatiably playful spirit. Her timing was also perfect. The message read simply, "Give 'em hell, Girl!" She closed her email and met Charles in the hallway. They walked together to the third floor conference room.

Charles Lewis was a tall distinguished-looking Black man whom Katherine considered both thoroughly brilliant and among the most decent human beings she had ever known. Their mutual respect and admiration had grown over the years into an unshakable allegiance, one that made their participation in departmental politics far more tolerable for each of them. It was a comradeship that reached beyond their shared experience as minorities in physics. They were both members of another minority, one that was just beginning to emerge in the physics community. Though they each had just a glimmer of what this emergence was all about, the ideas that drove it were as much a part of them as their gender or color.

"*Butterflies 101!*" The words were unmistakable. They had come from inside the conference room. The voice was that of their colleague, Lloyd Spector, whose sarcastic aspersion had been accompanied by another unmistakable sound — the sound of his eyes rolling in belligerent contempt. Charles looked at Katherine. She smiled as if to say she was not surprised. She had known that once her butterfly course had become a reality there would be repercussions within the department. She had also known that Lloyd Spector would be the first to express his displeasure. Charles opened the half-open door and followed her into the room. There stood Lloyd Spector with Harold Thurman and two other members of the executive committee. There was an awkward silence, then some superficial small talk about candidates for the deanship. Then they all took their usual chairs around the conference table.

There were seven on the committee, all in attendance. Katherine was pleased to see Bob Gurzick arrive. Bob's presence was always comforting to her. His Nobel laureate aura extended to his humanness in a way that made him uniquely and universally respected in the department. He could always be looked to for his dispassionate voice of reason, which she knew was likely to be needed on this particular day. Phil Robertson, across the table, was generally uninterested in departmental affairs, which made him an almost always silent member of the group. The other three senior faculty, Harold Thurman, Lloyd Spector, and Nick Tullman were deeply vested in the department and rarely without opinions about matters affecting it. They had been comrades at Michigan since the beginning of time and all shared in the visible field of

Godliness that had been the exclusive domain of physicists since the Newtonian era.

Everyone in the room was a tenured professor, widely published, with a stellar record of achievement in their respective field. Together they represented elementary particle physics, condensed matter theory, condensed matter experiment, nuclear physics, biophysics, and astrophysics.

Katherine was regarded in the astrophysical community as a leading cosmologist. She had been a feather in the University of Michigan's cap since the early eighties when it wooed the young Princeton star back to her home state and became one of the first institutions to grant tenure to a female physicist. She was now grappling with a theory in quantum cosmology to which she devoted every available hour. She was widely pursued by graduate students as a teacher and mentor, and had recently been the recipient of the College of Literature, Science, and the Arts Faculty of the Year Award, largely for her elementary physics courses at the undergraduate level. Two years earlier, Katherine had published *The Relevance of Nature*, the book she had written over the previous ten years. It had become a mainstream bestseller and continued to receive attention. Four of the old guard around the table were colleagues from whom she had never heard a syllable spoken about her book. A female in physics becomes gifted at subtext. She knew that her standing in the department, her popularity, and even the success of her book had been tolerated. Her latest offense was a high crime. A respected member of the physics faculty was teaching a course in butterflies.

Throughout the first half of the meeting the subtext remained buried in body language and in the almost audible deflections of eye contact. Dialogue was casual and cordial. They were all in agreement on the tenure decision they had been working on for months. Their assessment had been rigorous and was conclusive

— tenure would be granted. Charles gave a report on the new program the Institute for the Study of Complexity was launching. Most of the group stared at the table as he cited the departments with which he was now working – Biology, Computer Science, Sociology, Economics, Population Studies — the impressive list went on. Katherine was deliberately quiet. Everyone knew she had enthusiastically endorsed Institute status for the program Charles had founded for an interdisciplinary study of complex systems. The Institute was now housed in the department under his leadership. Though the program had been given perfunctory approval, the majority in the room had privately opposed it. Bob Gurzick's unanticipated remark far exceeded anything she would have wished to say. "I think it's great, Charles. I have no doubt we'll see complexity theory advance in the coming years beyond all our expectations." His comment provoked another fluctuation in the energy in the room.

The tension grew palpable as the group proceeded down the list of agenda items toward the one they all knew was an explosion waiting to happen — "The LS&A Initiative for Undergraduate Education" — the program under which Katherine's butterfly class had been launched. When they arrived at the item on the agenda she did not hesitate.

"Yes, as you know the Initiative that was outlined by the Dean . . ."

"You mean *Gustafson*," Lloyd Spector interrupted, not disguising his disdain.

"Yes, Lloyd," Katherine said, "Dean Gustafson is gone but the Initiative is still very much alive."

Wendy Gustafson, the former Dean of the College of Literature, Science, and the Arts, popularly known as "LS&A," to which the physics department belonged, had recently left the university to be president of a progressive private college. For years it had been openly discussed around campus that she and the previous U-M administration had not seen eye to eye. Given the general attitude toward the previous president, only a small minority of faculty had been unsympathetic to her plight. That minority was well represented in the room.

"Well, like everything else she started," Lloyd spurned, "this 'initiative,' as she called it, is hanging in abeyance now, isn't it?"

Nick Tullman chimed in with measured exasperation. "At the rate of dean searches around here, it could be years."

Open criticism of interminable search processes was a U-M epidemic. Over the past few years efforts to fill a number of vacant deanships had dragged on for endless months placing decision-making on hold in countless areas and with far-reaching effects. Faculty proposals went to department chairs, who were held up on decisions awaiting authorization from interim deans, who were reluctant to move on issues without approval from the provost. The provost was decidedly interim himself and he reported to a brand new president. People at every level were embroiled in the time-consuming conundrum of prioritizing. The deanship of LS&A was one of the positions that for months had been in what had come to be known at Michigan as "the perpetual state of interim."

"Actually, the Undergraduate Initiative is moving ahead and is fully expected to be championed by the new dean," Charles said, "whenever he or she comes aboard."

"Our new president has declared it a priority," Bob Gurzick followed.

Lloyd erupted, "It's now a *priority* to teach *butterflies* instead of quantum mechanics?!"

Katherine looked across the table at Lloyd. "Lloyd, may we please look at what the Initiative is about?" Her hand was placed on the document in front of her, a copy of which had been placed in front of each person in the room. "Surely you won't reject the program before you've . . ."

"What I r*eject*, Katherine, is the idea of a physics professor who's been awarded tenure by the same painstaking process we've just concluded here today spending her time teaching undergraduates how to *think*. If they do not have the skills, they don't belong here. *We're* here to train the smartest ones available and to turn out *physicists*. We're here to do research. Not to be nursemaids to undergraduates. That's something any junior faculty member can do. I resent your involvement in it and I think it's a miserable reflection on the department."

Katherine sat silently for a moment while she worked hard at concealing the effort it took to appear composed. "Lloyd, I'm sorry you find my involvement objectionable," she said. "I can't tell you how strongly I believe that these types of courses can make an enormous difference — for all students," she emphasized. "They can help give them clarity about the paths they choose. They can enrich their commitment to education, their experience of education. And those we do turn out as physicists may actually be better physicists given this kind of opportunity."

"To learn about butterflies?!" Lloyd thundered. "Did Harvard and Princeton teach you about butterflies?!"

"Harvard and Princeton are not the same places they were then, Lloyd. Harvard and Princeton are learning too. The same ideas are emerging everywhere. Because they make sense. We're responding to changing needs. In many places programs like these are in embryonic conceptual stages. Ours is in action."

"It's an *experiment*," Lloyd snapped. "In her own words, it's an *experiment*."

She looked at him pointedly. "It is as experimental as anything has ever been before being proven valid, Lloyd."

He did not appreciate her instruction in the fundamentals of science.

"The butterfly course I am teaching is my experiment. One I

believe to have merit."

"Well, with all due respect, Katherine, I seriously question the merit of your parading this experiment in the academic community. This exploration in — what did Gustafson call it? — *authentic learning?*" He blurted the initial discharge of an exasperated laugh designed to sound dismissive. "And what is it that she thinks has been going on here all these years?"

Nick Tullman spoke up with a little less rancor. "Well, whatever she had in mind, our esteemed dean has departed. An event it would appear the institution has survived."

The group was accustomed to Nick's languorous sardonic manner, the bite of which he generally softened a bit when he addressed Katherine.

"This LS&A Initiative," he asked, "this was actually faculty driven, wasn't it?"

"It involves faculty from throughout LS&A," Katherine said. "Fine people — in English Literature, Philosophy, Psychology, History — I was proud to be asked to participate. There are three of us offering elective courses in this initial phase. Over time, faculty from a number of disciplines will design other courses. We'll rotate responsibility if that makes the most sense. The idea is to have each student take one Initiative class during their undergraduate . . ."

"But you did not join in this endeavor as a representative of the physics department," Lloyd challenged.

"Not any more or less than the other faculty involved are associated with their departments," Katherine said. "It's not about departments, Lloyd. It's simply about learning. And each of us is approaching it in our own way. Mary Claire Henley from English Literature, for instance, is using literature as a tool but in a very different way than it is normally presented. My class happens to be about butterflies. The other . . ."

"My point is that you are *not* associated with this department in this endeavor," Lloyd stormed, "Not in teaching students about butterflies!"

"Lloyd . . ." Katherine's heart was pounding. She sat quietly for another moment and then continued as calmly as she could. "I can only assert again that I believe it has great value and ask you to read the proposal. I would also assure you that the course I am teaching was proposed and approved in accordance with the department's curriculum committee guidelines."

"I believe Lloyd's point is well taken, Katherine," Harold asserted in his most official department-head voice. "Your involvement with this program and this use of your time presents some curricular concerns which are unprecedented, and I believe the fact that the department is involved by association is a valid issue and should have been addressed by this committee."

"My involvement was approved by this committee," Katherine said.

All except Charles were caught off-guard by her statement. Charles had already reached for the Minutes book and was examining its contents. "April seventeenth of last year," he said as he read from the minutes. "Carolyn Lloyd, Curriculum Committee Chair, presented a report on the LS&A Initiative for Undergraduate Education, including a proposal and course outline for Professor Ayers' course to be presented under the banner of the Initiative." Charles continued casually. "As I recall, that particular report did not elicit much attention. The record shows no discussion. There are a number of other things here that I expect we found more pressing," he said with the slightest emphasis. "In any event, Katherine is right. It was approved." He looked around at the others. "Unanimously," he added, punctuating the impasse.

In another moment Harold Thurman spoke up in a manner befitting his usual style. Harold generally preferred to move away from contentious issues at meetings, especially when they could be handled at a later time in a less forthright manner. "We do have a couple more items that really should be addressed today," he said. And then he broached the next subject on the printed agenda — "Meeting with the President."

"As you know, our new president is meeting with each of the departments. And as he is favorably disposed to informal gatherings, he has invited me to bring a couple of faculty members to the President's House for dinner."

The President's residence was another topic of widespread intrigue at Michigan. The new president Jonathan Delcourt and his wife had revived the tradition of keeping residence in the restored 1840 President's House that for years had been used only for special functions. This decision had generated another weather report on faculty attitude toward the new administration. The overwhelming majority found only positive implications in the chief executive's deliberate presence at the center of campus. The minority view was once again well represented in the room.

"I guess it's a regular hub of activity now," Nick Tullman said in a patronizing tone. "Lots of wining and dining donors."

Phil Robertson was also amused. Until now he had been effectively absent, except during the brief bout of turbulence which had moved him to momentarily peer out from behind his enormous eyebrows.

"The dinner would be on a weekday evening," Harold continued. "As for the challenge of deciding who should participate," he hesitated, "I was thinking just now that perhaps it would be appropriate, since we'll be talking about the department, to bring two of our most vocal representatives, Katherine and Lloyd."

This evoked just enough laughter to break some of the tension in the room. Yet Katherine noticed an awkwardness in Harold that exceeded his usual discomfort with humor. She also observed that Lloyd was not at all surprised by Harold's startling invitation. It was of course predictable that Harold would want Lloyd to join him for such an event. There was deep personal history between them. But why her? And why this bold leap of extending such an invitation to specific faculty members? It was noticeably out of character for Harold to be so openly undemocratic.

Bob Gurzick exerted his usual calming influence. "I think Katherine and Lloyd are excellent representatives of the department," he said. The others concurred.

"Well then, Katherine and Lloyd," Harold said, "if you're agreeable, Karen will be speaking with you about dates." He glanced at the tape recorder as if to remind his secretary. "Katherine, I know you're out Mondays and Fridays this term and have a lot of travel planned, so we'll steer for a mid-week date to preserve your research time." He hesitated again. "And our last item, provided we have no other business . . ." Once again there was unease in his demeanor. "I've been giving considerable thought to the framework that is in place for committee roles and responsibilities and I think the department would benefit from some reassessment and perhaps some revamping. I just want to let you know that I'll be consulting each of you and the chairs of the existing committees as we consider some possible restructuring."

Harold was of course referring to the curriculum committee that had endorsed Katherine's involvement in the Initiative for Undergraduate Education. It was also clear that the idea of "revamping" roles was not one Lloyd was hearing for the first time. Nick Tullman was also looking remarkably settled. Bob Gurzick was puzzled. "You're referring to the committees that report to this one?" he asked.

"Yes, we'll be looking at all of them," Harold said.

There was an elephant in the room again and it was not going to be acknowledged.

The superficial adjournment dialogue passed by Katherine like a silent movie. After exchanging a knowing glance with Charles in the hallway she passed through the double doors and into the stairwell on her way to her next class. The moment she was alone in the stairwell she took hold of the handrail and physically shook off the stranglehold Lloyd had had on her insides. She could not have disguised for another moment the feelings he had evoked in her. As she walked down the steps she felt herself spiraling downward inside herself. What were these inner alarms that stayed with us for lifetimes, she thought. Was it really her father that still plagued her after all these years?

Later that afternoon Katherine stopped by the physics department office to give Karen Rodzik, the department secretary, the copies of the Initiative document she had collected from around the table that morning. "In the event anyone should be interested in seeing it," she said with a slight roll of her eyes.
Katherine and Karen Rodzik shared a special affection for one another. When Karen looked up at her from her desk her face was aglow with the exuberance of a teenager with a juicy secret.
"*So*, you're going to be having dinner with Delcourt," she said in an enamored whisper.
Katherine had no way of knowing that Karen had this information before Harold had returned to his office that day, before she had listened to the proceedings of that morning's meeting.
"How exciting that he asked you," she said.
Katherine responded with a half-hearted smile, still a bit befuddled by Harold's invitation.
Karen was clearly titillated. "And you're the only one."
"No, there are three of us going," Katherine said.
Karen was emphatic. "I mean you're the only one he *asked* for."
"What do you mean?" Katherine asked her.
"The *president*. You're the only one he specifically asked for."
"What are you talking about?"

Karen's face was as insistent as her tone. "Delcourt asked Harold specifically to bring you," she said. "He wants to meet you!"

Katherine was incapable of concealing her stunned expression.

"You didn't know?" Karen asked. And then she peered at Katherine as she whispered excitedly, "Delcourt's secretary told me he *loved* your book."

Katherine's gaze rolled toward the window as she recalled the strangeness in Harold's demeanor at the meeting.

Karen's enthusiasm persisted. "Of course Delcourt would want you there. Are you surprised?"

Katherine looked at her. "Not as surprised as I was that Harold would," she said.

"Warrior Two."

The yoga teacher's voice was distant and soothing. Katherine loved this pose. It evoked a sense of fearlessness in the depth of her being.

"Now let's take the pose deeper. Strong legs. Really strong. Now extend both arms as far as you can . . . Now soft gaze over the forward hand . . . Fix your sight on a point in front of you . . . And *breathe*."

Katherine looked out over her fingertips into the softly lit Ann Arbor night. She inhaled the candle-lit gymnasium air and imagined her elongated arms stretching all the way from Earth to Vega. Consciously, deeply, she breathed again.

"Now twirl your hands down to the floor and step back to plank. Now slowly descend to the floor. Up into Cobra. Really stretch . . ."

Katherine flashed on Lloyd's face at the meeting and on the feelings he had stirred in her.

"That's right, breathe . . . Tilt your head all the way back . . . Eyes to the sky. That's right . . . Beautiful . . . And now slowly descend . . . relax your entire body. And with your next exhale, completely let go of all your thoughts . . . Clear your mind completely."

Three

Mary Claire's "September Soup Supper" was now a U-M tradition. Among her circle of faculty friends it was the one social event for which the most rigorous schedules yielded. Good friends, great food and Mary Claire's unique hospitality were an unbeatable combination. And no matter how much the gathering grew over the years her intimate Burns Park home accommodated it perfectly.

Everyone knew the program. Mary Claire was generally camped out in the kitchen. On the stove were four enormous vats of soup, each a different one, and all different from ones she had prepared in previous years. "Or at least as far back as anyone can remember," she would say. On the counter were the slightly worn peony-patterned pottery bowls that had caught her eye years earlier at the Ann Arbor Art Fair. Everyone would claim a bowl and make the rounds into the kitchen several times during the evening, sampling each of the soups. This year's offerings were: corn chowder with new potatoes, peppers and basil, hot and sour shiitake chicken, white bean with smoked turkey and rosemary oil, and winter squash with sage. The dining room table was covered with fresh warm breads, homemade lavash and cheese sticks, an array of delectable desserts, hot spiced cider, and Michigan wines. This arrangement kept the group moving in and out of the kitchen and around the dining room. By the end of the evening there were camps of conversation all over the house.

Katherine, Charles and his wife Debra, and Larry Lowenstein were the first to arrive and were quite content to remain in the kitchen surrounded by the warmth and aroma of Mary Claire's savory soups. This was also the perfect vantage for meeting all the other guests as they circulated through and invariably lingered for conversation.

"Mary Claire, is it true?" Debra laughed affectionately at her enterprising friend. "Zingerman's actually bakes the breads fresh for you?"

"Hey, Zingerman's never misses a beat," Mary Claire said.

"Wow, this is delicious," Charles remarked.

"That's the sage one, isn't it," Debra said to her husband. "I knew you would go for the one with sage."

Charles and Debra Lewis were among Michigan's faculty couples, Charles in physics and Debra in psychology. They joked among their friends that finding one another's fields completely inaccessible was key to their compatibility. Debra in fact maintained that psychoanalysis would be a lifetime proposition for a physicist because it would be a lifetime before the analyst understood a word the physicist was saying. In truth, they each had a remarkable grasp of the other's discipline and their sense of humor was just one of their marriage's obvious attributes. In recent years they were both visibly enthralled with parenthood which they had begun much later in life than expected. Charles had confided to Katherine that he was sure the timing had made a big difference both in what they were investing in the process and in how much they were enjoying it. Katherine and Mary Claire took great pleasure in watching the two of them whenever they spoke of the four-year old around whom their lives now revolved.

"Debra, I'm overdue for an Avery story," Katherine said. "Charles hasn't told me one in days."

"Oh, wow, an Avery story. We're well stocked with those, aren't we." She and Charles exchanged intimate grins.

"The darkness," Charles said to her softly.

"Oh, yeah," Debra giggled, "the other day he said to me . . ." She mimicked her precocious son. " 'Mom . . . What is darkness?' He says, 'I *know* how it comes and everything, but what *is* it?' "

"Now there's a question for dad if I ever heard one," Mary Claire asserted.

"That's just it. Charles wasn't there, right? So what am I going to say to a child who, when I say it's an absence of light is gonna say, 'What's absence, Mom?' and then, 'Why is it not there, Mom?' and then, 'Where does it go, Mom?' "

Charles joined in, "With Avery, you see, you have to give him something he can really chew on for a while. You tell him it's a region of four dimensional space-time devoid of localizable mass energy quanta."

"*Charles,*" Katherine pounced. "This poor child."

"Well, it's true," Charles laughed. "If you tell him it's an absence of light you're gonna be there for hours."

"Maybe days!" Debra followed. "This way he just sits there and stares off into the distance for a while with those eyes of his." Her face took on a vacant, wide-eyed expression.

"Those killer eyes," Mary Claire said, with obvious affection for Avery.

"Listen, I sympathize with the little guy," Larry Lowenstein jumped in. "I'm the same way with those dissertations you people dream up over there." Larry was referring to his many committee duties for physics department dissertations.

Katherine grinned at him as though he were being his usual entertaining self.

"I'm serious," he said. "They just keep putting me on those panels insisting they need someone from outside the department — that it's 'required.' So I sit through entire theses not understanding a single word."

"*Come on*," Charles groaned.

"It's true!" Larry protested. "From start to finish. They may as well be speaking Swahili."

Larry Lowenstein was a thirty-five year veteran of the philosophy department who maintained the demeanor of a Sixties refugee. Long hair, rumpled sweaters and worn jeans were not uncommon on campus. But Larry was also famous for the grungy tie-dye covered sofa that had been a permanent fixture in his office since the Johnson administration and the ancient embattled Volkswagen van he had driven for almost as long to which he fondly referred as "the beast." His lack of concern for cosmetics extended to whatever he had to say, whatever the company. He was known for his candor, his scruffiness, and his unparalleled expertise on the philosophy of space-time.

"I guess it's a good thing I got out, huh?"

Katherine looked at him inquisitively.

"Spent most of my undergrad at Cornell just bent on theoretical physics," he said.

"Really," she exclaimed. "And what changed your mind?"

"Didn't have the smarts" was Larry's matter of fact retort.

"*Right*, Larry," Charles wrangled.

"I'm serious! It's a whole different kind of smarts you people have, that complex, abstract strain of reasoning, especially at the higher math level. It's a kind of smart that's just not available to regular smart people."

"This is from the guy who wrote the textbook on statistical mechanics," announced Steve Whelan, the chairman of the philosophy department who had just appeared in the kitchen.

"Hi, Steve," Katherine said.

Steve took Katherine's hand and they touched one another's cheeks with longtime affection. "Is that your lemon meringue out there?"

he asked her.

"That's why I'm a bit blurry-eyed," she said. "I started it at eleven o'clock last night."

"She couldn't show up without her lemon meringue! I'd throw her out! Besides, she never sleeps anyway." Mary Claire was engaged in her usual routine of flitting in and out of the kitchen, each time expelling some of her excess energy stirring her soups.

"Hmm. And what do we have this year, Madam?" Steve asked lustfully, his face poised over the pots on the stove.

Mary Claire's description of her soups always became more animated as the evening progressed.

"What's the word, people! Do they like the guy from Yale?" Pantelis Marinakis boomed, announcing his arrival in the kitchen.

"Oh no, Pantelis!" Mary Claire headed him off. "We're not talking about the dean search tonight. You can tell us everything we ever wanted to know about Classical Studies or your sex life but we're not talking about the dean search. It's not allowed. And you have to try all four soups or you can't leave."

"Well, I'll tell you about Classical Studies, but if you ask me about my sex life I'm going to lie."

"I'm surprised you didn't say they were one and the same," Larry chided.

"So what's this about abstract theoretical minds?" Steve asked, joining the group with his bowl of corn chowder.

"Think about it," Larry Lowenstein said. "In the entire world there are no more than a couple hundred people engaged in unified field work. I mean the people who are seriously capable of the processes at that level. That is one damn *minuscule* minority! Kind of makes you wonder why we need a final theory at all, doesn't it? I mean, hell, whatever they find, they're the only ones who'll understand it. They could all just get together and make something up, who'd know the difference?"

Katherine grinned at Steve as he casually shrugged his shoulders. "Hey, I can dress him up," he said. "This chowder is great, isn't it?"

"You're not actually denying your involvement in complex abstract reasoning," Charles persisted.

"Oh ho, my friend," Larry remonstrated, "it's a very different thing, breaking things down and examining them. I'm just a color commentator up in the stands."

"Color*ful* commentator, more like it," Steve interjected.

"It's the people who are constructing brilliant theories, and even better, communicating them — that's where it's at."

"That's why I appreciate Katherine's writing," Debra joined in. "I'm actually able to grasp some of what's going on out there in the universe. It's all just so fascinating."

"You do have a way with language that's . . ." Charles was meditating on Katherine's style.

"Pretty atypical physicist, isn't she?" Mary Claire concurred.

"What do you mean?" Charles feigned offense. "What's a 'typical' physicist?"

Mary Claire was wielding her long wooden spoon. "And I'm here to tell you, she was the same way with literature that she is with physics."

"That's right, you two were undergrads together, weren't you," Steve said.

"Poetry class," Mary Claire said. "That's how we met." Her eyes opened wide. "*Hated* her. It didn't matter who it was — Auden, Donne, Blake — this little frothy freshman would spout off these deeply textured interpretations. Saw things no one else saw. We all just sat there agape."

Katherine leaned into Steve as she whispered, "She's never been 'agape' in her life."

"They're really not as remote as you'd think," Charles said thoughtfully, "literature and physics." He was ladling another bowl of sage soup. "They're both about recognizing relationships."

"But literature demands more heart," Katherine said, her gaze aimed directly at Mary Claire.

The two women looked at one another as they often did acknowledging their deep connection.

"I had forgotten you two met at Harvard," Larry remarked.

"They've been friends all these years," Debra said proudly. "Mary Claire came to Michigan just a couple years after Katherine."

"That's really something that you both ended up here," Larry said.

"It was a pact," Mary Claire said. "And pacts steeped in Auden, Donne, and Blake aren't pacts to be broken."

"The stuff sisters are made of," Debra said as she raised her glass to her two friends.

"Hey, that's right," Charles said lightheartedly. "And you were both only-children too. Worked out great, didn't it."

The look that passed between Katherine and Mary Claire in this moment was not one that would be recognized by anyone else in the room, even their closest friends. Charles' comment about Katherine's being an only child had brought about a heart-rending moment between the two women. Mary Claire was the only person in Katherine's life who knew her real family history, a history that had been too private and too painful for her to share with anyone else. Even Mary Claire had not spoken of it since the day Katherine confided it to her years earlier. She knew it was a subject that had been long buried. Her adept recovery ensured its passing completely unnoticed.

"Yeah, they did back flips to snag her from Princeton," she groused. "All I had to do was starve myself for a month on top of the Fleming building."

Larry faked an exaggerated expression of revelation. "That was you on top of the administration building all that time?"

"Worked like a charm," Mary Claire said to the group's laughter.

Though Mary Claire Henley's endearing effervescence was always embellished a bit at her annual party, the feeling behind it was as authentic as her jet-black hair. By most accounts she was the heart of the English Literature department where her infectious love of literature was as irresistible to her students as her exuberance for life was to her friends. Yet Katherine knew like no one else did the depth and durability of the qualities that drew people to Mary Claire. She had been a faithful confidant and friend since their first freshman term at Harvard. They now shared the kind of bond known only to old friends — an intimate and abiding involvement in one another's histories, hopes and dreams. There were few things in either of their lives that they valued more than one another.

Mary Claire was the mastermind behind the Initiative for Undergraduate Education. Over the past number of years she had developed the program and enlisted the support of faculty throughout LS&A. Charles' wife Debra, from the psychology department, was among them.

"So, how do you think it's going?" she asked Mary Claire.

"The early reception is just what we'd hoped for," she said. "We'll see where it goes from here. Katherine's class is causing a real stir."

"She means in *our* department," Katherine said, rolling her eyes.

"Yes. We do have our share of stir, don't we," Charles said, smirking at his colleague. "Poor Lloyd," he said with both fondness and exasperation. "Some days I think he just wants to be put out of his misery."

"I wouldn't mind putting him out of his misery," Mary Claire grumbled.

"I heard about this," Debra said to Katherine in a supportive tone.

"I witnessed a pretty priceless exchange in the Help Room the other day," Charles said. "I wish I could have gotten it on tape."

Larry and Steve had launched into department talk and had moved over by the corner windows. Katherine, Debra and Mary Claire drew close to Charles as he quietly began his story.

"I had arrived a little early. Lloyd was about to go off duty and a student had just approached him as I was coming in so I heard the whole exchange. She was an undergrad in Theisen's seminar. A philosophy student," he added with emphasis.

"Oh no," Katherine said, shielding her eyes from the ensuing blow.

"I wish you could have seen this fervent young face looking at him," Charles went on. "She says, 'I really wanted to speak with Professor Theisen after class but I had to get to my ethics class.' And then she assiduously repeats, probably verbatim, what Theisen had said about superconductivity. She says, 'Professor Theisen says we don't really know how it works yet but we know that when we do understand it, it will definitely be an application of what we already know. He said that Electricity & Magnetism is a complete theory, that the book is closed.' " Charles looked at Katherine. "Does that sound like verbatim Theisen?"

"Oh my gosh, I can hear it coming."

"She says, 'I asked Professor Theisen — If we don't really know anything about it, then how can we know that our understanding will come from what we already know? And *he* said — because there is nothing else there.' And then she looks at Lloyd, perplexed, and she says, 'I don't understand what he means by that.' " Katherine winced as Charles continued, now fully impersonating his cantankerous colleague. "He says, 'Let me put it to you this way, *young lady*. We know all the words in the English language come from the English alphabet, don't we?' "

"You're right, this scene is priceless," Katherine said.

"So what did this brave young woman say to that?" Debra asked her husband.

Charles continued. "With this look of absolute purity, she says, 'But how do we know that something brand new won't be communicated in a language we don't even know yet?' "

"Well bully for her!" Mary Claire cheered.

Charles and Katherine looked at one another pointedly.

"Then Lloyd snaps at her, '*Young lady*, I am talking about the language of *science*. After you have learned it you can come back and ask me questions!'" Charles could not help his laughter. "He looked at me like he was going to blow a gasket. He says, 'Charles, I'm *expected*.' And he storms out of the room."

"The old coot," Mary Claire growled.

"And let me guess," Katherine said, "then you and the budding philosopher had a long talk and she left thinking that physics was a pretty fascinating subject after all."

"Mary Claire, these cheese sticks are to die for!" Sally Taylor declared, returning to the kitchen for another choice of soup. "I'd be broken hearted if you ever stopped making them."

"No, it's her flourless chocolate cake," Debra stressed. "That's the one thing that can never go."

"I'll keep my eye on it for you, Debra," Sally said, shifting her eyes greedily as she wandered back into the dining room.

"So, Katherine," Debra perked up, "I hear you're going to be having dinner with Delcourt. You'll have to tell us all about it."

Mary Claire's eyebrows danced. "She's also been invited to a mystery conference."

Katherine looked at Charles. This was her first opportunity to talk with him about the invitation she knew he too would find interesting. "Well, it's not a complete mystery in that I know it's hosted by the Finn Foundation. So, of course, I accepted."

"Absolutely," Charles remarked.

The Herbert B. Finn Foundation was one of the most prestigious foundations in the world. They had supported much of the groundbreaking science of the past couple of decades.

"It's actually been on my calendar for almost a year," Katherine said. "It was just confirmed today."

"Albert Finn phoned her personally," Mary Claire said emphatically.
"Now, is Albert the son?" Debra asked.
"The brother," Charles said. "He's been the chair since Herbert died."
"It's got to be something important, don't you think, Charles?" Mary Claire asked. Then she saw that the very same thought was being processed between Charles and Katherine. They were conferring in their familiar non-verbal collegial fashion.
Katherine shrugged a little. "All I know is they've invited a couple hundred scientists from around the world and from a broad spectrum of disciplines. And Albert Finn asked me to be there. So I'm going."
Charles quietly conjectured, "Science in the new millennium?"
"Whatever it is, it's sure completely out of the mainstream," Katherine said. "I haven't heard another word about it."
"The turn of the millennium," Charles said. "Gotta be."
"It's at Sundance, in Utah," Mary Claire said.
"End of the month," Katherine said, still looking at Charles. "And another four days at the end of the year."
"Ute country," Charles proclaimed. Native American culture was one of Charles' passions. "And another beautiful place you won't see," he added, referring to Katherine's demanding conference travel.
"How was Paris?" Debra asked Katherine.
"It was good. Exhausting. But it was a good conference."
"Good heavens, I couldn't do it," Debra said. "The jet lag alone takes up two days for me."
"I actually managed a quick visit to the Musée d'Orsay," Katherine said. "I couldn't be in Paris without just a little bit of being in Paris."
"And you've got Aspen coming up too, haven't you?" Charles said.
"Unified Symmetry," Katherine said, "the following weekend."

Debra looked at Katherine. "Just how do you keep this up, woman?"

"What are *you* talking about? I don't keep up with Avery!"

"Nobody keeps up with Avery," Debra laughed.

"Anytime you want to give him up, Debra," Mary Claire appealed to her friend, "you know where to bring him."

"I sure know where he'd eat well, Mary Claire."

Charles was still intrigued. "It'll be interesting to see what this is about. They're the only ones who could command that kind of full spectrum participation."

"I'm sure curious," Katherine said. "Not to mention honored. And I've never been to Sundance."

"*Robert Redford's* place," Mary Claire hummed as her eyebrows danced again.

Debra turned to Charles. "Someone else was there for a small conference, who was that?"

"Joanne Morgan was there for their summer theater program," Mary Claire said. "She raves about the place."

"Redford's been pretty outspoken for the environment," Charles said.

"Supposed to be great skiing," Debra said. "You'll have to take another day in December."

"Katherine, ski? Ha!" Mary Claire quipped.

"No need to be obnoxious about it," Katherine reproached her.

"She is obnoxious, isn't she," Charlotte Newberg agreed, just arriving in the kitchen. "And I hear she's got a mean hot and sour."

"Charlotte! How are you?" Charles enthusiastically greeted his colleague.

Charlotte Newberg was the director of the U-M Humanities Institute which provided a forum for faculty, fellows, and guest speakers in a wide range of humanities disciplines. Each year the Institute established a theme upon which all research and presentations were focused. This year's theme was "Emergence." Charles had explained to Charlotte that 'emergence' took on special meaning to complexity theorists as they studied the dynamics inherent to complex systems. Charlotte had found the idea fascinating and had invited one of the leading thinkers on complexity theory to be one of the guest lecturers in this year's series.

"Looking forward to our date," she said to him. "Sure hope we'll see some of the physics department there."

"You know we'll be there," Charles assured her, referring to himself and Katherine.

"Wouldn't miss it, Charlotte," Katherine followed.

Charlotte grinned at Charles. "I think he still wonders why on earth a humanities outfit wants him."

"Oh, he's a pretty enlightened guy," Charles said. "I'm sure he knows it's the best company around."

Charlotte warmed to her colleague's adulation.

"Charlotte, did you see Marsha out there?" Mary Claire asked her. Her mind was racing with the same adrenaline that propelled her around to all of her guests. "I want you to hear what she's planning for the Initiative."

"I didn't see anybody," Charlotte responded. "I was too busy eyeing the desserts. Good grief, Mary Claire, you've outdone yourself."

Charlotte's soup bowl arm trailed behind her as Mary Claire pulled her by the other arm, eager to connect her with another proponent of interdisciplinary ventures at Michigan. "Hey Weiying!" she called with her party voice a few decibels up from her usual. "Bout time you got here!"

Charles looked at Katherine as he snuck another bowl of sage soup. "She doesn't let up on the Initiative, does she?"

Katherine shook her head. "I'll tell you, if any bit of it bleeds into the mainstream it'll be a direct result of that woman's particular brand of passion and perseverance."

"I hear her Initiative class is a big hit too," Debra said to Katherine.

"What's she doing exactly?" Charles asked Katherine.

"Oh, it's so Mary Claire," Katherine said. Then she delighted in sharing some of Mary Claire's account of what was happening in her class. "She's always insisted that it's the somatic experience of literature that's what it's all about, you know. She's actually banned writing instruments from the lecture hall. She has them choosing whatever literature speaks to them — and they have absolute freedom in their choice of material — and then they read it interpretively for the class. This is after they talked in the beginning about other modes of learning, about early societies where knowledge was passed on through the spell of performance and the visceral identification with poetry and verse. The students were baffled at first, of course. But now they're eating it up. Doing everything from Proust to Harry Potter. One student even brought in . . ."

There was a bit of an uproar in the other room. Someone had told a great joke or a popular colleague had made a splash entrance. Moments later Mary Claire returned to her soup pots and surreptitiously turned to Katherine mouthing a single word, "David." The jovial sound from the other room was now a familiar one. Katherine had heard it many times. David Maize was just one of those people who brought life to life. When he entered a room he filled the space like an exploding supernova. And whoever else occupied the space relinquished it gladly, just for the opportunity to be in his company. He was the kind of man who took a woman's breath away. Katherine remembered.

David was exuberant as he crossed the threshold into the kitchen. "Hey! Go Maize!" Charles cheered. The two men locked in a hearty grip of a handshake. Debra's face lit up as her cheek touched the cheek of their art professor friend.

"How are you, David," Katherine said warmly.

He wrapped his arms around her and they held one another like old friends.

"How's life?" Charles asked him.

"Life's great. How 'bout you?" David responded as he turned and looked into Katherine's face.

"We heard about your show in New York," she said.

"Heard it was stunning," Mary Claire called to David, again moving swiftly.

"Oh, thanks, it went pretty well."

"Still have the same studio out on Pontiac Trail?" Charles asked.

"Yeah, I love it out there." David looked at Katherine again. "I've been spending most of my nights out there lately too. I'm thinking about letting go of the apartment in town and just winterizing the barn."

"You mean, live at the studio?" Debra gawked. "In the barn?"

"Yeah. It's a great space," David replied.

"I saw you on your bike one day last week," Charles said. "Out by the art department."

"Yeah, I've been biking in a lot lately. It's great."

"Heard you were in Alaska this summer too."

David inhaled a deep breath, again looking at Katherine. "Yeah. With a Sierra Club group. Joel and I did the same trip he did a few years ago, remember?"

"I do," Katherine said. She looked at Charles and Debra. "Joel Scannell is with the School of Natural Resources. A great guy."

"He said I'd never be the same again," David said. "Boy, was that an understatement. I understand now why he said it felt ridiculous to him to try to put it into words."

"Well, now you have to," Debra urged. "Tell us about it. Where did you go?"

"Hey! Go Maize!" exclaimed John Taylor, bursting into the kitchen.

"How are ya, David? Katherine. Charles and Debra." There were greetings and handshakes all around. John briskly rubbed his palms together as he inhaled the bouquet from the soup pots. "I hear we've got a good spicy one."

"Sally said you had an Athletics meeting. On a Saturday evening!" Mary Claire squawked as she ladled hot and sour soup into his bowl. "What's so important you have to meet on a Saturday night?"

"Hey, that's my line," Sally Taylor said, returning to the kitchen.

"What?" John gasped as he feigned a serious expression. "You mean there's something more important than athletics?"

"You know what I would like to know," David boldly announced. Everyone looked at the playful conniving grin on his face. "I'd like to know if anyone knows *anybody* who's actually been to a Michigan game." He accentuated the question with exaggerated tension. "You know, like actually *been* there, in the stands?"

Katherine immediately rolled her head and moaned in an exaggerated expression of protest. "Oh, he is haranguing me still. As if it were some kind of inconceivable crime that I have not been to a football game."

"You've never been to a game?" John blurted. He was looking at Katherine incredulously.

Sally pretended to catch her breath in astonishment. "What? And you've not been struck by Wolverine lightning?"

John Taylor was genuinely stunned. "All these years and you've never been to a football game?"

"Oh, no. NO, no." David was embellishing the moment. "We have to get the full canvas here. She has not been to a *game*. Not any game. And that's not even the best part . . ."

"Don't even think about it," Katherine jumped in. She could not keep a straight face.

"Do you know how many years . . . " David continued.

"He just loves this!" Katherine interrupted him again. "He has gotten more mileage out of this. He's going to tell you how many years I didn't know what 'Go Maize!' meant."

The group began to erupt.

David's expression intensified. "What are there, twenty four thousand employees of the U? Do you think there's another person in the entire system who doesn't know that Michigan's colors are maize and blue and that 'Go Blue!' has been the most ubiquitous Ann Arbor expression for the past century?"

Charles' laughter rose above the group's.

"And God knows the physics department is not exempt from Wolverine fever," Debra said as she dug her fingers into her husband's side.

"And she keeps hearing 'Go Maize!' right?" David continued. "Everywhere we go, somebody's hollering 'Go Maize!'"

"Well, I thought it seemed an *appropriate* expression," Katherine said, "given his personality." The entire group was enjoying a hearty laugh. "But I had no idea why everyone used the same expression."

"This is too funny," Sally snorted.

"Of course the only thing that prevented him from enlightening me was his perverse pleasure at my abysmal ignorance."

"How could I possibly pass up such a singular opportunity," David said as he reveled in the blush of Katherine's face.

"So, tell them, David," Mary Claire goaded. "I love this story."

"Traitorous wench," Katherine growled.

"Okay, so this has gone on forever, right?" David continued. "She's hearing 'Go Maize!' everywhere we go. And she never remarks or asks or anything, right? It never comes up. And then one night we're in the Prickly Pear and she hears somebody say 'Go Blue!' And she turns." David gave his best exaggerated impression of Katherine with an inquisitive look on her face, turning her head slowly, her eyes searching. He was milking the story for the sheer bliss of the moment. Charles was laughing uncontrollably at this point.

"This is too much," Debra chortled.

Then Charles heralded through his hysterics, "She's looking for someone named *Blue, right*?!

David's audience laughed with great enjoyment as he continued to tease with obvious affection his female physicist friend.

Four

It was almost eleven. The remaining guests were deeply engaged in small group conversation. In the kitchen the soup pots were cooling, the steam had vanished from the windows, and only the slightest evidence of flourless chocolate cake remained on the five peony-patterned dessert plates on the kitchen table. The intensity in David's voice reflected in the faces of his four friends as they sat around the table and watched him and listened.

"Nineteen million acres. And it's joined with another nine million acres set aside by the Canadians. It's the largest area on the planet deliberately preserved for creatures who've never known anything but primordial wilderness." He looked at Katherine. "You have to be there to believe the vastness and the wonder of it. It truly is a mystical place, there is no other way to describe it. The most elementally stirring, rearranging experience I've ever had." He fixed on Katherine's face as he began the story he was eager to tell.

"There were twelve of us. We flew for two solid days in increasingly smaller aircraft to get to our camp which was a gravel ledge overlooking the Jago River. For two weeks we were a good five hundred miles from the closest manmade device of any kind. Our tents and provisions were all we had. And you have to understand that with the caribou . . ."

"David," Debra interrupted, "did I read that they're the only deer species in which males and females both have antlers?"

"That's right," David said.

"Well, I like 'em already," Mary Claire said.

"There are about a hundred and fifty thousand in this particular band," David continued. "And they all make the fifteen-hundred-mile migration each year from their winter range to their summer range. The pregnant females depart first. They make their way to the North Slope of the Arctic Plain where all in a ten-day period some forty or fifty thousand of them drop their calves."

"Fifty thousand," Mary Claire whispered, her eyes opened wide.

"It's a massive birthing that literally becomes a feast," David said. "Every animal in the area that can possibly prey on caribou calves is completely satiated. And they can't possibly eat them all."

Debra drew back in her chair, aghast at the image.

Katherine had been sitting very still, intent on David's face. She spoke with quiet understanding, "And some survive."

"Over millions of years they've evolved this behavioral adaptation to the threat of predation." He looked at Debra, drawing her back into his story with his eyes. "And then there's a second wave of migration, the males and the other females, all coming to gorge themselves on the lush summer plant life and hoard their reserves for the following winter. And they share this boundless nutritional spread with hundreds of other wildlife. We saw musk oxen and jaguars, tundra wolves — countless species of migratory birds. I can't tell you how overwhelming it is to stand quietly in the middle of this immense, untouched, utterly intact organism — an exquisitely complete ecosystem. You can actually feel the rhythm of eons of perfectly ordered cycles." David's passion intensified. "There is a pounding vibrational power in the earth that we can't begin to imagine. Not until we've experienced the earth of another time — with all of its wild creatures." He shook his head in awe. "There really are no words for it."

"You're doing just fine," Katherine said emphatically.

Mary Claire was also enthralled. "It's like you're still there. The place is still in you."

"Oh, wow, is it ever." David looked at her gratefully. He moved forward again in his chair as he remained intent on his story. "Now you have to understand, the caribou migrations never occur on exactly the same route. It's impossible to predict where their trek will be each year. Joel has been on this trip a number of times. And our guide, this incredibly fearless soul, a real warrior for the wilderness — he'd taken this same journey for thirty years and never experienced what we did. The gods were really smiling on our little pack of humans. We woke up one morning to find ourselves right in the middle of the caribou trek." He became visibly moved. "For thirty-six hours a gentle river of caribou flowed all around us. As far as we could see in any direction — thousands and thousands of these magnificent creatures, slowly steadily walking, instinctively bound for their calving grounds. It was like bearing witness to a pilgrimage to the promised land. Joel and I, all of us, we were totally undone by it. We had found ourselves right in the middle of something we could only pay homage to."

"And your guide had never experienced this before?" Mary Claire asked.

"He said it was the experience of his entire career. I can't imagine anyone who wouldn't be completely rearranged by it — for life."

Katherine shook her head in wonder. "And of course it would happen when you were there."

"I feel like the luckiest man alive," David said. "And I'll tell you, there are consequences. There is a level of discontent that comes from an experience like that. An inescapable sadness, an outrage at what we're doing to the earth. And it doesn't go away. You can't be there, experience that place, and ever look at life the same way."

"It's the Arctic National Wildlife Refuge?" Debra noted.

"Yeah, and if some have their way," Charles said, "we'll go in and suck all the oil out of the place, power up our SUVs for a few more years."

David was solemn. "I'll tell ya, I'd personally ride my bike every day for the rest of my life just to save a blade of grass in that place."

Katherine had been examining David's face. "And how is your painting? How is your work since you were there?"

He looked at her with deep affection and then his blue eyes grew large and round. "It's big," he said with a wide grin.

She could not help responding to the expression she knew so well. "You and your enormous canvases. How perfect that you would have an experience like that."

"You know," Mary Claire said thoughtfully, "when I hear a story like this it really makes me wish I were a hardier stock."

"*You?*" Katherine exclaimed.

Debra concurred with an enthusiastic grunt.

"Oh, I have no doubt my spirit would thrive," Mary Claire said. "But I don't know if I'm cut out for it physically. I mean, we're talking wilderness here," she stressed. "Five hundred miles from anything?!"

David's veneration was constant. "As wilderness as we'll find on the planet."

"You and Joel must have really bonded," Katherine said. "An experience like that."

"Incredible. I owe him big for talking to me about it."

Debra stirred a little. "Well, it's been wonderful," she said, looking at David and then at Mary Claire.

"Yes it has," Charles said as he stretched his arms wide. "Home to the babysitter."

"Your sensational soup soiree was another huge success," David said as he gently stroked Mary Claire's arm.

"Your sensational, sumptuous, September soup soiree," Charles said.

"Your salacious, succulent, sumptuous . . . "
"All right, all right, I get it. The party was a hit," Mary Claire said.
"As always," Katherine added.

Mary Claire was forever true to another established custom — that of refusing any post-party assistance from her guests. "House rules," she would say as she escorted her friends to the door. Tonight there were hugs all around and Katherine elicited a commitment for Sunday morning yoga from Mary Claire, provided it was a reasonable hour. When David offered to walk Katherine home, Mary Claire, ignoring Katherine's glare, obligingly insisted. "I know it's Ann Arbor," she said. "But let him walk you anyway."

It was a perfect September night. Summer had lingered just long enough to catch the hint of crispness in the air. A slight mist hung over the park which was barely lit by the moon and the neighboring streetlights. David perched himself on top of the single picnic table, as Katherine knew he would. She wrapped her skirt around her legs and sat beside him on the cool wet wood. Old friends sitting in the park looking at the moon, she thought. Life was so amazing. It just kept streaking by.
"So how are you really, Katie?"
"I'm good. I'm really good. I miss my parents."
"That was really a rough one," he said softly. "Losing both of them so close together."
"But I've been busy. When I'm home I'm buried in my theory, which is good."
"They were good people, Bill and Marion. I liked them a lot."
She looked at him. "And they liked you."
"Your book is gangbusters, I know that. And this Initiative thing, you think it's gonna take off?"
"I hope so," she said.
"Mary Claire sure seems happy about it."

"She deserves to be. I've never seen anybody work harder at anything."

"Your being involved sure lends some punch to it."

She rolled her eyes. "It's certainly drawn a few punches in our department."

"I'll bet," he snickered.

"You can just imagine how they're loving the idea that one of their own is slumming in the 'soft' disciplines."

He laughed with a bit of relish. "Yeah, I sure can."

David had always been a little resentful of the deference paid to physicists. He was rightfully resentful of the arrogance he had encountered among some of Katherine's colleagues.

"I just really think it's a step in the right direction, you know?"

"Do I ever," he said.

"And then the ones who decide they really do want physics," she shrugged, "we'll teach them physics. We've got that part down."

"I think it's great. And the butterfly thing is fabulous. What made you decide on butterflies?"

Katherine almost instinctively began telling David about her butterfly dream. She knew how he would appreciate all of the details of her inspiration. Yet it was Mary Margaret's presence in the dream that had made it so powerful. And as close as Katherine and David had been, she had never told him about Mary Margaret. He had no idea that she once had a sister. A sister who died when they were both young. Like most of the people in Katherine's life, David thought she was the only child of Marion and Bill Ayers. There was another whole part of her life that even he knew nothing about. Mary Claire was the only person she was able to talk with about her butterfly dream.

She shrugged a little. "Who knows how things come to us."

"Well, I know you don't think so, Madame Butterfly," he teased, "but you really are an artist too. We just work in different mediums."

"Interesting thought," she said as she stared at the sky.

"If the rest of us had any idea what it is you do out there, I'm sure we'd discover that this theory stuff of yours is the most creative work there is."

Katherine looked at the moon as she pondered the idea.

"So things are pretty much the same in the department?" he asked.

"Oh, I'm getting a little better at it, I guess," she said. "If we want to work entirely unobstructed we kind of have to work in a vacuum, don't we."

David erupted with one of his uniquely expressive sounds. "And I don't think the machinery we're in exactly qualifies as a vacuum. Last time I looked it was a bureaucracy as thick as any government and a hierarchy as delineated as a colony of royals." His impish sarcasm became even more exaggerated. "And you, my dear, are among the royalest of the royals."

Katherine made no mistake about rolling her eyes this time.

"It takes a lotta years for artists to make peace with the kind of machinery we've got around us," he said. "Sooner or later we either get out, or we just get it. These institutional monstrosities have their own inbred survival instincts. They hold tight to them. Veritable *fonts* of radical ideas," he mocked, "so long as the really radical ones are generated in a manner *befitting tradition*. Anything remotely resembling unanointed progress can sure get gnarled up in all that tradition."

"You're in that place again, aren't you?" She was watching him with a knowing grin. "You've been doing this as long as I've known you, Mr. Maize."

He looked at her quizzically.

"You were in New York again with your art, and in Alaska with your other passion. You always have a hard time coming back to the 'machinery.' "

"I guess it's because on some fundamental level I know I'm in the wrong business. And I do mean business. We still call it education. The truth is, it's business now. It's about business and for business and it's damn big business itself. We can puff up our pigeon feathers all we want about what it is that we do, but we're kidding ourselves if we think we're not on the GNP train with everybody else. Hell, we're the ones stoking the fire."

He looked at her and recognized her familiar smirk.

"You're doing your *art*," she admonished.

"And believe me, I have a lot of moments when I can justify a whole lotta machinery just to keep doing it," he admitted. He rested his elbow on his knee and ran his fingers through his hair. "Tell me something." He looked at her. "You wanted me to go to New York, didn't you? Just chuck it and move to New York. Just go for it."

She looked at him pointedly as she marked her words. "Because it's what you've always wanted," she said. Then she saw his spontaneous response to her.

"God, you look sensational," he said.

She instinctively looked away.

"And how about love, Katie? Are you seeing anybody? The way you look, something is making you happy."

"I am happy. Work makes me happy. Mary Claire makes me happy . . . Love? Love makes me confused."

David let out an explosive sigh. "Professor Ayers, you are the only person on the planet who is not confused about anything." The awe in his declaration carried a slight tinge of exasperation.

"That's what you think," she chuckled.

David sat silently for a moment and stared at the night sky.

"I thought about you every minute, Katie. Out there in the wilderness. There wasn't a moment you weren't with me."

After a moment Katherine said softly, "It sounds like a truly magical place."

"For the rest of my life there will be a part of me out there in

Alaska. And for the rest of my life I'm gonna be wondering how the hell I could have let you get away."

Katherine sighed a little. "I remember more than once when I'd have given a lot to hear that."

His gaze dropped from the sky. "Ancient history, huh?"

She leaned into him, gently nudging his shoulder with hers. Then she fixed again on the star-speckled sky. "You know, out there, between the age of those stars and the age of the universe, there is a vastness so ineffably boundless it eludes the highest powers of imagination. The caribou in the wild may have a better sense of it than we do. Out there, every time a fluctuation occurs, suddenly there appears what we call a 'virtual pair.' They're pairs of virtual particles that spontaneously pop into and out of existence." She flicked her fingers gracefully toward the sky. "There's one. There's one. They can't be measured directly but we do know that every single one of them has its own effect on the universe."

He was watching her intently. "And what was our effect on the universe?"

"It was a good one," she said tenderly. Then she glanced at him and smiled. "Sometimes it takes a little while to get the whole canvas, you know."

He could not help smiling. Then he became serious again.

"I learned a lot, Katie."

"I know," she whispered.

"When I think of the way I've worked for things, even fought for things that mattered in my life. And the one thing that mattered most I wanted to just kind of . . . fall into place without disturbing a *paintbrush*."

His emphasis on this particular word touched a chord in her. No other image could have more effectively expressed the clarity of his understanding.

"I wanted you to just fit into *my* life, you know? But I had no idea what my life really was. Not until I got down to real life. And you were there. You were everywhere." He turned to her. "You're part of me, Katie. You always will be."

She slipped her hand underneath his and slid her fingers through his. "I have to say, it's really nice to hear."

They continued looking at the sky as the moon and stars grew brighter. And then he asked, "So why is it that some of those particles out there take so long to figure it out? That there's only one thing that really matters a damn. That's an honest to God relationship with one of those other particles."

"They're all just finding their way through the universe," she said. "Their own way, their own time."

"I think they're all just too damned attached to the path of least resistance."

She pushed against him again. "Is that what that condition is called?"

They grinned at one another. Then Katherine drew a deep breath as she looked again at the moon. "Mary Claire says it's what makes the world go round — all of us chasing around, searching for that one person who'll make sense out of life for us. She says what we all want is someone to connect with, like Emerson says, 'with the simplicity and wholeness with which one chemical atom needs another.'"

"Now there's a description of a virtual pair, huh?"

"I think when it happens like that there is definitely some universal force at play," she said. "I guess I want to believe that's true — that some people just belong together and that they do find each other."

"And when they do," he said, "they need to recognize that that's their moment."

"Their moment?" She looked at him.

He smiled. "Did you see the Japanese film *After Life*?"

She shook her head.

"There's this way station — out there," he gestured toward the sky, "where people go after they die. And each person is asked to choose from all the experiences in their life the one moment they most want to remember. They're asked to describe it in detail, everything they remember about the experience and how it made them feel. Then their memory is recreated for them in perfect detail, and they relive it over and over again for all eternity . . . And that's their heaven." He turned to her and looked into her eyes. He was as vulnerable as she had ever seen him. "I finally figured it out," he said. "You were my moment."

She drew in close to him and whispered to him tenderly, "I remember some pretty heavenly moments myself."

David sat silently for a moment and then he raised his voice in a sigh toward the sky. "So, why is it that virtual pairs don't stay virtual pairs?"

She smiled at the perfection in the metaphor. "Actually, what makes them virtual is the ill-defined energy. When the right energy goes into them they become real. The potential is always there. There are always flickerings." She looked at him. "Even profound fluctuations."

He was struck by the words. "That's a good description of us, huh? A . . ." They pronounced the words together, "*profound fluctuation*." They laughed an intimate laugh.

David looked at her as though he were about to admit something for the first time even to himself. "You know what I think? I think on some level I knew I just wasn't the right guy for you. I think we both did." They watched one another closely while he took comfort in his own honesty. "We both convinced ourselves that I was the one holding back because we both knew there was a part of you I would never have. I guess I always felt like that part of you was being faithful to someone else. Someone I could never be."

Katherine was intent on his face. "You know, I don't pretend to know anything about love," she said, "but I'm pretty sure that when a woman loves a man she doesn't need him to *be* anything." She looked into his eyes. "Except the one who loves her."

He thought for a moment. "So if he just loves her, maybe he gets to know the part of her she keeps hidden and protected?"

Katherine was struck silent. She had always marveled at David's intuition. Though she had withheld from him some of her deepest self, she could never quite escape his penetrating eye. She responded to him now with the same honesty. "And maybe the part of her that she keeps hidden and protected is the part that most needs to be loved."

His sigh this time was an emphatic one. "Professor Ayers, you are the last person on earth to ever be confused about love. You know what you want like no one I've ever known."

Katherine was thrown by his statement and then she thought about it. "Actually, I think what comes through so strongly is that I know what I don't want."

He looked at her with piercing conviction. "You don't want anything less than the whole thing."

"And you know," she confessed, "I really have no idea what the whole thing is."

"You must," he said. Then he waited for her to turn to him again. "You made me believe in it."

Katherine closed her eyes and absorbed the lovely feeling his words had evoked. She leaned into him as he wrapped his arm around her.

"You know I'm always gonna be here, right?"

"I hope so," she said. "I can't imagine not having Mr. Maize in my life."

His tone now assured her that he was resigned, even a little contented.

"Blows my mind, you know," he pondered. "The idea that all that stuff out there can be rendered somehow intelligible with that high math of yours. It's a language most people will never even encounter, much less be conversant in. And it's the one that's told us the most of what we know about the world."

"And when you do understand it, you know it's the only thing we can really depend on."

"The only thing?" he challenged.

She smiled. "Like you said, only people who've experienced it would understand why I would say such a thing."

"Oh, now there's a physicist's statement for you," he chided beneath his breath.

She pulled away and looked at him pointedly. "Well, I certainly wouldn't want to depend on way stations in the sky that deliver us to our personal heaven!"

"Ah, that's right, you don't believe in anything out there, do you?"

"I believe in everything out there," she stressed. "Just none of the things we've imagined there to be. When you've experienced what's really out there, it's hard to understand why we would need to imagine anything else. What's actually there is that amazing." She looked at the moon. "The moon alone is enough to inspire me for a whole lifetime of believing."

David fixed on the moon. "Yeah, I really liked hearing that it may have had more influence on life on Earth than we begin to understand. That made sense to me."

Katherine was touched by his recollection of something she had said in her book and by the fact that it had made an impression. She watched a wisp of a cloud as it rolled across the moon. "The effect it has on us is sure something, isn't it?" she said. "I don't think that's something we're going to understand anytime soon."

"We sure feel it though, don't we," he said. He continued staring at the moon. "You know, out there in Alaska for the first time it made perfect sense to me why you do what you do."

She smiled without diverting her gaze from the sky. "Yeah, I'm out there for the same reason a part of you will always be in the wilderness in Alaska. It's the sense of being part of something more magnificent than we can begin to comprehend."

David sat quietly for a moment captivated by the moon. And then as though he had suddenly been struck by an electric bolt he jumped off the table, stood tall, drew a deep breath and engaged his entire diaphragm in a wail at the moon. Then he whirled around and faced her, extended his hand, bowed before her, and with gallant affection he said, "May I have this dance, my lady?" And before she could utter a sound he whisked her off the table, took her in his arms and waltzed with enormous strides in the wet moonlit grass. And he sang, and she laughed, and he howled at the moon again.

Through her laughter Katherine half-heartedly reprimanded him, "David! We're going to be arrested."

"Ah!" he cheered, "I can see the headlines now." He dramatically waved his hand across an enormous newspaper in the sky as he bellowed, "Wild Man Art Professor Molests Moonstruck Astrophysicist." He whipped his head toward her. "Sell a lot of books," he teased.

She socked his arm with her fist and he faked a dramatic response. Then they walked through the quiet September night toward her home.

"So you and Mary Claire are gonna do yoga in the morning, huh?"

"No," she said casually.

He looked at her.

"I'll call her and she'll say, 'Oh, let's go to Angelo's for breakfast instead.' And that's what we'll do. She deserves a little indulgence."

"And you?"

"I deserve a little indulgence too."

Five

Jason looked quite impressively prepared standing next to the enormous image of a butterfly he had projected onto the screen in front of the lecture hall. He was using a pointer to draw attention to each of the figure's individual parts as he described their functions.

". . . And each of the two compound eyes contains as many as six thousand light-sensitive structures called 'ommatidia' which are grouped under a lens or cornea which is composed of an equal number of hexagonal prism-shaped lenses. The optic nerve carries the visual message from the ommatidia to the brain where it's received as an integrated, erect image . . ."

"All right, Jason, I'm going to stop you here for a moment," Katherine said. "Jason has provided us with this nice large image," she said to the class. "I'd like to ask everyone to take a close look at the drawing."

Jason stood back and enjoyed a moment of pride in his visual offering.

"Let's imagine that Jason has not told us anything about what we see here in front of us. We have not yet heard the words 'thorax' or 'ovipositor' or 'ommatidia' or any of the other words he's introduced us to."

The students looked at the drawing.

"Before we had any of these words to describe the parts of the butterfly, did the butterfly have the same parts? Did they function in the same ways?"

The students thought for a moment and then "yes" came from a number of them.

"And before we had any language at all, when we were capable of doing little more than grunting at one another . . ." There were a few grunts of amusement as Katherine again directed their eyes to the drawing. "Did the butterfly have the same parts? Did they function in the same ways?"

More students joined in the affirmative response.

"So the butterfly had all of its parts and all of the same processes occurred before we ever invented big juicy multi-syllabic words like 'integument' and 'polymerization' and 'ommatidia'? Imagine. How did the butterfly manage without us?"

The class was stimulated. Jason was a little deflated. He had worked hard on his presentation and looked forward to citing the prestigious science journals he had consulted in the process.

"Jason has done a wonderful job of presenting the physical composition of the butterfly," Katherine went on. "As he continues to share more of this information, let's be aware that the words we have placed on the parts and the processes of the butterfly are our own inventions. We're not really concerned with the words. Instead, let's look closely at the butterfly, the design of its body and what it is capable of."

When Jason reached the end of his presentation, Katherine acknowledged a young woman.

"You said it has six thousand, what did you say?"

"Light-sensitive structures," Jason replied. "And each one is linked to another complex lens."

"So is that why they're able to see so much more than we do?" the student asked.

Jason faltered a bit.

Cynthia immediately came to his rescue. "I have that one," she called out. "I'm working on butterfly vision."

"Great," Katherine said. "We look forward to hearing about what the butterfly sees that we do not."

As Jason started toward his seat she asked him to please stand by for a moment.

"We agreed that in developing an understanding of a living creature that its physical structure is a good place to begin. Let's look for a moment at what this approach does for us." She again directed the class's attention to the large drawing of the butterfly. "Jason, would you point, please, to any one of those individual parts of the butterfly?"

The tip of Jason's pointer fell on the proboscis.

"The straw-like tube the butterfly eats with, right?" Katherine said. "Let's imagine for a moment that everything else on the drawing is not there. There is only this little tube with which the butterfly eats. What function does it serve?"

After a moment someone responded, "None."

Then another student said, "Without a body, there's no reason to eat."

"Not much use, is it?" Katherine said. "Jason, will you touch another part of the body?"

Jason pointed to the antennae.

"How about the antennae? All those sensory nerves and microscopic receptors. Are antennae any use all by themselves?"

The students were wagging their heads.

"Antennae can be very handy devices," she said. "But they wouldn't be much use without the rest of the butterfly, would they?" She saw that her point had been made. "So," she continued, "when we approach an understanding of the butterfly by examining its parts and their functions, what is it that we're doing?"

"We're breaking it down," said one of the students.

"We're reducing it," said another.

"We're reducing it to its parts, aren't we," Katherine said. "And what are we missing when we do this?"

"How all the parts function together," said one of the students.

"The whole butterfly," Cynthia said.

Katherine looked around at the students. "What else is there about the butterfly that is not represented in its parts — or even in the functions and the processes that together make up the whole butterfly?" She referred again to the drawing in front of the room. "Imagine that instead of this illustration we have an actual butterfly here in front of us, a huge, brightly-colored, winged creature. What about the butterfly would we still be missing even if we were looking at an actual butterfly?"

"You mean a dead butterfly?" a student asked.

"I don't know," Katherine said. "Is it alive?" Her tone suggested this was an intriguing course to pursue.

"If it were alive it would be flying," said another student. "It wouldn't just sit there for us to look at it."

"It would be flying, wouldn't it?" Katherine stressed. "It would be living the life of a butterfly. And what do we know of those elements that breathe the actual life into the butterfly? That transform it from a collection of nerves and lenses and membranes and all of its parts into a beautiful living creature? Is that something we can see by examining its physical structure? Is that something that can be broken down into parts?"

It was not long before Jason and his fellow students were observing with interest the lively discussion that had emerged from his basic instruction on the anatomy of the butterfly. Jason was followed by several of his classmates whose presentations sparked the same stimulating discussion. Katherine would ask a question that began a dialogue and then students would ask new questions and point out new perspectives. They had joined one another in a pursuit of understanding, newly engaged by the delicate winged creature that had previously been a mere flitting bit of color in the peripheral landscape of their lives.

They learned that butterflies have indeed been around since long before humans had invented words like the ones they heard in Jason's presentation. Butterfly fossils in Green River shale in Colorado dated them back at least as far as forty-eight million years, which meant that butterflies had lived on Earth for at least forty-four million years before the appearance of the earliest humans. They learned that as members of the animal kingdom butterflies share lineage with everything from protozoa and dragonflies to gazelles, mountain lions, whales and human beings. Together with their moth cousins they constitute "Lepidoptera," from the Greek, meaning "scale and wing," the second or third largest order of insects, after bees, beetles and ants, depending on which entomologist is counting. They learned that insects were the first species to master flight and that the butterfly is among the most highly evolved of all the insects, distinguished by its profound metamorphosis from the form it is encased in at its earliest stage of life to its magnificent winged adulthood.

Aaisha had prepared a series of drawings that illustrated the dramatic transmutation from tiny egg to worm-like caterpillar to stirring chrysalis and then emerging butterfly. At each stage she described in detail the transformative processes of "splitting shell" and "shedding skin" and "dissolving organs" and "rebuilding structure." "And as it hangs from the pupa," she said, pointing to one of the final drawings, "the butterfly pumps blood into its veins and dries its wings. And within a couple of hours its wings are fully spread and ready to lift the little beauty for its first flight."

Aaisha emphasized the dramatic changes the butterfly undergoes by again calling attention to its mouthpart. "You see, here, in the early stages, the biting jaw of the caterpillar allows it to chomp on its host plant. Later," she pointed to the proboscis, "its mouth transforms into a sipping-straw that it uses to siphon nectar from flowers. At each stage the butterfly has very specific ecological requirements. And it transforms itself to accommodate its needs. The entire process, from quiescent egg to the final winged imago state, is a transformation that is virtually unparalleled in nature for its sheer wonder."

The subject of metamorphosis inspired particularly spirited discussion. What was nature's intention in drawing forth from a tiny egg, a hairy little worm, and finally one of its most splendid creatures? Why had nature imposed a life of such radical change? The butterfly had to repeatedly transform itself in order to survive. Was its winged finale perhaps nature's way of rewarding the creature for having endured such processes?

Sarah's project on the word "butterfly" identified its Anglo-Saxon origins in "butterfloege," or "flying yellow butter," which referred to the male Yellow Brimstone butterfly prevalent in England. She invited the group on a frolic through butterfly language that introduced, among others, the French word, "papillon," the Me-Wuk "hul-lah-kah-tee-wah," the ancient Greek "psyche" and the Russian "babochka"— the last two of which identified the butterfly with the human soul. She then treated her classmates to a sampling of names from the almost twenty thousand known species of butterflies, obviously choosing those with the greatest entertainment value. It also escaped no one's notice that the names she had selected evoked images they all observed on the U-M Diag and in the hallways every day. There was the "Great Purple Hairstreak" and the "Dingy Skipper," the "False Grayling" who is always accompanied by a "Deep Blue" female, the "Painted Lady" and the "Small Pearl-bordered Fritillary." Sarah went on, "There are the Great-spangled, Purple-edged, Red-spotted, Silver-studded, Long-tails, Short-tails, Swallowtails, and Ringlets . . ."

The popularity of butterflies in general, both as objects of appreciation and as subjects of scientific research, took much of the class by surprise. Jeni reported on the great number of work and leisure-time activities that the enchanting winged creatures provide for people all over the world. She emphasized the amazing reliability of the butterfly's precise behaviors which makes them one of the most widely studied organisms in population, environmental and ecological research. She then cited astonishing statistics on the growing numbers of butterfly museums, gardens and centers, especially in the U.S., which draw thousands of tourists daily. She summed up her detailed report with, "Human fascination with butterflies is definitely on the rise."

Hailey recognized this as the perfect lead-in for her report entitled, "The Magnificent Monarch Mexican Migration," about an event which draws thousands of tourists to Mexico each year. "In one of the world's most spectacular migrations some two hundred and fifty million butterflies fly in a huge migrational funnel all the way from the Eastern U.S. to a forest of Oyamel fir trees in the Michoacan Mountains of Mexico," she said. "There they cling to the trees in serene stillness for the entire winter until the spring sunshine warms their wings and the thick blanket of insects explodes into an ascending swirling flurry — like flying fragments of black and orange stained glass!" she exclaimed. "The sight is so thrilling that people come from great distances just to see it." She stressed that the most fascinating thing about the Monarch migration was that these tiny creatures not only fly this great distance but they also find their way to the same precise location each year.

"Now, that may not seem so amazing until you realize that they've not only never been there before, they are the *fourth generation* of the butterflies who were there the previous winter! You see, the group that survives the winter in Mexico heads to the

Gulf Coast where they lay their eggs in habitat that is suited to their offspring. And then that generation flies to the Great Lakes region where they also reproduce and die. Then *their* offspring make their way to the East Coast where they spawn another generation. And they complete the circle by heading back to Mexico!" Hailey was exuberant. "This is an insect that weighs less than a dime that flies across an entire continent of unknown terrain to the exact home of its great-great-grand parents!"

Isaiah, who had been visibly engaged in Hailey's presentation, eagerly followed with his own. He had learned that the Michoacan Mountains Monarch Reserve had created quite a controversy in Mexico where the government was working to prohibit logging and protect the Monarch's winter home. He was especially excited about the long conversation he had had with one of the leading experts on the Monarch migration, Dr. Lincoln Brower, whom he said had been incredibly generous with him on the phone.

"If there is such a thing as an 'expert,' " he said to Katherine, "this guy is definitely it. He's been studying the Monarch migration for years. Been to Mexico many times. And he's very concerned about the future for the Monarchs. For one thing, there are all kinds of disturbing environmental trends that could threaten their winter habitat in the coming years. And he's also concerned that the Mexican government will be able to withstand the pressure from the logging industry, which is a huge threat to the only place where the Monarchs can survive. I've included in my hand-out all the information he gave me about why it's so important to protect the Monarchs, that it's so much more than just preserving this miracle of nature and the pleasure of watching it. By protecting the Monarchs, and pollinators in general — he explained it all in some detail to me — we're actually protecting ourselves."

Isaiah had learned that the Monarch's migration habits had also prompted protective legislation in parts of the U.S. He read for the class an actual city code from Pacific Grove, California, where another group of Monarchs migrates en masse each year:

> *"It is declared to be unlawful for any person to molest or interfere with, in any way, the peaceful occupancy of the Monarch butterflies on their annual visit to the City of Pacific Grove, during the entire time they remain within the corporate limits of the city, in whatever spot they may choose to stop in . . ."*

He informed the class about the Endangered Species Act and other legislation that protects threatened species and natural habitats, explaining that butterfly trading was now more than a popular hobby, it was a thriving business with rare species commanding thousands of dollars. "In some places, legislation is strictly enforced," he said. Then he shared with the class some of the intrigue surrounding an Oregon case that had caused quite an uproar in the "butterflying community." "A collector was seized by authorities for capturing an endangered butterfly," he said, "and was slapped with a three-thousand dollar fine, three years probation, and three-hundred hours of educating the public about laws protecting wildlife. Those Oregon folks are serious!" he exclaimed.

"Yes we are!" a student called out.

It was clear that Melodee had struggled with her topic. She nervously reported what she knew the class had already learned, that the average life span of the butterfly was a couple of weeks. She cited a few species that were generally more long-lived, including the Monarch which spawned three to four generations in a year. And the "Gonepteryx rhamni," the pronunciation of which made her even more nervous, held the record for the longest life — they survived sometimes for almost a year. Yet the fact remained that most butterflies lived in their adult winged state for no longer than a couple of weeks.

"I just don't get it," she said to Katherine. "I mean, it just doesn't make any sense. Especially after all they go through to get to *be* butterflies. I tried to find something that would explain why they live for such a short time but I just couldn't find anything."

"Maybe there is nothing that will answer that question for us, Melodee," Katherine said.

Melodee sighed in relief. "It's not that I didn't try. And I was thinkin' about what you said about what the butterfly accomplishes in the short time it's here, you know? But no matter what I came up with it just sounded so stupid. I mean all they do is eat and have sex!"

This drew a round of laughter from the class.

"It's true!" Melodee said. Her anxiety melted away as she raced through her explanation. "Everything I read said that all the butterfly is interested in is, uh . . ." She shifted her gaze as she recalled the exact wording, " 'Sustenance, survival, and reproduction.' So, do they just reproduce and die? I mean, I just don't get why they live for such a short time."

"Well, let's see," Katherine said. She had glanced at the clock and knew they had a few more minutes. "We haven't lacked for ideas yet." She smiled as she looked around the room. "Who wants to give this one a try? Why does the butterfly live for such a short time?"

"Maybe their time is different than our time," Tim offered.

"Yeah, maybe they have nine lives, like cats," called out another student.

"No, seriously," Tim said. "Maybe time is completely different to butterflies than it is to us. Maybe two weeks is an eternity to them."

"Interesting idea," Katherine said. "In fact, we're still trying to figure out what time is, aren't we? Some of our greatest minds have grappled with the concept of time. Yet the most we know with any certainty is that we know nothing with any certainty. We have this illusion of something that runs in one direction — today comes after yesterday and before tomorrow. The caterpillar would look forward to being the butterfly and the butterfly would remember being the caterpillar. But these concepts are human inventions, aren't they? Who knows that the butterfly doesn't have a completely different experience of time." She paused for a moment. "What do you think, Sir Robert?"

Katherine had noticed that Robert Pritchett, the man in the back row of the lecture hall, had not been participating in any of the discussion.

Robert immediately responded, "Einstein would say the butterfly's experience of time depends on how fast it's moving and its relationship to the speed of light."

This drew a wide grin from the teacher. Robert had indeed been participating in the discussion.

"You're probably right," she said. "He may also have said that it was tough enough to figure out the human concept of time, let alone the butterfly's." She continued to smile. "And do you care to make a conjecture of your own?"

"About the speed of light?"

Students around Robert Pritchett giggled.

"About why the butterfly lives for such a short time."

"Well, like you said, maybe it isn't such a short time for the butterfly."

Katherine nodded at Melodee whose hand was again in the air.

"Well, when I was trying to find something that would explain more about why they live for such a short time, or I mean, maybe it's a short time and maybe it's just different, but what I was thinkin' was about how we say 'only the good die young,' you know? Like when children die, and no one can really explain it, it's just a mystery, you know. And I was thinkin' that maybe that's the way it is with butterflies. Maybe they're just not supposed to live very long."

Katherine sat motionless. The weight of her upper body was poised on her straight arms, her palms gripping the edge of the desk. She was looking at Melodee but her gaze went right through her.

"Well, anyway," Melodee said nervously, observing Katherine's frozen expression. "That was one of the things I was thinking when I was tryin' to figure it out."

In a moment Katherine focused on Melodee again. "Perhaps it's one of those questions that there really are no answers to, Melodee."

In the next moment she was up off the desk.

"*So*," she exclaimed. "It's been a very full hour and a half. We'll continue on Thursday. We look forward to all of the interesting things we've yet to discover." She scanned their faces. "And remember . . ."

She smiled as she arched her pointer finger in the air.

The students stopped and looked at her.

"Consider the butterfly's perspective," she said.

Six

Katherine cherished her weekends at home in Ann Arbor. They were precious time for early morning walks and uninterrupted days with her theory. She would often set out in the quiet hours and take one of her familiar routes through the neighborhoods to the Arboretum, the university's park-like conservancy affectionately known as the "Arb." The silence and sanctuary of its rolling hills and rich foliage had beckoned her regularly for years. Her walk on the winding path through the trees to the river now felt like a visit with an old friend.

She could hear the river's welcome pouring through the trees on the path's final bend, where all at once the silence would be infused with the teeming cry of the rushing stream. It was years earlier when she first identified the rock formation in the river that was responsible for the dramatic sound. An extraordinary grouping of boulders formed two adjoining arches that together stretched the full expanse of the river. The exuberant interplay between the steady rocks and the dashing stream flushed out the deep current and created the verve and force that gave the river its thunderous voice.

She had come to think of him as "the river man," the wiry, eccentric looking man with his weather beaten face and worn clothes who was ever-present at the river. Up to his knees in the rushing water, hidden under his rumpled hat, he was always there, like a doting elder, tending the rocks — aligning this one, balancing that one, re-securing their intimacy with one another. How wonderful, she thought. He recognized the enchantment nature had bestowed in this seamless rock formation and had taken it as his charge to watch over it, to maintain it.

She had never observed the man communicating with anyone. Not people anyway. She had no idea why he chose this particular morning to speak to her. She was sitting on the riverbank where she often sat for a few minutes before resuming her walk. Suddenly the man began to speak.

"It took nine years to build it," he said. "Ever since I just take care of it."

She looked again at the formation of boulders in the river and saw it with new and astonished eyes. "You *put* the rocks there," she said. She was completely stunned by the revelation. The river man was much more than a guardian of nature. He was a co-creator in an environmental sculpture that was the very essence of this magical site. She marveled at the thought of all the thousands of people who had lingered there in that very spot over the years and had never known of the enormous difference one man had made in their experience. She raised her voice to be sure he would hear her. "It's really quite amazing," she said. "I had no idea it was a work of art. A human work of art, I mean."

The man did not look at her, he did not respond. Instead he stood in the water and as though he were addressing a large audience on the riverbank began his elaborate tale about his creation in the river. He pointed to the two adjoining arches in the river. He then pointed downstream to another grouping of boulders Katherine had not noticed before. There, the two arches came together in a point, forming the closure in a larger shape. The image took her breath away. It was a heart. The man had placed an enormous heart in the middle of the river.

"Love and compassion. That's what it says," he shouted. "Love and compassion."

When the man spoke these words Katherine was moved to look into his eyes and experience a direct connection with him. Yet the man did not look at her. He did not respond. He suddenly seemed even curiously unaware of her presence. "The heart of Christ," he said loudly. Then he pointed to the sky. "The Lord summoned me to dive to the bottom of the river and turn over the boulder. There, on the bottom was the face of Jesus. The Lord commanded me to build the heart and to tend it," he said. "The Lord gave me vision and the Lord gave me strength so all would bear witness to Jesus . . ."

Katherine sat as the man continued his fervent depictions of visions and voices and labors for Christ. Her gaze drifted back to the flowing water whirling about the rocks as it hurried downstream. What a lovely sensation it had been, she thought, the moment she had beheld the work of art. There had been such perfection in it. A heart built of rocks in the middle of the river signifying love and compassion.

"The Christ Jesus is the only salvation!" the man hollered, as his evangelistic expression grew steadily more fierce. "Come to Jesus or be forever damned!"

Katherine felt the back of her neck seize up. Her throat tightened. Though her better judgment flashed through her awareness she was powerless against the urge to speak. She gripped her outward composure and looked directly at the man, smiling. "Wasn't it the love and compassion that Christ was about?" she asked him.

The man stopped short, though he continued to evade her gaze.

Katherine remained fixed on him. "Wasn't that the message he wanted to share? The message there in your beautiful heart? Isn't that what Christ was about?"

The river man's face contorted with scorn. He spewed his next words as though he were expelling a vile taste. "Jesus alone can save the soul!" he said. "The Christ Jesus is the only salvation!"

Katherine's entire body began to tense up as she heard her father's voice thundering in her ears. "Christ Jesus is the only salvation! Come to Jesus or be forever damned!" She saw in the river man's face her father's face, his eyes filled with rage, his fist raised toward her mother. She jumped to her feet and backed away from the river. As evasive as the man had been toward her, he was clearly agitated by her attempt to leave. "The Christ Jesus is the only salvation," he screamed at her.

As quickly as she could turn from the river and resume her walk she was back on the path moving swiftly, freeing herself from the river man's grip. With every breath she was expelling the sound of his voice, the sound of her father's voice.

She was only a short distance from the river when she was startled by another voice.

"Morning," said the groundskeeper who had come up behind her on the path.

"Oh, good morning," she said.

"He's harmless," he said with a casual smirk as he gestured toward the man in the river.

Katherine observed the park attendant's easy expression. Yes, she thought, the river man was harmless. His words were harmless.

"He really put those boulders there himself?" she asked.

The ranger shook his head in good-natured exasperation. "Yeah, he's been doin' those rocks for years," he said. "We just let him be." Then he veered off the path toward the Peony Garden. "Take it easy," he called to her.

Her stride was now as deliberate as her effort to redirect her focus. Both her heart and her gait were finding their way back to a steady pace. She looked ahead at the glistening green of the clearing before her where the sun was just beginning to cut through the dampness. The sight of an early morning runner ahead was a comforting one. When she arrived at her favorite spot in a scenic stretch of the Arb she sat by the large oak tree near the top of the hill. She felt the familiar bark against her back and the moist earth seeping through her jeans. And then it came to her. She and Mary Margaret had always run to the tree at the far end of the yard, as far away from the house as they could be. There they would wait for their mother to come, to know that their mother was safe. Her heart lunged as the realization hit her. "I'm still running to the tree, aren't I, Mary Margaret? Still running from our father's voice after all these years."

It was only moments after she had resumed her walk again that thoughts of work began to creep in. Today her time with her theory would be interrupted by the public lecture she had to give at noon. Her step quickened as she began formulating the outline of her speech.

As she walked up the final hill on her way out of the Arb, again she felt the energy of the rushing river. She saw the sparkling water bounding over the rocks, flowing through the river man's heart. His words resounded in her mind again, the only words she would allow to remain — "Love and compassion. That's what it says. Love and compassion." She picked up her step and briskly walked toward home.

The popular Saturday "What is Physics?" series was designed to introduce the public to the U-M Physics Department and to some of the latest developments in the field of physics. It was presented each week in the main lecture hall of the Dennison Building and featured a faculty presentation accompanied by questions and answers. The series was well attended — a diverse group of physics aficionados, local retirees and other interested Ann Arborites, students at all levels, and local press. Karen Rodzik, the department secretary, had informed Katherine of the multitude of calls they had received that week so she was not surprised to see the lecture hall was full. Her colleague Brandon Troxtel, who coordinated the series, introduced her as a theoretical physicist and a member of the astrophysics faculty, explaining that her specific field, cosmology, was a study of the universe as a whole. He asked if the physics students in the room would please refrain from asking technical questions in this forum in order to encourage more general questioning from the audience.

Katherine looked out at her audience. "Why study the universe?" she began. "Does increasing our knowledge of the origin or the nature of the universe have any direct impact on the human experience? Did it improve the human experience to learn that the Earth was not flat but round? To discover that Earth was not the center of the universe? To find that the world as we knew it was in fact an infinitesimal fraction of the boundless, expanding, perhaps multiple universes we now explore? Indeed, human civilization owes much of its progress to the unceasing pursuit of knowledge. Our entire evolution has been marked by one unanticipated discovery after another.

"How can we justify spending precious financial resources on space exploration and research when there are pressing problems right here on Earth? Communication satellites, Earth observing systems that monitor global warming, military satellites that make it possible to enforce arms control treaties — all of these things are the products of space exploration and research. And if before these things were realities we had decided we could not justify the enterprise, we would never have discovered the potential that awaited us in space.

"Before speaking about what we know about the universe, it is important to emphasize how recently we know what we know. Just as the history of human existence is a mere blink of an eye in the most recent history of the universe, our understanding of the universe is recent, short-lived, and ever changing. A century from now we will be occupied with questions that at the present time we do not have the knowledge to ask. And whether it is the time of Newton, or of Einstein, or of the great minds of centuries from now, we can never anticipate when the things we discover will make it impossible to imagine the conviction we could have had about our previous world view.

"We've come a long way since mythological gods and titans rode their fiery chariots through the boundless beyond — controlling the sun, creating storms, and deciding the fates of the mortals below. Today's cosmology reveals a profoundly beautiful, elegantly-ordered universe governed by its own immutable laws. Science is continually providing us with more understanding of these laws. And the universe continually reveals itself as a boundless reservoir of mystery.

"Our present cosmology is rooted in Einstein's conception of the universe. When we peer through high-powered telescopes into the distant reaches of space, for instance, we are actually looking back in time to the earliest epochs in the history of the universe. Space is not what we imagine it to be either. Rather than the vast empty stage upon which matter plays out its dance, space is actually a member of the cast of characters, a complex dynamic structure that yields in graceful response to the bodies that inhabit it.

"When all of the evidence has been weighed, we believe it will indicate that approximately fifteen billion years ago the universe began in a single cataclysmic event in which space and time themselves came into being. This event, which we call the Big Bang, involved heat beyond measure by available instruments and power beyond our comprehension." She went on to describe each of the early stages of the universe's evolution — it's initial vacuum state, its transformation to a hot soup of particles and antiparticles, its next emergent phase when the energetic forces that were borne out of the Big Bang split from one another and distinguished themselves as separate dynamics. "And about a billion years later," she said, "some of those particles of matter began to coalesce and to form stars and galaxies.

"Today we know that Earth and all of its inhabitants emerged from a supernova — an exploding star," she explained. "This means that the Earth and everything on it, including the two-legged creatures in this room, consists of the same essential elements as the stars we observe in the night sky. We humans in fact owe our very existence to the explosions of stars and to the universal forces that for eons carried those stellar elements until one day they united to form the substances of which we are made."

The audience was silent and attentive as she spoke spontaneously, guided by the cursory outline she had prepared that morning. When she finished her broad-stroke picture of the universe as it is currently conceived, she cited some of the enormous questions that consume cosmologists today: What is the nature of the mass that makes up the universe? What is its origin? How did galaxies form? Will the universe continue to expand? She highlighted some of the research being done at the University of Michigan and by cosmologists worldwide. Then she wrapped up her speech by saying, "Obviously, this was a very brief time in which to talk about something as vast as the universe. I do want to leave the allotted time for questions."

Before she had finished her sentence a student reporter from *The Michigan Daily* had her hand in the air. She had been writing throughout Katherine's lecture and was poised with her pen as she posed her question.

"Professor Ayers, would you answer one basic question? The name of this series is 'What is Physics?' Would you tell us please what your response is to that question?"

Katherine smiled. "Well, in the words of one of my undergraduate students whom I overheard yesterday . . ." She gasped as she mimicked the student's revelatory expression. "Physics is everything! And everything is physics!"

There was an audible response of enjoyment from the group.

"One can understand why she is so excited about physics, since there is nothing else."

The group continued to laugh.

Katherine shifted her inflection to that of an aside. "For those of you who are unfamiliar, her statement is not to be confused with the 'Theory of Everything.' " A number of people in the room were having a good laugh. "The Theory of Everything refers to a slightly more comprehensive 'everything' than I'm sure even this enthusiastic student had in mind . . . On a more serious note," she continued, looking at the young woman who had asked the question, "though I can appreciate how she arrived at such a conception, I would respond a little differently to your question. I would say physics is the study of life at its most fundamental level."

The reporter hurriedly wrote on her pad.

"That would be my answer," Katherine added. "You will certainly hear different answers from different physicists."

The young woman discharged an emphatic sound.

"I take it you have discovered this," Katherine said.

"It's like asking artists What is art?" the young woman exclaimed. "I've asked each of the speakers in this series the same question. Their answers are so different. One said it was 'the study of the physical world and the rules that govern it.' Another said it's 'the study of matter and its interactions.' Someone else said it was 'understanding nature and how it works.' "

"And it's hard to tell if we're saying completely different things or the same thing in completely different ways," Katherine said sympathetically. "I think it's probably a little of both. Just as with art and with every other profession, I'm sure, there are no two physicists alike. And we all have our own ideas about what it is that we do." The woman was nodding as Katherine spoke. "In fact, some say theoretical physics is a lot like art. We may be two distinctly different cultures but we seem to understand one another surprisingly well, especially when we talk about 'process.'"

Katherine acknowledged another young woman who spoke up with self-conscious eagerness.

"Is it hard being a female physicist?" she asked.

Katherine smiled. "Well, I won't ask if there is an inherent supposition that it is hard being a physicist."

Again laughter rumbled through the room.

She looked again at the young woman. "Are you studying physics?"

"Yes," the girl said with youthful pride. "I'm going to be a freshman here next year majoring in physics."

"And I'll bet that is your mother next to you."

"Yes," the mother spoke up. "I'm also very interested to know what kind of experience you've had, being that women are such a minority in the profession."

"Yes," Katherine said thoughtfully. "Three percent is certainly a minority. I recently read that there are fewer women in physics than in any other enterprise save military combat." She thought for a moment. "The thing I found most troubling about that statement, even beyond the statistics, was the reference to military combat as an 'enterprise.'"

She observed the number of young women in the room and then looked again at the high school senior. "Your question is a good one," she said. "If I had had the opportunity to ask it of a woman when I was where you are now, I would have benefited, I'm sure, from her perspective. So I will do my best . . . We tend to think of gender barriers as those that prevent women from flourishing in persistently male professions. But there is another side to that equation which is often overlooked. It is true that historically women have been denied access to physics. But far more consequential, physics has been denied access to women. When we take a close look at how profoundly our lives have been shaped by physics we see that women have had very little voice in deciding the course of the *human* enterprise. Electric power, computers, radio, television, telephones, air travel, the Internet — these are all children of physics. As are laser-sighted guns and guided missiles and supersonic fighter-planes and atomic bombs." She browsed the faces before her. "Everywhere we look in Western society women are carrying at least an equal share of the responsibility for home and family and community. If women were also equally vested in our world-shaping professions, it's hard to imagine we would not at least reassess some of the ideas to which these professions continue to cling." She looked at the young woman's mother. "Some even suggest that when men and women are true partners in science that the greatest benefits will be reaped not by women, but by science."

There was an enthusiastic response from a number of the students in the room.

Katherine looked again at the high school physics student. "If it sounds as though I am suggesting you should become a physicist because you are female, on the contrary — I can think of no worse way to enter any profession than with gender consciousness. I would be far more concerned with whether I was a member of a much more significant minority — those who have identified what they truly want to do with their lives. If you are, and physics is what you want to pursue, then I'm sure you will deal with whatever challenges come your way. The challenges are certainly there. But life is a challenge, isn't it? Whatever we decide to do with it."

The young woman nodded at Katherine.

"So, we'll see you in class next year," she said with a smile. Then she acknowledged a young man in the center of the room.

"Yeah, Professor Ayers, you talked about why we do research, and that all made sense, but what I wanna know is, what good does it do us to have satellites that monitor the environment when it hasn't made any difference in how we treat the environment? I mean, no matter what we learn about how we're destroying the earth we can't seem to change our priorities one bit. And we're spending millions of dollars investigating Mars and discovering planets and exploring the universe. Shouldn't we be spending our resources on research and education about what we're doing to our own planet?"

Before Katherine could respond she was taken aback by an abrupt remark from the rear of the lecture hall. The student who had asked the question turned toward the back of the room in response to the statement neither he nor Katherine had clearly heard. The man in the back of the room repeated his remark. "Read her book!" he said.

Katherine then recognized the man in the last row of the lecture hall. It was Robert Pritchett from her butterflies class. She smiled. "I believe the gentleman in the back of the room is defending my rather vociferous advocacy for the earth and for eco-sustainability," she said. Then half-chiding she asked Robert, "Mr. Pritchett? Do you have some further thought to express?"

Robert boldly articulated his response. "The more knowledge we have of the universe the more difficult it is to think of the earth as separate from the universe and the more we see that environmental degradation flies in the face of what the universe is about."

Katherine was stunned. She could not have managed a more adroit response to the young man's question. Even more striking was the fact that in all of the critiques of her book there had not been a more astute articulation of its message about the environment.

"Well said," she said to Robert. "I'm not sure I have heard it put more succinctly."

She looked at the young man who had posed the question. "I agree that education which increases our respect for the earth is absolutely essential. And increasing our knowledge of the universe is, in my view, an important part of that education."

She nodded in response to the hand of a distinguished looking white-haired man in a sports jacket. She had noticed his profuse laughter at her joke about the Theory of Everything.

"I wonder, Professor Ayers, if you would comment on the Anthropic Cosmological Principle?" he said. "I can't pretend to understand it well enough to be asking questions about it, but do I understand correctly that in its strongest version it suggests evidence of God, or grand design, so to speak?"

Katherine's neck began to tighten as she flashed on the face of the river man. She hesitated only a moment and then responded decisively.

"No. Grand design is not inherent to the principle. Very briefly, for those of you who are not familiar, the Anthropic Principle deals with the emergence of intelligent life in the universe. It is therefore an easy target for extrapolations that belong in realms other than science. The Anthropic Principle was put forward in several gradations, the strongest of which has been interpreted by some to suggest that the emergence of human life in the universe is an integral part of the universe's evolution. Some even suggest that our conscious reflection on the universe is a significant aspect of this evolutionary phase." Her smile was subtly dismissive. "It is hard to resist being philosophical when we speak of the emergence of intelligent life. We are, after all, the intelligent life we're speaking of. But the Anthropic Principle as a scientific theory neither supports nor denies whatever one chooses to believe about God, or grand design, or the purpose of human existence."

The man in the sports jacket graciously hesitated before asking another question. "So when people ask you to comment on the existence of God, you do what most scientists do and refer them to the theologians?"

Katherine was steadfast. "If I am being asked as a scientist, you are correct that it is not my role to comment on spiritual matters. Science and religion are separate domains."

The man was nodding at her with a knowing smile.

"Where I might depart from the response you are obviously familiar with is that I would not refer such a question to a theologian."

The man looked at her with heightened curiosity.

"As a scientist I cannot comment with any authority on art or literature either. But if someone approached me for advice on what they should feel in response to a particular work of art, I would not refer them to a critic."

The man's expression transformed. He watched Katherine closely as he articulated his conjecture. "You would refer them back to the work of art?"

"Yes," she said simply. They smiled at one another.

It was only a moment before another young man, obviously a student, had his hand in the air.

"Yeah, Professor Ayers," he said eagerly, "when Stephen Hawking was asked if he believed in God, he said 'If by God you mean the embodiment of the laws that govern the universe.' Do you agree that God is simply the embodiment of mathematical laws?"

She was not surprised that she had been unsuccessful at ending this particular discussion.

"I agree that the universe is governed by mathematical laws," she said. "I do not confuse this scientific reality with conceptions of God."

There were again a number of hands in the air.

"We're really out of time," she said. "But we'll take one more question. One with a quick answer," she added with a grin. Then she gestured toward a young woman.

"Professor Ayers, you said that we are all made of the exact same elements as the stars are made of, that we evolved out of the exact same material."

"That's right." Katherine nodded. "Stars that exploded long ago produced carbon and nitrogen and oxygen and the other elements of which every atom in our bodies is made."

"Well, I understand that science is not about design or purpose and that it doesn't comment on the meaning in things, but I mean, doesn't that scientific fact alone tell us something really important about ourselves and the universe?"

Katherine looked at the girl attentively. "And what do you think it tells us?"

"Well, I think it says that we're totally connected to the universe and to everything in it. It's like physical evidence that we're all part of the same thing." Her face expressed her appeal to Katherine. "Isn't that what it says?"

"Yes," Katherine responded. "It does tell us that we are all part of the same thing. I think it also tells us that the thing we are part of is something quite amazing." She smiled warmly at the young woman and then again scanned her audience. "And I can't think of a better note on which to close," she said. "Thank you. I have enjoyed your attention and your questions very much."

She smiled at her audience in response to their applause as she left the room.

That evening, as tempted as she was to skip yoga and work straight through the night, she knew that if she did she would regret it the next day. She so looked forward to spending the entire day with her theory. For years she had struggled with the same debilitating pain in the back of her neck which was clearly aggravated by long hours at her desk. She had learned that regular yoga made all the difference in both her comfort and her stamina.

Her favorite yoga teacher worked with a small group of faculty women at the YMCA on Saturday evenings. The moment she was behind the wheel she was glad about the decision.

When she pulled up on William Street next to the Y she sat for a moment and stared through the windshield. A couple of young lovers were strolling along the sidewalk, their arms wrapped tightly around one another. Saturday night, she thought. And this was her life. Work, teaching, travel, and the yoga that kept her going.

As she walked from the car she came up behind the couple on the sidewalk, meandering aimlessly, completely oblivious to the world outside their embrace. She heard their breathy euphoric giggles and watched his fingers tangle in her hair. Breathe with intention, she said to herself, anticipating her yoga teacher's instruction. And with her next breath she filled her lungs.

Seven

" . . . The tachyonic nature of preheating in hybrid inflation implies that instead of the production of gravitinos by a coherently oscillating field . . ."

Throughout her lecture Katherine had been glancing at the doorway, diverted by something she had not yet identified. When she finished her talk she looked to investigate the distraction. There was indeed an elderly woman standing in the hallway. She had been unobtrusively hovering, watching her and listening. Perhaps one of the locals who attended the community lecture, she thought. It was not until the students had cleared the room and the woman stood alone inside the doorway that other thoughts began to occur to her. Suddenly she was seized by the woman's silent gaze. This was a visitor from another time. Another reality. A reality Katherine had left behind long ago.

The woman had entered the room and stood motionless. Her expression betrayed deep emotion.

The words came involuntarily from Katherine, "Aunt Agnes."

"Katie," the woman said.

Again Katherine uttered her thought in no more than a whisper. "I remember."

The woman gripped her handbag with both of her hands. "I recognize you too," she said. "They told me this might be a good time to . . . try to see you . . . that this was your last class for the day."

The next silent moment was an eternity for both women.

"Yes, it is," Katherine said.

The woman clenched her handbag again. "I'm here for my fiftieth reunion . . . The medical school, you know . . . I hoped, I thought maybe we could . . . have a cup of tea or something . . . maybe go for a walk." She released her handbag to one hand and nervously gestured with it toward the window as she smiled awkwardly. "The campus is so different, I don't know where I'm walking anymore."

"Yes, it's changed a lot since you were here," Katherine said. She picked up her leather folder and cradled it in her arm. "Yes, we can go for a walk."

Inside the elevator Katherine remained fixed on the elevator buttons. "How are you?" she asked.

Her aunt was looking at her as though the sight of her took her breath away. "I'm well . . . I'm very well," she replied.

"You're here for your reunion," Katherine said. "How is it?"

"Oh, it's just starting tonight. We're having a dinner at the League."

"That will be nice," Katherine said.

When they reached the sidewalk the lithe white-haired medical graduate examined her surroundings. As she gazed to the right, down South University Avenue, her breath quickened. "Oh my goodness," she whispered with sentimental devotion, "Martha Cook."

"Still going strong," Katherine said.

As they walked along the sidewalk toward the Martha Cook residence hall, the alumna's reorientation to the campus provided a welcome distraction.

"Oh, and the Clements Library."

"Yes, still a gem," Katherine said. "The tall building behind it is the new extension of the Graduate Library. That would have been the main Library when you were here."

Agnes' gaze flitted back and forth between the passing students and the buildings.

"The library is one of the finest in the world," Katherine said.

"Yes, isn't that wonderful. That was true even in my day," Agnes said.

When they arrived in front of Martha Cook the two women stood on the sidewalk and looked into the face of the historic building. Katherine observed her aunt's expression as she longingly observed the residence of her youth.

"It does have a noble presence, doesn't it," Katherine said. "I've always been particularly fond of this Law Quad area."

"It's so nice to have some things that never change," her aunt said.

"Or at least give the illusion," she replied.

As they resumed their walk Katherine gestured again toward the ivy-covered walls on their left. "I remember the first time I visited here with my parents," she said. Both women felt the atmospheric pause after the word "parents." "They wanted so much for me to come here. They held Michigan in such high regard. And of course they would have loved to have had me close to home."

"I'm sure they were very proud when you went to Harvard," Agnes said.

Katherine looked at her. "You knew I was at Harvard?"

"Oh, yes. We . . ." Agnes did not finish her statement.

In a moment Katherine resumed the cursory conversation that was filling the chasm between the two women. "I was a teenager when we first drove through here, when they first tried to put the idea into my head. I remember looking out the car window at those grand walls covered with green. The Law School made such an impression."

"But you wanted to be a scientist," Agnes said proudly.

"It seemed to be the place where I was most comfortable," Katherine said.

Katherine could see the wave of nostalgia that overcame her aunt as they strolled past the old familiar buildings — the President's House, Tappan Hall, the Museum of Art. As they crossed over State Street toward the Michigan Union she suggested a cup of tea. Her aunt was visibly thrilled.

"You know, in my day women weren't allowed to go in this way," she said as they walked up the stairs and approached the doors of the Union.

"Yes, I know. I think we definitely should, don't you?"

From the moment they stepped over the threshold at the front entrance of the Union, Agnes' fascination was palpable. She watched the students as they roamed in all directions, a sociocultural mélange of twenty-first century youth. She could not take her eyes off one young woman in blue jeans and a sweatshirt with a backpack slung over her shoulder.

"My, but things do change," she said.

"Yes, they do," Katherine agreed.

Sitting at the small table in the Union cafe Katherine found herself looking into the face of an intimate family member she had not seen since she was a little girl. She saw her own fragility about their meeting reflected in her aunt's eyes. They both leaned back in their chairs as the waiter placed the tea pots and cups on the table. Agnes unconsciously dipped her tea bag.

"So, things seem quite different to you," Katherine asked.

"Oh my, yes," Agnes said. "It's been almost forty years since I've been back."

"That's a long time."

Agnes was visibly hesitant. "I didn't know if you would . . . well, I didn't know what to expect."

Katherine slid a saucer over near her aunt's teacup and spoke to her gently. "Perhaps it is strong enough for you now."

"Yes," she said, unaware of her tea. "Thank you."

"So, have you been a pediatrician all these years?" Katherine asked, trying to resume their casual conversation.

"Yes, I have. Well, I'm retired now, of course. But I practiced for nearly forty-five years. Spent most of them in the Point Reyes area. In the same office, in fact, for many years."

"Sounds like you enjoyed it."

"Oh, I loved my work. I miss it."

"And do you have a family?"

"Oh, I never married," Agnes said. And then with a tentative smile she added, "Had too busy a life I guess." She looked at Katherine again, examining her face at every opportunity. "I can hardly believe you've not married."

Katherine was obviously taken aback by her aunt knowing anything about her life.

Agnes reluctantly confessed, "The truth is, I do have an old friend who has kept us up on things." She looked solemnly at her niece. "We did hear Marion and Bill passed away. I'm sorry, Katie."

"Yes . . . thank you," Katherine replied. She grasped the warm teacup in the palm of her hand.

"And within a month of one another," Agnes said. "That was quite something."

In a moment Katherine responded.

"Well, it would be if you didn't know them," she said softly. "From the moment Mother's illness became serious Dad said that whenever she went he would be following right behind her. He said it with such certainty. And that's exactly what he did. Just drifted off after her in his sleep one night." She picked up her teacup and steadied herself. "They really loved each other."

Agnes looked at her reverently. "They were good parents to you."

"They were the best parents I could have had," Katherine said.

Agnes' effort to contain her emotions floundered. "We wanted so much to see you . . . to let you know." She reached for her handbag in an effort to regain her composure. "We did try. Did you know that we tried?"

Katherine felt her intestines tremble inside her even as she sat perfectly still. "Yes, my mother . . . Marion told me," she said. She stared out the window for an uneasy moment. She knew what her anxious visitor was waiting for her to say. "How is my mother," she said flatly as she felt her intestines lunge.

Agnes' eyes filled with emotion as she seized the relief she experienced in her niece's inquiry. "She's well," she said. "She is very well now."

Katherine adjusted herself in her seat. It was taking every bit of effort she could summon to maintain her composure. "Was she ill?" she asked.

There was another silence as Agnes carefully considered what she would say. Then she labored with her words. "Katie, what happened . . . when you were young . . . such a terrible thing. For all of you. It affected your mother . . . deeply. I don't know what you know about what happened to her."

Katherine dragged her stir-stick in her teacup. She wondered what organ was quivering deep inside her. "I know that she went to live with you in California," she said. "And that the courts decided I would live with my parents. With Marion and Bill."

Agnes looked searchingly into Katherine's teacup where Katherine's gaze was aimed.

"But your mother was not able to live with me for a long time," Agnes said. "She was in the hospital. She was very ill. I mean, in her mind. In her heart. Because of what happened. It was years before she came back to herself again. What happened was extremely hard. For everyone." She looked into her niece's eyes. "That's why it was so good that Marion and Bill were such good people, that they were there for you."

"My parents were wonderful people," Katherine said. And then she saw in her aunt's pained expression how much she had involuntarily punctuated her statement.

Agnes' voice faltered. "I just wish you could know how much . . . how very much your mother loved you. How much she loves you."

The tension in Katherine's neck was becoming unbearable. "She's all right now then?" she asked as disinterestedly as she could manage.

"Yes. Yes, she is. And she's doing such . . ."

"Well that's good," Katherine cut her off. "I'm glad she's well." She could not bear to hear another word about the mother that had left her long ago.

Agnes began again, obviously struggling. "Dear, there is so much more that . . ."

"Agnes," Katherine interrupted her again. Then she spoke to her as gently as she could. "I know this was not easy for you. And I appreciate all of your feelings." She stopped again. She was working hard at her tone. "But my *mother* died." She looked directly into her aunt's eyes. "My parents are both gone now. And that's still difficult for me. Some days it's very difficult." She grasped her teacup in her hand. "I'm glad that my birth mother is well. I'm glad she's happy." She sat back in her chair. "Some things are just better left behind."

The two women sat silently for a moment while Katherine sipped her tea and Agnes stared into her own teacup, searching, surrendering. After a moment, she lifted her gaze to meet her niece's. "I understand," she said softly.

Katherine drew a long breath. "Agnes, I truly am glad you're both well. I'm glad to know that you are. And I wish you both the best."

Agnes' eyes expressed her sincere resignation and then her genuine gratitude just for the opportunity to look at her niece again. "It's been such a long time," she said.

Katherine responded warmly, "Yes, it has."

Both women sat for a moment silently sipping their tea.

"So, have you kept in touch with any of your classmates?"

Agnes ventured a smile. "A couple of them, yes. I'll be meeting my old friend Virginia Lane at the League in a little while. We'll go to the dinner together. It's kind of exciting, really, seeing all our old chums."

"I'm sure you were quite a close group then."

Agnes livened a little. "They say the classes are now fifty percent women. And we thought it was really something having twenty three in our class."

"Twenty three women was pretty amazing fifty years ago, wasn't it."

"They had only one or two at other schools," Agnes said proudly with obvious devotion to her alma mater.

"Being a doctor wasn't something women were expected to want to do then, was it," Katherine said.

"Oh heavens, no. Of course everyone expected to have a family then. In my day they called it an 'M.R.S. degree,' you know — girls going to college. I don't know what came over me. I just always wanted to be a doctor. Just like you wanted to be a scientist, I guess. And with my work over the years I've felt as though I've had lots of children." She appealed to Katherine with her eyes. "Do you know what I mean?"

"Yes," Katherine said thoughtfully. "Yes, I do."

"Helen wanted to be a doctor too," Agnes said, completely unaware of speaking again of Katherine's mother. "I suppose because I was her only role model. There's twelve years between us, you know, so she was young when I was in medical school. She wanted so much to go to Michigan. That was her dream."

"Really?" Katherine said, denying her own surprise and her interest.

"But then she fell in with that . . ."

Katherine again felt her muscles begin to clench.

"Oh, I guess if your mother can bless his memory, I certainly can," Agnes said. She looked at her niece as she checked herself. "I won't talk of things we shouldn't talk about."

As they withdrew again to their teacups Katherine observed her aunt's face. It was the face of a kind woman, a woman who would choose to spend her life caring for children. She began to feel compassion for her. She could see how difficult this overture had been for her.

"I do remember your visits," she said.

Her aunt looked at her.

"You used to bring me those little orange jelly candies."

Agnes' face brightened with the glimmer of reminiscence. "You remember the orange candies?"

Katherine smiled. "They were my favorite."

"I know," Agnes said, thoroughly gratified.

"I felt a lot of love from you, I know that," Katherine said.

A warm glow overtook her aunt. "I stayed with you once, you know. When you were just a baby. Neal's mother died and he and Helen went to Kentucky. I'll never forget holding you in my arms. You cried and cried like you would never stop. And then finally you drifted off to sleep. We bonded with one another, you and I. I've never forgotten that." She examined Katherine's face and hair as though she were deeply satiated by the sight of her. "And now you're a beautiful woman. I was so proud, watching you in that classroom. I wish so much your mother . . ." She stopped herself. "I'm sorry, dear."

Agnes' unsteady gaze drifted toward the window where the light caught her pale blue eyes. They were almost the blue of her mother's eyes, Katherine thought. For years she had dreamed about her mother's pale blue eyes.

Agnes continued, again almost completely unaware. "It's just that . . . she's my baby sister, you know? I think that's just the way it is with sisters." She stopped short, devastated at the thought of what had just passed her lips. She looked into her niece's eyes, visibly heartsick with remorse.

Katherine sat perfectly still. Then she steadied her focus in her aunt's eyes and attempted an understanding smile. "There is no feeling on earth more abiding than the feeling between sisters."

Agnes was tormented. "I'm so sorry, dear. So very sorry."

Katherine sat silently for another moment and then she decided to share something with her aunt that she knew would find its fullest measure in that very moment.

"Charlotte Brontë said that the feeling between sisters is one that 'no passion can ultimately outrival' — that 'love itself cannot do more than compete in force and truth.' " She held tightly to the side of her cup as she looked again into Agnes' eyes. "Charlotte and Emily Brontë were very close."

Agnes was moved by the Brontë quote and by the forgiveness she saw in Katherine's eyes. She joined her niece as they retreated again to the casual conversation that had been their salvation. After a while Katherine rested her fingers on her aunt's wrist. "Shall we go?" she said to her softly.

Again they walked the long corridor through the Michigan Union. When they arrived at the front entrance, just inside the large double doors, Agnes stopped. With a slight wave of her hand she called Katherine's attention to the doorway where her small pale eyes were fixed on a vision. "There used to be a tall slender man here," she said. "Standing right there." She pointed to the side of the doorway. "He was all decked out in morning clothes and tails. Like the quintessential British butler." She smiled at Katherine. "He wore gray striped trousers . . . and a full wing-back collar." She was gradually recalling each fine detail. "And white gloves. And a tall top hat too — which of course he removed whenever he was inside the building," she said. "Oh, he was a picture. He stood there in that doorway, right there, until he was as old as I am. Maybe even in his nineties. Just like a tree, he was. Like he had grown there out of the ground and was always going to be there."

The image Agnes was conjuring was fascinating to Katherine. She was finding some relief in it from the intense emotion that had overwhelmed her body. It was also in that moment that she began to grasp the enormity of her aunt's experience, returning to Ann Arbor after so many years.

"Everybody knew him," Agnes continued. "And everybody knew why he was there. You had to be a member to come through that door."

"You mean you had to be a man," Katherine said.

"That's right. We could come in, if we minded and didn't call attention to ourselves. But we had to come in the side door. We couldn't come through here. And you know, he was so elegant and aristocratic we all respected him. We wouldn't dream of coming through when he was there."

"It's so amazing," Katherine said. "Hard to believe, really."

Agnes shrugged. "That was just the way it was in those days."

Katherine gently placed her hand under her aunt's arm. "I'll walk you to the League," she said.

Agnes turned and looked at her. Her pale blue eyes beamed.

Katherine's walk from the League to Burns Park that evening was almost involuntary. She only vaguely experienced her feet stepping one in front of the other until she arrived on Mary Claire's front porch. Mary Claire immediately recognized that something extraordinary and distressing had driven her there. She quietly studied Katherine's face all the while she took her things and poured some wine and they sat in their familiar chairs at the kitchen table. There Katherine slowly began telling her about her visitor and about the feelings their visit had evoked in her.

". . . 'Mother'. . . It's just so difficult to hear that word in relation to anyone but Marion, you know? I just tensed up so terribly." Katherine was massaging the back of her neck. "My mother stopped being my mother long ago." She erupted, "Oh, Mary Claire, she is a sweet sensitive woman. I felt for her. I really did. I could see how much it meant to her. I just honestly wish she hadn't."

Mary Claire was deep in thought, carefully observing Katherine's face. She hesitated a long time before she spoke.

"Katie, I've been wrestling with this for a while. I know how much you've been missing Marion and Bill and I just didn't know if it was the right time."

Katherine looked at her. She could see that Mary Claire was dealing with emotions she rarely saw in her. "What?" she asked her.

Mary Claire proceeded slowly and carefully with what she had to say.

"Do you remember, in Chicago, when Marion and I had a long talk. I told you she was teary-eyed because she was so moved by your speech. Well, you know that was true. But she also talked to me about something else, something that had been weighing on her for a long time." She waited for another signal in Katherine's eyes before she continued. "She knew that I was the only one you had told about what happened years ago. She wanted me to know that not even you knew the whole story. She needed to share some things that you had never been told."

Katherine sat motionless watching her friend. "What was I never told?"

Mary Claire drew another breath. "Katie, your mother didn't actually go to California. And it's not true that she stopped being your mother. Your aunt took her to California. Your mother was in shock for a long time after what happened. And they really did try. Your aunt tried for years through a lawyer to enable your mother to see you. She knew that seeing you might make the difference in making her well again. You see, because your father fled and because there were still possible charges, it was all extremely difficult. But your Aunt Agnes did pursue it. And later she and your mother pursued it." She looked deeply into Katherine's eyes. "Your mother was even willing to come back and face prosecution. She tried desperately to see you for years." As she spoke she watched Katherine's gaze slipping away from her. "The courts refused her, Katie. The judge had picked Marion and Bill personally and he said he would see that any interference was severely prosecuted. Well, you know how tormented Marion would be about wanting you to know all this. But she didn't want you to be hurt anymore. My God, you were a child. What you went through was more than most adults . . ."

Katherine was now staring out the window. Mary Claire watched her intently.

"Katie, do you know it was almost a year that you didn't speak? You didn't say a word. Marion and Bill were beside themselves. It was no wonder they were so careful about what you were told. And no wonder the judge protected you. But, Katie, your mother didn't leave you. It almost destroyed her to lose you. Marion said she believed in her heart that it was wrong for the State to take you from your mother."

Katherine was now staring into the distant past. Slowly, she began to speak again. "I remember, I was about eight or nine, I guess. I remember them sitting me down on the sofa, explaining to me that my mother loved me, that she wanted very much to see me. They said that California was just so far away and she wasn't able to get back to Michigan."

Mary Claire let out a sigh of admiration. "Marion and Bill just didn't have the skills for deception."

"It was just so obvious that they were lying, you know?" Katherine turned from the window and faced Mary Claire. "But I thought the lie was that my mother still loved me."

Mary Claire struggled with her own emotions.

Katherine turned again toward the window. "I could never reconcile the deep feeling that she was trying to get to me, you know . . . that she would come . . . with the reality that she never did. And then one day I just started denying it all together . . . how much I needed her."

"And she needed you," Mary Claire whispered.

Katherine's gaze was locked in the distance. She was remembering things she was now understanding for the first time. "Marion tried to tell me when my father died. She tried to talk to me about my mother then too. She really tried. I just had no place for it, I guess."

"How could you?" Mary Claire said. She was watching the slow, difficult absorption that was visible in Katherine's expression. She spoke to her gently, "That day in Chicago, after your speech? Marion was so proud of you. She told me that from the moment you came out of yourself again, that day when you were little, she knew you would do something important with your life. She said she saw it in your eyes. She said that from that day on you behaved as though you would never be lost again."

Katherine sat very still, the tears slowly rolling down her face. "There wasn't a day with the two of them that I didn't feel I owed them my life."

Mary Claire laid her hand on Katherine's. "But what you gave them, Katie. What you gave them."

Katherine was dazed and distant. As distant as the events she had revisited during the past few hours. "That day . . . the day when I finally spoke to Marion?"

"When you were little?" Mary Claire said gently.

"She was there."

Mary Claire supported her with her voice. "You mean Marion?"

"Mary Margaret," Katherine whispered.

Mary Claire was physically seized. She sat holding Katherine's hand as she began to weep.

"She's with me all the time," Katherine said. "Just as vivid as she was in that dream."

Mary Claire was barely able to speak. "Your butterfly dream?" she said.

As Mary Claire sat silently watching her friend she became intent on Katherine's eyes. She recalled the same eyes years earlier in the park at Cambridge, the day Katherine confided in her about her real family history. She remembered the moment when she suddenly understood the precision with which her extraordinary friend approached everything in her life, when she understood how she had come into such a deep understanding of poetry and literature and why she had chosen instead to focus on science. As she looked into those same eyes now, for the first time she was imagining what those eyes had seen when Katherine was just six years old.

Mary Claire had known that Katherine's father had been violent and fanatically religious and that he had denied care for Katherine's little sister Mary Margaret when she was dying. What she had learned from Marion were the parts of the story that Katherine had been unable to tell. She learned that Katherine too had pleaded with her father to take her sister to a doctor. She too had been forced to kneel and pray at her sister's bedside. She had watched her sister suffer until the very end. The last time Katherine had seen her family she had watched her mother beaten and her sister die. And then she had been ripped away by the State, never to know that her mother had not abandoned her. For the first time Mary Claire was vividly imagining what the woman before her had endured as a young girl. She did not know how she would ever find the words to express her compassion.

"Do you know . . . in all the years I've known you . . . you have never called me anything but 'Mary Claire?'"

Katherine slowly turned to her and searched her eyes.

"It's true," Mary Claire said. "In all the multitude of times it would have been far more convenient to use a syllable or two less than 'Mary Claire,' you never did. You have never called me anything but 'Mary Claire.' "

Katherine's bewildered stare remained fixed on her.

"Do you remember that day sitting in the grass in Cambridge when you first told me about Mary Margaret? You said you had never called her anything but 'Mary Margaret,' that you just couldn't bring yourself to ever shorten her name, that she was just a 'Mary Margaret' — that that was who she was." The tears welled up in Mary Claire's eyes as her smile persisted. "In all the years I've known you there has never been a time you've said 'Mary Claire' that I have not been touched."

The tears ran down both of their faces as they held one another with their eyes.

Mary Claire drew a deep breath and exhaled. "I can't even imagine losing a sister, Katie. And to lose her the way you did . . . My heart just bleeds for you." She squeezed Katherine's hand.

Katherine turned her hand to meet her friend's. "I know it does," she said. And then she added, "Mary Claire." And then they both let go a sigh of a laugh and another soothing sigh as they held tightly to one another's hands.

"You have been a sister to me," Katherine whispered. "You have."

Eight

"... My shimmering wings are the resplendent emblems of nature's intrinsic beauty. The diaphanous film you see is carpeted throughout with millions of ultra-fine scales arranged in intimate proximity and intricate patterns that absorb and reflect light. This magical coating of filmy flakes imbues my wings with their magnificent color and dazzles my observers with the illusion of iridescence. Though my wings are what you notice most about me, they serve much more than the aesthetic eye. They carry me to the flowers. They flutter when I see my love. And they glide on the wind enabling me to soar."

Marisa was a pretty blonde. The sight of her standing in front of the class adorned by a pair of glistening silken wings had captured the attention of everyone in the room. The men were particularly alert. Her ingenious visual presentation combined with her artfully crafted narrative held the class throughout. Her colleagues learned all of the details of how the warmth from the sun's rays enables flight, about the significance of colors and markings in species recognition and survival, about the fragrant hormonal scales that play a role in courtship. Every interesting detail about the wings of the butterfly had been blended into her melodious monologue.

After compliments from Katherine and the class, a number of hands were in the air and several students questioned the same thing. Had Marisa said that the shiny color on the butterfly's wings was an illusion? What did she mean, an 'illusion'?

"It's an optical illusion," Marisa explained. "It appears to be a bright iridescent color but what we're seeing is actually a response to light. Without the light, the color doesn't exist."

"You mean it's not as bright," stated another student, trying to comprehend her meaning.

"No, it's like when you see oil on the surface of a mud puddle in the sunlight," Marisa said. "If you look at it from a certain angle you see color and shine, but from another angle it's just a mud puddle. It's the same way with the Blue Morpho butterfly. It's so bright blue it looks like flying blue foil. But as it flits in and out of sunbeams it alternates between being incandescent sapphire and dull drab brown. It's all illusion. It's the light."

The students were looking at Katherine.

"The bright iridescence we see coming from some butterflies is the effect of what we call 'thin film interference,' " she said. "Marisa's example of the mud puddle in the sunlight is a good one."

Katherine could see that Steffen was eagerly engaged. Steffen was the one student in the room whom she knew. He was a bright young physics student who had been in her undergraduate class the previous year. "Steffen? Would you like to tell us about what causes this effect?"

Steffen immediately replied. "Yes. On the surface of the butterfly's wings the thin terraces formed out of a cuticle-like material create interference in the light wave. The metallic and iridescent qualities are generated by these three-dimensional structural scales refracting the light."

"But, I don't get why you say that the color is not really there," Melodee said.

"Colors are never really there," Steffen asserted. "What we perceive as color is actually our eye's photoreceptors' response to light. It's our brain's interpretation of differing gradations of energy. Each color is a different gradation."

Katherine observed a number of students' blank expressions. "What we've happened upon here is the fascinating subject of light," she said. "What light is, and how it works, is a subject that has intrigued formidable minds since human beings have been wrestling with the mysteries of nature. In fact, our desire to understand light has been at the root of our most significant scientific revelations. And yet light remains quite a mystery."

She glanced at Marisa who was folding together her glitter-streaked butterfly wings. When Marisa looked at her, Katherine was suddenly struck. The image from her butterfly dream flashed before her. She again beheld her sister Mary Margaret as a beautiful butterfly surrounded by light. It took her a moment to regain her focus.

"As Steffen has pointed out," she said, "there are things we do understand today about light and color. And as we have seen, sometimes what science tells us turns out to be quite counter-intuitive. For Marisa to tell us that the butterfly's luminescence is not really there kind of flies in the face of what our instincts tell us, doesn't it. Just like the idea that we're revolving around the sun rather than observing it rising and setting."

The fact that Jack eagerly volunteered his presentation on butterfly mating immediately following Marisa's captivating presence in the front of the room seemed to have been lost on everyone but Katherine. She carefully concealed her amusement with his enthusiasm.

"Males and females are two entirely different creatures," was his opening declaration. "The male is always interested."

There were a number of giggles from around the room.

"It's his job to see his genes are passed on. Females, on the other hand, are much more discriminating. Not all of them agree to mate. Some are choosy about color. Others require elaborate courtship rituals. It is therefore important for males to recognize signals that indicate the female is not receptive. One of them is hard to miss — she flies away. Other females assume a posture that makes it physically impossible to mate. This too is easily recognizable as a negative response. Yet another sign of disinterest — the female rapidly flaps her wings, battering her harasser and sending him on his way."

Jack's classmates were enjoying themselves.

"When the male does meet up with a willing female, attraction is at first a matter of chemistry. The female releases hormonal fragrances called 'pheromones' that entice the male. The couple sits quietly for about thirty minutes to an hour, depending on the species. Then they engage in a spiral flight that can last for quite a while before the pair drops to the ground and continues their fitful dance. Some flutter slow and low. Others are prone to circling, stroking or fluttering. Occasionally a couple will exhibit bizarre or frenzied behaviors. Purplish Coppers, for instance, have been known to face-off and stroke one another's wings with their antennae. The male Barred Sulphur perches next to the female and waves his forewing up and down, dragging the edge of it along her antennae. The Little Yellow male, on the other hand, is real straightforward. He simply buffets the female for a few seconds before whisking some pheromones onto her antennae, rendering her agreeable to mating."

Jack blushed a little as he glanced in Marisa's direction.

"Female butterflies are another story," he continued. "They can be ferocious in their quest for the ultimate mate. And it actually pays for them to be picky," he explained, "because males offer a wide range of both genes and nutrients that are passed during the mating process and can greatly affect the chances of their offspring's survival. In certain species, the females are famous for their intense selectivity. One species, the Empress Leilia, is extremely particular.

She mates only once in her life, so she wants to be sure she gets just the right mate."

Jack wrapped up his detailed and rather colorful depiction of butterfly mating behaviors with his own bit of color. "Entomologists continue to observe butterfly mating practices as they seek to explain some of their bizarre behaviors. No doubt, as with the mating practices of other species," he said pointedly, "certain behaviors will continue to elude those seeking reasonable explanations."

Jack's presentation was a hit. The response from his buddy, Paul, the one who had offered him up as a golf idol the first day of class, could be heard above the others. "Spoken like a champion," he called out as Jack was returning to his seat.

"I'm sure he's referring to your golf prowess," Katherine added.

The class was having a good time.

Melodee spoke up as she asked Jack, "Was all that true? I mean, was it all really true about butterflies?"

"Yep," Jack replied. "Took it right out of the science journals. Just supplied a few adjectives," he said proudly.

"Very interesting," Katherine said. "Well done."

And as the class was settling down she said, "So. Who's next? How about you, Tim? Have you found some interesting things about 'imago'?"

"Uh, yeah, I found a lot," Tim said. "But I haven't really put it all together yet."

"Well, why don't you just share some of what you've found?"

"Well," Tim said as he leafed through the papers in front of him. "The word 'imago' means 'image' or 'mental image.' It's from Latin. There are two definitions." He read from one of the pages. "One is 'an insect in its final adult winged state.' The second is 'an idealized mental image of a person.' It's a term used in psychology. I found some psychotherapies which refer to it as the ultimate goal of a 'transformative journey.' So it looks like in both cases it refers to kind of a final fully-formed state of being."

"And do you know when the word was first applied to the insect and when it became a psychological term?" Katherine asked.

"Uh, I would have to . . ." He again leafed through his pile of papers.

"That would be an interesting thing to know, wouldn't it. What else did you find about the imago state of the butterfly?"

Tim spoke spontaneously now. "Well, the butterfly is one of the insects that goes through a complete metamorphosis to reach this final state. And, like we talked about, it goes through a lot. In the early stages it literally digests itself from the inside out and goes through a kind of death because a lot of its old body dies. And then it forms a hard shell around itself and just lays low for another stage and kind of has to pull itself together again out of this soup that's left over from all the previous stages. And then new enzymes are released and there is all of this converting of tissues and . . . What's really kind of amazing is that there is this one little bit of tissue. And inside of this tissue is a special group of cells called the 'imaginal bud.' It stays in the butterfly all the way from the egg stage to the winged adult stage. So even with all of the dramatic changes it goes through it still has this little part of itself that survives everything. In the beginning this 'imaginal bud' doesn't really serve any purpose. And in the stage when the caterpillar is being transformed it just kind of stays hidden and protected. But later on, it's the gene inside these cells that supervises the whole reconstruction of the body. The butterfly literally has to rebuild its entire being. And it's the 'imaginal bud' that's been there from the very beginning that's responsible for the whole process. Without it, the butterfly would never be a butterfly."

Katherine acknowledged Aaisha who had been waving her hand.

"So the word 'imago' applies to any creature that goes through a metamorphosis?" she asked.

"It's the name for the final state after a complete metamorphosis," Tim said. "And the butterfly's metamorphosis is so radical it's like one animal disintegrates and a completely different one appears. Achieving 'imago' is no small thing for a butterfly."

As the students responded to Tim's findings they remarked about the vast amount of information they were all finding on the Internet — scientific studies and a myriad other sources in all of their subject areas. They had also discovered that butterflies were an extremely popular logo for many Internet businesses and organizations. Two of the students, Frank and Collin, who were computer science majors, had begun designing a website where the class would be able to share the information they were gathering. And since the turn of the millennium was approaching and was very much on the minds of computer science majors, they had several times raised the question of what the class would do if computers crashed when the clocks turned to 2000. Katherine marveled as she often did at the technological resources the group before her had little memory of ever being without.

Ming Jie and Cherie had teamed up on their topics. Together they informed the class about butterfly adaptation and survival and about the symbiotic relationships between butterflies and other living things. Cherie, a second-year art student, displayed her drawings in front of the class while Ming Jie, a junior in industrial engineering, talked about the amazing techniques the butterfly has evolved over millions of years that are responsible for its survival.

"The female butterfly can identify out of hundreds of plants in her habitat the exact one that will support her offspring," she said. "And she lays her eggs on the part of the plant that is at just the right stage of growth and with just the right sun exposure to give her eggs the nourishment they need. The butterfly's knack for plant recognition is in fact so reliable that botanists often depend on butterflies to identify specific plant species."

As Ming Jie described the butterfly's intense attraction to flowers, Cherie's drawing changed to that of a Pearly Crescent butterfly hovering about a stalk of deep blue delphinium. She was demonstrating the butterfly's preference for deep hues of violet, purple and blue, just as Ming Jie was describing.

"Among the thousands of species of butterflies," Ming Jie continued, "there are also thousands of plants and flowers that they have profound relationships with. We heard about the importance of the Mexican Oyamel fir trees to the Monarch butterfly. Well, other species have similar relationships with specific plants and trees. The Hessel's Hairstreak, for example, cannot survive without the Atlantic white cedar. This came to light when the citizens of a small town in New York worked hard to prevent a movie theater complex from coming into their community because it would have meant destroying two Atlantic white cedars. They later discovered that these two endangered trees were also the home of the Hessel's Hairstreak, an endangered butterfly. By saving the trees the community also rescued the Hessel's Hairstreaks, who for a century or more have depended on the great old cedars for their shelter."

Ming Jie then talked about the host of brilliant guises and deflections butterflies have developed over the years to confuse would-be predators. Among their many survival techniques was a thing called 'mimicry' by which palatable butterflies' wings evolve to mimic the patterns of other species that birds have learned to avoid. "Some even grow eyespots on their wings to serve as false targets so birds won't strike their head or body," she said. "Others will perch themselves on rocks with the same speckled pattern as their wings. And they all strategically avoid white birch which will make them more visible and instead alight on brown tree trunks the same dun color of their undersides. One species is so adept at survival that as a caterpillar its rear inflates and takes on the pyramid-head shape of a snake, thereby discouraging its adversaries from sneaking up behind it." She paused while the class laughed at Cherie's drawing. "Other butterflies will extract toxic substances from plants that make their bodies distasteful and poisonous to their assailants."

The survival behavior that evoked the most astonishment among the class was the mutually supportive relationship scientists have discovered between caterpillars and ants. "Caterpillars actually sing out to ants," Ming Jie explained, "attracting them with the same frequency and pulse rate as the ants' own communication signals. The ants are then seduced to remain next to the caterpillar by a tantalizing fluid the caterpillar emits from its nectary glands. And in exchange for the tasty meal the ants assume a defensive posture, protecting the caterpillar from predators. They actually become their bodyguards!" she exclaimed. "And this relationship can continue into adulthood. Butterflies have even been observed laying their eggs in the vicinity of ants' nests where their larvae then mimic the behavior of ant larvae. Then worker ants actually come and carry them off to their nests where they remain for many months of ant care and feeding," she said, "until one day they surface from the nest, spread their wings and fly! Foster butterflies!"

After Ming Jie and Cherie's report Katherine joined in the class discussion from the third row seat where she generally sat during student presentations. "And do all of these behaviors inspire any new thoughts about the 'imaginal bud' Tim told us about?"
Tim immediately responded. "Yes. Those genes inside the imaginal bud not only tell the butterfly how to rebuild itself but also how to survive."
Katherine shot up from her seat and headed to the front of the class. "For millions of years the butterfly has passed on that imaginal bud, hasn't it. And what a treasure of information is stored in that

tiny cell. How to survive. How to avoid the bird's attack. How to join forces with ants. How to take advantage of the safe harbor of trees. How to actually grow spots and change colors. In that tiny bud, in that little piece of tissue, in all the soupy remnants from its earliest stages of life — is a survival manual. And generation after generation, for millions of years, it's been passed on."

Tim waved at Katherine. "What I don't get is how scientists can know what they know about butterflies and say they don't have intelligence."

"Come on, man," Paul groaned. "They don't even have brains."

"You mean they don't have brains like our brains," Tim responded. "Okay, they've got a few. . . " He looked at Jason. "Whaddaya call 'em?"

"It's just three ganglia fused together," Jason said. "It receives stimuli from the antennae and the eyes."

"I'm not talking about their brains," Tim asserted. "Besides, a lot of scientists say we're just beginning to understand all their behaviors and what's going on. I'm saying that everything we have learned about them, to me, says there's intelligence there."

"I agree," said Cynthia. "I think they demonstrate amazing intelligence."

"Well, we know they don't *think*," Paul contested. "It's not like they have *real* intelligence."

"They just know how to survive," Jason said. "Like all animals. Animals have their own kind of intelligence."

"Well, we've raised another interesting subject," Katherine said. "So what kinds of behaviors suggest intelligence to us?"

Melodee was titillated. "Yeah, they have a lot of behaviors that are just like ours."

"Okay, let's look at those first," Katherine said. "What butterfly behaviors have we learned about that strike us as human-like?"

Paul jumped in. "The males always wanna do it and the females are always choosy."

The class laughed.

"Jack pointed out some interesting courtship and mating practices, didn't he," Katherine said. "What else?" She looked around at the hands in the air. There was a steady stream of responses.

"Some remain in the meadow where they were born for their entire lives and others wander wide distances."

"And some mate instantly when they meet a prospective mate and others look around for a long time for a suitable partner."

"Some species form tightly closed populations with distinct geographical boundaries."

"Yeah, and some hang around in groups in the same trees in the evenings!"

"And in some species the oldest ones in the colony are the first to select their perches."

"Oh yeah, and remember they observed in some species that one of the butterflies goes around in the morning and wakes up the others in the colony?"

"They go through radical changes throughout their lives and have to adapt in order to survive," Cynthia said.

Katherine smiled. "There are others too, aren't there?" she said. "And do these behaviors suggest intelligence?"

Most of the group responded affirmatively. Paul held his ground. "Animal intelligence," he said firmly.

"All right," Katherine said. "For the moment let's consider intelligence all by itself without any labels. How do we define intelligence?"

"The ability to *think*," Paul asserted.

"No," Tim calmly disputed, "I don't believe it is the ability to think. I think *we* think it's the ability to think because that's our experience of intelligence. I think there are other kinds of intelligence besides ours."

"Okay, Tim," Katherine posed. "How would you define 'intelligence'?"

Tim was eager to pursue this train of thought. He spoke carefully as he thought through his definition. "It's an ability to know . . . and to communicate."

Katherine looked around. "Anyone else? Does Tim's description work for us? Paul?"

"I don't have a problem with it," Paul said grudgingly.

"Okay, and are there any butterfly behaviors that suggest the ability to know and to communicate that are not particularly human-like?"

It was only a moment before Tim had organized his thoughts again. "Yeah, their survival behaviors. They suggest incredible intelligence. And it's not at all human-like to cooperate with other living creatures. Not like caterpillars do with ants."

Cynthia immediately followed. "And their relationship with flowers is the same way," she said. "They're like co-conspirators in the continuation of life."

"Well, that's exactly what I'm saying," Paul groaned again. "It's just survival. That's all they're doing is just keeping their species alive."

"Do you hear what you're saying?" Cynthia asked Paul. "How can you say they're keeping their species alive and say there's not intelligence there?"

"I didn't say they *talk* about it," Paul said.

Several students laughed.

"Okay," Katherine interjected. "We all want to understand what is being said here. Paul, correct me if I'm not completely understanding you. In the case of the butterfly and the flowers, you're saying there is no intelligence — no way of knowing or communicating — but you think the butterflies and the flowers are actively engaged in behaviors that perpetuate their species."

"Yyyeah," Paul said with a slight hesitation.

"And you think the continuation of their species is the purpose of their behaviors."

"Yeah, but it's not like they plan it, or like she said, '*conspire*'!" Paul rolled his eyes. "It's not like they're actually communicating with each other."

"And Cynthia, you think butterflies and flowers do communicate."

"Absolutely," Cynthia said. "I think there is definitely communication involved. If we forget for a minute about our idea of language and really look at what's happening between these two creatures." She reminded the class. "The butterfly has inordinate sensitivity to color. And flowers display the most pronounced color in nature which is how they attract the butterflies. They even have markings on their petals that guide the butterflies to the nectar at the centers of their blossoms." She went on. "The butterfly needs the nectar for its nourishment. And while it's drawing nectar it gathers the flower's pollen which it then sprinkles in the area, creating more flowers. They have a complete mutually sustaining relationship. To me, that's communication."

Paul thrashed his upper body in exasperation. "But that's just *nature*," he protested.

The rest of the class was probing Katherine's expression. She was sitting perfectly still on the edge of the desk, her smile remained constant.

"It is nature indeed," she said. "That's one thing of which we may be certain." She glanced at the clock. "And I have no doubt we'll be continuing this discussion," she said as she smiled at Cynthia and at Paul.

As the students began to stir in their seats she added, "One more thing before you go." She tilted her head playfully, exhibiting an interrogative expression.

The students blared in her direction, "*Consider the butterfly's perspective.*"

Nine

When Charles Lewis suggested to Charlotte Newberg, the director of the Humanities Institute, that it might be interesting to include a complexity theorist as a guest lecturer in her "Emergence" series, he knew the idea would confound some of his physics colleagues. Charlotte understood to a lesser degree than Charles that for such an event it would be unrealistic to expect much of a showing from the physics department. Though the guest speaker, Christopher Luetzow, was an esteemed Stanford physicist, to many of his own he was among the misguided who had defected to the Santa Fe Institute and this dubious new field of complexity theory. Bob Gurzick and Carolyn Lloyd did attend the lecture along with Charles and Katherine, which made for a slightly more respectable showing from a department of ninety some physicists. As it turned out, the rest of the department was not missed. Rackham Auditorium was filled to standing room only.

Christopher Luetzow immediately connected with his humanities audience by pointing out that the most fundamental particle of matter, the 'quark,' took its name from James Joyce's *Finnegan's Wake* — evidence, he proposed, that physicists were capable of both literary insight and bouts of whimsy. He began his discussion of the concept of "emergence" by stating that the same essential dynamics that are present in a quark are present in everything else in the universe — in a tree, a human being, an ecosystem. Yet there are dynamics present in a tree, a human being and an ecosystem which are not present in a quark. Trees, human beings and ecosystems were his first examples of "adaptive, non-linear, complex systems." "Emergence," he explained, was one of the dynamics that brought complex systems into being. "At each new level of structural organization in a complex system," he said, "qualities *emerge* which were not present at previous levels in the system's development."

Many in the audience had attended the other programs in this year's Humanities Institute "Emergence" series. They had heard from a linguist about the emergence of new words in a language system reflecting the dynamics of a changing culture, and from a cultural historian about the emergence of democratic principles in developing societies. They had experienced a dance created by a choreographer-in-residence, called "Emergence," and heard from a poet about the intuitive bursts of insight and other "emergent" forces that are the lifeblood of every creative process. Christopher Luetzow's discussion of "emergence" as a dynamic inherent to all complex systems was a wonderful addition to the mix. In addition to shedding new light on the concept of "emergence" itself and on the exciting new field of complexity theory, his talk gave new meaning to the other events in the series. The response from the humanities audience surpassed Charlotte Newberg's most hopeful expectations.

The reception crowd had thinned by the time Charlotte reached Charles, who was now standing with Debra, Katherine and Mary Claire in their familiar huddle of four. The gleam of satisfaction that passed between them was well deserved. Charles' intuitive sense of the growing interest in complexity theory had been borne out even beyond his expectations. And Charlotte had been rewarded for her daring leap across the great divide between the humanities and the sciences. She was thrilled.

"Quite dynamic, isn't he," she said to Charles. "And I can see why he's been somewhat controversial in your neck of the woods."

"What was his remark that he said a lot of physicists would disagree with?" Debra asked Charles. And then she answered her own question. "It's hard to tell what is possible in the universe simply by looking at the rules?" She was now looking at Katherine. "Yes, well, we spend a lot of time looking at the rules. And for the rules," Katherine said.

"The truth is, Charles," Charlotte admitted, "I wish he had talked even more about complexity studies and exactly what it is they're looking for. Sometime I'd love a fundamental explanation. The non-scientist version," she stressed.

Charles chuckled. "Well, I'll be the envy of a lot of people if I can accomplish that. And not just non-scientists."

"It so depends on whom you ask," Debra said.

"The field is still defining itself," Charles explained. "That's one of the things that makes it so exciting. There are a lot of good heads working on complexity. They'd all define it differently — and all validly. Some are looking at analogies between physical systems and biological systems. Some are studying social systems. There are computer scientists, sociologists, economists, organizational theorists – so many people doing interesting work in complexity."

"Yes," Charlotte said. "But it's what you're all doing that's still fuzzy to me. I still want to ask, 'What exactly is complexity theory?'"

"Go ahead," Debra prodded her husband. "Give her your condensed version. In regular people's language," she added.

Mary Claire jumped in. "Now, what we should do is have Debra explain it," she said.

"Yeah, I'd like to hear that version too," Charles said, grinning at his wife.

"Well," Debra ventured. "The way it makes the most sense to me is that most of science is breaking things down, right? Ever since we found our way into the atom we've been so enthralled with what we've found, we keep digging deeper, breaking things down into smaller and smaller parts, looking at processes and patterns at the atomic level. What complexity theorists are doing is taking a step back and looking at systems as wholes. And they're finding that there are dynamics we would have missed altogether had we not looked at whole systems. Things like self-organization and adaptation and 'emergence,' " she said. Charles was watching his wife with visible adulation as she spoke. "And what's fascinating is that they're finding that incredibly diverse systems — from a single protein to a walking breathing creature — ecosystems, economic systems, social systems — they all exhibit some of the very same dynamics."

"Like the emergence of order out of chaos," Charlotte said, assimilating some of Christopher Luetzow's talk.

"And the most interesting one, of course," Debra continued, "is the tendency toward higher levels of order and increasing complexity — which seems to be present everywhere."

Charlotte appealed to Charles. "So do I understand correctly that a "complex" system is any system where a great many parts interact with one another and where the whole system kind of takes on a life of its own?"

Mary Claire jumped in. "That's what I love is that they call them 'complex' or 'non-linear' or 'dynamic' — they don't call them 'living' systems because the jury's still out on what actually distinguishes life." She became emphatic. "What's more *living* than a system where all of its parts work together toward some advanced state for the whole? And who's to say what's not a living system?! I defy anyone to tell me a creative work of literature is not a living system!"

"Well the brain that created it certainly is," Debra said. She looked at Charles. "The human brain is the most complex system we know of, right? Other than the universe itself."

The look on Charles' face told his wife she had unearthed an interesting question. "I guess unless you consider all of our brains together another complex system."

Charlotte was still probing. "I didn't quite get what he said about the Second Law of Thermodynamics."

"Well, the Second Law is one of those basic laws we've identified, right?" Charles explained. "Everything breaks down. Metal rusts, bath water cools, bodies run down. There are complexity theorists who'll tell you that what they're looking at are the dynamics that run counter to the Second Law. What is it in all these systems that causes them to create order and increasing complexity? What is it in a single fertilized egg that causes it to divide and to generate the quadrillion cells that eventually form a newborn infant? And what prompts the brain to constantly organize billions of neural connections toward a coherent device for thinking and learning?"

Mary Claire bounded in again, "So what they're really asking, bottom-line, is 'What is life's life force?'"

Katherine shared a broad smile with Charles. "She does have a way of cutting right to it, doesn't she."

"And when they've figured it all out," Mary Claire continued, "we'll know once and for all that it's all just one big complex system and that everything is connected and that the slightest fluctuation in any one of the tiniest parts affects the whole shebang."

Charles saluted her with his punch glass. "Mary Claire, you want to work on my next book with me?"

"So, what's more important?" Charlotte asked Charles. "Seriously. I don't understand why scientists look down on complexity theory?"

"Not all scientists," Katherine said.

"That's right," Charles followed. "There are many who're recognizing its importance."

"But I don't understand why all physicists don't," Charlotte said.

"Well, for one thing, as Debra said," Charles explained, "most of the advances science has made so far have happened by the opposite approach. We've learned an awful lot by getting inside of things and examining their most reducible parts. There are particle physicists who'll tell you there's nothing we won't eventually figure out by continuing to do just that. All this large picture stuff is just not science to a lot of physicists."

Katherine joined in. "But the most strenuous objection, of course, is to the foraging in realms outside of science."

"That's right, it's one thing to study physical systems," Charles said. "But the thing is, you don't have to look far to see that some of the very same dynamics are present in all kinds of other systems."

"Including those *soft* sciences," Mary Claire said in a dark scary tone. "Where those *humans* lurk," she dramatized, "like social systems and cultural systems. Can't be getting cozy with those *soft-headed* disciplines."

"But if the same dynamics are showing up everywhere it would be crazy not to look at that, wouldn't it?" Charlotte asked.

Charles grinned at her. "Couldn't agree with you more, my dear."

Debra smiled at Charlotte. "You just summed up his complexity program," she said.

Katherine and Mary Claire left Charles in high spirits that evening, he and Debra and Christopher Luetzow heading to their home to have dinner with Avery. Katherine and Mary Claire walked from Rackham across the Diag and onto the sidewalks leading home. Mary Claire too had a bounce in her step that evening, buoyed by the burgeoning interest in complexity studies. Her efforts for the Initiative for Undergraduate Education had earned her a deep sense of alliance with any endeavor that was bridging the gulfs between scholarly disciplines.

"So why is it that Lloyd and the gang are so infuriated by all this?" she said to Katherine. "It's not as if they're putting forward some kind of wacky theory that belies science, right? They're just communicating with other fields and looking at the larger picture."

"Yes, but as Charles said, that isn't what scientists do," Katherine said. "Scientists do science." She had punctuated the words with feigned smugness and then shifted to a serious tone. "And it's true, real science is done within specific disciplines. As far as people like Lloyd are concerned, to even open dialogue with other areas of research is to tamper with science at its core. What he's infuriated by are the scientists who are agreeing with people like you." She nudged her friend. "All of you loonies who think we should all be communicating with one another. Even communicating *within* the sciences," Katherine stressed. "He'd be completely baffled by an event like this Sundance weekend."

"Can't wait to hear what this is about," Mary Claire said.

"All the sciences together?" Katherine mimicked Lloyd. "Whatever for?"

Mary Claire shook her head. "*Butterflies 101*," she spurted, amused by Lloyd's ridicule of Katherine's Initiative class.

"I'm glad we decided on 'A Course in Butterflies,'" Katherine said.

"And is it ever turning out to be one.

"You said you had a flashback on your dream?"

Katherine's eyes opened wide. "In class, yes. This dream is so amazing the way it stays with me."

Mary Claire's kitchen had become the favorite spot for Katherine and Mary Claire over the years. They had spent countless evenings in the same chairs at the same antique table. And no matter how simple the meal, Mary Claire always lit candles. Tonight they spread her homemade pesto on crusty French bread to accompany their vegetable salads. Yet it was quite a while before Katherine could focus on anything but her butterfly dream.

"Did you ever have a dream that you just knew would never fade?" she asked.

Mary Claire sipped her wine. "I usually forget them. If we ever really forget them," she added.

"This one is still so powerful," Katherine said. "And so perfectly detailed. Yet when I think about trying to describe it in words . . ."

"I know what you mean. Dreams come through in their essence rather than in language."

"God, Mary Claire, it was so . . ." Katherine became intent on her effort to describe the indescribable. "It was the most beautiful butterfly . . . Just breathtakingly beautiful. And it was surrounded by the most magnificent light . . . Truly. It was as though the light itself were alive. And then suddenly the butterfly was Mary Margaret. And the light came from behind her and glistened all around her. It was the light more than anything that was so . . . And when she was Mary Margaret she was a child, you know? But she had the consciousness of an adult. It was as though she were speaking to me as a grown person. And she was so euphoric and peaceful. And what she was communicating . . . it was so . . . rearranging, as David would say."

"There was one thing she said that you did remember, right?"

"I'll never forget it. She said, 'Here or there, it is all the same life.'" She looked at Mary Claire. "But in the dream, what she was saying was something so much larger than the meaning of the words. Do you know what I mean?"

"I do." Mary Claire assured her.

"When I woke up that morning I just knew it had to be butterflies we would study."

"Well, you're sure doing it," Mary Claire said.

"There was so much she was telling me that I'm still just on the edge of understanding. In a way it was as if she were trying to tell me that I could be at peace with it all. With her, with my father, even the whole religion thing." Katherine shuddered as she recalled the river man's demeanor. "That fellow at the river Saturday morning."

"He really ambushed you, didn't he."

"It's so amazing," Katherine said. "No matter how much we may think we've evolved, that inner child is a powerful thing. And it's so interesting that Lloyd is able to evoke the same feelings in me."

"Funny, isn't it," Mary Claire said thoughtfully. "The guy at the river screaming at you for not buying into his particular religion, and Lloyd blasting you for stepping out of science."

Katherine was engrossed in the thoughts she was still processing about her dream.

"I know it sounds crazy but it was as though she was trying to tell me that it's all okay. She was trying to ease the feelings that still cling to my insides."

Mary Claire hesitated before expressing her next thought. "And did you get any feeling about your mother from the dream?" She knew Katherine was still struggling to assimilate the new information she had about her mother. She gently presented her next words. "I do think your aunt was right."

Katherine looked at her.

"I think she really loves her daughter."

Katherine looked away from her and Mary Claire hesitated again before she spoke. "I can only imagine how hard it's been for her all these years to honor your relationship with Marion and Bill."

Katherine stared at the candle flame. "I'm just not there yet. I don't know if I ever will be. I just can't imagine ever not thinking of Marion, you know?"

"She was a wonderful woman," Mary Claire agreed. Then she ventured a little further. "And you know she would want you to do whatever is best for you."

Katherine was still meditating. "What is it about dreams that . . ."

"Even physicists pay attention to them?" Mary Claire asked.

They smiled at one another as Katherine finally began eating her salad.

And then almost as if in turn, Mary Claire became contemplative. "You know, knowing you and Marion and Bill really was the thing that nudged me."

Katherine understood her perfectly. She knew that for some time Mary Claire had been considering adopting a child.

"God, it's such a huge step," she said. "Sometimes I think I'm certifiable to even be thinking about it."

Mary Claire had been married for nine years to Bob Henley, a U-M political science professor with whom she had maintained a good relationship since their divorce. Her one regret about their marriage was that they had not had a child. In the years since their divorce she had thought many times about the possibility of adopting on her own. The idea was increasingly on her mind.

"It's a never ending process, isn't it," Katherine said thoughtfully. "Even after you think you're completely reconciled."

"Even after your body's reconciled," Mary Claire followed.

In another moment her expression lifted as she raised her glass to Katherine. "And I'll say it again," she announced – "*Relevance* is a *helluva* child."

The sound of their glasses touching was the only sound necessary. They both knew how grateful Katherine was for Mary Claire's outlook on procreation. She believed strongly that there was more than one way for women to give birth, to create, to contribute to the world. She had been there for Katherine as she labored through her own processing, letting go of motherhood. It was a process that had finally come to closure for Katherine.

Mary Claire became immersed again in her own reflection on the idea of adoption. "I sure wouldn't be Marion and Bill," she said.

Katherine was warmed by the thought of her parents. "No, but you'd give to it every bit of what they did. Even together," she emphasized.

"You think so?"

"I think so."

Mary Claire played with her salad. "I still need some more time to just wear the idea."

"And you know I'm going to be here for you, whatever you decide," Katherine said.

Mary Claire brightened up. "What more could a kid want, huh? A certifiable mom and an astrophysicist aunt."

Katherine grinned. "Pesto is fabulous," she said.

"It is good, isn't it. Produce Station has the best basil."

Walking home through the quiet streets that night Katherine found herself whispering the word aloud — "home." She too had once had dreams of home and family. Marion and Bill had given her that too. She was reminded again of her own difficult processing on the subject of motherhood. It was a subject she really did feel at peace with now. Yet there was something else in life for which she still yearned. She looked up at the half moon and spoke to it as she walked along the sidewalk. "What is it that makes us hold onto things we have never really known?"

As she turned the key to her condo door she felt the wood give way the same way it had done for years. "Home," she thought as she entered the darkness. Was that something she would ever really know?

Ten

Seeing Cynthia standing in front of the class, Katherine was reminded of the Queen Alexandra's Birdwing, the species the class had learned was one of the world's grandest, unique to the rainforest of New Guinea, with wings that can span a full twelve inches. Cynthia was a tall, stately young woman who carried herself like the adult she was. Her presentation was every bit as polished as Katherine knew it would be. She captivated the class with all of the latest findings about the butterfly's extraordinary vision.

Her elaborate graphic display illustrated the full expanse of the electromagnetic spectrum of light. A threadlike marking in the middle of the chart indicated the sliver of a narrow range that is visible to the human eye, while the vast highlighted area represented the expansive visual scope of the butterfly. The graphic showed how the butterfly's vision can extend from well into the infrared, which humans know only through the feel of heat, all the way into the high-frequency ultraviolet radiation which is also invisible to the human eye.

Cynthia's detailed presentation underscored the butterfly's extraordinary relationship with ultraviolet light which is an important feature of the butterfly's visual experience, one we humans do not fully understand. She explained that for some species UV markings play a role in how they distinguish one another for mating. For others, whose ultraviolet patches are directionally iridescent, the light that emanates from them, flickering while they are in flight, is thought by scientists to have some role in behavior and communication.

"One of the other things I found interesting . . ." She was talking informally now. "The more I learned about their visual experience, the more I was fascinated by how they reflect the things they are drawn to." She looked at Katherine. "They have a direct and immediate need for the sun. They need it to fly, to incubate their ovaries, to live. And they reflect the light, which is what enables them to recognize one another and to mate, even to ward off predators. And it's the same way with color," she said. "Their intense sensitivity to color attracts them to flowers. And they are, in a way, reflections of flowers themselves. Remember, Kimberly said that early American gardening books referred to butterflies as 'flying flowers?' I just think it's so interesting that they are drawn to and absorb light and color, and they also radiate light and color into the world."

"It's true," Tim chimed in. "They've even detected unusual sensitivity to the polarization of light in butterfly cells. They have a built-in relationship to light that's written into their survival manuals."

"It's written into all our survival manuals!" Paul asserted in his now infamous condescending tone. "Everything depends on the sun. We can't live without it!"

"Yes, but we don't have light receptors on our sex organs that go off when it's time to pass our sperm, do we?" Tim said. The class laughed and stirred as he fired off his response to his classmate. "And our entire bodies don't automatically tilt in the direction of a sunbeam. And sunlight doesn't transform us from a dull, drab brown into iridescent. And we don't see infrared and UV rays. I'm saying their relationship to light is something beyond ours."

"Steffen, you look like you have something to say," Katherine said.

"It's just that all of these things have reasonable explanations," Steffen said. "The butterfly's broader range of electromagnetic sensitivity is explained quite fundamentally in the structure of its visual apparatus which has been explained in some detail." He looked at Tim. "As for the lights on their sex organs, butterflies are the first conclusive example of peripheral extraocular photoreceptors in the genitalia of arthropods." Steffen was oblivious to the stirring around him. "This photosensitivity is mediated by neurons that, through an axon in the abdominal ganglion, connect with motoneurons that control movement in the external genitalia. Electrophysiological measurements indicate that these receptors effect a marked increase in copulation success rates." He turned toward Cynthia. "And the butterfly is not reflecting the color of the flower. The butterfly and the flower simply appear to have color based on our photoreceptors' interpretation of the light."

"I'm not saying that they literally reflect the color of the flower," Cynthia responded. "I'm saying that I find it striking that they emanate the very things they're profoundly drawn to."

Mya's hand shot into the air. "Professor Ayers? Didn't you say that we don't understand light? That it's a mystery?"

"I did," Katherine said. "And what Steffen has told us is also true. We actually know a great deal today about how light works. We understand how the sun, which is a big ball of hydrogen and helium, generates light. We know something about how that light travels ninety-three million miles to Earth. We know how our photoreceptors respond to light and interpret color. And now, I see we even have some understanding of photoreceptivity in butterfly genitalia!" she remarked, acknowledging Ryan's discovery of a recent Japanese study regarding these special light receptors. "We have quite an understanding of the physical composition of light and of what light will do under certain conditions. The problem is that light also behaves in ways that are mutually incompatible.

Which tells us there is still a great deal we do not know." She observed Steffen. "Steffen, will you tell us what we know today about what light is?"

"Well, it's pure energy," Steffen said.

As Steffen went on with his highly technical explanation that was understood by no one in the room but Katherine, she diverted him by asking, "And what is the ultimate source of the energy?"

"Well, ultimately," he shrugged, "we don't know."

Cynthia looked at Steffen. "So, isn't it the same as approaching an understanding of the butterfly by breaking it down into its parts?"

"What do you mean?" Steffen asked her.

"Understanding how light works without understanding what it is."

Steffen replied in his unwaveringly precise manner. "It makes good sense to study how a thing works in order to understand it."

"Yes, but I'm just saying that it's not the only way," Cynthia said. She thought for a moment and then she formed her appeal to Steffen. "If you imagine the Blue Morpho in that moment when it's struck by sunlight and flashes that iridescent blue, and you realize that we have no idea what light really is — then understanding three-dimensional structures and refraction and photoreceptor apparatus, well, that just feels very limiting to me. I feel like there is so much more to explore."

"That's fine," Steffen said. "But the approach you are describing is not scientific. It has no basis in fact. You are just imagining things and exploring your feelings."

"I agree!" exclaimed Melodee in her high-pitched accelerated speech. "I mean with Cynthia. I was thinkin' about the Blue Morpho butterfly too, like we saw in Natalie's video, the way it shines so bright blue. Especially when you said that blue and violet have the most energy."

Steffen began to suffer in controlled agitation.

"What do you mean, they have the most energy?" Carlos asked.

Cynthia referred again to her diagram of the electromagnetic spectrum of light. "Blue and violet, at the far end of the spectrum, are the most energetic of the visible colors," she said. "Beyond the violet portion is the ultraviolet."

"Yeah," Melodee said. "So doesn't the shiny blue that comes from the Blue Morpho mean it's really high energy? Isn't that why butterflies prefer blue and purple flowers? Cuz they have the most energy in them?"

Katherine raised her eyebrows to Melodee. "Blue and purple are indeed high frequency colors," she said. "Perhaps that is precisely why the butterflies prefer them."

When Robert signaled from the back of the room and stood up from his desk, Katherine concealed her inordinate interest in what he would have to say. She had no idea what he had been working on for his presentation but she had no doubt it would be somehow provocative. Robert was a solid, imposing figure with a strikingly square jaw and pronounced forehead. His almost unwieldy, hulkish comportment was softened by the waft of his silken hair as he ambled down the steps of the lecture hall to the front of the class. There he stood without even a piece of paper in his hands glaring at the faces in front of him. His deep-throated voice filled the room. "My name is Hessel's Hairstreak," he said.

Though his opening was clearly an amusing one, the group did not stir. To Katherine's amazement they remained his captives almost without a blink of an eye until he yielded the floor. And Robert did not yield the floor for quite some time.

"I'm the one who lives in the Atlantic white cedar in Putnam County, New York," he said. "You heard the story."

A couple of students turned and looked at Ming Jie who had mentioned the Hessel's Hairstreak and the Atlantic white cedar.

"Some people have gone to a lot of trouble to save a couple

of old trees. They stood up to big business. The kind of business everybody loves — mega movie complexes with plenty of parking. The two old trees that are standing on the property are a good forty feet tall and nearly seven feet around. It took a little longer for them to discover me. The only thing special about my residence in this particular tree is that I can't survive anywhere else." Robert was intent on the faces in front of him. His steady tone and measured pace gave added emphasis to his words. "I'm not gonna remind you how nice it is just to have us around — grand old trees and gossamer wings. Some call it 'intrinsic aesthetic value.' I won't tell you that those noble centenarians have earned the right to stand their ground for as long as the earth supports them. I'm gonna tell you the part of the story you may not have heard before. Or if you have, you haven't paid it much attention.

"You call us 'endangered,' me and the tree. But the danger's much greater than you think. Around those trees, just like every other twelve-acre parcel of earth, live billions of other creatures. Oh, not important ones, some say. What could be more inconsequential than earthworms and roundworms and insects and mites? Except maybe algae, and fungi, and the trillions of microscopic organisms that hang around in the same place. Who needs a bunch of disgusting bugs and microbes, right? Well, every single one of those microorganisms is a worker in a system that's been operating the same way for eons. Together they produce and maintain the soil they live in. And the air around them. And the water below them.

"Underneath this particular plot of land there just happens to be a reservoir that supplies water to parts of New York City. And those tiny organisms all work together to filter and regulate the water that continually replenishes the reservoir. You see, those few smart citizens figured out that the entire self-generating system would be decimated and the reservoir below would be assaulted by the chemical waste of thousands of people and automobiles. They also thought that those two mighty trees that had been standing in the same place for more than a century should be left alone.

"But movie theaters and shopping malls have to go somewhere, right? What's a couple of old trees and a butterfly? Species are always disappearing from the earth! It's called evolution! Well, it's true. When Mother Nature's left to her own devices she just keeps producing more and more species. And the greater the diversity of species in the system, the greater its ability to withstand storms and droughts and quakes and other natural disasters. The problem is, since the arrival of technological man, Mother Nature is being taxed like she's never been before. She's now contending with all the human activity which is not only destroying the earth's resources but its systems for replenishing itself as well. Every year millions of automobiles and coal-fired electric plants and burning forests are pumping billions of tons of carbon dioxide into the atmosphere. Atmosphere that for eons has maintained precise proportional levels in its component parts. It's that delicate balance in the atmosphere that regulates global temperatures and patterns of climate, not to mention keeping the air breathable for living things. And the overload of carbon dioxide is just the beginning. Every year millions of tons of toxic chemicals are being spewed into the air. And millions more tons of hazardous waste and chemical fertilizers and pesticides are being dumped into the soil and the water — every year. A lot of those poisons are gonna stay around for thousands of years, some forever. With what you humans are doing to the planet, is it any surprise that the earth's becoming unfit for more and more of its inhabitants? Species are now disappearing thousands of times faster than they did for all the previous life of the planet. And guess what folks? Every time one of those species is extinguished — remember the job it did in cooperation with all the other workers in the system? Well, that particular species isn't gonna be doin' its job anymore. It's never gonna do it again.

"It's also not surprising that none of this has caused you much concern. You live in a part of the world where the least inconvenience is instantly remedied. The flip of a light switch. The touch of a thermostat. Hungry? Open the refrigerator. It's hard for you to imagine that many of your own species don't have enough food or water to keep their children alive. In other parts of the world, weather's not something you close the door on. It's an inescapable force that can wipe out entire populations. Populations that have never seen a bed. Or imagined a light bulb. Never heard of an antibiotic.

"Well, that's the problem, you say – overpopulation! Why doesn't somebody stop all those countries from having too many people and taxing the earth's resources? You might be surprised to know the truth, my friends. About a quarter of the world's population lives the way you do. And the way you live is consuming natural resources about forty times faster than populations for which refrigerators and automobiles exist only in dreams. And the biggest kicker is — those other parts of the world? They want to live the way you do. Who can blame them? And many of them are working hard to achieve that very thing. The problem is, ol' Mother Earth's havin' trouble dealing with what's here now. Scientists say that to even stabilize the atmosphere at its present carbon concentrations, global emissions must be reduced by fifty to seventy percent. Meanwhile, motor traffic and coal-fired electric plants and the other perpetrators of carbon emissions — they're escalating at staggering rates. And so is all the rest of the rampant contamination.

"But that's not true! you say. That's just a lot of hot air from those tree-huggin' environmentalists! People who are sayin' those things are alarmists! If the Earth was really in trouble we'd be hearing about it every day. From our government. From the media.

They'd tell us if the earth was being destroyed! Well, my friends, just who is it that you think is gonna step up to the podium and say, 'We're consuming ourselves right out of a planet. We've got to change the way we think. The way we live.' " Robert peered into his classmates' eyes. "Know anybody who's gonna announce that? To their constituency? Or their viewing audience? Or the people who buy their products?

"The people who are telling you that, why, they're just like those two old trees — 'standin' in the way of progress.'" He looked around the room. "And it doesn't really matter who's telling you, does it? Cuz as long as your latte's hot and that express air button on the dashboard keeps crankin' out a hefty breeze, you're gonna be thinkin' about other things. You've got places to go. Things to do. And let's face it, it's a whole lot easier to listen to the folks who're tellin' ya — 'There's nothin' to worry about. Nothin' at all.'

"The truth is all around you, my friends. But it's something you have to put together on your own. The first step is to know how things really are right in your own backyard, in your own community. And then you do what you can to steer 'em in the right direction. Just like those few residents of Putnam County did. Hey, they like movies as much as anybody. They want their grandchildren to see movies. And big old trees. Even Hessel's Hairstreaks. And they don't mind being called 'tree huggers'— because they know the truth. If every one of us was responsible for just as much of the planet as we can wrap our arms around, well, the whole situation could be turned around . . . But then, don't listen to me. I'm real partial to tree-huggers. They're hangin' on for dear life. Just like me."

Katherine watched the students' expressions as Robert took his long deliberate strides back up the aisle. He invited no questions or comments. In fact, as she glanced at the clock she realized his presentation would be the final words of the day, perhaps just as he had intended. She could not help noticing the face of the young girl she had observed the first day of class as the youngest in the room. It was a face that could make the devil be true, she thought. Her name was Breahn. Though her contribution to discussion had been negligible, no student had ever been a more attentive participant. Katherine was not surprised to see that Breahn had been visibly affected by Robert's speech. And though she made it a practice to not force meek students into the light, her calling on her in this moment was far from a breach of principle.

"Breahn? Is there something you would like to say?"

In a moment Breahn softly spoke. "I would just like to say thank you to Robert."

"Yes," Katherine said as she looked at Robert. "I would like to thank Sir Robert too."

In another moment Cynthia began a round of applause. Isaiah handed Katherine a copy of the printed materials that had filtered down throughout the room. It was Robert's list of recommended reading and web sites. His Hessel's Hairstreak monologue had been the product of copious research. And yes, she thought, as she quickly scanned the resources — some of the finest minds at work on solutions.

"I take it you had the statement about the butterfly as an indicator of environmental change," she said to Robert. "I'm curious. Did you trade for it?"

"No, it was assigned to me."

"Interesting," she said, with her familiar serene gaze. "But your interest in this project started before this class began."

"I've been working on it for a while," he said.

The class was slower to stir than usual. From their expressions it was clear they were anticipating some final remark from Katherine.

"The butterfly's perspective is in good hands," she said.

She smiled at Robert and at Cynthia as the class stirred to leave.

Eleven

The moment she arrived at baggage claim at the Salt Lake City Airport, Katherine spotted a K. AYERS sign conspicuously displayed by a young man in a Sundance t-shirt and a baseball cap. His eyes brightened and he whisked a stray lock of hair behind his ear when she extended her hand and smiled. "Hi, I'm Katherine Ayers."

"This is it?" he said as he eagerly lifted her bag.

She automatically crawled into the back seat of the Sidekick before realizing she was his only passenger. "An unfortunate habit among travelers," she said, acknowledging their immediate rapport. She buckled herself into the front seat at the highway convenience store where he stopped for her to pick up a bottle of water. They talked all the way to Sundance.

"An astrophysicist, huh?"

Rob had spent just enough time in college to know that "organized education" was not for him. He was a serious outdoorsman who was both knowledgeable and passionate about local history and Native American culture. He spoke of his employer with undisguised exhilaration, diverting his gaze with each detail that highlighted his familiarity with the famous film icon. At the same time he emphasized that his affinity for the Sundance mystique had nothing to do with the "Hollywood hoo-hah," as he put it. "He has respect for the land, you know? He keeps the place the way it was, the way it's supposed to be. And not just because it's cool, you know? I think he really has respect."

All the visible terrain between the airport and their destination confirmed Katherine's preconceptions of Utah. Except for a one-time stopover in the airport this was her first exposure to the state. "It's quite, well, brown, isn't it?" she said a little apologetically.

A wave of astonishment came over Rob's expression. "You just wait and see if you feel that way in a little while!"

From the moment they began their ascent toward Mount Timpanogos Rob took genuine pleasure in each glance at Katherine's face. "My gosh, it's beautiful," she said, more than once, swaying to her driver's fluid communion with the road. The sunlight streamed in from alternating directions as they climbed the smooth winding pavement that rolled like a ribbon through the glistening golden aspen groves dotted with emerald pines. Rob was beaming. "Not so dull and brown anymore, is it."

The Sundance resort was a little piece of heaven nestled at the base of Mount Timpanogos. Guest cottages were so respectfully placed within the rolling green woodland it was as though they had sprung up of themselves like wild grasses, embracing the trees that surrounded them. Rob had pointed out the "Rehearsal Hall" across the creek where the reception and meetings would take place and the gourmet restaurant in the large log cabin across the bridge. "You're one of the last to arrive," he said. "So I'll take you to your cottage and you can head over to the reception whenever you're ready."

Inside, her cottage smelled of rustic elegance — natural fibers, handcrafted furnishings, a stone fireplace, hand-made oatmeal soap. On the carved wooden table was a large manila envelope imprinted with The Herbert B. Finn Memorial Foundation logo. "Katherine Ayers" was hand-written on the face of it. Inside were a few pages with "Welcome to Sundance from the Finn Foundation" written at the top. It was a simple list of names — no titles, no institutions, just names and cities. She sat on the bed and eagerly scanned the list. From the names she knew it was clear this was indeed an unprecedented assembly. A number of Nobel laureates from the U.S., Germany, France, Belgium, Japan. There were physicists and biologists, geneticists, cognitive scientists — major names from every field and from all parts of the globe. She noted Nicholas Smuclovsky, her Stanford colleague, and Dave Carico, whom she had worked with at CERN; Jackson Howell from the Vatican Observatory; Yuki Ichikawa from Princeton who was now with SETI, Manoj Kapoor from the Tata Institute. There were top scientists whose names were now associated with the World Resources Institute, the Council for Ethical Genetics, Scientists for Global Peace, The Union of Concerned Scientists, The Living Earth Program — James Kohnke, the Johns Hopkins biophysicist and best-selling author. She was thrilled to see Heidi Eichler's name; they had corresponded after *Relevance* was published. And Alexandra Navas who had single-handedly corralled last year's conference on global climate change. She especially looked forward to meeting Claudia Hill, the author of *Regeneration*.

Albert Finn had said "a couple hundred scientists," she thought. In this age of precise specialization, there were no "scientists" anymore. There were high-energy experimental physicists, and membrane biophysicists, and mathematical cosmologists. Even more extraordinary was having them all together. People at this level met with leaders in their fields. They met with specific agendas. She again lifted the envelope. There was nothing else inside. Charles was right, she thought. Only the Finn Foundation could have accomplished this.

As she walked along the wooded path to the evening reception she recalled the sweetness in her parents' voices, the two of them on the extensions the way they had always spoken with her.

She thought of how thrilled they would have been to know the company she was in tonight. She yearned for their presence in her life again. She knew she always would.

A crowd was already gathered inside the Rehearsal Hall, wineglasses in hand. The faint roar of lively discussion rolled through the room. Katherine was accustomed to being one of few women in a group. She was also used to the looks — some admiring, some patronizing, some a mixture of both. There was something different about this group. She felt it from the first moment. And it was more than the way they responded to her. The usual tension that was felt among scientists when they were asked to convene — it seemed to be absent in this group. Perhaps it was the setting, she thought. Or was it Albert Finn's choice of scientists?

It was only a moment before her colleague from Stanford, Nicholas Smuclovsky, was hailing her from across the room. The man with whom he was conversing stood with him and watched her as she approached. She had always marveled at what a woman can discern about a man from his first glance at her. This was a look that spoke volumes.

"Katherine! How are you?" Nicholas trumpeted in his enduring Russian accent. "Michael Cavanaugh, another cosmologist," he said, introducing his friend. "Michael and I worked together at Stanford. He now heads up a private organization in San Francisco." Michael Cavanaugh took Katherine's hand and continued his steady gaze into her face. "Katherine Ayers. I'm delighted to meet you. *The Relevance of Nature* is an important book." He did not release her hand. "Really. I'm thrilled to meet you."

"Thank you very much," she said.

She recalled the name of a Stanford colleague, Michael Cavanaugh, from years earlier, though they had never had any contact. When she asked him about his San Francisco organization, Nicholas diverted them both by handing her her nametag and a glass of chardonnay. Then instead of responding to her inquiry, Michael Cavanaugh quickly asserted, "And we have something else in common." His gaze remained steadfast. "I never miss a Wolverine game. I did my undergrad at Michigan."

"Ah," Katherine smiled. "And I'm sure you miss Ann Arbor. Especially in February. You poor fellows, out there in all that ghastly sunshine."

"Actually I love Ann Arbor, even in February. I get back for a game whenever I can. Unfortunately, in recent years that hasn't been often enough. There's nothing quite like being there in the stands, is there."

"Katherine Ayers."

Katherine turned to be greeted by Albert Finn, a distinguished looking man with silvering hair and extraordinary eyes — dark but at the same time clear. To look into them was to see a long way into the man. What Katherine saw in Albert Finn's eyes was a steady sturdy soul filled with the equanimity of one who had learned many things, whose lessons had been hard and deep, and who had found his way to a serenity that flowed from his eyes in a ceaseless fortifying glow.

"I'm not surprised at the grip," he said, still holding tightly to her hand. "One should expect it — if they've read you."

"And I'm not surprised that you would respond in-kind," she said, acknowledging the strength of his reputation as well as his grip. "Men are sometimes apprehensive about a woman's hand." She smiled. "We learn as much from handshakes as men do."

"And more, I'm sure," he laughed. "I'm so happy to finally meet you. I was just about to make an official welcome. I'm delighted you're here." He placed his other hand on hers. "And I see you're in good company," he said with a parting smile toward Michael Cavanaugh.

Albert greeted a few others as he made his way to the front of the room and then he took the microphone and faced the group.
"Good evening . . . distinguished guests."
It was only a matter of moments before the entire group had stilled to silence and faced Albert Finn.

"First of all, I want to express my profound appreciation to each of you for the effort I know it took to keep this engagement on your calendars." He looked around the room. "I am gratified to interpret this as a testament to the fact that the Finn Foundation has over the years effectively represented our commitment to the same standard of excellence this assembly represents.

"I have referred to this as a gathering. My avoidance of the word 'conference' is a deliberate one. I'm sure you all noticed the peculiar absence of agendas and objectives. It is our intention to make this experience casual and enjoyable and to encourage a genuine sharing. For the next few days you will be in the company of one another. There is no press here. No students. No departmental colleagues. No government or funding agencies. And you'll notice your nametags do not reflect any institutional affiliations. This gathering does not involve the participation of any organization other than the Finn Foundation.

"We chose Sundance for its natural environment, and I must add, its commitment to the environment, for the intimacy and ambiance of the place, and last but not least — there is no better food anywhere." The group laughed. "In a moment we will see what the chef has in store for us. For this evening our agenda will be to relax and get acquainted, or catch up, as the case may be. And later, if you care to have a drink in front of the fire, The Owl bar across the way will be accommodating. Or you may prefer to retire to your own cabins and fireplaces. This altitude does make an evening fire a welcome friend. For those of you who are interested, breakfast will be served here in the Rehearsal Hall tomorrow morning from around seven thirty and we'll begin our visit at the civilized hour of nine. For tonight — enjoy."

The Sundance chef, true to his reputation, had created an epicurean sensation around which lively conversation flowed. After dinner, in The Owl, the roaring fire from the stone fireplace warmed Nicholas' cognac and the pot of herb tea Katherine had placed on the hearth. Michael Cavanaugh had been enticed to try his first cup of chamomile as he responded to the group's interest in their host, Albert Finn.

". . . He lost his parents, his only brother and his wife all in a few years," he said. "Spent the next six or eight completely alone. Traveled India. Spent years in the mountains of Tibet and Nepal. He really got in there with himself. He's one of the most extraordinary human beings I've ever known."

"He's been quite low profile with the foundation, hasn't he?" Nicholas asked. "Doesn't the staff pretty much run things?"

"Until now, yes," Michael said. "This is the first time he's been visibly involved."

"Someone said he has read everything every one of us has written," Nicholas said incredulously.

Michael was emphatic. "And everything every one of our colleagues has written. For the past ten years he's done nothing but read and meditate. And yet you'll never hear the man suggest he knows anything. He's always listening."

"You've obviously spent some time with him, Michael," Katherine said.

"He called me one day years ago and asked if we could meet. He arrived at my home on a Saturday morning — my wife and kids were away for the weekend. From the first moment there was this uncanny recognition, like we were already intimately acquainted. The next time we looked, we had talked the day away without any awareness of time passing."

"I heard he and his new wife met in Tibet," Nicholas said.

"At Lake Lhamo Latso," Michael said. He noted the inquisitive look on Katherine's face. "It's a magical place, high in the mountains. Albert and Diana are convinced they were drawn there to meet one another."

"My brother and sister-in-law own some of her art," Nicholas said. "She's quite a sculptor."

"They certainly have the same thing going on in their eyes," Katherine remarked.

Katherine had met Diana, Albert's wife, when some of the women in the group converged after dinner and visited for a while in the Rehearsal Hall.

"Well, it will be interesting to see what he has in store," Nicholas said, examining the color of his cognac in the firelight.

"You mean tomorrow." Michael smiled. "Believe me, it's guaranteed to be interesting."

"And if I'm going to participate with even half my wits . . ." Katherine reached for her handbag.

Nicholas immediately rose to his feet. "Yes. We'll walk you."

The sound of the rushing stream filled the frigid air as they crossed over the wooden bridge that led to the guest cottages. "So I'm over in the Pines," Nicholas said. "Are you two . . . or are you that way, in River Run?"

"Nick, you actually know the names of these places already?" Michael said, his eye on the path in front of them in the dark.

"I'm up in that direction," Katherine said, pointing to the hill on the right. And then she added, "Listen, I'm fine."

"I'm up there too," Michael said.

"Those are the Mandan Cottages," Nicholas noted.

"Always a step ahead," Katherine said, intending a deeper compliment to her colleague.

Nicholas received it with his big Russian grin she could hear in the dark. "Well, good night, you two. Sleep well," he said as he headed off on the path to his cabin.

Nicholas Smuclovsky was a brilliant cosmologist and a highly charged competitive personality. Katherine was enjoying their budding collegial relationship regarding their respective theories. Michael had told her at dinner that she should pursue Nicholas' Anthropic ideas with him sometime.

"What did you mean, you think that's why Albert invited him here?" she asked.

"Oh, I just think Albert's real interest is in ideas," Michael said. "Nick is known for his theory, of course, but in close quarters his ideas are his greatest charm."

"He's a charmer to be sure. Even in the realm of theory," Katherine said. She was savoring the pristine air as they continued uphill on the wooded path.

"And I'm finally meeting one of my other favorite thinkers," Michael said. "I've been a big fan of yours."

"Well, thank you again," she said. "I appreciate your being so generous the way you delivered me from my embarrassment at dinner."

"Not at all. I wouldn't have expected you to know my work. I'm off the beaten path these days. So to speak," he added, emphasizing the pun as he stopped at the clearing and turned around. "I've been off the beaten path for quite a while now."

"There seems to be an interesting mix here," Katherine said, referring to the group.

Michael's smile was sanguine. "Albert covers all the bases," he said. "It's the ground-breakers he's interested in."

They stood for a moment and looked back on the silent village speckled with nightlights. The fragrant breath of burning pine streamed from the chimneys and drifted on the cool crisp Alpine air.

"It's quite a place isn't it," Katherine said.

"Yes, it is. And I have a feeling it's going to be quite an experience too."

When they arrived at their cluster of cottages they looked at one another in the blanched light that shone from the fixtures that hung above their group of cabins.

"Well, Michael . . ." She extended her hand. "It's been great meeting you. I've really enjoyed all the conversation."

He was prolonging their handshake again with the same steady gaze into her face. "Nick is a kick, isn't he?" he said, obviously groping.

"Yes, he is." She squeezed his hand with an unmistakable friendliness. "Goodnight," she said as she turned away. "See you tomorrow," she called softly.

She could feel that his gaze remained fixed on her until she was inside her cottage.

He's married, she thought, as she closed the cabin door and fastened the latch.

The morning sunshine streamed through the windows of the Rehearsal Hall where the aroma of freshly brewed coffee infused the brisk air. On a buffet table the full length of the room was a festive display of every conceivable country breakfast offering, Sundance style. The juices were fresh, the pastries were warm and flaky, the granola organic, the bacon perfectly crisp. There was marked buoyancy among the occupants of the room, hearty appetites, laughter and cajoling. The previous evening had made an enormous difference in the comfort level of the group.

Katherine took a seat at a table where three men gestured to her with welcoming smiles. She knew of Franco Benedetto, the Nobel biochemist from Italy. The other two men's names were unfamiliar at first. Russell Downie, next to her, was a soft-spoken

Australian who exuded a wholesome sincerity in his welcome to her and his comments about her book. He identified himself simply as a biologist from Melbourne. Timothy Longmire was from Berkeley, a lean attractive man with long white hair and a distinctly California look about him. "Neuroscience," he said, eagerly shaking her hand. She then recognized his name. Charles had raved about Timothy Longmire's book about the brain. Russell Downie leaned into her at the first opportunity and quietly said, "Timothy is a brilliant complexity thinker."

It was about ten to nine when she saw Michael Cavanaugh standing in the doorway. There was something strikingly appropriate about his presence in the center of a large beam of sunlight that streamed through the open outbuilding doors. As she discreetly shifted her gaze back to Russell she peripherally observed his tall figure wandering by the buffet table and then approaching theirs.

"Good morning," he said to the group with a deliberate glance at Katherine.

Russell came to his feet and enthusiastically shook Michael's hand. "Russell! We didn't quite get to one another last night. How are you?"

"*Good*, Michael. Great to see you."

When Russell sat down Katherine casually remarked to him, "You know one another."

"Oh yes, everyone knows Michael," he said earnestly.

Michael Cavanaugh took the one remaining chair at the table. He and Timothy Longmire were also obviously well acquainted. He and Franco Benedetto introduced themselves.

"The orange marmalade is great," Katherine said as she eyed the pile of preserves next to the bagel on Michael's plate.

"Yes," he said as he looked at her with another deliberate smile, "I'm a big fan."

As Katherine continued conversing with Russell she could not help overhearing Michael's pronounced expression as he talked about "the waterfalls." She had seen them mentioned in the Sundance brochure in her cottage. Timothy Longmire then remarked about having begged off on the early hour. She noticed Michael's freshly showered appearance. He had hiked this morning, she thought. He had gone by himself to the waterfalls. She then heard him say something about staying on after the conference for a visit with the Utes on the Reservation.

"Have you been to Michael's Center in San Francisco?" Russell asked her.

"No, I haven't. He invited me last evening. This is the first time we've met."

"I'm sure he's eager to get you there."

"Have you known Michael long?" she asked.

"Oh, we've been good mates for some years now," Russell said. "We corresponded for quite a while before I finally got to the Center, oh, three years ago now I guess. It's funny, I ran into his wife a few months ago at Oxford."

"Is his wife a biologist too?" Katherine asked casually.

"Oh no, I mean we literally ran into one another. She's working in anthropology there I think. I thought it was quite a stroke of chance, seeing Michael's wife on a third continent. I guess I should say 'ex-wife' now. They were divorced a few years ago. Quite amicably, I think. That's always refreshing, isn't it."

"Yes, it is."

Katherine's gaze instinctively drifted to the other side of the table where Michael was talking with Franco Benedetto. It was only a moment before he greeted her gaze with another warm smile.

Albert Finn opened the morning session in the same relaxed manner in which he had spoken the night before. He expressed gratitude for the beautiful day, for the exquisite meal of the previous evening and, once again, for the "extraordinary opportunity represented in this gathering." Then he stood silently for a moment as he observed the attentive group.

"None of you had the opportunity to know my brother, Herbert. I am sorry for this. He was an extraordinary man. I am going to share something with you this morning that I have not shared with anyone but my wife, Diana. I do so because I feel the time is appropriate and because I think Herb would approve.

"I am grateful that my brother and I had some time alone together before he died. Often in life we do not share our deepest thoughts even with those closest to us. My brother's reflections on his life had a powerful effect on me. He said that when a man has wealth there is nothing he can achieve that will distinguish him beyond his achievement of worldly success, that even his philanthropy is seen as one of the privileges of wealth. He said that we should all have more than one chance at life. One to work hard and achieve something, and another to make a difference. His final words to me were . . ." Albert paused. " 'I wanted to make a difference.' I share these words with you now to give you a sense of the spirit and motivation behind the Finn Foundation's invitation to each of you to join us for this gathering.

"The group I see before me is as illustrious an assembly as one could imagine. Some of the finest minds of our time. Together you constitute the frontier of insight to the physical dynamics inherent to life, to the planet Earth, and to the universe in which we find ourselves. In addition to your international stature as leaders in your fields, I would like to point out if I may some other qualities you all have in common. This is of course by way of telling you a bit about why we felt that convening this particular group held some promise.

"You are all recognized for your fidelity to science. At the same time you recognize that the search for truth cannot be limited to the instruments of science. You see science in relation to the larger fabric of which it is part, the fabric of humanity. You have raised important questions about humanity's role in the evolving universe. And you have all stepped forward on behalf of the inheritors of this sacred planet of ours and this incalculably precious thing called 'life.' The people in this room are all fulfilling a purpose that reaches beyond the role of science, and which is bravely redefining the role of scientist. It is my hope that you will all find this time together invigorating, especially to the ideas you share.

"Not long ago, this ground we're standing on, this wonderful place that is now called 'Sundance,' was the home of Native Americans, the Utes. It was of course not they who identified themselves as 'Native Americans.' The Utes were here long before 'America' was even a glimmer of an idea for the men and women who came to this continent with their own dreams of home and family and freedom.

During those formative years of our nation, just a little more than two hundred years ago, all of our significant minds of science *and* the humanities could be comfortably convened in one room in Philadelphia's Philosophical Hall. The American Philosophical Society's members in fact numbered just about the same as the group in this room. And they were all conversant on the entire sphere of Western knowledge, which at that time — it's almost impossible to imagine – could still be seen *whole*.

"Two hundred years, through most of your lenses — you, who investigate the beginnings of life, the beginnings of the universe — two hundred years cannot be described even in terms for the most infinitesimal quantities. But the world of knowledge that has emerged in this ineffably brief period of time — this is something for which we have meaningful words. Words like 'boundless,' and 'global,' and 'emerging,' and 'self-reproducing,' and 'intricately interconnected,' and 'universally accessible.'

"I have wondered what we would see were we to look through one of your lenses at the immense, burgeoning organism that is today's world of knowledge. I wonder especially if the proliferation of tightly-focused specializations would not appear as an increasing disassociation, even a disintegration. I know many of you share these very thoughts; you have expressed them far more eloquently. Some of you have turned your lenses to the world of knowledge itself and to the phenomenon of human consciousness.

"One might think that such a gathering of great minds today can be no more than a fleeting grasp at an integration of ideas. We must all return to the world in which we live and to the speed at which it is moving. Perhaps our time together can yield no more than a gratifying exchange with one another — this in itself will have been a worthy purpose. And perhaps as we coalesce, the dynamics that emerge and the relationships that form will reveal some higher purpose. As I told my brother Herb recently — I do still chat with him now and then — we will have done our best to create the opportunity.

"What is our agenda? I thought long and hard about this. It was when I stopped thinking about it that it came to me. The plan is a very simple one. For the next few days we'll be spending most of our time with the four individuals we now see sitting at our tables. Given the experience of last evening, I believe it's likely that at least one of them is someone with whom you have some relationship, however new. In addition to honoring these connections, we wanted to save you the trouble of thinking about where you would gravitate."

The group stirred a little as many looked around at the colleagues at their tables and at other tables throughout the room.

"We will be together as small groups, except of course during mealtimes when we'll all be together again here in this room. And we'll convene again as a full group for our final hours. There are seven blocks of time between now and then. They're identified on the schedule which you'll find on your tables. You will also find seven white cards placed facedown that will remain where they are throughout our time here. The staff has been alerted to this. At the beginning of each segment of time, you will please draw one of the seven cards that will give you your topic for discussion.

"As you know, we have placed another year-end engagement on your calendars. That time will again be hosted here at Sundance. We hope you'll all be able to manage the full four days. The first two will again be spent with the members of your group of five, wherever you choose to convene." He smiled and dropped his inflection. "Perhaps it would not break your hearts to take in a little skiing while you're here. During those two days we hope you will revisit your topics in the added light of your reflection during the interim. For the final two days we'll all be together again and share our ideas with the entire group.

"It's a simple plan, interspersed with some great food and the magnificent surroundings that await you outdoors. It is my hope that when we leave here in a few days we'll all assess this time as well spent."

Katherine, Russell, Franco, Michael and Timothy looked at one another. Franco was the first to speak. "Well, we are an excellent group!" he said with a touch of Italian gusto.

They all smiled as they began to warm to the idea of simply embracing Albert's plan.

Timothy examined the schedule. "Looks like we begin now," he said.

"Katherine, will you do the honors?" Russell said warmly.

Katherine reached for the pile of white cards and picked up one, leaving the others face down in the center of the table.

"Leadership," she said.

"That's it?" Timothy said.

Katherine showed the others the card. The single word was printed in bold letters.

"Leadership," Michael said. Then he smiled an affirming smile.

The next few days at Sundance were as rich with intellectual stimulation, gourmet indulgence and invigorating communion with nature as any three days Katherine had experienced. Their group's rousing discussions spilled over into long hours of early morning exploration and evenings in front of the fire. One morning, Michael led a sunrise expedition to the waterfalls above Sundance. And for one of their afternoon session they ventured via the gondola into the hills that were ablaze with color. They were all operating on very little sleep and yet they were thoroughly energized.

Katherine was drawn out of herself in ways she would not have thought possible with brand new acquaintances. She was also extremely challenged. The very next topic she unsuspectingly drew from the pile was the last one she expected to face at a meeting of scientists. It took every bit of adroitness she could muster to disguise the unease with which she was seized. The single word printed on the card was "God." She instinctively looked at Michael Cavanaugh. The expression on his face told her he was not only not shocked, he was delighted. His response made her even more uncomfortable.

Albert's surprising agenda was about the very synergy of ideas to which Katherine was firmly committed — to the knocking down of walls between disciplines of thought. He had also laid bare the one demarcation that was absolute in her mind, the one boundary she could not cross — the wall between science and religion. For Katherine it was more than the commonly held divide between "fact and faith." It was the very barricade that had kept her safe all her life from the world on the other side of that wall. A world filled with the painful memories and impossible emotions she had pushed behind her long ago. Albert's seven words deliberately placed together more than challenged her faithfulness to science. They tested her most finely honed skill of survival — the cerebral dexterity that was her shield.

To her own astonishment her participation on each of the seven topics was equally spirited — as much on the subject of "God" and "Leadership" as it was on "Science." She not only rose to the challenge, she found the experience an exhilarating one. She and her four colleagues had collided under conditions that were somehow intrinsically magical. They had fused with one another in the powerful compound of their collective ideas. The entire weekend of deeply probing discussion was thrilling to her. And she knew her four new friends all felt the same way.

It was late the final night when Michael again walked her up the hill to their cottages. When they stopped at the clearing in the same spot where they had stood on their first night, the intimacy between them was not something they could have anticipated just a few short nights before. It was a feeling of profound connection, one they shared with their three comrades, Russell, Franco and Timothy. For Katherine and Michael, the alchemy of the previous days had also crystallized the magnetism between them. Yet their time together had also flushed out a powerful resistance in Katherine. Throughout Albert's surprising agenda, throughout all of their deep discussion, it had been Michael Cavanaugh who had challenged her most.

She was sure he was one of the most riveting minds she had encountered. Rarely had she been exposed to such a consistent flow of startlingly original thought. Yet some of the ideas he had wielded with such certainty had shaken her most fundamental bearings. Did he have any idea how deeply he had provoked her? Or how many times she had completely rejected him in her mind? At the same time, throughout the entire weekend she had been filled with the same anticipation she was feeling in that moment, standing there next to him in the dark. There had not been a moment since their eyes first met when she had not reveled in his gaze, when she had not looked forward to the next time he would look at her again. As they hugged one another goodbye, there on the hill overlooking Sundance, the feeling was as undeniable as it was unsettling. Michael Cavanaugh was a brand new enigma in her life, as was the way he made her feel.

Heading back to Ann Arbor, both exhausted and reeling, she stared at the clouds through the airplane window. The intoxication of the previous days consumed her. All of the ideas that had flowed from those seven simple words, she thought. She looked at the note pad on her lap where she had written the seven words. Albert had deliberately placed them on cards, she marveled. The order was undetermined. They might easily have drawn them from the pile in any other sequence. Surely other groups had. She looked at the order in which their group had approached them. Then she wrote the words again, rearranging the sequence.

Leadership God Science Universe One Humanity Spirit
Science Leadership One Spirit God Universe Humanity
One Humanity God Science Universe Spirit Leadership

Her gaze rolled toward the clouds in the stark blue sky. She saw the sparkling water cascading over the rocks in the hills above Sundance. She smelled the breath of burning pine adrift the midnight air. She felt Michael Cavanaugh's penetrating gaze. Her head fell back and she closed her eyes.

Twelve

"... 'I had scarcely taken my foot off the poor insect when, like a censuring angel sent from heaven, there fluttered through the trees a butterfly with large wings of gleaming gold and purple ... It shone only a moment before my eyes, then, rising among the leaves it vanished into the blue skies above. I was silent, but an inner voice said to me, 'Let not the creature judge his creator, here is a symbol of the world to come — just as the ugly caterpillar is the beginning of the splendid butterfly, this globe is the embryo of a new heaven and of a new earth whose meagerest beauty infinitely surpasses mortal imagination . . .' "

"That was lovely, Shawn. Thank you. And she wrote that in French?" Katherine said.

"Yes, it's from *Five Essays Written in French* by Emily Jane Brontë."

"And this one is just called *The Butterfly*," Katherine noted.

Melodee waved at Shawn. "So she steps on a caterpillar and then she sees a butterfly?"

"And in that moment she understands that death is just a part of life," Shawn said, "that life is about constant change." She looked at Katherine. "I had no idea she wrote *Wuthering Heights* when she was in her twenties. That's so amazing."

"She was a gifted young woman," Katherine said.

"And she died so young," Shawn remarked. "She was only thirty."

"What was it she said?" Katherine asked thoughtfully, " 'Nature is an inexplicable puzzle'?' "

Isaiah handed Katherine a copy of the essay that was being distributed around the room while Shawn recited again from the text. " 'Nature is an inexplicable puzzle. Nevertheless, we celebrate the day of our birth, and we praise God that we entered such a world.' "

Katherine remained silently thoughtful.

"And it's funny," Shawn said, "I found this right after we read the Ray Bradbury story about the boy who went back in time and stepped on the butterfly."

"And I found another one!" Marisa called out. "My aunt actually told me about it. It's an author that she said everybody was reading back when she was in college, Richard Bach. It's from his book, *Illusions*. He says," she read from the page in front of her, " 'The mark of your ignorance is the depth of your belief in injustice and tragedy. What the caterpillar calls the end of the world, the master calls a butterfly.' I'll be adding it to the website today," she said.

Marisa was referring to the "Butterflies in Literature" section of the website Frank and Collin had set up for the class. It was one of the tabbed sections on the site along with "Butterfly Facts," "Butterfly Species," "Extraordinary Features," "Butterflies and the Environment" and a growing number of others. This section listed all of the works of literature the class was finding that made use of the butterfly as a symbol. Marisa's discovery brought the total to sixty-two, Frank reported, and more were being added all the time.

"Authors use butterflies and caterpillars a lot," Angela remarked.

"Because they represent change and transformation," Grace followed.

"Because they're writing about life," Cynthia said.

Katherine relaxed on the edge of the desk. "It's a very reliable image, isn't it? The sight of a butterfly evokes feelings of enchantment and wonder, of unearthliness and beauty. It's a powerful image. "

It would have been hard for Katherine to pinpoint exactly when she knew her butterfly class was going to have special meaning for her even beyond what she had anticipated from this extraordinary course she had dreamed up. She had known that butterflies would be a subject of interest for students and that the shock value alone of an entire course devoted to them was likely to get their attention. She had been confident too that a study of butterflies could be used for a broad exploration of the learning process. On some level she had also been curious about what she might learn about the powerful image that had appeared to her in her dream. It was not long into the course when she saw there was more to this idea than she had ever imagined.

Hannah and Emma had developed another impressive project on the butterfly as a symbol. Their written report opened with an illustration from a classic Greek fairy tale depicting Cupid's wife, Psyche, as she was often portrayed in Greek and Roman art, adorned with beautiful butterfly wings. The caption reminded the class that in Ancient Greece, the word "psyche" applied to both the butterfly and the soul. The selected collection that followed showed how the butterfly had served since antiquity as a symbolic image in art, ritual, legend and mythology, from simple romantic tales to the philosophy of sages.

There were legends from the East, like the one about the Chinese emperor who in the midst of his extravagant garden parties would release hundreds of caged butterflies that would fly directly to the fairest beauties in attendance, enabling him to choose the women upon whom he would bestow his imperial favor. Another story, well-known in China, told of a man who lost his love at a tender age and mourned her all his life, never marrying another, until one day his love returned to him in the form of a white butterfly and the man happily died and joined his love.

There were many stories from Japan, where the butterfly has

been featured for centuries as a central figure in art and culture, and where poets and painters have themselves assumed the names of butterflies, like Choumu (Butterfly Dream) and Ichou (Solitary Butterfly) and Chohana (Butterfly Blossom). The ancient Japanese Butterfly Dance was a revered tradition in the Imperial Palace for many years, performed for emperors by beautiful dancers in resplendent winged costumes. And in literature and drama the butterfly has been cast in leading roles in many famous works. "The butterfly has in fact been of such significance in Japanese culture," Emma said, "that even in recent years in the province of Mutsu there remains a custom of naming the youngest daughter in the family 'Tekona,' which in the classical Mutsu dialect means 'butterfly.'"

The class listened intently as Hannah and Emma shared what they had found about the numerous ancient societies in which butterflies were believed to be messengers from God. Their association with the human soul and with spiritual transformation dated back, they reported, to the earliest references to the insect in Eastern thought. In Mycenae, for instance, around 1500 BCE, it was believed that the butterfly contained within itself all of its previous incarnations as well as the promise of future generations. In ancient Chinese Taoist philosophy, Chuang Tzu, a follower of Lao Tzu, was known as "the butterfly philosopher" because of the famous story he was known to have shared with his students. He said that he had dreamed he was a butterfly, and that when he awoke he did not know whether he was a man dreaming he was a butterfly or a butterfly dreaming he was a man.

With their series of compelling tales Hannah and Emma showed the butterfly's significance in the rituals and mythology of indigenous peoples all over the world, from the tribes of Sumatra and Manipur to North America Indians. "According to Papago legend, for instance, butterflies were introduced into the world when the Creator wanted to give a special gift to the children of the tribe. He gathered together the brilliant colors of sunlight, flowers, leaves and the sky and put them into a magic bag, and when the children opened the bag the beautiful winged creatures flew out. Among the Blackfoot tribe, it was customary for women to embroider butterflies on small pieces of buckskin which they tied in their babies' hair when they wanted them to sleep. The mothers then sang a lullaby that summoned the butterfly to hover about and protect their infants during their slumber.

"Many tribes recognized the butterfly as a symbol of regeneration and rebirth," Hannah said. "The Mexican Aztecs believed that their warriors, after passing through death, would return to the earth to experience the life of the butterfly. Aztec braves looked forward to an existence of pure being when they would suck the bliss from flowers and bask in the intoxication of eternal peace and boundless joy. For the Hopi, the butterfly is among the sacred Katsinas, spirit mediators with the Divine, that participate in seasonal ceremonies and appeal to the Creator on behalf of the tribe. For other tribes, the butterfly has played an important role in the medicine of their shamans. To call upon an animal in the Shamanic tradition was to be drawn into the creature's essence and to share in the creature's strength. The butterfly was summoned specifically for wisdom and courage in the art of self-transformation."

After Hannah and Emma had taken the class on their global exploration, from the carved images on the walls of caves to the popular legends and folklore alive today, they concluded their report by saying, "Since humanity first contemplated the mysteries of life, the butterfly has been a ubiquitous symbol for the rebirth and transformation of the human soul. For cultures all over the world it has signified the absolute wonder of life itself."

Lucas was the first to commend Hannah and Emma on

their research and report. Lucas was among the students whose participation had dramatically increased as the semester had progressed. Since his own presentation on the commercial butterfly market he had initiated class discussion a number of times.

"It's interesting that all of these ancient societies thought of them as sacred," he said. "I mean, we collect 'em and buy 'em and sell 'em and stuff — just like everything else you can make a buck at, y' know? We use 'em for research and medicine and stuff. But it's not like they have any real value to us. Not like they did to these ancient societies."

"That's true with all animals," Jason said. "We don't think of any animals the way earlier societies did."

"And why do you suppose we've evolved away from this kind of thinking about animals?" Katherine posed.

"It's pretty hard to have reverence for something you control," Robert said. Many of the students turned in their seats to look at Robert as he spoke. "Just look at how we relate to animals now. We pick over their flesh in the supermarket and we round them up in zoos for our entertainment. We select a few species to serve us and amuse us as pets. The others we abuse. After all the brutality we've brought down on them, it's pretty hard to think of them like they matter, like they're actual living creatures."

"Yes," Marisa said, "we couldn't be much further from relating to them the way the shamans did."

Katherine asked Emma to remind the class.

Emma located the passage in their report and read it again. "Shamans believed that all animals should be approached with the humility that comes from honoring every living thing as a teacher and from seeking oneness with all that is."

"Well, we don't have witch doctors anymore either," Paul grumbled, obviously disparaging the idea of Shamanism.

Hannah quickly responded. "Actually, I didn't know before I did this research that Shamanism is the most ancient form of healing there is. It's been used for thousands of years and it's still practiced today in places all over the world."

Paul continued with tempered annoyance. "This stuff is interesting and everything but it's still just superstition. I mean, I can't believe there's anybody who doesn't think it's a little touched in the head to treat a flying insect like it's someone's spirit, or soul, or some messenger from God or something. I mean, gimme a break. People just needed to believe in those things so they made 'em up, that's all." He sniggered dismissively. "People just want to believe in stuff like that."

"We all believe in what we want to believe in," Cynthia said.

"Yes, and it's what you believe in that makes you who you are," Marisa said.

"Yeah," Paul groaned under his breath.

"You know, the other thing that's important to understand," Emma said, "is that 'medicine' didn't mean the same thing to these societies that it does to us. The shamans were the healers of the tribe but they were also much more than that. 'Medicine' to them meant anything that improved a person's connection to the universe and enabled them to live in harmony with themselves and with the world around them. Shamanism was more of a spiritual practice."

Cynthia chimed in, "Well, I thought the whole thing was fascinating. You did a really great job." She looked at Hannah who was seated nearby. "One thing that really struck me was that on the medicine wheel of the shaman, in the example you gave, the butterfly was the animal that guides you on your path of 'illumination.' "

"Yes," Tim exclaimed.

"Whaddaya mean?" Jarrod asked.

"Didn't you notice all the references to light?" Tim said. "When the butterfly was in that particular spot on the shaman's wheel, it was a guide to 'illumination.' And in the Haiku poem, the butterfly quivers in its sleep because it's dreaming of the light. And in the story from the ancient Egyptian mystery school. . ." He was thumbing through his copy. "Where they talk about transformation, they talk about the 'vision of the light' and being surrounded by 'teachers of light.' "

"I don't understand what you're saying," Steffen said.

"Just that it's interesting that in all of the butterfly legends the light has a special significance."

"Light is always associated with spiritual rebirth," Marisa said. "And a lot of these stories were religious stories."

"I don't think they were religious," Angela blurted, obviously a little ruffled. "There was only one religious one. The one where the butterfly was a symbol of the Resurrection."

"Yeah. The others weren't religious at all," another student agreed.

Isaiah responded to Angela's remark, "Just because they're not your religion doesn't mean they're not religious."

"And I'm saying they're religious in nature," Marisa explained. "The Native American beliefs about the sacredness of all living things — that is their religion. And the Tibetan ideas about impermanence and rebirth — that's an important part of their religion."

Katherine could see that Ming Jie had something to say. With a little encouragement she spoke up.

"Taoists believe in the sacredness of all living things too," she said. "Chuang Tzu's story of the butterfly dream was used to illustrate the Taoist belief that everything in the universe from the lowest to the highest is part of the same universal One. It's very similar to the Native American belief that all things are part of the same sacred wholeness. Chuang Tzu taught that everything is continually in the process of destruction and construction, just like the butterfly. He said this was the perfection of life — that it was in constant transformation."

"And whose words do those remind you of?" Katherine asked.

The students looked at her.

She repeated Chuang Tzu's words, "Everything is in the process of destruction and construction."

"Emily Brontë," Shawn responded.

"Emily Brontë's lesson from her butterfly, right?" Katherine said.

"She saw in nature that change and transformation are what life is about," Shawn explained.

"Now her vision was very religious," Angela remarked.

"Yeah," Melodee followed. "Emily Brontë's essay did have a religious message."

"You don't have to talk about God to be religious," Marisa asserted.

"Yeah" came from a few other students.

"Well now we've hit upon a fascinating topic, haven't we," Katherine said. She looked around at the group. "And no matter how long we discussed it I'd be very surprised if we managed to reconcile the differing notions about what constitutes religion." She smiled at Ming Jie.

"And there'd be just as many people convinced there's only one true religion," Robert asserted.

"Yeah. *Theirs*," Jason followed.

"Religion's just inherited anyway," Jack said. "It's like genes — you get what you get. It's just whatever family and culture and part of the world you're born into."

"Yeah," Isaiah said. "It's not like you have any say in it."

Angela was agitated. "Well, you make it sound like it's no big deal what religion you are. I think it's a lot more important than that. It's like Marisa said, it's what makes you who you are."

Marisa calmly corrected Angela. "I said it's what you believe in that makes you who you are."

"Well, isn't a person's religion what they believe in?" Angela asked.

"It is if that's what it is for them," Marisa replied.

Katherine's smile persisted. "A fascinating subject indeed," she said. "One we could easily discuss until the end of the semester. And yet what might be equally fascinating is to look at what is being said here by two people as far afield in geography and family background and belief systems as Emily Brontë and Chuang Tzu."

"And they're both saying the same thing," Tim said.

"Remarkably similar, aren't they?" Katherine agreed. "And what was it that they both perceived as the essence of life?" she asked.

"*Transformation*" was delivered from a number of students.

"And what was it that Emily Brontë was referring to in her essay?" Katherine perused the students' faces. "Isn't the transformation she is talking about something beyond that of a single creature?" The students examined the essay again as Katherine read from the text. " 'Here is a symbol of the world to come. This globe is the embryo of a new Heaven and of a new Earth, whose meagerest beauty infinitely surpasses mortal imagination.' " She looked at the group. "What is this 'globe' she's talking about?"

"She's talking about the world," Isaiah said.

"She's saying that it's going to be transformed, just like the butterfly," Hailey joined in.

"I think she's talking about humanity," Breahn said. "I think the globe is the 'imaginal bud' of humanity."

Katherine was taken aback, first by the comment and then by the fact that it had come from Breahn.

"I agree," Tim said. "I think she's saying that we're still in the caterpillar stage. And that it's our destiny to be transformed. That just like all living things have genes inside of them that make them mature and grow, humanity is the same way."

"She's saying that we will reach 'imago'," Breahn said.

"And what a perfect symbol," Katherine pondered. "A creature whose every part undergoes dramatic transformation. Its gnawing jaws into a sipping straw. Its worm-like body into an upright featherweight structure. Its many legs into a pair of diaphanous wings." She paused a moment as she looked again at Breahn.

"Breahn, do you have something you want to share with us?"

Breahn was among the students who had not yet made a presentation to the class. She nervously explained her situation to Katherine.

"Well, my statement said that some butterflies exhibit signs of love and courtship," she said. "And Jack and Genevra talked about some of their courtship behaviors when they talked about mating and reproduction." She hesitated. "But I did find this article in one of the science journals that had this one little section called 'butterfly love.' And it said that some butterflies have been observed kissing."

There were murmurs of both amazement and amusement.

"They've seen Zebra butterflies kiss," Breahn continued. "They're in New Zealand. And this article said there's a lot we don't understand yet about butterfly mating behaviors and that some things suggest that there is more going on than we think. And I . . ."

"Oh, *right*," Paul interrupted. "Now we're supposed to believe they have *feelings* too."

Paul was not budging from the naysayer role he had established for himself. He was even taking a bit of pleasure in it.

"Well, how do we know they don't have feelings?" Marisa asked Paul.

"Yeah, it's not like we *talk* to them," Carlos said, obviously revisiting Paul's earlier remark.

There were giggles from around the room.

"I'm serious," Marisa continued. "All of the studies say their whole existence is about mating — that that's the one thing they're focused on."

"So they can reproduce!" Paul blurted. "So they can keep butterflies around!"

"Well, maybe it's more than that," Marisa persisted. "Maybe they really do experience love, or their version of love, how do we know? Maybe they're so focused on finding a partner because they don't want to miss experiencing butterfly love. I mean, procreation is one of the outcomes of human love. But the thing we pursue isn't procreation, is it? It's love."

Paul thrashed about in his seat. "Oh, *come on.*"

There was a flurry of laughter and remarks from around the room. "Professor Ayers?" Breahn timidly waved her hand. "I wasn't finished with . . ."

"Oh, yes Breahn, please," Katherine said.

The class began to settle down.

"Well, I really couldn't find much of anything about butterfly love or feelings, but . . ." She hesitated again. "Well, the fact that they kiss — I thought it was pretty amazing." She was looking at Katherine with an apologetic expression. "Well, I wrote a poem. Is that okay?"

The class quieted down to hear Katherine's response.

"Yes. Of course that's okay. It's more than okay. We'd love to hear your poem."

Breahn stood up next to her desk rather than coming to the front of the room. Katherine slid back onto her desk and sat attentively. The class stilled to silence and waited for Breahn to speak. Slowly, softly, she read her poem:

If you should wake one morning
with the memory of a dream
like rain drenched flowers in the new day sun
If you should turn
with feelers softly feeling
to find what it is you left behind
And slip

half wanting, half knowing
back into the enswathe of balmy bliss
You will see me there
with wings that flutter
and the light that sings of glitter
as I leave

The class was still and silent.
After a moment Katherine said, "Breahn, that was lovely." She was making every effort to cover her astonishment. "What a wonderful way to deal with your topic. Really. That was lovely."
She was glad to see that students near Breahn were complimenting her on her poem and that Tim immediately spoke up about her mention of light. "You see. It's there again in Breahn's poem," he exclaimed.
Then Mya asked Breahn, "They really have seen butterflies kiss?"
Breahn nodded.
"So is it a Zebra butterfly in your poem?" Shawn asked her.
Breahn shrugged. "It's just a butterfly."
"Well, we know it's not an Empress Leilia," Marisa said.
"How do we know that?" Jason asked.
"Because the butterfly in Breahn's poem leaves her lover," Marisa said. "The Empress Leilia mates only once in her life."
"That's right," Katherine said, glancing in Jack's direction. "The Empress is highly selective, isn't she? She mates for life."
She glanced at the clock. "Well, we've been all over the map again this week, haven't we? How butterflies fly." She bowed in Steffen's direction. "How they offer early warning signs about atmospheric fluctuations. We're learning quite a bit about their environmental sensitivity, aren't we? No wonder they're so heavily studied by scientists." She looked in Ben's direction. "And how they're advancing our understanding of population dynamics . . .

And 'Butterfly Economics.' " She acknowledged Chad, repeating his phrase, "Small changes can have big consequences." Her gaze continued to roll around the room. "Carlos and Daniel told us everything we could possibly want to know about male butterfly puddling. Or is it muddling?" The students laughed. "And Sue has introduced us to the butterfly as a totem animal on the Enneagram, the ancient Sufi system that most of us are hearing about for the first time . . . And the butterfly as a symbol in literature and in life." She smiled at Hannah and Emma. "We've even heard a butterfly's perspective on love," she said as she smiled at Breahn. "And what a nice way to finish up the week."

Katherine raised her voice as she addressed the disbanding group. "I can hardly wait to see what else you're discovering," she said. Then she warbled a little with an obvious tongue in cheek, "You butterfly experts, you."

She and Isaiah exchanged grins.

Thirteen

It was late October before the dinner with the president could be arranged. Harold and Lloyd, who had attempted to disguise the event's significance in their own spheres of priority, were both in their best suits that day. Lloyd had an obvious haircut. His best effort to deflect attention from the earnestness with which he approached the event was to casually remind colleagues that Delcourt was a humanities scholar. In other words, there was nothing momentous or daunting about a meeting with a liberal arts president. It would be, after all, incumbent upon the physicists to adjust to the "lay" understanding.

As is often the case with eventful days, this one had spiraled into greater complexity. The message had come during Katherine's afternoon lecture that Harold's mother-in-law had died and he and his wife were on their way to Florida. She and Lloyd were to proceed with the meeting with the president without him. She had run home to change after a full day and had returned to the department in just enough time to spend a few minutes with Charles before he left for the day. He would be leaving in the morning for Santa Fe. It was a hectic time for both of them. They welcomed the quiet moment and the chance to reconnect.

Charles stretched back in his chair as he often did, his large hands cradling the back of his head. "So, it's you and Lloyd, eh?" Katherine's expression left no need for words.

"You and Delcourt are going to hit it off. I get the feeling he's a pretty straight-up guy."

"He seems to be."

"He called me today."

"*Delcourt?*"

Charles laughed. "Believe me, I had the same reaction."

"The president called you?"

To say that it was highly irregular for the president of the university to bypass the forty-nine layers of institutional decorum that stand between the president's office and individual faculty members would be an understatement unsurpassed in the annals of academia. Delcourt's simply picking up his phone and ringing Charles at his desk constituted a major event.

"What'd he say?" Katherine asked eagerly.

Charles was peering at her with a big grin. He had barely recovered from his own astonishment. "He wants to meet." He shrugged. "Wants to know more about the complexity program. Said it's been high on his list since he arrived. Sounded genuinely interested."

"Well, what do you know," Katherine marveled. "This fellow is becoming quite intriguing."

"I'll say."

"Mary Claire said he set aside a huge block of time to talk about the Initiative. And they've pulled her in on the dean search too. He really seems to be digging in."

"And in all the right places." Charles' grin was immovable.

"Does Harold know?"

"I have no idea if he spoke to Harold. I let Karen know about the call and that we set a lunch."

"Well, very interesting," Katherine said. "Now I do look forward to dinner tonight."

"You'll have to send me an email, let me know how it went." Charles was as chipper as she had ever seen him. "So, did you finish

Longmire's book?" he asked her.

"Isn't he something?"

Charles chuckled, "He's got my vote."

Charles was thrilled with Katherine's newfound connection with Timothy Longmire, the Berkeley neuroscientist whom he held in high esteem since his book on complexity and the brain. Katherine had taken great pleasure in informing Charles that the feeling was mutual, that Longmire had commented to her at Sundance that Charles' book on complexity was "one of the finest out there."

Charles beamed as he revisited the comment. "Pretty 'out there' himself, isn't he?"

"Oh my gosh, you have no idea. They all are. Especially Cavanaugh. And complexity is so much a part of their language. I really do want you to meet these guys."

Charles was the only one of Katherine's physics colleagues with whom she had shared a word about the Sundance weekend. He had not been as shocked as she had thought he might be about Albert Finn's agenda, and he had smiled broadly when he learned that Timothy Longmire was among the invitees.

"I'll bet Longmire had some interesting things to say on a few of those subjects," he snickered.

Katherine grinned. "He was the first to comment on the subject of 'God,' she said. Then she recalled Longmire's words exactly — "Well, we're all equally qualified and equally unfit on the subject, aren't we."

Charles was chuckling again. "He went through a whole psychedelic period, you know. I'll bet there aren't too many other members of the National Academy who've been to places he's been."

"That's just it," Katherine said. "They're all bluebloods."

"No kidding. That's quite a list."

"I just didn't expect some of the other things they'd have in common. Russell Downie also had a period with hallucinogens years ago. He's done some serious work with the Aborigines and with Amazonian Ashaninkas. And Michael Cavanaugh also has a huge affinity for ancient cultures. Something they all share with Albert Finn. Between the bunch of them they've been with indigenous peoples all over the world." She observed Charles' nonverbal response. He was finding this Sundance group increasingly interesting. "Cavanaugh and Albert were in Tibet together last year. And I told you Cavanaugh has spent a lot of time with North American tribes."

"Yeah, you said he stayed on in Utah with the Utes. I'd love to hear how that went."

"I should send you his email." She smiled. "The five of us have a group-serve."

"So you're all still communicating, huh?" he asked as he paid close attention to her expression.

Charles had sensed in Katherine that the Sundance experience had drawn her into some uncharted territory even beyond what she had shared with him. He also perceived how much she was looking forward to returning in December and seeing the same group again. He especially wondered if he were not picking up a little extra sparkle when she spoke of the San Francisco cosmologist.

"He spent three days with their spiritual leader," she said. "Sounded like quite an experience."

"I'll bet."

"He asked him about the butterfly for me."

"Oh yeah?" Charles stretched back in his chair. "And what's a Ute spiritual leader's read on butterflies?"

"He said all animals are our spiritual elders, that they all have something to teach us. He said one of the lessons from the butterfly is that each of us has our own unique dance."

Charles smiled. "Dance has real significance to the tribes. He tell you about the Sundance?"

"The fellow who drove me from the airport told me a little about it. Said it's an important spiritual ceremony."

"As old as the wind," Charles said. "You'll have to ask Cavanaugh about it. I'd love to hear what their spiritual leader had to say about the Sundance."

"I guess all of this indigenous research has something to do with this Center of his."

"And you don't know any more about it, huh?" Charles asked.

Katherine looked at him curiously. "They're very low profile. Can't find a thing on Cavanaugh or the Center on the Internet." She looked at him incredulously. "He said they don't plan to have a website."

"Interesting," Charles said.

"He's a fascinating guy. *Bizarre*. But fascinating. Everyone who knows him thinks he's one of the more extraordinary minds around."

"Yeah?" Charles said as he continued observing her demeanor.

"And for Nicholas Smuclovsky to say they were sorry to lose him at Stanford." Her expression conveyed the weight of such a statement from her Stanford colleague.

"He knows his stuff, huh?"

Katherine was emphatic. "And not just physics. He's a real 'omnivore,' as Timothy says. Biology, anthropology, politics, literature. He's got one of those brains that holds onto everything and is constantly synthesizing." Charles watched her as she reflected. "But my point is that he has to be brilliant to get away with some of his outlandish ideas." She shuddered.

Charles was amused. "Sounds like this Center of his is something interesting."

"And he's sure tight-lipped about it. With me, anyway. He and Albert both just kept saying that I need to come out and see what they're doing."

"Albert Finn funds it?"

"And Michael runs it. And he brings in people from all over. Longmire and Russell Downie and a number of others who were at Sundance have been there for different projects. With Cavanaugh, I have no doubt it's something 'out there,' as you say." She glanced at the clock. "Hey, we've gotta get going. Quick, I need an Avery story."

"Oh, and I've got a good one for you." Charles' face was bright. "The other day he's examining the inside of his apple, right? It's cut in half. And he says, 'Dad? Which seed does the apple's life begin in?'"

Katherine absorbed the question, "Which seed does the apple's life begin in. This guy is too much, isn't he? And what did you say?"

"I said the one that's powerful enough to affect all the other seeds." Katherine smiled admiringly at her friend.

"So then he picks out the one he thinks was responsible, right? He says he's gonna keep it cuz it's fulla powerful energy."

"He is one special child," Katherine said as they rose to their feet. Then she looked at Charles pointedly. "I can't get over Delcourt," she whispered.

"You'll have a good time tonight," he assured her. "You two are going to handle Lloyd just fine."

"Maybe we'll talk about complexity all night," she said impishly. "Drive him totally crazy."

"That'd do it all right," Charles chuckled.

"Hope Santa Fe is good and productive. And nourishing," she added.

"It always is," Charles said. "Send me an email," he said as he locked his office door.

Katherine observed the familiar eagerness in his step as he strolled down the hallway toward home. "Love to Debra and Avery," she called after him. Without turning he waved his hand in the air.

Katherine picked up her coat, locked her office door and walked down the two flights of stairs to the inside entrance of the Randall Building. Lloyd Spector was standing in the doorway making every effort to appear nonchalant. They walked together through the crisp autumn evening to the President's House.

All along South University Avenue Lloyd remained fixed on the sidewalk in front of them. "So he's a literary fellow," he said, enunciating the word. "What else do we know about him?" He was obvious about expending little energy on the inquiry.

There had been such a plethora of press on Delcourt during the months of his candidacy it was hard to imagine Lloyd was not aware of his background, his wide-ranging scholarship, his national reputation.

"Have you met him?" he added with an equal measure of disinterest.

"Just briefly," Katherine said, "at the inaugural reception. His speech was impressive. You've really not heard much about him?"

"I know he was at Princeton. I know he's here now."

"He seems to be garnering respect in pretty short order," she said.

"You mean his provost appointment."

Katherine ignored the tinge of sarcasm in Lloyd's tone. "The swiftness with which he moved was certainly to his credit," she said. "And I think she was a good choice."

President Delcourt had appointed Elizabeth Dwyer as his second-in-command, the new provost of the university. Her previous appointment a few years earlier as Dean of Engineering had been a national sensation, a female dean of a major engineering school. The fact that she was one of only two women in the department added surge to the flurry of press and attention, not to mention the undercurrent in the College of Engineering. Dwyer had since become a visible and respected dean on campus. Moreover, with Delcourt's reputation as a deep humanist, this embrace of the quantitative disciplines was a significant move. Many felt that his decisive action had been exactly what the institution needed. The response campus-wide had been overwhelmingly positive.

Lloyd, on the other hand, was a proud member of the klatch of academicians who had long ago confused cynicism with erudition. He never relinquished the edge he was convinced his particular brand of hubris gave him. Had the new president joined forces with another humanist, Lloyd would have been the first to indict him. The appointment of an engineer, on the other hand, was renounced as a self-serving gesture, a strategic ploy to prolong the presidential honeymoon. Though they did not speak another word on the subject, Katherine was well aware of her colleague's opinion — that the only way a humanist could work with an engineer was if the engineer were a woman.

"I'd like to know when the two of them are going to get into the trenches and move on this deanship," he asserted. "It should be a priority."

"From what I've heard, they both agree with you," Katherine said. "I think they're genuinely committed to finding the right person."

"Well, we'll see if we can't be literary," Lloyd said dryly as they arrived at the sidewalk leading up to the residence. "It should be a decent meal anyway."

It had been a number of years since Katherine had been inside the President's House, which was now tastefully appointed reflecting an elegant individual style. The Delcourts had obviously made the residence their home. At the same time their choice of decor created the same distinct atmosphere of eminence and official welcome as the stately exterior that had graced the campus since the university's earliest years.

Jonathan Delcourt greeted them with a hearty handshake and earnest welcome. He addressed them as "Katherine" and "Lloyd."

"Jonathan or Jon, whatever you prefer" was his way of putting faculty at ease. He was a robust round-faced Iowan whose sense of himself was the quality that most set him apart. In addition to his intellectual prowess and commanding presence, he was a bona fide member of the monarchy; his Ivy League credentials and comportment cast a compelling aura of credibility. Yet one sensed that just below the surface of his composed demeanor lurked a vigorous streak of restlessness or daring. He was the youngest president in the institution's history, a formidable mountain climber, and his romance with his wife of thirty years was visibly alive. Whatever would be said of the university's new leader, one thing would be clear to all who encountered him — Jonathan Delcourt was his own person.

Appetizers were barely on the plates in front of the president and his two guests before Lloyd launched into a laborious exposition on the U-M Physics Department. He sounded like the personification of the department's glossy graduate studies brochure, citing specific fields of research and highlighting special projects and international collaborations. He was especially emphatic about the role the department played in the university's leading status in research funding. At the frontier of atomic, molecular, condensed matter, high energy, and space research, Physics was heavily supported by the National Science Foundation, the Department of Energy, NASA and other federal and foundation sources. They were not dependent on the private fundraising that was critical to other departments of the university.

Delcourt smiled at his dinner guests. "Yes, I believe you have the distinction of being the first to sit at this table for whom funding issues are not the underlying thrust of the agenda."

Lloyd continued his extended discourse, oblivious to the fact that it had been unsolicited by their host. It was clear to Katherine from the president's comments that he was well aware of the department's strengths and the significance of its collaborations.

He had also been thoroughly briefed on its funding. He remained nevertheless thoroughly attentive to Lloyd, all the while including Katherine in his eye contact. He then effortlessly led conversation to his own topics of interest.

"Like everyone else, I suppose, I'm fascinated by the quest for an ultimate theory."

Lloyd stabbed a red skin potato with his fork. "It's the most important work going on."

Before Lloyd could embark on what was sure to be a rudimentary exposition on unified field theory, Delcourt dissuaded him masterfully. "It's a staggering thought, really — the idea that an ultimate force that unites all of the other forces of nature could actually be something identifiable in the physical realm."

"It wouldn't be the first time science has revolutionized our understanding of the world," Lloyd responded.

The president stirred. "Which reminds me, Lloyd, you didn't mention one of your other banner projects, the complexity program."

Katherine felt Lloyd bristle. She knew that as far as he was concerned the only thing the complexity program had in common with physics was that it was run by a physicist and housed in the physics department. He was visibly labored in his civility on the subject. When the president asked if they saw complexity theory as the wave of the future, he did not hesitate.

"The fad of the future perhaps," he responded. "Trying to refit the principles of dynamic systems to economic systems and social systems and every other system on the planet has nothing to do with physics."

"Then I take it you don't see complexity theory as part of a larger trend away from reductionism," the president asked.

Lloyd could not restrain himself. "As fashionable as it is in some circles to bad-mouth reductionism, science *is* reductionism.

Reductionism is science. *Holism* is for *poets*."

Delcourt cheerfully responded, "Yes, I guess my poetic sensibilities are showing, aren't they?"

Katherine noticed the subtle grin on Delcourt's face as he appeased Lloyd. In the next moment it was a straight-on smile and he was looking squarely at her.

"Katherine, there are few books I've enjoyed more than *The Relevance of Nature*."

"Well, thank you. I'm thrilled to hear it," she said.

"My wife was sorry she couldn't be here tonight too. She's quite eager to meet you."

Katherine was delighted, though a little uncomfortable. As hard as she had worked over the years to not be affected by her colleagues' indignation, she could not be completely at ease with the president's adulation in the company of Lloyd.

"She attended your lecture," Delcourt said. "The Saturday public series."

"Oh really. I didn't know that. No one told me she was there."

"No, she wouldn't want them to." Delcourt smiled. "She especially enjoyed the Q&A. I understand you had the place in quite an uproar with your joke about the Theory of Everything."

Katherine smiled. "It was a good group."

"I love that term — 'Theory of Everything.' It's so interesting the way expressions emerge and latch onto things, isn't it? 'Big Bang' and 'Theory of Everything.' "

"Yes, that's exactly what happens," Katherine said. "'Theory of Everything' is actually kind of being abandoned by physicists these days."

Lloyd brusquely interjected, "Most of us never used it."

"And why is it being abandoned?" Delcourt asked.

Katherine's smile was playful. "Oh, I don't know, I think maybe they decided it wasn't such a good idea to mislead people that we were actually looking for a theory of *everything*."

Delcourt laughed. "It does sound a bit ambitious, doesn't it. Even for an ultimate force of nature."

"And the universe has a way of reminding us that 'everything' includes some pretty infinite and elusive things," Katherine said.

"At the same time," Lloyd interjected, "science continually reminds us that it is only a matter of time before mysteries are unlocked."

Delcourt pursued Katherine's comment as he smiled at both of his guests. "And it's our understanding of the universe that's really the holy grail, isn't it? Isn't that what unified theories and string theories and all of physics is ultimately about — understanding the universe?"

Lloyd's discomfort was palpable. Katherine was affected by it. She smiled at the president as she patted her lip with her napkin. "Yes, well, you're asking a cosmologist."

"I find it fascinating," Delcourt went on, "this idea of a 'cognitive imperative' or 'cosmological urge' as it's been called — the idea that we come into the world with a desire to make sense of it, that it's an actual biological urge. I read one theory that infants stop feeding when they're intrigued by something in their environment because our drive to understand the world around us is even stronger than the need for food."

Katherine raised her eyebrows. "And if the infant happens to be Einstein," she said, "the desire to make sense of the world grows into an 'inexhaustible longing'."

" 'An inexhaustible longing to behold harmony,' " Delcourt cited Einstein, noticeably pleased with the new tenor of conversation. "And was his comment inspired by the desire or the harmony, do you think?" he asked.

Katherine smiled. "An interesting question. The harmony is definitely there. I also think there's something to the idea that we're born with a desire to understand it. And of course some say the two are inextricable."

As the evening progressed and the president addressed his own agenda with his guests, he continually returned to the thoughtful dialogue with Katherine that he obviously found stimulating. He also returned regularly, almost rhythmically, to issues about which he deferred to Lloyd. His dexterous social manner accommodated the sensibilities of everyone in the room, including the catering staff. Katherine knew that even Lloyd could not help being impressed with the new humanist at the helm, though he would of course find every reason to deny it. He was sure to be especially incensed about the president's comments on one subject in particular.

"Katherine, the Undergraduate Initiative is something to which the provost and I are completely committed. We've invited Mary Claire Henley into the next phase of the interview process for the LS&A deanship because we feel it's such an important component."

"Yes, I was delighted to hear that. Mary Claire is the absolute architect of the Initiative."

"She's quite a force, isn't she."

"She'll be a great asset on the dean search," Katherine said.

"And I've heard nothing but great things about your Initiative class," Delcourt said. "I was quite taken with your proposal. It was the first thing I read about the Initiative."

Katherine was both surprised and delighted by the president's comments, though she knew her colleague would find them revolting.

"I should also tell you," Delcourt confessed, "I've had a unique vantage for assessing your course's value."

She looked at him.

"One of my oldest friends, my old Amherst roommate, has a freshman in your class. My godson, as a matter of fact, Isaiah Jalen."

"Ah." Katherine smiled.

"I had dinner with them recently. We spent the entire meal

listening to our young man talk about your butterfly course. Isaiah's parents are convinced his entire experience at Michigan has been influenced by the enthusiasm that has overtaken him in your class."

"Well, thank you. That's wonderful to hear."

"The department is getting a lot of great feedback, I'm sure," Delcourt said to Lloyd.

"About Katherine's class?" Lloyd remained fixed on his meal. "Yes, well, Katherine is very talented," he said, with a bite that was discernable only to Katherine. "Our concern in the department of course is that students who respond in the way you have described to this kind of experimental course will have difficulty adjusting to the rigors of academics. After all, we don't want to mislead students about what will be expected of them in actual course instruction."

Without a moment's hesitation the president responded. "Well, correct me if I misrepresent the Initiative, Katherine, but I think one of the objectives is precisely that — to ensure that we do not mislead students in their pursuit of learning. To instead give them the benefit of a close look at the process of learning and at knowledge as a whole. I think of it not so much as experimental, as fundamental, to promote clear thinking at an early stage in their studies. Their pursuit of specific disciplines will surely benefit from a stronger sense of what it is that they bring to the process."

Katherine could not help being thrilled by the president's keen grasp and endorsement of the Initiative.

Delcourt's expression brightened. "Isaiah's father couldn't be more excited about your course. He's always been a big Whitehead fan. You should have heard him chanting — 'Eradicate the fatal disconnection of subjects! What you teach, teach thoroughly!' "

"That's Whitehead?" Katherine asked.

"One of his essays on education," Delcourt said. "Whitehead would have loved your class . . . And I'm a bit chagrinned to tell you about another triumph to your credit for which I am personally indebted." The look on the president's face revealed the child in him. "You've actually turned my godson's father into a Michigan fan," he said, "which in the case of this particular Yale snob is more of an achievement than I can tell you. I'm not sure whether he is more pleased about his son or disappointed to have the wind knocked out of his pomposity," he laughed. "Believe me, you've done me a great service."

Delcourt was enjoying himself, as was Katherine. She turned and looked into her colleague's face. Radiating from Lloyd's pupils was the constrained disdain he was managing to keep from affecting his facial muscles. She could not help sympathizing with his deep discomfort at the same time she felt bolstered by the president's support. She smiled at Lloyd in sincere resignation. "Lloyd and my other colleagues in the department are aware of the Initiative but they're really not familiar with the substance of the courses."

"No, we're not," Lloyd said. His contempt was only slightly veiled at this point. "We are also believers in teaching what we teach thoroughly," he said. "And we teach physics. We have some attachment to the idea of Katherine's teaching physics."

Delcourt was convivial. "Yes, I can certainly appreciate that. There is only so much we can ask of any one faculty member. I promise to be mindful of this, Katherine," he smiled at her, "or I may become the worst offender. I did plan to impose on you for your input on the Undergraduate Initiative. I expect to become more involved as we plan for its future."

"Of course," Katherine said.

"Lloyd, I look forward to taking you and Harold up on the department tour. I especially look forward to seeing the new optical labs and the detector pieces we're sending off to Fermi . . ."

Her home computer read 11:36 p.m. when she sat in her robe and adjusted her eyes to the screen's illumination. As she dashed off a spirited message to Charles she delighted in each detail about the evening with the president and especially his comments about the complexity program. She then perused her roster of incoming messages, persuading herself all the while that she was not looking for a particular one. The warmth she experienced at the sight of it intensified when she saw that the message was not a group email this time but one for her alone.

Go Blue! Your colleague has got it right! What you're missing here is that it's not just the game but the whole experience — the tailgate, the walk to the stadium, the spirit around you in the stands. And best of all — the marching band! Your deficiency in Wolverine spirit is a condition that must be remedied, my dear. And we must add SKIING to that list! Your four musketeers are all banking on it. (Judging from our group emails, especially Franco's latest, we're going to be busy talking again too.) I'm really looking forward to it.

p.s. I'm beginning to like the sound of "Cavanaugh."

She sat for a moment and stared at the screen. Her smile was a deep, true, alone in the dark smile. She scrolled down to read the message to which he was responding.

Greetings, Cavanaugh,
Deceived you? I did no such thing! How could I possibly have deceived you about something as thoroughly non-existent as my football consciousness?! It never occurred to me that I should immediately declare what my colleagues consider my most abominable shortcoming. But since you are clearly as severely infected with Wolverine's disease as anyone in my vicinity, I must share a story one of my colleagues just

shared with me: He informs me that he has been in attendance at every home football game since 1960, and his father attended every one from 1904 to 1963. So between the two of them they have not missed a game in almost a century! Is this sickness or what?! Have to run! Have a great day, Cavanaugh.

She scrolled back up to Cavanaugh's last line: *I'm beginning to like the sound of 'Cavanaugh.'*

She crawled into bed and laid her head on the pillow and stared at the ceiling in the dark. "Cavanaugh," she whispered, with a deep, true, alone in the dark smile.

Fourteen

"...The word 'soul' comes from the Gothic 'saiwala' and the old German 'saiwalo'," Niko read from her report, "both of which are connected to the Greek 'aiolos,' which means 'quick-moving, twinkling, iridescent.' And the Latin and Greek words for 'soul' and for 'spirit' also evolved from words associated with wind, or 'moving force' or 'life force.'"

Hannah had been listening intently to Niko's findings. "You can really see in the language that ancient societies believed the soul had an invisible breath body and that it manifested in the butterfly."

"You said you found a couple more examples, Hannah?" Katherine asked.

"Yes. In ancient Egypt, the Shilluk people said their leader Nyikang communicated with them often after his death in the form of a butterfly. And the Finno-Ugric peoples, back as far as about 10,000 BCE, believed their soul left their body as a butterfly when they were asleep. This was their explanation for dreams."

"Interesting," Katherine said. "We've heard this now from a number of cultures, haven't we."

"Yes," Hannah said. "And some of them believed that the butterfly that appeared in their dream was their own soul, and others believed it was the soul of another who was communicating with them."

"And some believe they are one and the same," Ming Jie said.

"This all certainly gets more interesting as we explore more deeply, doesn't it?" Katherine said. "Cynthia and Paul?" She smiled. "We know you're both dying to pounce on the latest materials you've shared with us."

Paul plunked his hand down on the pile of articles he had distributed to the class. "Well, this makes it pretty clear," he said. "All of these studies say animals are instinct driven, that it's just simple cues from the environment triggering instinctive behaviors." He read from one of the articles, "Their communication systems can be impressively sophisticated but they are neither invented nor taught; they are purely instinctive."

"Okay, Paul," Cynthia said in an obliging tone. "I just want to be clear about what it is that you're saying makes us unique. It's language, right?"

"It's not me," Paul exclaimed. "It's the whole scientific community!" Again he referenced the article, "Abstract thought. Symbolism. Self awareness. These are uniquely *human* capabilities."

"My point is that it all comes down to language, right?" Cynthia said. "Abstract thought is performed in language. It's described in language. It has its entire identification in language."

The students who were aligned with Cynthia in this on-going debate were quietly cheering her on, while Paul had his own group of comrades who though fewer in number were more given to clamorous outbursts.

"Yeah, so, what's your point?" he said. "Animals don't have language. We do."

"So you think the fact that they communicate in ways . . ."

"I'm telling you, there's not a scientist on the planet who'll back you up on this," Paul remonstrated. "It's not just that they don't speak our language, it's that they don't *have* language." His body language indicated that the case was concluded. In another moment he was facing off with his colleague again. "We've studied their brains!

And their behaviors! And their communication systems! We know they operate on instinct. The only thing they're programmed to do is *survive*. Just reproduce and survive. The facts are all here." He again struck the pile of papers in front of him. "We have language. Animals have instinct."

Shawn could not contain herself. "But this scientist says language *is* instinct," she said, referring to one of the articles Cynthia had copied for the class.

"That's right, Paul blurted. "And he also says that some leading scientists disagree with him."

"That means there's disagreement, Paul," Cynthia replied. "The point is, nobody knows anything for sure."

"So what if language is instinct?" he persisted. "That doesn't change the fact that we think and animals don't. It's a scientific fact."

"Well, once it was a scientific fact that the Earth was the center of everything," Amanda interjected.

"It makes a huge difference if language is an instinct," Tim said to Paul. Then slowly and deliberately he began his case. "We have butterflies in the midst of birds . . ."

Paul began to thrash and growl at the thought of revisiting another of the examples the group had been foisting upon him.

Tim remained steadfast. "The butterfly actually alters the pattern of its wing movements to mimic the pattern of another butterfly that birds don't eat, because those butterflies extract toxic substances from plants in order to protect themselves from hungry birds. And the birds actually *discriminate* among the butterflies based on the subtlest variation in their wing movement patterns to ensure they'll be *dining* instead of *dying*. Now, you say there's no intelligence in these behaviors, that they're just instinctive, for survival. And we're saying that if language is instinctive then we humans may have different tools but they are still tools for survival. We're saying that of course we have a more complex existence than animals.

But that doesn't mean that survival isn't exactly what drives us too. It especially doesn't mean that there are not other forms of intelligence besides ours."

"We're saying that we don't begin to know everything about the animal experience or what they're capable of," Cynthia said. "And there appears to be a lot of intelligence there."

Paul inhaled a long exaggerated breath.

Cynthia made one last stab at their argument. "Paul, you keep saying their communication is just chemical. Well, whether communication occurs in chemicals or in words, it doesn't really matter, does it? Isn't it possible that it is just a different language? One we don't understand?"

Paul was quiet for a moment. He had been thrown a bit off guard. "Ashlyn," Katherine said, "you've been trying to say something."

Ashlyn was one of several who had been flagging Katherine.

"Well, I just wanted to point out that when we look at animals we see them and we form our ideas about them in language, you know? I mean, like, we say things like 'queen bees' and 'worker ants' and 'mother hens.' We use words like 'rival' and 'court' and 'mate' and 'social hierarchy,'" she read from the pages in front of her — "all words that make sense out of what we're seeing, for *us*. Like Cynthia said, language defines everything for us. And when we look for intelligence in nature, we're looking for signs of our intelligence. For the kind of intelligence we understand."

Katherine nodded in Shawn's direction.

"I just wanted to share something else Nabokov said," Shawn said. Then she read from *Nabokov's Butterflies* which had been referred to a number of times during recent weeks' discussions.

" 'Human intelligence . . . inasmuch as it is a gift of nature, and a perpetually repeated one, cannot fail to exist in the warehouse of the bestower.' " She looked at Katherine. "I think he's saying that of course intelligence exists in nature, because we're a part of nature."

"But we don't see ourselves as part of nature," Robert spoke up from the back of the room. "We think of nature as some kind of *backdrop* — like it's just the *scenery* for the current run of the human drama. When in reality nature spent millions of years on the whole production, like Nabokov says, for the 'future applause' from the 'inevitable spectator.' That's us!" he said. "We're supposed to be applauding! Instead, we've embarked on this insane Baconian mastery over nature."

Not all of Robert's colleagues always understood his comments, though they were invariably taken in by his intensity. Joe's approach to things was one to which every one of his classmates could relate. "Nobody's talked about the fact that not all humans ever get past the reptilian brain," he said. "If our brains are supposed to be so advanced, how come a lotta people live their whole lives never doin' anything besides these things listed here under the reptilian brain?" He cited some of the words in one of Paul's articles. "They 'hunt' and 'nest' and 'groom' and 'mate' and 'breed.' They 'hoard food' and 'defend their territory' " He became more intense as he went on. "They 'reject species different from their own.' And how about this one?" he said emphatically, " 'Their behaviors are programmed and even ritualistic but there is no hint of playfulness or joy.' How many humans do you know like that?!" he said. "Havin' the capacity for abstract thought isn't the same as usin' it."

Paul jumped in. "Well, no one's saying all humans are geniuses," he challenged. "Some are smarter than others. Just like some animals are smarter than others. It's the smart ones that survive."

Immediately there was pandemonium in the lecture hall.

Paul was swift with his defense. "I didn't mean they're *smart*!" he protested. "That's just an expression!"

Katherine laughed with the group. And then she sympathized with Paul. "It's just *language*, right, Paul?"

Tim spoke up as he waved at Katherine. "I have some more interesting stuff on Jung's concept of 'imago'," he said.

The previous week, Tim had led the class on an expedition of Carl Jung's ideas about the psychological term, 'imago.'

"Man, you are really into this stuff, aren't you," said Scott.

"I am too," Mya said. "I'm glad he's into it. It's interesting."

A number of students concurred.

"The whole 'imago' thing is a lot clearer in Jung's book, *Symbols of Transformation*," Tim said. "He talks about humanity's collective nature, how we inherit systems that have developed over millions of years, just like the Monarchs with their migratory instincts. He says that we carry in our unconscious selves the whole plan for our patterns of behavior. And the parental imago is part of that plan. He says its influence on the psyche of a child is so powerful that we should wonder how such a responsibility could be given to ordinary human beings, that the parental imagoes are so dynamically charged that the slightest difficulty in adult life can reawaken memories of childhood and reactivate them. He says they're especially tied up with feelings about religion, that our religious feelings are rooted in our unconscious memories of early childhood emotions in relation to our parents."

"Didn't Freud say that too?" Daniel asked, recalling Tim's earlier discussion of Freud.

"Freud said that divine figures are rooted in the father-imago," Tim said. "But Jung saw both the father and mother imagoes as extremely powerful."

"I agree with what Tim was saying last week," Mya said. "I think Jung's concept of imago does refer to a final state of being. It's just that for humans it's kind of a whole complex of all the imagoes he talks about — the God imago and the parent imagoes and all the things we have to deal with in order to achieve that feeling of being whole, you know?"

"It's complicated for humans," Melodee said.

Katherine had been sitting very still. "Yes," she said to Melodee. "That it is."

Genevra spoke up. "So, do we know now that the psychological term grew out of the entomological one?"

"What do you mean? This is all etymological, isn't it?" Isaiah said.

"*Entomological*," Genevra stressed.

"'Etymology' and 'entomology' are awfully close, aren't they, Isaiah," Katherine said. "'Entomology' is the study of insects. 'Etymology' is the study of . . ."

"*Words*," Isaiah said sheepishly. "Got it."

"It's another 'compartment,' you know," Katherine said grinning.

"That's what's so cool about this class," Isaiah said. "No compartments."

"And no 'experts,' " Aaisha said.

Katherine looked at Aaisha, obviously pursuing her comment.

"Well, in other classes," Aaisha explained, "there's always someone who knows more than everybody else, you know? In this class we started out with some people who knew more about physics, or biology, or the Internet, or whatever, but we were all pretty much equal on the subject of butterflies."

"Yeah, we all knew nothing," Carlos said.

"We know you know more about a lot of these things we've been talking about," Isaiah said to Katherine. "But you haven't been telling us we were right or wrong, you know?"

"You haven't directed us," Niko added. "It's more like you're exploring with us."

Katherine was intrigued. "I was thinking just now when we started in on Jung again." She smiled at Tim. "I was imagining a Jungian expert in the room with us."

"Oh, wow," Lucas said.

Several other students chuckled, appreciating Katherine's thought.

"And how would that have changed the dynamic, do you think?"

"Oh, forget it," Tim said. "We would never have had that discussion."

"And why not?" Katherine said.

"Because there'd be someone to tell us what's what," Tim said. "They would have told us all about Jung's ideas. Instead, we've been able to explore our own ideas."

"And have we been at any kind of disadvantage, do you think?" Katherine asked. "Not having the perspective of a Jungian scholar? Someone who could talk with us definitively about Jung's concept of 'imago'?"

"Well, that depends on whether it was more important for us to understand Jung's ideas or to think about our own," Cynthia said.

"Yeah, if we were going to be psychologists," Mya said, "it would make sense to listen to someone who's studied Jung. But what we've been doing is completely different."

Katherine perused the student's faces. "What we've been doing in this class is not the kind of thing most people have participated in or had the chance to observe. What would you say to someone who sincerely questioned the value of what we've been doing?"

Lucas spoke up immediately. "Well look at everything we've learned," he exclaimed.

"We've learned quite a bit, haven't we," Katherine concurred.

She was heartened by the affirmations from around the room.

"In the beginning I didn't get it," Isaiah spoke up. "Like what the point was of learning about butterflies. But like, the other day on the Diag I passed this girl who had a butterfly on her book. You know, one of those stick-on things? And I was like . . . " Isaiah became animated. "Wow, we *know* butterflies like nobody else on the planet!"

There was a swell of laughter and consensus from the group.

"I know," Melodee exclaimed. "The other day a friend of mine said she had butterflies in her stomach, and my other friend said 'I wonder where that silly expression came from anyway.' And I was able to tell them the whole story — the ancient Chinese story about the lady who ate a butterfly, and how the expression became popular with the aviators in World War II — the whole history. And they were like, 'What's this butterfly class anyway?' "

Grace was waving her hand. "The day we talked about the Hans Christian Andersen story?" she said eagerly. "We had a discussion in my philosophy class and I brought up that one line from Hans Christian Andersen's butterfly — 'It's not enough merely to exist.'— And I told them about our discussion in this class, and people were saying, 'Your butterfly class? What's a butterfly class?' Most of them didn't know anything about the Initiative courses."

"I think a lot more people know now," Ben said.

"We've learned so much about butterflies," Cherie said, "but there's hardly been a subject we haven't discussed besides butterflies."

"That was the whole idea, wasn't it?" Joe asked, looking at Katherine.

Melodee jumped in. "I've learned more in this class than most classes I've ever had!"

"And what do you think has been the most valuable thing we've learned?" Katherine asked.

Isaiah responded immediately. "How much there is to learn."

"Yeah," Sarah said, "and about something as simple as a butterfly."

"I think the way we've gone about it has a lot to do with how much we've learned," Isaiah said.

"And you have all played an enormous role in deciding the way we've gone about it," Katherine said. Then she sat for a moment and contemplated Isaiah's remark.

"Not all classes can be approached in this way," she said. "We have other objectives in other types of courses. The hope, of course, is that experiences like this one can give us some perspective on learning. And our own perspective on learning can be the most valuable tool we have — for any learning experience."

Cynthia spoke up. "And isn't that what real learning is about? Developing your own perspective on something to the point that your own ideas begin to emerge?"

"Yeah, real learning is so much more than just understanding a subject," Ashlyn said. "It's understanding your own thoughts on a subject."

Katherine listened attentively as the students continued to express their thoughts on the experiment they had all had a hand in defining.

"And have we created any new knowledge, do you think?" she asked them.

"I think we have," Mya said. "We may not have furthered a particular study but we've created something brand new. Something unique."

"And what is it that we've created?" Katherine asked.

Tim thought through his answer as he spoke. "Well, we have a perspective on butterflies that's probably never existed before," he said. "Like, if you think about it, not even the scientists who spend their whole lives studying butterflies know what we know about them. I mean, they know a lot more about specific things, like Mya said, but like, for instance, does the evolutionary biologist who's studying lipid energetics in Monarchs know what the neurophysiologist knows about butterfly vision?" He was glancing at his colleagues who had reported on these studies. "And the behavioral ecologist who's looking at caterpillar defense systems — does he know what the developmental geneticist knows about wing patterns?"

"And do any of them know about the butterfly's role in literature, or Shamanism, or mythology?" Mya added.

"No kidding," Joe agreed.

"We even have some perspective on the butterfly's perspective," Isaiah said as he grinned at Katherine.

Katherine acknowledged Hailey.

"What's been the most interesting thing to me," Hailey said, "is seeing how much scientists know about butterflies and yet there's nobody putting it all together, you know? I mean, even in all these studies where the butterfly is an indicator of what's happening to the environment — there are so many of them. But like, one study tells you that butterflies are moving northward every year because of rising temperatures — And another one tells you how the Bt-contaminated pollen travels from genetically engineered corn to the neighboring milkweed plants and how lethal it is to the Monarch caterpillars — And another one tells you about the impact of deforestation on butterfly stratification — Just look at all the information we've seen in all of these studies!" she exclaimed.

"And we've been exposed to just a fraction of the science," Katherine said.

"But all this stuff just gets published for other scientists, you know?" Hailey stressed. "And then more scientists do more studies and the findings get more specific. But like, whose job is it to put it all together? I mean, all this stuff about what's happening to the soil and the air and the water. Whose job is it to tell people how important it is to do something about it?"

"That's not what science is for," Steffen asserted.

"Steffen?" Katherine encouraged Steffen to repeat his statement so the class could hear.

"It's not the role of science to tell people what to do with scientific information," he said. "Science generates information about the world. It doesn't make judgments."

Katherine was struck by Steffen's statement and disappointed when she glanced at the clock. The discussion he was opening up would have to be postponed. Robert, however, was not about to let the statement go unanswered. He was his usual fiery self as he leveled his reply.

"Well, when science generates information that tells us our survival may be in jeopardy if we don't make some changes, there's kind of an inherent judgment that we might want to make some changes, don't you think?"

Cherie chimed in. "For some people, it doesn't matter what science tells them. Their minds are made up and nothing's going to change them."

"Yeah. Even though they know nothing at all," Jason said. "It's amazing what people will dig in their heels about — when they don't have a clue what they're talking about."

Cynthia spoke up. "The important thing to remember is that there really is no one whose job it is to put all of this information together. It's really up to us."

Katherine looked at the group thoughtfully. "Yes, Hessel's Hairstreak was right, wasn't he. At the end of the day, it really is up to each one of us." She scanned the eyes in front of her. "We have to learn for ourselves what the truth is. And decide what we think is worth speaking up about."

"It's just like with Kafka," Isaiah said.

Katherine looked at Isaiah, delighted by the connection he had made. He was referring to their earlier discussion of Kafka's *The Metamorphosis* and what they thought 'imago' meant to Kafka, as a person and as an artist.

"Achieving your final state of being is more than just realizing your own possibilities," he said. "It's also speaking up about what you think matters."

Katherine smiled. "Isaiah, I'm sure Kafka would be heartened to know we were closing on that note." She gestured to the class. "See you on Thursday."

Fifteen

They were blue violets. As beautiful bright blue as Katherine had ever seen. Their electric blue hue glowed in the diffuse December light from her office window. The small florist envelope that had accompanied them had been addressed in a bold artistic hand, "The Empress." Inside was a plain white card with the words "Empresses Rule!" in the same hand. A warm smile spread over her face. "Go Maize," she whispered.

By now, Karen Rodzik, the department secretary was straddling the door jam, her head poised in anticipation. "Empress?" she said. She could see she would be extracting no further information. Katherine was intent on her computer screen examining her list of incoming emails. "Beautiful, aren't they?" she said.

There was a noticeable hesitation in Karen's demeanor. And then she asked, "Is Charles going to be at the meeting?"

Katherine turned and smiled at her, appreciating her sensitivity. "I'm meeting him in a few minutes. We'll head up to the meeting together."

Nowhere does the current of political subterfuge reverberate more palpably than in the web of academia. Karen was keenly aware of the departmental strife surrounding Katherine's participation in the Initiative for Undergraduate Education. The popularity of her butterfly class was only adding fuel to a fire. Lloyd Spector continued to lobby the executive committee to the extent that Nick Tullman and Phil Robertson were now unable to look Katherine in the face when they passed her in the hallway. It was known throughout the department that today's executive committee meeting would be a showdown, and that Katherine would be in the minority.

When she sat with Charles in his office before the meeting her interest was in something far more consequential than departmental politics. Charles' lunch with the president had taken place the day before.

"You really want to hear about this now?" he asked.

"Absolutely," she said. "It's exactly what I want to hear about. Something wonderful."

"Well, it's pretty wonderful." Charles grinned as he stretched back in his chair.

"Where did you go?" she asked him.

"The Gandy."

Katherine was tickled at the thought of Charles in his suit having lunch with the president at the Gandy Dancer. He had lunch so regularly at Ali Baba, the casual Middle Eastern restaurant not far from the office, his falafel sandwich and lentil soup simply appeared on his table the moment he arrived. It was the standing joke among his friends who called him the "King of Ali Baba."

"I'll tell you, I'm impressed," he said. "He seems to be right on the mark."

"That's my take on him too," Katherine said. "I'm not at all surprised complexity's one of his interests."

"And it's far from casual," Charles stressed. "It wasn't until later in the conversation that he let on just how much he's read. It's definitely a passion of his."

"And he was really interested in your take on it all," Katherine said, delighted with her friend's enjoyment.

"Wanted to get right at it," Charles said. "What's the essential question? Where are we headed with theory? And he was very interested in where I saw the Institute going. He even seemed savvy about the climate here in the department."

"Oh, I told you, he glossed right over Lloyd's comment at dinner. It was as if he just wanted to confirm his suspicion about how Lloyd would respond."

"Listen to this." Charles was upbeat. "He says, 'Well, I'm just an interested bystander but my impression is that scientists generally are either particle people or they're process people.' He says, 'Clearly, complexity attracts process people, who although they're outnumbered are kind of an emerging group, aren't they?' "

They smiled at one another.

Katherine was reveling in Charles' contentment. How well she recalled his demeanor during the strenuous and even hostile opposition to his launch of the complexity program. The Institute's niche in the department, its funding and support, all continued to be an uphill battle. The idea that the new president of the university had a genuine understanding of the program's value was a long overdue boost for his morale.

"So, did you talk about funding?" she asked.

"You kidding?" Charles erupted. His expression immediately provoked laughter in Katherine.

"Oh, yeah, Charles," she said with contrived nonchalance, "when the president asked you to lunch, did you happen to mention funding?"

"Gee, never occurred to me," Charles chuckled. "He wanted to know the whole situation." Charles sat erect in his chair. "I told him straight out, complexity studies just don't fit in physics. Or in any department. It's about authentic collaboration — hard sciences, social sciences, economics, humanities, all working together. I told him the most brilliant complexity thinkers, when they do stay at universities, are eaten alive by joint appointments. They spend their time straddling departments and fighting with bureaucrats and begging for money. Hell, academia is the last place for a science that hasn't even hung its hat in the scientific community."

"Did you say that to him?"

"It was straight talk. All of it. And if he wasn't listening he sure gave a good impression."

"Oh, I have no doubt he heard every word."

"Next time I'm introducing him to Ali Baba." He snickered.

"You're meeting again?!"

"Yyyep." Charles was in rare form.

"And you're actually taking him to Ali Baba?" Katherine laughed with delight.

Though Charles' meeting with the president had certainly roused interest in the department, not all of his colleagues were sharing in his elation the way Katherine was. Nick Tullman was brazenly condescending as the executive committee convened in the conference room. He lackadaisically remarked about how each new president over the years had taken his time observing the various projects on campus. "They especially enjoy basking in the limelight surrounding underdogs and other programs that have some appeal in popular culture. In the end, it all boils down to nothing."

The subtlety with which his colleague was belittling Delcourt's attention to Charles' complexity program was not lost on Lloyd Spector. "Just biding time," he said, "before they're held accountable for any real decision-making."

"Talking about the deanship again?" Harold Thurman said as he entered the room and took his seat at the head of the table.

"We're talking about Charles' meeting with Delcourt," Bob Gurzick said, clearly pleased. "I think it's great he's taken an interest in the Institute."

"Yes, how did it go?" Harold asked Charles in a perfunctory tone.

"I haven't had a chance to speak to you."

Harold's resentment of the president's attention to Charles' program was as difficult to disguise as his preoccupation with the start of the meeting. His mission was clear — to assuage his friend Lloyd's mounting fury and forestall the onslaught of a major siege. The role of arbiter was one for which even he recognized he was woefully ill-suited. He opened the meeting straightaway by presenting the group with copies of his memo announcing the appointment of a new "Curriculum Advisory Committee." The group consisted of five faculty members with whom he had long-standing ties, including none other than Lloyd Spector. He then proposed that the executive committee deal with pending curriculum issues after the new committee had had a chance to make its recommendations.

"I want to assure everyone that, although we will of course continue with our present commitments, any future proposal of involvement in extra-departmental courses will be reviewed first by the curriculum committee. And I'm sure you all understand that our needs in the department are such that they will always be priority."

Lloyd was not appeased. "Let's all just be clear about what we're talking about, shall we?" he said. "Katherine, would you tell us what truth there is in reports that an esteemed member of the physics faculty is leading students in a debate about *U.S.– China relations?*"

"Yes, Lloyd, it's true," she said. "Our discussion of the plight of silkworm workers in China evolved . . ."

"And the identity issues of Franz Kafka!" Lloyd sarcastically stormed. "And the rest of the physics department is evidently missing something that we're not delving the depths of *Darwinian theory!*"

"Lloyd, we've already established . . ." Bob Gurzick attempted to speak.

"Do you know that serious students are confused by this type of free-for-all?" Lloyd trounced. "This no grades business. This *mayhem* that I'm sure you think is all very Socratic and progressive. Do you realize this is a disturbing interruption of serious academic pursuits?"

Katherine looked directly into Lloyd's eyes. "Lloyd, if there are students who are confused, either by Initiative courses or by the absence of grading, I'm certain they are fewer than those who are confused or disheartened by education generally."

"And now it's our concern that students are disheartened by education?!" he fumed.

"It seems to me, Lloyd, if it's not our concern, it sure should be," Charles said.

The group was momentarily struck silent. Katherine's heart was pounding so furiously it took her a moment to achieve the calm with which she responded.

"Actually, I think it's worth sharing a bit of the discussion you mention, Lloyd — the discussion of Darwin's ideas. It was started by one of the few seniors in the class, who, by the way, elected the class because they had heard about the Initiative and were interested in its mission. This young man led the group in an examination of the present state of the world as a 'hyper Darwinian time,' as he called it, a time when a small segment of the global population was flourishing while billions teetered on the edge of survival. The class discussed their way to what they understood to be Darwin's central idea, that survival belonged to those most adaptable to change. They then had an incredibly thoughtful dialogue about the change and adaptation that needed to happen in order for the world to survive. And yes, this and the other discussions you mentioned all came out of a very ill-defined, loosely guided study of butterflies. And there is no doubt in my mind that the class is fulfilling an extremely valuable . . . "

"It is not a matter of what's valuable, Katherine," Lloyd cut her off again.

This time Bob Gurzick spoke up determined to finish his remark. "Well, it's clear that what's unchangeable here is that Katherine's participation in this program was approved by this committee. We've established that. And we've agreed that there will be a review before any future commitments are made. So it would seem that the sensible course at this point is to wish Katherine well with her class and to move on with our agenda."

That evening Katherine persuaded Mary Claire to join her for a yoga class and afterward they went to The Earle for dinner. They had spent an evening at The Earle every couple of months for as long as they could remember. Their visits were now almost ritualistic — two Gorgonzola and walnut salads, a loaf of French bread, and two glasses of merlot in a quiet cozy booth where they could talk.

Katherine became intent on her wine glass. "Somehow yoga and wine just don't quite . . ."

"Oh, it's good for the soul," Mary Claire said dismissively. She could hardly wait to talk about the Initiative meeting with the president and the deans that had happened that afternoon.

"So, Charles likes him too?" she said eagerly.

"Charles is ecstatic," Katherine assured her.

"Well, he's sure aboard the Initiative," Mary Claire said.

As Katherine observed her friend she thought "ecstatic" was a pretty good description of her too. "I'm so glad it went well," she said. "I knew it would."

Mary Claire then launched into her detailed description.

"They know it's going to be a challenge," she said. "The response in physics is just the tip of the iceberg. It pits Initiative classes against other classes. It undermines institutional status. And of course some deans think the absence of grading is just one step away from rampant anarchy — Everything we knew was coming. But the feedback from students and from *parents*," she stressed, "has really grabbed their attention. Delcourt and Dwyer are both completely signed on." She leaned in to Katherine. "Delcourt told the deans it wasn't about grades, it was about encouraging students to direct themselves which was the only way to promote real learning." She sat back in her seat. "He's definitely aboard."

Katherine raised her glass to her friend. "Congratulations, my dear."

She reached into her handbag and handed Mary Claire a paperback edition of Alfred North Whitehead's essays.

"This is from Delcourt's friend who has a son in your class?"

"He sent it with the nicest note." Katherine grinned. "Evidently Delcourt told him I drew a blank on Whitehead and education."

"Oh!" Mary Claire was enthused again, remembering something else that had been said at the meeting. "Dean Whitley from the Law School said, 'Why butterflies? What do butterflies have to do with physics?' Delcourt says, 'The fact that it has nothing to do with a specific discipline is part of the point, John.' " She peered at Katherine.

"He really does get it, doesn't he," Katherine said. "And, you know, it may be *mayhem*," she rolled her eyes, recalling Lloyd's remark, "but listening to those kids today . . ."

"What'd they get into today?"

"I told you we spent quite a bit of time on *Nabokov's Butterflies*. Today they had this great debate about whether Nabokov was a scientist or a writer. You'd've loved it. They started out with the premise that he had to be one or the other because scientists and writers are two completely different species. And then one of them brought up Goethe."

Mary Claire's eyes opened wide.

"One of the seniors," Katherine said. "I told you there are four, right? I think the mix of grade levels is really important too. Especially having a few seniors like these particular four. "Anyway, you know where they ended up?" Katherine fixed on Mary Claire. "Goethe and Nabokov were *thinkers*. And thinkers shouldn't be pigeonholed into any one field. They decided that society should simply acknowledge its great thinkers as thinkers and forget about categories and labels."

The two women looked at one another with a shared sense of gratification. And then Mary Claire began to reminisce.

"Reminds me of a huge argument Bob and I had years ago when I said Herodotus wasn't a historian." She sipped her wine. "I said he was just a thoughtful guy who was inspired to write about the events of his time. For the life of me I could not get Bob to understand how I could possibly say that the 'father of history' was not a historian."

"Because 'history' wasn't in anyone's frame of reference," Katherine said.

"Exactly! Not if he was the 'father' of history!" Mary Claire's snicker became a sigh. "Some of our better moments actually, fighting like idiots about ideas."

"Well, the little winged wonders are sure filling this group with ideas. It's so incredible, Mary Claire, the way this is playing out."

"I'm sure their teacher has a little to do with that."

Katherine looked at her thoughtfully. "Do you know that in Tibet one's teacher is revered even above one's parents? Teachers are shown the highest respect in Tibetan culture."

Katherine had no secrets from Mary Claire. They both knew this was another piece of information Katherine had obtained from the California cosmologist. She looked at her friend sheepishly as she admitted, "He has taught me a lot about Tibet."

"And you're sure there's nothing abrew here, huh?" Mary Claire probed.

Katherine was almost convincing as she shrugged off the idea. "We're just so radically different."

"Maybe not so radical as you think."

"He challenges my whole sense of reality, Mary Claire."

Mary Claire was playfully dismissive. "I'm tellin' ya, it's California. They're on the edge out there."

"Believe me." Katherine rolled her eyes. "This guy takes 'on the edge' to brand new edges. I don't know if I'm more astonished by his ideas, or confounded that they could come from a physicist."

"Like what?" Mary Claire asked.

"Like references to the 'great stream of creation,' and 'the entire numinous universe,' and the 'divinity at the center of the universe'!" Katherine's head rolled right along with her eyes.

"Is that what has you freaked about his guy? You think he's religious?"

"Trust me. This is not standard cosmology language."

"Well, you know me," Mary Claire said. "I think Blake hit it on the head — 'The only true religion is education.' "

"Absolutely," Katherine concurred. Then she looked at her friend. "It is interesting though that Blake's work was saturated with religion."

"Part of his education," Mary Claire quipped.

"I suppose. I don't know. Whatever it is Cavanaugh believes, there's this amazing kind of certainty about him that's just so . . . compelling."

"Compelling is good. We like compelling."

"Compelling is great, isn't it? It doesn't show its head often enough." Katherine's expression shifted to an affectionate smile. "I have to say, Mr. Maize has turned out to be more of a mensch than I ever expected."

"You talked for a long time last night, huh?"

"It's more that we really talked. We don't talk often anymore but . . ."

"You really talk," Mary Claire followed. "There's nothing quite like someone you used to love, is there?"

"He actually seems to be enjoying being friends," Katherine said. "He's definitely better at it."

"So tell me about the Empress thing," Mary Claire said.

"The Empress Leilia is a butterfly that's made a reputation for herself by insisting on mating only once in her life." She looked at Mary Claire. "I told him they must wonder in their short lives if maybe mating isn't going to pass them by altogether . . . He kept asking me what was up. Thought maybe I'd met someone and he didn't turn out to be what I'd hoped."

Mary Claire was watching Katherine, understanding perfectly how David would have arrived at such an idea. "Empresses Rule," she repeated the phrase. "He's definitely one of a kind."

She leaned toward the lamp on the table and began flipping through the Whitehead book.

"I did read *The Aims of Education* once upon a time."

"You never mind my highlighting," Katherine said.

"Hey, that's what books are for," Mary Claire exclaimed. "As long as they belong to you." Then she read aloud some of the lines Katherine had highlighted on the pages in front of her. " 'The solution which I am urging, is to eradicate the fatal disconnection of subjects which kills the vitality of our modern curriculum. There is only one subject-matter for education, and that is Life in all of its manifestations . . . the joy of discovery . . . an intimate sense of the power of ideas . . . the beauty of ideas'."

"Look at the one, what's it called, 'The Function of a University'?" Katherine said.

Mary Claire flipped to the essay "Universities and their Function" and again read from the highlighted passages.

" 'This growth of universities, in number of institutions, in size, and in internal complexity of organization, discloses some danger of destroying the very sources of their usefulness.' " She lifted her gaze to her friend's and then returned to the book.

" 'The whole point of a university . . . is to bring the young under the intellectual influence of a band of imaginative scholars . . . to preserve the connection between knowledge and the zest for life . . . to enable students to construct an intellectual vision of a new world . . . A university is imaginative or it is nothing.' " She looked at Katherine. "Now there's a guy I could take to bed."

Katherine grinned at her. "That's what he's here for."

Mary Claire slipped the book into her bag and then beamed a lofty smile as she raised her glass to her friend. "To the Empress," she said, "who waits for her true mate."

Katherine sipped her wine and then returned to her introspective stare at the lamp on the table. "Don't you think everyone is determined to find their true mate? That everyone believes that's who they're marrying?"

Mary Claire looked at her squarely. "I think every one of us knows exactly what we're doing when we do it. We don't always pay attention to what we know, but we know."

"Are you saying you knew Bob wasn't your true mate?"

"I'm saying there are few people who make a conscious decision that it's worth waiting, whatever it takes."

Katherine looked at her. "Somehow I think it's not quite so complicated for butterflies."

Mary Claire sighed. "Yeah, and either it's getting a whole lot more complicated or a whole lot more people are acknowledging how complicated it is. Do you know, when I was eleven and I told my best friend that my parents were getting divorced, she didn't know what I meant? We didn't know a single other kid whose parents were divorced. Now I know few people who haven't been there. But then I guess there are a whole lot more Empresses too, aren't there. Amazing, isn't it? How radically the culture changes in just a couple of decades? God knows it was a given we'd have children, even when we were in college."

It was only a moment before Mary Claire realized she had raised the subject of Katherine's aunt. She proceeded sensitively. "Your aunt must have been quite a woman, not marrying in her day. Not to mention becoming a doctor."

Katherine was staring at the lamplight on the table. "She said my mother wanted to be a doctor too . . . I do wonder sometimes if it's not all tied up together, you know?"

"If what's tied together?"

"The Empress thing. Maybe David's right. Maybe I'm out there trying to figure out the universe because it's easier than figuring out why someone who wanted so much to have love in her life hasn't found it."

Mary Claire pushed her face forward into Katherine's. "Did your kids by any chance turn up any research on how rare the males are that are suited to female Empress butterflies?"

Katherine remained thoughtful. "I just wonder if their incessant selectivity isn't connected to feelings they're not even aware of, you know? If maybe their early experience of family was just so d . . . "

"Dysfunctional?" Mary Claire balked. "God, that word makes me crazy."

"Actually I was going to say 'dark,' but I guess 'dysfunctional' is the word, isn't it."

Mary Claire erupted. "It cracks me up. This contrived notion that *some* of us come from dysfunctional families. That *some* of us have dysfunction in our lives." Her words burst forth in a constrained restaurant whisper. "Good God, *life* is dysfunction. That's what we're here for! To try to make function out of dysfunction! We're all filled with the same force that all the complexity theorists are trying to figure out. To be alive at all is to be trying your damnedest to make order out of disorder. Function out of dysfunction." She fell back in her seat. "That's why we all want so much to be in love. It's the one place where, at least for a little while, there's a sublime sense of order."

Katherine smiled as she again raised her glass to her friend.

Mary Claire sniggered. "What's that stage some butterflies go through — diapause? Where they're knocked senseless temporarily and then resume their growth? That's what divorce is for some of us caterpillars." She sipped her wine. "I don't know, I think maybe we all have exactly the family experience we're supposed to — and that true love shows up exactly when we're ready for it to." She reached for the bread. "We're the lucky ones, Katie. The chaos we had to find our way out of was exceedingly visible. For most people it masquerades in all kinds of subtle, indiscernible forms. They spend years just trying to identify it."

Katherine smirked at her. "Ours was clear, undeniable dysfunction, huh?"

"Besides," Mary Claire said, "if we'd had the choice, we'd never have been happy with simple lives."

"You know, it's funny," Katherine reflected. "When Cavanaugh asked me if I'd ever been married, his reaction was the exact opposite of what I usually get from people."

"He wasn't aghast?" Mary Claire said.

"No. I was completely bowled over. He just looked at me thoughtfully and then real calmly he said, 'I'm not surprised.' God, it was so refreshing."

"And you really don't think there's something happening here, huh?"

"No," Katherine said. "I mean, there's definitely some attraction."

"Now that part I figured out," Mary Claire teased.

"We're just violently incompatible on such basic things," Katherine said.

"Well, now, you don't know for sure that he's . . ."

"He's *wacky*, Mary Claire."

Mary Claire laughed. "Well, wacky's good."

"No, I mean seriously wacky." Katherine leaned across the table and glared at her friend. "He thinks the universe *communicates* with us!"

Mary Claire was thoroughly amused. "Well, maybe it does! No, really," she said as she returned Katherine's glare. "When you think about it, is that any wackier than *Big Bang* theory? Or some of these other theories you all come up with?"

There was no mistake about the reprimand in Katherine's expression.

"I'm *serious*," Mary Claire pressed her. "You spend your life with this stuff so you take it for granted, but *think* about it. The idea that the universe just happened all of a sudden out of nothing? That human beings appeared out of the stuff stars are made of? I mean, come on, what's not wacky about any of it?"

Katherine boldly retorted, "Those are things we have evidence of."

"Yeah, and some people think we have some pretty powerful evidence of a universal intelligence." She glared again at her friend. "You've said some things not too far from that yourself."

Katherine was taken aback.

"So how much of a reach is it to think that intelligence communicates?" Mary Claire insisted.

Katherine's expression was right on the edge of acquiescence. "Oh all right. I'm just not communicating the depth of his wackiness."

"The depth of his wackiness," Mary Claire echoed. She was enjoying herself immensely. Then she doggedly faced-off with her friend. "He's fascinating, right?"

Katherine half-heartedly conceded.

"And there's definitely chemistry," Mary Claire persisted.

Katherine wrestled with her feelings for a moment. She was getting ready to tell Mary Claire the truth, to hear the truth herself. She leaned toward her. "I've been asking myself how many thousands of people we meet in our lives before we meet another one of those precious few, you know? The ones who suddenly appear and their very existence makes you feel completely different than you've ever felt before."

Mary Claire's face dropped. "God, I'd walk down the street naked to have that feeling again."

Katherine let out a disgruntled sigh. "So, why does it have to be so complicated?"

"You mean, why does he have to be wacky?" They both started to laugh. "What can I say?" Mary Claire said, "It's the complex systems that are the interesting ones, right? I'll bet you anything he's got some kind of turmoil in his background too."

"Turmoil?" Katherine said.

"Turmoil," Mary Claire insisted. "All the most interesting people have some kind of painful inner turmoil left over from their childhood."

"You think so, huh?" Katherine was humoring her.

"And you know what else?" Mary Claire peered into her eyes. "It's the ones who come along once in a couple thousand that remind you you're *alive*."

Katherine's surrender was visible.

"And guess what, kiddo," Mary Claire persisted. "That kind of feeling doesn't happen to one person. It happens to two."

Katherine's face transformed. "I do think about him," she said.

"Now, believe it or not, I figured that one out too."

Katherine grinned at her and then grumbled affectionately, "You're incorrigible."

"So you're still emailing?" Mary Claire was upbeat.

"All five of us. Had another one today. They really want me to ski."
Mary Claire's eyes opened wide.
"Not in this lifetime," Katherine said dismissively. "Come on, ready to go?"

As they walked up the indoor stairwell from The Earle, Katherine exclaimed, "Do you know that butterflies are twenty-four hundred times more sensitive to smell than we are?"
"There really is something here with these little winged wonders, isn't there."
"I had no idea," Katherine replied.
When they reached the sidewalk outside The Earle on Washington Street, Mary Claire stopped. "Well, I have to confess," she announced, "I don't think 'master yogini' is ever gonna be on my epitaph."
Katherine drew a deep December breath. "Oh, but there's something about the breathing that's just so . . . nourishing," she said. "Don't understand it exactly but there's definitely something to it." She stood on the sidewalk facing the street. "I have to show you this one posture I'm doing all the time now. It's so great after you've been sitting at the desk for a long time."
"Here?" Mary Claire protested.
"Come on, there's no one around. Look. You place your feet firmly, about a foot and a half apart and spread your arms wide." She demonstrated. "Think of a butterfly. You stretch your arms and your hands and your fingers as far as you can, and then your head falls back. Just really stretch. Feels sooo wonderful."
"Good grief, you look like a hood ornament."
Katherine laughed. "Come on. Try it," she said. She was still stretched in a full winged position.

Mary Claire was walking away from her now. "I've never seen her before, officer," she said to the night. "I have no idea who this woman is."

Katherine laughed as she ran and locked arms with her friend. "Oh yes she does, officer. She's known me all her life."

Sixteen

So, if we ask, 'What's the butterfly's purpose in life?' — that's a metaphysical question, right?"

"That's a good example, Grace," Katherine said. "Some would say that to explain the butterfly's purpose in the physical web of life is to explain its purpose. But we could certainly argue that that's a metaphysical question too, couldn't we."

"Like, why they live for such a short time," Melodee said.

"And, why they're able to see so much more of the spectrum of light," Tim said. "Not how, but why."

"And the question we asked at the beginning of the semester," Jason said. "What is it that actually breathes the life into the butterfly — that's a metaphysical question, isn't it?"

Katherine raised her eyebrows. "What constitutes life is a big question even in the physical sciences," she said. "It is certainly also a metaphysical question."

"So, metaphysical questions are the ones we can't answer, right?"

"Well, that's an interesting way to put it, Isaiah."

The class had been reflecting on the lessons inherent to the butterfly's experience and perspective when they found themselves in a discussion of what distinguishes the metaphysical from the physical.

"Physics examines what the world is made of and how it works," Jason said. "Metaphysics asks the deeper questions like 'why' and 'for what purpose.' "

Cynthia followed. "A physicist discovers patterns in the natural world and transcribes them into mathematical schemes," she said. "But the questions of why there are patterns and where they come from and what they mean — those are things a metaphysician contemplates."

Robert spoke up from the back of the room. "It wasn't an accident that Aristotle's metaphysics came last," he said. "Physical science always eventually leads to metaphysics. What we've been doing with butterflies is a good example. We started out examining its body and we've gotten more and more metaphysical as the semester's progressed."

"Another keen observation, Sir Robert," Katherine said.

She had explained to the class that "metaphysics" or "after physics" was originally coined by Aristotle's first editor three hundred years after Aristotle's death, referring to the part of his writings that were placed after those that dealt with the physical sciences. The class had discussed the fact that "physics" was at one time called "natural philosophy" and that science had evolved over time to be both highly specialized and completely separate from what was now known as "philosophy" and "metaphysics."

"Professor Ayers?" Melodee spoke up. "As a physicist, do you deal with metaphysical questions?"

"Philosophers deal with metaphysics," Jack said.

"Physicists do too, don't they?" Daniel asked.

Katherine could not resist asking Steffen if as a physicist he would be dealing with metaphysical questions.

"Well, the underlying questions are always there," he responded. "But a scientist must abstain from metaphysical inclinations as they only undermine the soundness of science."

Katherine was intrigued. "And how about moral and ethical questions?" she asked the budding physicist.

Steffen held his head perfectly still as he considered his response. "Moral and ethical questions are also outside the domain of science."

Katherine casually pursued his premise. "Well, what if as a physicist you found yourself in a situation where ethical issues were unavoidable. For instance, let's say you were one of the leading nuclear minds in the world and you were asked to participate in the creation of the most powerful weapon ever made. And you knew that without your expertise it could not be built."

Steffen looked at her. "Well, fortunately, I would not be in that situation because . . ."

"We already have the bomb," Paul asserted.

"Yeah, don't we already have enough bombs?" Mya asked.

"We have enough bombs right here in the United States to end the world as we know it," Katherine said. "And as many people are unaware, the weapons we have in our arsenals today are a thousand times more powerful than the most powerful bomb dropped in the last global war."

"A thousand times?" Sarah whispered, horrified at the thought.

Isaiah looked at Katherine. "Has a scientist ever refused to build a bomb?"

"As a matter of fact, one of the discoverers of nuclear fission refused to participate in the development of the atom bomb," Katherine said. "Her name was Lisa Meitner. Germany's first female physics professor." She saw that even Steffen did not give his usual nod of recognition. "Though Otto Hahn took the Nobel Prize for the discovery of nuclear fission, scholars now tell us that Lisa Meitner, Otto Hahn's thirty-year collaborator, was a true partner in the discovery and in fact the first to articulate it."

"And she refused to work on the atom bomb?" Isaiah asked.

Katherine nodded. "Of course others expressed remorse after the bomb was dropped," she said.

"Wow," Ashlyn said, as the realization penetrated. "Just imagine if they'd all refused."

"Then we wouldn't have any national defense," Jack said brusquely. "That's what bombs are for. To defend ourselves."

"Well, I know it's a radical idea," Cynthia jumped in, "but some of us don't believe military might is a defense against anything. It may even provoke the very aggression we want to avoid."

"I agree," Cherie said. "I think it just provokes your enemies to have the most powerful weapons."

"Professor Ayers?" Melodee spoke up. "Do you get involved in nuclear weapons?"

Jack sputtered, "She's an astrophysicist."

"That's not what I meant," Melodee said. "I wanted to know if physicists get involved in nuclear issues, like banning weapons and stuff."

"Yes, they do, Melodee," Katherine responded. "Many physicists feel it is their responsibility to speak out on nuclear issues."

"Physicists are the only ones who know the full extent of the threat," Robert called out.

"Then you do speak out against nuclear weapons?" Niko asked Katherine.

"At every opportunity," Katherine said. "Backing off on weaponry is something I feel strongly about. And nuclear waste is a disaster we haven't begun to deal with. Unfortunately, unless there is a major catastrophe fresh in our memories we become complacent about the fact that there is tremendously hazardous waste in our midst for which we have no real solutions."

"Lisa Meitner?" Shawn asked, clarifying the name. "So if she was a partner in discovering nuclear fission, how come she didn't get the Nobel too?"

"Well, that's a good question," Katherine said. "It's too bad we're not able to ask Otto Hahn that question. The short answer is that she was a female in physics at a time when women were not at all accepted in the profession. She in fact spent a good part of her early career working in the basements of buildings where her collaborators worked because women were not allowed in the labs." She looked around at the students. "More important, regarding the years surrounding the elucidation of fission, she was a Jew living in Germany. So she was forced into obscurity throughout her career. It was only in recent years that scholars brought her achievements to light. Today an element on the periodic table is named in her honor."

"But that's not the same as a Nobel Prize, is it?" Sarah asked.

"No, Sarah. It's not," Katherine said.

"So physicists do get involved in moral and ethical issues," Ashlyn asked.

"Some do," Katherine said. "Like every other profession."

"But you don't get involved in metaphysical issues?"

"Some do that too," Katherine said thoughtfully. "A precarious undertaking, scientists commenting on the metaphysical. When it is done, there needs to be a crystal clear distinction between the science and the non-science." She smiled at Steffen. "Although it is debatable whether science is undermined by our inclinations toward the metaphysical, there is no question that a scientist's credibility is undermined by assertions not grounded in science."

"You mean, if you were to make a statement like, for instance, that the Big Bang happened at the hand of a creator," Joe posed, "your reputation as a cosmologist would be weakened?"

"Oh, it would be more than weakened," Katherine responded. "The question of whether or not there was a creator involved in the origin of the universe is not a question for science. A cosmologist deals with the *physical* evidence of the *physical* origins of the universe."

"And we'd also have to define 'creator' to have that discussion,"

Robert hollered from the back of the room.

Shawn had been studying Katherine's face. "Professor Ayers?" she spoke up. "In your book, in the introduction, when you were talking about the study of the universe, you said you could not imagine a more 'stark confrontation with the unknowable.' "

Katherine recognized her words from *The Relevance of Nature*. "And that sounded as though I were saying that cosmology is inherently metaphysical?"

Shawn nodded.

"Well, there is surely no field of inquiry that sits more directly on the tributary between physics and metaphysics," Katherine explained. "But science is about discovering the things we can know, the things we can articulate — in the language we share with the universe, which is mathematics."

Ashlyn spoke up. "Can you tell us the most fascinating thing you've learned about the universe?" She and her colleagues were enjoying this digression.

Katherine pondered the question. "I think the most fascinating thing to me is the idea that only one billionth of the sun's energy reaches Earth and yet the force of that energy is powerful enough to propel all of the life on the entire planet. Imagining the energy that exists in the universe — it's breathtaking at times."

"One billionth?" said an astonished Mya.

"It's no wonder we always think of light in a spiritual way," Grace pondered. "Because light is literally the source of life. I mean, light is what gives us life. It's what makes life possible."

"If we have any doubt, we should try living without it," Jason remarked.

Cynthia spoke as she processed her thought. "It's so fascinating that we can even know how a butterfly's eyes process light and yet we don't really know what light is."

Tim jumped in. "What's really interesting is that we've had to build

technology in order to see the light the butterfly sees naturally."
Katherine contemplated Tim's thought. "It is interesting, isn't it."
"I still think they're uniquely tuned into the light," Tim said. His enthusiasm had not been dampened in the least by Steffen's 'reasonable explanations.' "It's like they thrive on the energy in a special way."
"Didn't someone say that the reason butterflies evolved from moths was so they could fly in sunlight rather than at night?" Isaiah asked.
"That's a theory, yeah," Scott said.
Katherine was reflective. "I think we'd be amazed to discover just how profoundly connected we all are to the light, to the energy from the sun. It's the most fundamental connection between the universe and every one of its inhabitants. Everything from the simplest protozoan to the complex creatures who've been engaged in all this interesting discussion." She smiled at the group and then at Tim. "And butterflies certainly do exhibit that connection in extraordinary ways." She rested on the edge of the desk. "So, what other lessons have we learned from our little winged friends?" She was returning to their earlier discussion. "What else has the butterfly's perspective taught us?"
Jason began. "Well, we all have to start out as lowly, wormy caterpillars inching along in the dirt, one foot in front of the other, to get where we want to be."
"To be what we want to be," Cherie added.
The students were again contemplating what they had learned from their exploration of the butterfly's experience of life.
"Life is about constant change," Ming Jie said. "Whether it's Heraclitus' 'constant flux,' or Chuang Tzu's 'tranquility in disturbance,' or Emily Brontë's 'destruction and transformation' — everything is constantly changing."
"And to achieve our ultimate self we have to be open to change," Marisa said, "even in our values and our thinking."

"How do you mean, Marisa?" Katherine asked, intrigued by her comment.

"Well, the butterfly has to continually change its whole value system really," Marisa explained. "Because it has to constantly adapt to new sources of sustenance and to completely new ways of being. But if it does, and it survives all the changes, then it's ultimately able to spread its wings and fly. To dance its own unique dance, like the Native Americans say."

Ashlyn brightened up as she added, "And to have a mutually sustaining relationship with the most beautiful creatures on the planet — the flowers."

"Mmm. That's a nice thought, isn't it," Katherine remarked.

"It's also important to remember that the butterfly's extraordinary vision is something it grows into," Marisa said.

"That's right," Cynthia followed. "The caterpillar has barely any vision at all. The ability to see so much is something that comes to the butterfly in the later stages of its life."

"And who knows that it's not even *because* of all the challenges it goes through?" Marisa said. "Maybe that's how it develops its extraordinary vision."

Katherine's expression indicated a keen appreciation for the thoughts that were being expressed. In a moment she nodded in Hailey's direction.

"Yeah, we all go through metamorphoses in our lives," Hailey said. "And sometimes it can feel like you're going through a complete breakdown and like there's barely enough left of you to face the next stage. But we all have to let go of what we were in the past and allow ourselves to grow. That's the only way we can grow."

"And sometimes the changes that happen in our lives are really difficult to understand," Shawn said. "Like if the caterpillar doesn't know he's on his way to being a butterfly then when he's coming apart at the seams and falling to pieces he must feel like life is over for him, when it's actually just beginning. Just like sometimes, when change hits us hard and we can't make sense out of why it's happening, we have to remember that something really great may come out of it, we just don't know yet what it will be."

The students watched Katherine as she sat quietly listening.

"You have to hold onto your dream of having wings," Mya said.

"And remember that everything is fleeting," Hannah added. "Beauty, freedom — it's all fleeting."

"Because life is *short*," Melodee asserted.

There were a few snickers.

"Yeah, so you have to smell the flowers!" Paul blurted, thoroughly amused with himself.

Some of the students laughed. Others continued thinking.

Melodee spoke up as she raised her hand. "I think their short lives tell us that it's not just where you're headed that's important but all of the things you have to go through to get there, they matter too."

"Yeah," Breahn said. "Every single moment is precious to a butterfly."

Katherine observed Breahn's face again. The face that could take one's breath away. And Isaiah in his front row seat. Robert, in the back of the room. They were all in the same places they had staked out the first day of class. Yet the eyes in front of her now looked directly into hers. The women had long ago stopped examining her shoes and her earrings and her naked ring finger. The men's brief self-conscious glances were now steady and secure.

"So," she addressed the class. "Have we learned everything there is to know about butterflies?"

Melodee's voice rose above the other spontaneous exclamations. "I never would have believed how much there was to learn about them! We could never learn it all."

Katherine smiled at Robert. He too recalled his comment from the first day of class. "There will always be more to learn about them, won't there," she said.

"Yeah, and it's cool that you chose butterflies," Jason said. "But no matter what you chose, there would've been a whole lot more to learn than we'd ever have believed, right?"

"That's a good point, Jason," Katherine said.

"It's like you said in the beginning," Emma said. "Learning is a constantly evolving process. And we've learned a lot more than anyone could have taught us, because it's what we've been processing ourselves and learning from one another."

Katherine was smiling at the group. "And have we contributed anything to humanity's knowledge of butterflies?" she asked.

The class thought for a moment.

"Yes," Cynthia responded. "Knowledge doesn't have to be written down to be carried on or to be contributed to humanity. What we've been doing has its own intrinsic value. And that makes it a worthwhile contribution — to our lives anyway."

"And we're humanity, right?" Carlos said.

Shawn jumped in. "I think what's made it so interesting is that we haven't had any end-goal in mind, you know? Like, we weren't trying to learn a certain amount of information or to pass a test or anything. It's like Isaiah said, it's been more of an exploration."

"We don't retain everything we learn anyway," Robert said. "The real learning happens, like you said, in the process."

"Professor Ayers?" Jason asked. "How did you know how this class would turn out? I mean, because this has never been done before, right? And there were no requirements or guidelines or anything. So, I mean, how did you know that it would work out the way it did?"

"That's a good question, Jason. This really has been an experiment. And I had no idea how you would respond or how things would develop. I had some hopes. But I have to say I never imagined the enormous scope of what we would discover, even about butterflies," she said. And then she added in fun, "Who taste with their *feet*?!" The class had learned that the mother butterfly has taste receptors on her feet and that she gently drums her feet on a plant in order to taste it and determine its suitability for hosting her young.

"That is so amazing," Melodee said.

"Professor Ayers?" Grace asked. "Are you going to be teaching this class again?"

"I don't know, Grace. There are a number of things to be considered. Other people to weigh-in on that decision."

"With all the flap about the Initiative," Robert said, "the decision's probably moving all the way up the food chain to the top administration, isn't it?"

Katherine was not surprised that Robert's savvy extended to university politics, and she was never surprised at his candor.

"Well, as we've learned," she said, "change doesn't always come easily." She looked around at the students' attentive faces. "It is certainly the hope of those most involved in the Initiative that these classes will continue." She paused for a moment, still pondering their remarks. "I'd like to go back to one of your earlier comments. I'm curious about whether anyone has felt that what we've done here has affected your approach to your other classes."

"Definitely," Melodee asserted.

A number of students concurred.

"I ask a lot more questions," Sarah said.

More students joined in, affirming Sarah's comment.

Ashlyn spoke up. "Yeah, and don't you think that asking questions is a really important skill in itself?"

Katherine's expression let Ashlyn know she had made an excellent point. "You're absolutely right," she said. "The ability to ask questions is a very valuable skill."

"I look at language differently now," Joe said. "I see it more, you know? Like the word 'expert.' And even the idea of language. I think it is our tool for survival. That's why it makes good sense to learn how to use it."

Melodee jumped in. "I see all of my classes differently now."

Katherine was intrigued. "And how is that, Melodee?"

"Well, like we said, everything is broken down, you know? Like the scientific studies and the subjects we learn in school, everything is separated into specific areas. It's like we talked about in the beginning, how in biology or math or other subjects they wouldn't be interested in learning everything about butterflies, cuz everybody's concentrating on their own thing, you know?" She glanced in Steffen's direction. "And I understand that it's important for people to study things real specifically, to understand them thoroughly. I understand and I agree with that. But it's also important to see things all together, you know? Like, the way we've looked at butterflies. And the way we should be looking at all of the things that are happening to the environment and, well, lots of other things too. Cuz everything is so connected, you know? Everything affects everything else. I'm not sayin' this very well, but . . ." She appealed to Katherine with her eyes.

"I believe I understand exactly what you're saying, Melodee," Katherine said. "And you may have put your finger on precisely what this class has been about. In fact, if that's a message we take away from this experience, I think we can consider it a success."

"Professor Ayers?" Isaiah looked at Katherine thoughtfully. "Why did you pick butterflies anyway?"

There were murmurs of resonation from around the room.

"Yes," Marisa said. "What made you decide on butterflies?"

Katherine thought for a moment about what she would say. "Well, I knew I wanted it to be something we could examine from many different perspectives. Something that would provide us with an interesting experience . . ."

Racing through her mind was the thought of Lloyd and her other colleagues learning that she had not only stepped out of physics to teach this bizarre course, she had actually told her students that the idea came to her in a dream. She hesitated another moment as she observed the students' rapt expressions. "And the truth is," she said, "during the time when I was thinking about what our subject would be, I had a dream. A very special dream that inspired me to learn about butterflies."

A number of the faces in front of her lit up, and then the chorus of comments continued.

Katherine stood silently and perused their eager faces as the words rolled through her mind again. "A Course in Butterflies."

Seventeen

The truth was, Katherine was terrified of skiing. She could not have imagined the force of nature that would compel her to voluntarily leap off the side of a mountaintop on a pair of skis. Yet there she was. She had actually arranged an extra day in advance of the group's arrival, determined to learn. The "compelling" force that had prompted such aberrant behavior was one she was not entirely ready to acknowledge. Mary Claire had had no problem identifying it, or describing it in frank language.

Her ski instructor had been with Sundance for years. There was never a moment when he was not right beside her, assuring her that she was safe. His manner was so gently persuasive, to her amazement it happened before it had even registered that their lesson had ensued — she was skiing. By the end of the afternoon they were gliding from the Wildflower Run at the top of the mountain all the way down the slopes to Center Aisle, the very course she had identified on the map and fantasized about mastering. Though her instructor informed her that this was a common experience with skiing, she could not help feeling thrilled about her triumph. The exhilaration was something she could only have compared to that of a major theoretical breakthrough.

Spirits were high the following day when they all jumped on the gondola together energized by the prospect of the days ahead. All around them the glistening white hills of Sundance stood stark against a bright blue sky. As disoriented as Franco and Russell might have been from their long flights from Italy and Australia, they were both alert and enthusiastic. The two Californians were also eager to be on the slopes. When they disembarked at Wildflower and stood overlooking the mountain, Katherine's heart pounded. She was on her own now. There was no instructor by her side. Sheer terror began to take hold of her.

"You can do it," Michael whispered. "Just exactly like you did yesterday. You'll be fine." He had pulled his sunglasses from his eyes and was peering into hers with the same winning smile she had recalled many times.

When she pushed off she felt as though she were jumping headlong into a dark abyss. Fear and exhilaration merged as one. Halfway down the slope she began to feel the fluid movement of her body swaying from side to side as the blades below her carved their way through the powdery snow. All in a moment she felt it. The wind in her face, her hair streaming in the wind. She was experiencing it for the first time. This was the ecstasy known as skiing.

"I never understood it before," she said to the group at their quiet dinner table in the Sundance Tree Room. "I couldn't imagine why people were always so rabid about it."

Michael took great pleasure in her expression. "Yeah, nobody's ever lukewarm about skiing," he said. "You either don't do it at all or you can't wait for the next opportunity."

"I think I've narrowed the fear down to trees and people now," she said to the group's laughter.

"Your ski instructor was right," Timothy said. "It's your yoga practice that's saved you from what you might be feeling right now."

"You've taken to it beautifully," Russell said to her warmly.

"And it's taken to you beautifully," Michael said. His dark green eyes gleamed at her in the candlelight.

From the moment they were together again, Katherine and her "four musketeers," as Michael called them, they were all energized by the same camaraderie they had experienced in September. Their conversation was as effortless as their descent of the mountain slopes. They glided from topic to topic as provocative ideas continually emerged from the seven central concepts Albert had placed in their charge — Universe, God, Spirit, Science, One, Humanity, Leadership.

After dinner, around the fire in The Owl, they had a good laugh recalling their first moments together when Katherine drew their first word from the pile. They marveled at all of the ground they had covered since then. The single word "leadership," which at first had seemed such a straightforward concept, now stood for something far more complex.

Russell began again in his amiable manner his case for a worldview that was not so fixated on hierarchy. "In the entire living world," he said, "there are no leaders. Not the way we think of leadership. Life just continually emerges. Intricate interdependent networks imbedded in other networks. It's all interdependence."

"Well, I agree completely that we need to rethink top-down systems," Timothy said. "But I really think there's something cockeyed about this idea that's being bandied about now that human systems should simulate the natural world and be purely self-organizing. As far as humans are concerned, I'm inclined to think we need more leaders, not fewer."

"And Russell, I'm not completely convinced that there are no leaders in nature," Katherine said. She rested her teacup on the hearth. "I keep coming back to the bird formations — they're just so fascinating to me. And even if it is learned behavior and, as you say, they're taking advantage of the aerodynamic wave in the atmosphere that's created by the lead bird — we still don't know there's not leadership going on, do we?"

"Well you're absolutely right," Russell said. He was upbeat about this particular concession. "We really have no idea if there is leadership there or not. We know that the lead bird changes. That's certainly interesting learned behavior."

Franco jumped in. "We don't know if there's leadership until we know where the lead bird is headed," he exclaimed, "and if the flock arrives."

"That's right," Timothy concurred. "Leading a group in a particular direction is a very different thing from the kind of top-down dominance Russ is talking about."

"It's the difference between leadership as dominance and leadership as influence," Michael said. "A real leader is a teacher. People like Gandhi and Mandela and Havel — people naturally followed them. And I don't think that kind of leadership is as rare as we think. It's not the kind we hear about too often. We're all saturated with a real misguided conception of 'national leadership' and 'global leadership.' But the real teachers are out there. They're everywhere. Quietly moving humanity forward."

"That's an encouraging thought, mate," Russell said.

"You know, one of the most interesting things I learned from the Utes was that Native Indian words for their leaders didn't translate into anything resembling 'chief.' Indian 'chief' was the white man's invention." Michael's reprove seeped through in his tone. "The name for the guy in charge as we were negotiating our command of them. The real Indian 'leaders' were the elders and the braves that the tribe looked to for counsel because of their dignity and their wisdom and because they faithfully represented the interests of their people."

"You had quite an experience with the Utes," Timothy remarked to Michael.

"Yes, I appreciated your email account," Franco said. "It was quite an education for me. Even learning Utah was named for its native people. And there is an actual 'Sundance?"

Katherine had asked Michael on the gondola if he would tell them about the Sundance.

"It's their most sacred spiritual ceremony," he said. "Albert was here to observe one last summer. He was blown away by it."

"They dance for several days, don't they?" Russell said.

"Without food or water," Michael said. "It's about as intense as it gets, dancing in the hot sun non-stop for days. The sun of course represents the creator and the source of all life. And since the creator is unimpressed with material things, they believe all we have of value to offer is ourselves, our own sweat and suffering. It's kind of a rite of passage for a young man, the first time he's called to participate in the dance. They say it comes to them in a dream-vision." He looked at Katherine. "For the Utes it's traditionally the men who dance. But the whole family comes together and participates, singing and drumming and supporting the dancers. They believe that by enduring the physical exhaustion and the suffering that great power comes to them from the creator. Power that's to be used in service of family and community. Ah Kah Nooch, their spiritual leader," Michael enjoyed referring to his new friend by his Ute name, "told me that what they're really asking for is enlightenment for all humanity."

Russell looked at Michael. "It sounds like maybe Albert had good reason for choosing Sundance."

Michael smiled at him. "Oh yeah, there's not much that gets by Albert."

The following morning in the resort's rustic Foundry Grill their breakfast conversation kept them at their table long after the breakfast dishes had been cleared. The subject of "Humanity" had once again led them to the single enigma with which all of science grapples — human consciousness. And on this subject they had in their midst a fascinating savant. Timothy Longmire's agile hands waved in the morning sun that streamed through the windows where they sat with their mugs of coffee.

"Well, memory is the defining feature, isn't it?" he said. "We are most definable as conscious beings by the continuum of memory. And yet what we consciously recall is just a drop in the ocean of what's actually accessible. And in ways we're not even aware of. It's mind-boggling really. I think most learning occurs in ways we're not conscious of too. More and more I'm convinced that's the primary purpose of dreams."

Katherine was sitting directly across from Timothy. She was suddenly utterly fixed on his face.

"The Ashaninkas say that everything we know we know from plants and from sleep," Russell said. "From hallucinations and dreams," he explained. He was smiling at Michael. "I figure they've had who knows how many thousands of years to look at the situation."

Michael grinned at his friend. "You think maybe they learned a few things, huh?"

Katherine earnestly pursued Timothy. "You think our dreams are about learning?" she asked him.

Timothy looked at her. "If I told you I had a dream in which I was bestowed with a complete comprehension of time — that would give cause for amusement, yes?"

She was his captive.

"And yet, I have not a shadow of doubt that while I was in this particular dream-state *time* was completely within my grasp. Pretty exciting moment, let me tell you. Just that sliver of a second when I was returning to consciousness and was fully aware of my revelation. Of course within seconds I had no recollection of it. Not a whit. Not consciously anyway. Chances are, if I did I wouldn't be able to handle it. The interesting thing is that what I did get from the dream was the answer to a question I'd been carrying around for several days prior. It was during a period when I was hooked on seeing and on-line systems."

"The alternative visual pathway you talked about in your book," Katherine said. "I recall the tennis player example."

"That's right, it's something professional tennis players intuitively exploit. It's a direct subconscious pathway that bypasses the optic nerve tract which is faster than the conscious visual pathway. In tennis terms, that means they're able to return the ball before they actually see it. It happens all the time. Anyway, it was during this intense period with the neuro-physiology of seeing juxtaposed with the neuro-physiology of dreaming."

Timothy was now looking at Michael who continued his thought. "And you started thinking about dreaming as an alternative pathway."

"Exactly. For lobs from the other side of the net, so to speak." They smiled at one another. "And then, voila! I have this dream in which I'm staring right into the face of a crystal clear understanding of time."

He noted Katherine's anxious expression.

"You're saying that the dream persuaded you that we receive from some other . . ." She was stunned by her own thought. She had almost said the word "dimension," a word that to even be considered by a physicist in this context was, to say the least, startling to her.

Timothy was observing her entire thought process in her expression. His grin was bright. "You didn't know quite how mad your mad scientists were, did you?"

As playful as Timothy was, Katherine could see that he was both serious and clear-headed about the thoughts he was articulating. And from the expressions around her, she knew he was being completely understood. Skiing was not the only thing that was challenging her out of her comfort zone, as her ski instructor had put it. This was a brand new realm she was entering. And her response to it was as surprising to her as the way she had taken to skiing. She glanced at Michael who was watching her attentively. He smiled brightly. "You know why Albert arranged for the skiing, don't you?" He was exuberant as they rose to their feet. "As a preventative from cerebral combustion," he laughed.

The sustained discourse that naturally emerged from their group was indeed put in balance by the delightful diversions of Sundance. They all laughed as they headed out of the restaurant to another sunny day on the slopes.

That evening they built a fire in Russell's cottage and Franco opened the wine he had toted with him from home. They all knew it was time to pursue the comment he had made in one of their group emails. They also knew they were headed into deeper waters than they had been in together previously. Katherine was privately bracing herself. Franco had said that he wanted very much to revisit their discussion on the subject of "God." The subject Katherine had carefully avoided all her life. On some level she welcomed it this time. There was a part of her that wanted to know what Michael Cavanaugh's beliefs were really about.

They had found in September that their individual philosophies on the subject of God were quite unanimously shared. They had easily arrived at a consensus and then had distilled their thoughts into a statement — one which they all acknowledged was more about "religion" than "God." They had also discovered during their mealtime discussions with their other colleagues that they had all arrived at statements remarkably similar to their own — "Ideas about God that promote harmony among all peoples and all faiths represent religion's highest purpose."

"With a little reflection," Franco said, "I could not help thinking how civilized we all were."

Katherine could hardly believe her ears when Franco confessed to the group that throughout their last time together he had carefully avoided his own deeply trying issues with religion. She listened intently as he explained that he had since decided that perhaps this opportunity had presented itself for a purpose, one that for him was a deeply personal one. The story he then shared with his four new friends was one he said he had wanted to share for almost fifty years. And as his comrades heard it to the end, they came to know the tender heart of their illustrious Italian friend.

Franco Benedetto's mother had died when he was a boy. His father's deep religious faith had sustained him through his grief and through the challenge of raising his four sons alone. Franco too had been a devout Catholic throughout his youth. But when he was about twenty years old he experienced something that changed him completely.

"There is no other way to describe it," he said. "It was a mystical experience. I had hiked by myself one day up into the Dolomites. And as I looked out at what I was sure was all of Austria . . . it's not something I can put into words, really, except to say that it was a communion with God. I believe I experienced the oneness you've talked about, Michael. It happened all in a single moment. But what happened in that moment changed me forever."

Franco explained that after this experience he had gone to his priest, whom he loved, and had eagerly shared every detail of his experience. Yet he came away with a deep sadness that he had not been understood. He knew that if his priest had grasped the magnificence of his revelation he would have been overjoyed. He would have celebrated the immense blessing that had been bestowed upon one of his parishioners. Instead Franco remained painfully alone with the most profound experience of his life. Until he discovered Augustine, he said. Saint Augustine was his liberation.

"His ideas about illumination and self-knowledge, about divine emanation in the intelligible world — I felt that my experience was completely understood. And then I discovered Bruno and Cardano and their ideas about divine light being present and accessible in every living thing. About a universe that is unified and alive and an open path to God." Franco looked at Timothy. "Cardano believed that a true union with God was most likely to occur in dreams," he said. He stopped for a moment and looked around at his friends. He was cherishing the opportunity to speak from his heart. "It was with the Gnostics that I found the truest expression of my experience." He recalled the words he had remembered all his life. "It leaves one forever with the memory of the possibility that one is ultimately a body of light." He looked at Michael. "This was not language I could ask my father to understand."

The irony of Franco's being led away from the Church by saints and priests and martyrs had been completely lost on his father whom Franco said had never recovered from his son's 'abandonment of God's Church.' Franco's expression transformed to that of a hurt young boy as he described the feelings of rejection that continued to afflict him even as he watched his father grow old. "It is so hard to accept the reality that my greatest joy in life is the very same thing he considers his greatest failure," he said. He was rubbing the arm of his chair as he visibly restrained his emotions. "My father was a tomato farmer whose son was given a Nobel Prize. And yet I know that in his heart he would have preferred to have his son be a Catholic." Franco paused for a moment as his friends waited for his next words. "There are moments when I look into his eyes and I am so very sad that he will leave this earth not knowing the most important thing he will leave behind . . . The depth of his son's faith." He picked up his glass and tipped it slightly. "I'll tell you, my friends, I would trade my Nobel for that."

Katherine laid her hand on Franco's. She saw in his face the deep wound that was still inflamed after so many years. They both turned as Russell dropped a large log on the fire.

Michael had leaned forward on the sofa. The light from the flames flickered on his face. "You know, I think Albert was very deliberate in his choice of the words 'God' and 'Spirit,' rather than 'Religion.' He was acknowledging what believing is really about. Whenever anyone could be denied their own path to God, it's not about God or spirit. It's about how much people need reassurance that the way they have chosen is the right way."

With a final purge of emotion Franco explained, "You see, for my father it is impossible to believe that a relationship with God that does not occur through the church could be a real relationship."

"I know," Michael said. "And it's a very new, very Western attitude, really. As you said, the early Christians, the Gnostics — they communed with God in a very personal, visceral way. Like the Sundancers in the native community for thousands of years. And the whole realm of Eastern thought. It's completely devoted to a direct, non-conceptual experience of God."

Franco looked at Katherine. "I particularly wanted to ask you, Katherine . . ."

Katherine masked her discomfort with his turning to her in this moment.

"We didn't really talk about our personal faiths last time," Franco said. "That's one of the things that struck me too. But you did say you were not a religious person."

Katherine drew her legs up next to her on the sofa.

"And yet when we were discussing spirit, I had the feeling we were talking about the same thing."

Katherine hesitated only a moment. "I think so too," she said. "I just think of spirit and religion as two separate things."

"I thought about the Einstein quote you cited," Franco continued. "And this is something you and Michael can both speak to. I have often wondered if theoretical physics isn't inherently spiritual. If the search for explanations about the order and the beauty of the universe isn't in itself a religious activity. It seems to me that the very exploration of objective reality is a way of satisfying spiritual hunger."

"Oh, I think it definitely is," Katherine said.

"What was the Einstein quote again? Timothy asked her.

"Well, I'm paraphrasing again, I'm sure," she said, "but he said that anyone who is not lost in rapturous awe at the power and glory of the mind behind the universe is as good as a burnt out candle."

Michael was sitting with her on the sofa. She could feel him watching her as she spoke.

"Einstein didn't subscribe to any religious doctrine or practice either," she said. "And of course some still contend that he was an atheist. But I think that what he referred to as 'cosmic religious feeling' was as deep a reverence for the mind behind the universe as one could achieve in a lifetime of religious practice."

"You know, Einstein was quite eloquent about religion himself," Michael said. "He identified deeply with Spinoza and Buddha and Democritus and Francis of Assisi, all of whom were at some time regarded as godless. And yet they were all imbued with the highest kind of religious feeling."

"Let me ask you a question," Franco said as he looked at both Michael and Katherine. And then he paused in a way that emphasized the importance of his question. "Did he believe in '*God*'?"

Katherine took only a moment. "Yes, I believe he did. I believe he had a profound belief in God. And I think he would have been a great one to sit and talk with about conceptions of God and what God means — to him, to you, to each of us. As long as no one was prepared to define God for anyone but himself."

"He didn't believe in a God in man's image," Michael said. "Or in limiting God to something definable. When you think about it, isn't that the ultimate reverence?"

Katherine turned to Michael both stunned and thrilled by what he had said.

"Then tell me something else," Franco said. He was watching the fire now. "Do you think in his private heart Einstein remained a Jew?"

"Well, being a Jew is about more than religion, isn't it?" Timothy said. "Jews are a people." And then he immediately followed with, "Of course, I guess growing up in any strong religious community can feel like a culture and a people too."

"Oh yes," Franco said solemnly.

Michael understood Franco's question. "You mean, do we ever really lose the faith we're born into?" He thought about this for a moment. "I think in Einstein's case it was the faith he grew into that was his real genius. His real 'faith' was his unqualified openness to the truth." He looked at Franco. "And isn't that the most essential prerequisite for a genuine search for ultimate truth? An absolute preparedness for the unknown? An openness to the unknown? Whatever it may be."

Katherine was engrossed in Michael's question when Russell spoke to her.

"I'm interested, Katherine. You said neither of your parents participated in religion either. That's pretty unusual here in the States, isn't it?"

For as far back as Katherine had ever allowed her memory to take her she had always thought of Marion and Bill Ayers as her true parents. Never had she gravitated to that reality more than she did in this moment. She was as reverent as the group had seen her.

"My parents were unusual people," she said. "Their virtue came from a deeper well than religion, I think. Neither of them had ever set foot in a church. And yet they were the 'holiest' people I have ever known." She was looking at the fire. "I've actually had a good number of significant people in my life who've never subscribed to any form of religion — and who are among the most deeply ethical people I know. I mean, truly and deeply ethical, you know? To the point that their own integrity is their religion."

"Yes, I know what you mean," Russell said. "And isn't that the highest aim of religion? To produce that quality in people?"

"You said you had no religion in your upbringing either," Franco said to Russell.

Russell smiled. "Religion never really got on in Australia like it did here in the States," he said. "We were originally a penal colony, you know." He grinned at his friends. "A lot of healthy disrespect for authority. It's still a small percentage of Aussies that take to religion. Not something I was raised on at all."

Franco was intrigued. "And somehow I got the impression you were a believer too."

Russell gave him a big smile. "Well now, that came to me in the church of biology, mate. You can't possibly look at the living world and not see design, can you?" He looked at his friends thoughtfully. "It's funny. I've spent my whole life in a profession that still defines DNA as an inert chemical — at most, a chemical language. One that just happens to be present in and oversees the construction of every living thing — including organisms as staggeringly complex as conscious human beings," he stressed. "And yet it would be preposterous to imagine DNA possessing consciousness itself, wouldn't it." He looked at his friends incredulously. "We're celebrating having cracked the code of a language, yet we've missed the essence of what's being communicated. Biological evidence," he said, "that all living things are fundamentally bound to one another — that we're all the outgrowth of a single consciousness." He smiled at Katherine. "I think the mind behind the universe must find that very amusing."

"Now there, you see," Franco said, "We do refer to God in personal terms without necessarily believing in a personal God."

"Of course," Timothy said. He was lying restfully on the floor in front of the fire. "Some of us even participate in monotheistic religion when we actually subscribe to a much more abstract conception of God."

Katherine was incapable of disguising her complete astonishment when Timothy revealed to the group that he was a practicing Jew. She had thought of Timothy Longmire as perhaps the least likely candidate on the planet for participation in any form of organized religion. He smiled at her in a way that let her know he understood her reaction.

"There was a time," he said, "when I could not have conceived of an intelligent, thinking, religious person." He rolled over onto his side and shared the story of his dramatic turnabout.

It began, he explained, when he promised his wife that their children would be raised in the Jewish faith. What followed, he said, was the biggest surprise of his life. "From my first experience at Temple I discovered a community unlike any I had known. I think that's the soul of organized religion anyway, don't you? Community?" He continued to smile with both affection and amusement at Katherine's stunned expression. "I'll never forget my very first day. The first Rabbi I'd ever encountered in my life, mind you. And on that particular day he was making a persuasive case for atheism. Can you believe it?" Timothy looked at his friends. "He said that there is one time when every one of us should be passionate nonbelievers — when we encounter another human being who really needs help. He said that in that moment we should believe that there is no other being, supreme or otherwise, who is going to be there for that person — that there is only us. He said it was much more important to help a person in need because it's the right thing to do than because any religion tells us we should." He smiled at Katherine. "That day that Rabbi became my Rabbi." He rolled back onto his back on the floor. "And he's been my Rabbi ever since."

"What a great story," Russell said.

Franco was deep in contemplation. "And you know, I believe that in that moment when we reach out to a person in need — that is when God is most present."

"Exactly," Timothy said.

Katherine decided it was time to ask the question she had wanted so much to ask.

"So, Michael, are you Buddhist?"

Michael looked at her. "Am I Buddhist?" he said, absorbing the question.

"I say that only because you've talked quite a bit about Buddhist philosophy," she said.

"Well, if I am, I guess I'm also Panthentheist and Taoist and Sufi and Eckankar . . ." The more he thought he continued, "and Gnostic Christian and Kabbalist, and probably a lot of tribal religions that don't have names. If I'm anything at all, I guess I'm all of the above."

"Michael's put a lot of energy into spiritual traditions," Timothy said.

Michael looked at Katherine thoughtfully. "I don't subscribe to any particular one but I certainly respect the basic tenets they all share."

"And what do you think is the most pronounced thing they all share?" she asked.

He reflected for only a moment. "Well, all of the great initiates carried the same simple message, didn't they. 'Do unto others,' 'Human affection' — They all said to just love each other. And as far as I know none of them said, 'but only love the ones who believe what you believe.' He responded to Franco's smile and then lounged back on the sofa and looked at Katherine. "I guess I have talked a lot about Buddhist ideas," he reflected. "They're so often on the mark for me. And the Dalai Lama really made an impression on me." He stretched his arm across the back of the sofa. "Albert and I were in Dharamsala last year with a small group and we spent a little time with the Dalai Lama. We had asked beforehand if he would share some of his thoughts on global issues, and his assistant suggested we identify whatever questions we thought were most important. So the group got together and decided on what we thought were the most pressing global issues." Michael recalled their questions: "How do we save the earth? How do we address the widening gap between the rich and the poor? How do we educate our children for the future? How do we help oppressed people of the world? And how do we bring true spirituality and deep caring for each other into all of our lives? The first thing the Dalai Lama said was that if we could answer the last question we would answer all the others."

Russell pondered as he watched the fire. "That really is the question, isn't it. How do we get people to simply care for one another."

"The Dalai Lama said he could only offer the same suggestion as any simple monk. He said all each of us can do is try to live that way ourselves."

"Yes," Franco whispered.

"I think that idea is far more powerful than we know," Michael said.

"I've found Buddhist ideas pretty settling too," Timothy said, still lying restfully on the floor. "Especially since Michael's enlightened me about how compatible they are with other concepts of 'God' or of a 'universal mind.'"

Katherine was intent on Michael. "And do you believe that God, or whatever the universal mind is, has ultimate power over our lives? Or does that belong to us?"

"I believe they're inextricable," Michael said. He smiled

affectionately as he watched her assimilate his response. "That's why I'm especially inclined toward religions that espouse that everything in the universe is an attribute of God rather than separate from God."

Katherine took another moment. "Then when you say you believe that everything in the universe is infused with 'divine' energy, you're not referring to the kind of divinity that's normally associated with an intervening kind of personal God." Her statement was a question.

Michael pondered, "I think it's more like what Einstein was responding to with his 'cosmic religious feeling.' To imagine that any anthropomorphic concept could correspond to it would, I think, diminish it considerably."

When she looked at him this time she could not escape the transparence that came over her. The feelings he had evoked in her were impossible to conceal. It was more than being struck by a newfound alliance. A warm rush of magnetism had been freed inside her. She could feel it radiating in her expression. The firelight flickered on their faces as they looked at one another.

The group's ruminations continued until the early morning hours as they talked and stared at the fire and languished in the cozy comfort of one another's company. The resort was dark and silent and the snow crunched beneath their feet when Michael, Timothy and Franco finally dropped Katherine at her cottage. The morning sun would soon awaken them for another full day, this one with all of their other colleagues from around the world. As she lay in her bed in the dark, she stared at the wooden beams above her and wondered how she would ever sleep.

Eighteen

It was nothing short of amazing that every one of the two hundred invitees had seen their way clear to return to Sundance. This was powerful testimony. The sense of unity was apparent in every pair of eyes, in the flow of laughter that reverberated throughout the Rehearsal Hall. Albert's plan had been an ingenious one. Some of the finest minds in the world had again converged, free of their professional facades, and were relating with one another like spirited elements in a synchronous living organism.

The Finn Foundation encouraged a completely open forum for their final two days together. Microphones had been placed throughout the room giving ease and intimacy to their full-group discussion. There was a togetherness among them that began with early breakfast and ran a lively course until the late night hours. By the final day they were like an enormous extended family in the final throws of a bracing reunion.

It was mid-afternoon on their final day when they all began to observe that the lines between their topics had blurred. It was as though Albert's seven concepts had merged together as one. One Universe God Science Humanity Spirit Leadership. Their now free-flowing dialogue showed all the signs of a single determined purpose. And no doubt in keeping with Albert's ingenious plan, some of their most significant ideas came from their effort to articulate just exactly what their time together had been about.

They had talked a great deal about science and religion and about the increasing dialogue between the two. Many in the room had in fact participated in "Science and Spirit" conferences which were now being hosted by even the most established institutions. Scientists in every field who were also devout Christians and Muslims and Jews were now speaking more publicly about how the findings of science could be viewed through the eyes of believers. A mere decade ago, they noted, a physicist could not write a popular book without endangering his or her reputation. Today, popular science flourished and with a plethora of books by physicists with "God" in the title. Even the hardest of all the sciences was yielding to what many called a "spiritual revolution."

Religion too throughout the West was showing new signs of openness and dialogue. Interdenominational worship was experiencing explosive growth in the United States. In today's world it was virtually impossible to remain isolated with the ideologies of one's given religion. The life of Christ was now examined by millions through the eyes of journalists and preeminent scholars. The Pope and the Dalai Lama spoke on international television. Rabbis wrote popular books about awakenings to Eastern philosophy. Catholic priests explored tribal wisdom. Even "Science & Spirit" conferences, they noted, were now opening up to Eastern religions and other systems of spiritual thought beyond the major monotheistic faiths. Was all of this evidence that people of all faiths were increasingly acknowledging the essence of religion rather than the form?

After examining the "spiritual hunger" that was showing itself in both science and religion, they turned to the subject of the deeply personal experience of "spirit" that had driven much of their most vibrant dialogue. A visual gleam passed between Katherine and Franco that was soon endorsed by their three cohorts when James Kohnke, the famous geneticist, summed up the full group's discussion. "Science and religion are both coming to the same realization," he said. "The authentic spiritual awareness that gives value to the human experience is not something that is reachable either by scientific proof or by religious doctrine. It is something that can only be achieved in the individual human psyche. Or perhaps in the human soul."

As Katherine listened to her colleagues' reflections on their final day together she marveled at how they had increasingly delved into deeper levels of thought, into heightened levels of courageous exposure. They were expressing ideas that in other company might have completely shattered their reputations. And they shared them now with a newfound liberty, fortified by the alliance that had formed in the remarkable assembly around them. For Katherine there was one crowning moment of insight that came from this extraordinary event she had been part of. It began when Wallace Vandemere took the floor.

Wallace Vandemere was well known to everyone in the room. He was a Cambridge biologist who had been with the University of Chicago for many years. He was also clearly the eldest person in the room. When he rose to speak the entire group gave him their earnest attention. He began with a smile in Albert Finn's direction. "First, I think I should point out, Albert, that not all of us peer into high-powered telescopes. Some of us have trouble seeing through our bifocals." Quiet laughter rolled through the room. Then Wallace continued, slowly enunciating his words. "You know, someone once said that it is less than five percent of the population that advances civilization. I don't know how scientific that analysis was but I think few would argue that it's a small percentage of humans that actually 'move humanity forward,' as Michael Cavanaugh puts it. It seems to me that what we've been doing here is examining just where we all fit in that picture.

"The accepted view, of course, has always been that science is about what is, not about what should be. The idea that science deals exclusively in facts has come to mean that scientists deal exclusively in facts. The question is, are we now being called upon to reexamine that premise? If we really believe that scientific advances are the most worthy contribution for scientists to make to the advancement of civilization, then we can continue to relegate the responsibility for leading humanity forward to the artists and the educators and the other passionate souls for whom the idea of nudging humanity forward is what gives them a reason for living." He paused a moment. "But I think we all know that humanity looks to science not just for humanity's understanding of the world, but also for humanity's understanding of itself." He looked around at his colleagues. "And I don't believe there is a single person in this room who doesn't believe that science should have a real voice in that dialogue.

"It's true that we and many of our colleagues are stepping forward now on all kinds of issues. Many of those issues have their greatest champions right here in this room. What we've not yet begun to communicate is that unless we resolve this central conflict of man against nature there is not a single one of those other issues that will matter a damn. Not bioethics or the weaponization of space, not even nuclear catastrophe, which may be just a more expedient version of what we're doing to the planet already. We have not begun to communicate the absolute precariousness of humanity's moving forward at all, given our present course." He continued looking around the room at his colleagues. "The fact is that no one can offer absolute certainty about where we're headed or just how grim the future will be, given our present course. The indications, however, are undeniable. We may well find ourselves in a situation where it will be impossible to imagine we could have even suspected what was coming and not changed our course altogether." He paused for a moment as he looked toward the window where a bright beam of light streamed into the hall. "And yet, as long as the majority, particularly in this country, are able to draw water from their faucets and walk out their doors into reasonably clean air, the real crisis is one of perception.

"Clearly, this is not a problem that can be relegated to political leaders." There was a somber swell of consensus from the group. "Or even to the impassioned troops who are on the front lines every day for the environment. The fact is that the people who are wholly knowledgeable about our global ecological crisis all hang their hats in the scientific community. And never before have the stakes been so high for seizing responsibility for our knowledge." He became even more resolute. "There is not a scientist on the planet who should be able to hold his or her head up until our fellow human beings understand that we are the first species in the entire life of the planet to become a geophysical force. One that is altering the earth's climate. And destroying the integrity of the atmosphere. And devouring natural resources at a rate that would only make sense if we were the last generation on Earth." His mounting intensity evoked solemnity among his colleagues. "We have got to somehow get the message across. And to those who can change our course. Who can adapt our inventiveness and our thinking and planning to include the fate of our planet in our priorities." He looked around at his colleagues again. "We all know some of the great minds that are hard at work on solutions. Solutions that make great economic sense as well. But these people have little voice in the world. They have especially little voice with those making critical decisions." He looked over at Albert again as he processed the thought that came to him. "Albert, perhaps the people who should be here at Sundance are the corporate leaders. Exploring the same concepts we've been exploring here together. Perhaps the future of the planet is really in their hands."

Katherine was not surprised that Michael Cavanaugh was an eager participant in the dialogue that flowed from Wallace's remarks. When he stood he expressed his allegiance to Wallace with the admiration due a tribal elder. Then he spoke to the group with the same ease of expression his four cohorts had come to know in their San Francisco friend.

"I do think we have good cause for the hopefulness we've all felt here together. Not just about our comrades in science — there are definitely more of us speaking up now — but about humanity in general. I find I'm often reminding myself that every new heightened level of consciousness has always begun with a few. And there are far more than a few of us now. There are people all over the globe who know the truth in their bones — even before it's ever put into words for them. People who also see our global predicament as an opportunity to discover our true identity as human beings. As cohabitants of the planet Earth. And those people are finding one another. We're all connecting with people every day who speak the same language. The language that comes from a powerful sense that we're coming together as a species. Not just through the Internet and through trade and communication and through the tentacles of consumerism that are reaching around the globe, but in the deepest reaches of our humanity.

"I think the real 'reconciliation' we've been talking about here is not just about science and religion. It's a much larger reconciliation of humanity with itself. That's why so many of us are turning to our roots. We're hungry for what the natives of all our lands have to teach us — because we know they are an important part of our identity and our nature as a species. And we know somehow instinctively that it's time to decide what our nature truly is — and to determine our course accordingly."

Michael looked around at his colleagues. "We've talked so much about this burgeoning spirituality, for lack of better words.

It's seeping into all our language — in science, in medicine, in popular culture. There are even enlightened leaders emerging in the corporate community." He looked over at Wallace again. "And I for one will continue to take my lumps for believing that this phenomenon of spirit is something more powerful than the other commotion going on in the world. I really believe that it's the force that will redirect our course. I believe it's already beginning. It's the young people in our classrooms who are . . ."

Katherine watched him as he spoke. She could feel that her colleagues around the room were listening to his every word. She recalled the moment they met, there in the same room, the moment she knew that someone significant was entering her life. She thought of the many times since then when she had been shaken to her core by his outrageous ideas, when it had been impossible to reconcile the attraction she felt for him with the ideas he espoused. Yet she had never ceased being completely captivated by the sheer brilliance of his, what was it? – his mind? – his faith? His devotion to whatever it was that inspired his . . . *hopefulness*, she thought.

When Albert Finn stood up and took the microphone she was sure he had been reading her mind. "I remember my reaction to Michael the first time we met," he said. "Our conversation that day was a lot like the ones we've had here." The group sat attentively as Albert reflected. "I vividly recall my reaction to his *inexhaustible optimism*. His belief that this new consciousness, this emerging spirituality, even our environmental crisis, are all part of a very purposeful confluence of events. One that is moving us to a higher state of being. At the time I thought that maybe my new friend was just a little naïve about the world, about the realities of what's happening in the world, and to the world." He let out a slight laugh. "I didn't know him well enough yet to know that Michael knows exactly what's going on in the world — all over the world," he stressed. "I remember asking him that day if there weren't plenty of other times in our history when people believed they were in the midst of a spiritual awakening. I called his attention to the fact that humanity hadn't changed much, that we were still killing one another and judging one another and ignoring one another's suffering. I remember saying, 'The same ideas have emerged over and over and yet they have never taken hold.' " He looked over at Michael. "I'll never forget his response. He said, 'But that's exactly what makes me hopeful! The fact that the same ideas keep emerging over and over.' " He emulated Michael's exuberance. " 'We forget how very short human history *is*,' he said. 'And even in our infancy these ideas are deeply imbedded in our psyches. And they are relentless about manifesting!' He said, 'We can't help but eventually discover the power of our own consciousness.' "

As she listened to Wallace and Michael and Albert on their final day together, Katherine experienced the sensation of being directly on the pulse of an enormous turning point in time. The beginning of a brand new millennium, she thought. She recalled Charles' astute observation. Albert Finn's Sundance event had indeed been a meditation on science in the new millennium. It had been that and so much more. She scanned the faces around her. She could feel the deeply shared sense of that higher purpose Albert had envisioned in their coming together. It was perhaps not something that would ever be fully captured in words, yet it was profoundly felt by everyone in the room.

It was late in the evening when they finally disbanded from the Rehearsal Hall. It was a mild starlit night and the air at Sundance was crisp and clean. Katherine and her "four musketeers" again found their way to The Owl, where they and other groups of their colleagues lingered for their final hours. Franco had staked out a place near the fire where they relaxed once again with their tea and brandies. There, Katherine sat quietly for a moment and perused their seemingly random group of five. Some remarkable force had been at play in their convergence, she thought. She observed Russell's serene demeanor. He was a man who was truly gentle to his core. And Franco's passionate heart she had come to love. Timothy's long white signature locks, his incisive mind and keen wit. When she looked at Michael, a warm glow came over her. And "Cavanaugh," she thought.

It was Russell who proposed in fun that they each identify how they would change their lives given the opportunity. He qualified his query by saying that the change had to be something other than the obvious, a breakthrough in their research. Instead, it should be something entirely apart from their scientific work. The group found his challenge an enjoyable one. They all agreed that it would be hard to imagine fulfilling lives that did not include some continued teaching and writing. They all agreed that they would read more literature. Russell then asked what they would each add to their life that was altogether outside of the intellectual. He focused first on Katherine, as he generally did. She thought for a moment about what was absent in her life that she most wanted. Had she been totally honest about the first thing that came to mind, she would have said she wanted a great love in her life. She glanced at Michael's attentive eyes. And then at Russell's. She wondered if her Aussie friend was not purposeful in his questioning.

"I would love to have a garden," she said. "I've often fantasized about having a wonderful garden. And I would spend much more time outdoors and be more physical, I think. I don't know that I'll ever be a serious skier," she laughed, "but I'd love to hike more and just be all around more physical. I'd do more yoga." She raised her teacup to Russell and grinned. "Don't get us too carried away now with this balanced human being stuff."

"It is fun to think about though, isn't it," Timothy said. "My wife would sure have some ideas."

His comment resonated with Russell and Franco. Then Russell turned to his San Francisco friend. "What about you, Michael?"

"Oh, that's an easy one for me," Michael said. "I'd spend a whole lot more time outdoors and in the mountains." Then he wistfully added, "And I'd listen to a lot more music."

"What kind of music?" Franco asked.

"Oh, I'm pretty eclectic."

"Michael's a real equal opportunity kinda guy," Timothy said.

They all laughed at the obvious reference to Michael's smorgasbord approach to spiritual traditions.

As their time together wound down, Katherine found herself connected to Cavanaugh's every word, warmed by his every glance. She was now imagining listening to music with him. And hiking in the mountains. And cooking together. And burrowing in for long talks in front of the fire. He had asked her what her plans were for New Years. She wondered what the holidays held for both of them. Increasingly, her whole body was giving way to an overpowering anticipation. How she looked forward to being alone with him again.

It was Russell again who made the overture toward their staggered departure from The Owl. And subtle as he was, his suggestion was not lost on Timothy and Franco. There were warm embraces all around as they expressed their farewells and then Franco, Russell and Timothy were off to their cottages. Katherine and Michael were not long behind them.

The crisp quiet nights of Sundance had been the perfect backdrop for the little time they had had alone together. This time they walked very slowly through the silent December twilight. Their breath was visible in the cold night air, yet Katherine was warm.

"You did say it was guaranteed to be interesting," she said.

"And then some, huh?"

"I guess you know that in the beginning I didn't really understand why I was included," she said.

"Our truth comes through in our language sometimes even before we recognize it ourselves," he said.

"How do you mean?"

"I mean you can't read your book and not know with certainty that the universe is a thrivingly divine organism or that it's calling upon us to recognize our purpose in it."

Katherine was stunned. "You saw that in my book," she said incredulously.

"Absolutely," he said.

She knew it was what Michael brought to the reading of her book that made the difference in what he had found there.

"Well, I definitely see the universe as a single organism — and very much alive," she said. "That was one thing that was clear from the start that this group had in common. And I'm a little more comfortable with your use of the word 'divine' now," she said. She looked at him pointedly as she added, "You notice mine was not one of the books with 'God' in the title."

They both chuckled.

"You do have some discomfort with the personal God thing, don't you?"

"I'm not sure I've bought into the idea that the universe speaks to us either," she said.

Michael laughed. "I guess God and the universe are so much the same thing to me, I talk about them both in personal terms. Human terms," he added. We don't have a lot of other choices, do we."

"I suppose not," Katherine conceded. Then she smiled at him as she confessed, "I guess you also know there were moments when I was sure I'd been confined to close quarters with a California *New Age Guru*." She had emphasized the words even as Michael started to laugh. "Didn't know how I'd ever reconcile my terror with my attraction."

Michael was delightfully amused. "There is a lot of silliness that gets lumped under that label," he said. "Especially in California. And I can't imagine two words less deserving of negative connotations, can you? God forbid we should actually be entering a 'new age.' "

Katherine acquiesced. "Whenever we put words on things something happens to them, doesn't it. And I guess there's not really anything to be done about that either."

"Which is exactly what we've been saying about religious beliefs," he said. He spoke to her gently. "I understand that for you, the fact that what you believe is private and personal is part of what keeps it sacred. That kind of privacy is definitely something to be cherished."

She looked at him appreciatively. "Yes, it is."

They strolled silently, close to one another. In a moment, Michael remarked, "That was quite a conversation you were having with Albert and Diana earlier."

"We were talking about the students," she said. "I was telling them how encouraging it is, the things the really thoughtful ones think are important."

"It's true. Ask any twenty year old who's interested in issues at all, the issues to them are the environment, human rights, responsible global thinking and planning."

"Albert was especially encouraged that they think Americans are too comfortable to care about anything that matters."

"Boy, and let's hope they hold onto that, huh?"

"Some of them will," she said confidently. "They'll be part of that network you talk about."

"Did you hear Russ say that every time he comes to the States he feels like he's arriving at the center of the universe?"

She smiled. She too had found Russell's comment about the U.S.

a telling one.

"It's amazing, isn't it?" He shook his head. "So much of the world keeps up on our elections, our music, our films, our scandals — seems almost on a daily basis. Yet it takes decades to get the word out about the real crises in the world. Maybe when your students are running the country the influence they have in the world will be focused on some more important things."

She looked at him. "Do you ever feel guilty about being so comfortable? I mean, we're a pretty comfortable bunch, don't you think?"

"No question. People who do what they love are the ultimate elite," he said.

"And we're comfortable," she stressed the word again. "We're educated. We're traveled. We spend our time with the best and brightest. Not to mention being treated like royalty by people like Albert and Diana."

"I wouldn't call it guilt exactly, but I know what you mean," he said. "I do think Albert picked a group for whom comfort translates into responsibility."

"For moving humanity forward?" she said.

"In every way we can, yeah," he said. "Of course, part of moving humanity forward is never losing sight of the fact that the vast majority of people on the planet aren't the least bit affected by what some minority of Western intellectuals think they're doing to move humanity forward." He was emphatic. "Believe me, Albert and Diana are more aware than most. They do this kind of thing because they think it's important, but they also do so much more that no one ever knows about. They both believe that the only kind of compassion that really matters a damn is the kind that pulls a person out of his or her own comfort. They're among the Americans who've made a huge difference. And in places where few people care to."

"That's the feeling I get from them," she said.

They had arrived at the clearing again, the same spot where they had stopped on their first night. They turned and beheld the hills of Sundance.

Michael brightened up. "It must feel great to know you're a champion skier now, huh?"

"Well, I'm no champion," she laughed, drawing her hood close to her neck. "But I did do it," she said proudly.

Michael examined her face in the twilight. "I'm sure you do anything you put your mind to."

She felt the warmth from his body next to her as she stood looking at the snow-covered scene. She recalled the moment at the top of Wildflower when he had peered into her eyes and encouraged her to take the leap. The ecstasy she had experienced on the slopes had had more to do with him than with the skiing. She longed to see that expression again, the one that had persuaded her to take the plunge into the blissful unknown. There was a moment of stillness between them. Then she looked up at him, knowing full well the effect his gaze would have on her. His expression was a contemplative one.

"You said you had trouble reconciling your terror with your attraction?"

She was not surprised that that particular remark had not escaped him. She feigned embarrassment for only a moment and then looked into his eyes.

"And have you reconciled them now?" he asked.

From the depth of her heart she was eager to respond. And then she saw the apprehension in his face. It was more than apprehension, it was conflict. Conflict about this very moment. Her heart plunged. She had never been so sure of anything as she had been that Cavanaugh would seize this extraordinary thing that had taken hold between them. Cavanaugh, who believed in everything. Were they really going to say goodbye? There, where the paths diverged to their separate cabins? To their separate lives? She examined his expression. Mary Claire was right. It was the kind of feeling that does not happen to one, it happens to two. It was there in his eyes. It had been there since the moment they met. Yet it was not going to be pursued. She could feel it in the air between them, in the cold that was nipping at her face. They would be taking their separate shuttles to the airport in the morning and returning to their long-distance friendship. It would be many months before their paths would cross again. She began to shiver. She turned her body toward him, her hands buried in her pockets. "I won't see you in the morning."

"Yeah," he whispered. "We're out at the crack of dawn." Then he looked deeply into her eyes.

Katherine remained buried in his gaze for as long as she could stand it, then quickly she wrapped her arms around his neck. When he held her it felt for a moment as though he would not let go. "You're a special one, Cavanaugh," she said.

"I'm gonna miss the sound of that," he said.

"Me too." She hugged him tight. "I'm gonna run up and get warm. Take good care."

She did not look back, though she knew he had not moved. She could feel him standing there at the clearing, motionless. At the top of the hill when she knew she was out of sight she stopped running. A deep dark numbness was filling her insides, spreading through her entire body. Only her breath before her was alive, as though it belonged to someone else. Inside her cabin she closed the door and laid her forehead on the cold hard wood. She remained there motionless for a long time.

Nineteen

It was the first day of spring. Not the official first day. The first day when all at once the grass is alive and the air is fragrant and every breeze carries a chorus of birds chirping and wings flapping as though it were the first day of life itself. Katherine missed the springtimes of her youth. She remembered stepping out into the yard in their small Michigan town and experiencing that first glorious blast of green. There were four distinct seasons then. They took their equal turns and then stepped aside for the next dramatic blow to the senses. The transitions were less pronounced now. The seasons were blending together more with every passing year. And people were busier now. Their lives were too full of other things to notice the first day of spring.

She looked out the window of the westbound 747. Interesting, she thought, the gravitational pull she had always felt from California. The connection she felt with Cavanaugh was still with her too, though she told herself every day that time healed all imaginings. This particular trip was one she had imagined all her life. How appropriate that it was happening on the first day of spring and in a brand new millennium. The greatest climatic impact of the past season had come in the fine linen envelope she held in her hand. Was it even necessary to read it again, she thought. Was not such a letter committed to memory at first blow? As she slipped her hand inside and pulled out the letter, she recalled

Albert Finn's extraordinary eyes. She thought of how grateful she was for his presence in her life.

Dear Katherine,

I hope this finds you well and happy. I have thought of you many times since Sundance. Diana and I both look forward to spending some time with you. And I remain eager to introduce you to the Center.

My reason for writing to you now is an important one. And though I would love to be sharing these thoughts with you in person, perhaps it is best that they come to you this way. I hope you will find some quiet, private time to absorb them. I trust the powers that have urged me to share them, and can only hope the highest purpose will be served.

When she first read the opening of Albert's letter she had thought somehow that he was going to say something about Cavanaugh. She never dreamed what awaited her in his long, hand-written letter and in the story he said he needed to share.

My first wife, Julia, my partner for twenty seven years, passed away eleven years ago. Julia was one of the great teachers in my life, especially during our final year together. She believed that her cancer served the purpose of bringing her into contact with people she would not have known under any other circumstance. One woman, whom she encountered soon after her diagnosis, was a powerful influence on this amazing attitude. She is known in the healing community as a "medical intuitive." To my mind, she is simply an intuitive, and a gifted one. She is sought out now by people from all over the country and yet she remains the private unassuming soul she has always been. Her intuitive gifts came to light years ago when she saw a threatening obstruction in the heart of a man who had no symptom that anything was wrong. Surprisingly, he responded to her urging and immediately saw a doctor. The next day he had surgery that saved his life. In the years since then this woman has helped many people, many of whom were misdiagnosed or were in treatment to which they were not responding. She has saved many lives. But that is not always the purpose of her meeting the people who come to her. My wife Julia believed she was the spirit who came to assist her own spirit in its departure from this world. I am inclined to agree.

Since Julia's passing, this remarkable woman has remained a steadying spiritual force in my own life. Today we sat for hours in her beautiful garden and talked as we have done many times over the years. But this was the first time she shared with me her deep personal history. It was an intimate sharing, one I cherish as sacred. And yet I am compelled to share her story with you. I do so believing strongly that I was called to, and trusting you will understand why.

The woman I am speaking of is Helen Dalton. She grew up in a small southern town where she married young and then moved with her husband to the Midwest. By her early twenties she found herself in circumstances she could hardly believe were her own. She and her two daughters were completely dependent on a man who was a deeply troubled personality. More than once she was critically injured at the hand of her husband. Her greatest fear was of his threats to her children should she ever leave him. It was her love for her two daughters and her determination to give them a better life that in her darkest hours gave her the will to live. When one of her daughters became ill, her husband forbade medical care for the child. He said he would allow no interference in the work of the Lord. When Helen described the circumstances of her daughter's death, it was difficult to imagine how a person survives such an experience. Yet when she told me the rest of the story I saw what had been her deepest heartbreak. Her other daughter was taken from her by the State and adopted by another family. Her greatest agony was in the empathy she felt for her surviving daughter. Being separated from her was the most impossible thing she endured.

By now, Katherine, you understand why I came home this evening feeling that the hand of fate connected us today. It connected us, I believe, the day we met. Helen knows nothing of this connection. She does not know that I am sharing her story with you. As you read on, please know that I am passing this story along with the same caring I felt today for my dear friend Helen.

 After the tragedy of losing both of her daughters, Helen became very ill. She said that in many respects she had ceased to live. It was her sister who cared for her for years and eventually nursed her back to life. And her life since then, Katherine, has been living proof that sometimes the greatest tragedies give birth to miracles. Over the years of her illness her sister took her for walks each day at the Point Reyes National Seashore. There, they regularly encountered the same park ranger. One day Helen spoke to the man. He was the one whose heart she looked into when her gift first presented itself, the man who later said he could not help trusting the look in her eyes. (Helen says that broken hearts always recognize one another. The man she spoke to that day was in deep grief over the loss of his wife and son in a terrible accident.) That forest ranger, now retired, is Helen's husband, Larry Dalton. Their lovely home in Inverness, a quiet little town about an hour north of San Francisco, is near the Point Reyes National Seashore, where Larry continues as a volunteer ranger and Helen continues her regular walks by the sea.

 When I asked Helen if she knew anything about her daughter she said that it was many years before she was able to think of her without feeling that her heart was being torn from her breast. Yet she thinks of her now with peace in her heart. Her eyes glowed as she spoke of her. She said she was a beautiful woman and a brilliant scientist and teacher. She said that the people who raised her had loved her as their own and that her daughter had embraced them as her true parents. When she told me this I could see how unbearable it had been for her to accept this reality. And yet she said there had not been a day when she had not been filled with gratitude for the virtue in this couple's hearts, the people who had taken care of her daughter. It was they most of all who convinced her of how uniquely fitted we all are for the parts we will play in the lives of others.

Later in our visit I noticed a couple of books on the bench in the garden where Helen had been sitting. When I saw that one of them was *The Relevance of Nature*, I of course commented on your book. In that moment I saw in her eyes the same depth of feeling I had seen when she spoke of her daughter. I knew in that moment that her daughter was you.

Katherine, more than any other person in my life, Helen has taught me that there is purpose in every one of our encounters in life. Ironically, after she confided in me today she did not know why she had done so. She said that I was the only person other than her husband with whom she had shared her history. I told her that perhaps sometime the reason would reveal itself.

There is something else that I want very much for you to know, Katherine. It is something I have thought about many times since Sundance. The moment I met you I was struck by how strongly you reminded me of one of the brightest spirits I have known. Helen Dalton was the person I was thinking of. Today on my way to Inverness I was struck again by how important it was for the two of you to meet. I decided that when you came to visit we would arrange a visit with Helen. I want you to know that these thoughts have been in my mind since our meeting last September.

I would also like you to know that I have some understanding of the time it takes to heal from such a loss as the one you recently suffered in both of your parents. There is no doubt that your heart will know what is right for its own healing and for perhaps reaching out to another heart. Whatever you decide, you have our affection and our friendship whenever you wish to have it. Diana and I would love to have you stay with us when you are next in San Francisco.
Yours ever, Albert Finn.

It had been many years since Katherine had imagined seeing her mother. Yet how well she recalled the private fantasies to which she had clung for much of her youth. Somehow she had known even before her aunt's visit. It was when Mary Margaret came to her in her dream that she first began to feel that she would see her mother again. Perhaps Albert Finn was right. Perhaps we all have purpose in one another's lives. What she knew for certain was that the course he had laid out for her was one she could not turn away from. She had to see the woman who was once her mother.

A strange mixture of longing and trepidation began welling up inside her the moment the plane touched down in San Francisco. It rolled through her in waves as she drove along the Pacific coast northward from the city. The terrain was dramatically different from that of her childhood imaginings about the place where her mother lived. She had not imagined the Golden Gate Bridge in the morning light, or the fragrances that wafted through the car along the winding ocean highway, or the tiny village tucked between the lavish national parklands and the tranquil waters of Tomales Bay.

Inverness was indeed a quiet little town. The lady in the general store knew exactly where to direct her. From the moment she saw the street sign, her heart began to pound. Quivering inside her was the frightened little girl she had thought she had left behind years ago. The adrenaline pulsed in her eyes and in her ears as she sat in the car by the side of the road and observed the fence and the foliage that obscured the house from view. Her mind raced with every conceivable thought that would heighten her anxiety. How would she feel if her mother did not recognize her? How would she react if she did? What would they say to one another? Albert had given her his word. Helen Dalton would not be expecting her. The opportunity was there for her to change her mind at any time. He had also told her that Helen would be leaving that evening for Portland to be with a woman who was dying. No sooner had she put her hand on the car door handle than her heart began to throb with the next bout of anxiety. What if her plans had changed? What if she was not there?

As she stepped toward the fence her heart skipped a beat at the sight of a woman emerging from the gate. She was a frail looking woman, her hair extremely short, her face ashen and drawn. Katherine was taken aback when the woman looked at her as though the prospect of speaking to this approaching stranger was one of sheer delight. "Hi, I'm Jane," she beamed. "She's in the garden," she said. Then she smiled again brightly and was on her way.

Katherine stood inside the gate and faced the path in front of her. Her entire body was instinctively bracing itself for some kind of cathartic upheaval it did not begin to understand. She stepped along the large smooth pieces of dark green slate that were embedded in the earth. As the path diverged to the right and led around to the back of the house, the foliage that lined the path became dense and high and filled with radiant color. Bright bougainvillea and rhododendron bushes lined the path until it opened up into a large open sanctuary. This was the garden Albert had spoken of, she thought.

A large matriarchal oak tree would have been the focal point for an artist painting the scene. And everywhere throughout the yard were clusters of flowers of every color and variety. Near the oak was a carved wooden bench with bright yellow cushions on the seat. Closer to the house was a white wrought iron table and chairs on a cleared area with a floor of the same green slate as the garden pathways. Her eye and then her step were irresistibly led along the pathway lined with flowers — tall proud stalks of columbine and belladonna, delphinium and snapdragons, pride of Madeira, and lily of the Nile. She followed along the path until she reached the intended destination. There, sculpted in stone was a beautiful winged angel overlooking the scene. Katherine looked up at her ethereal face, her hands gracefully outstretched toward her visitor, her gown flowing as though she had just touched down from above. Her delicate feet were arched in a downward pose and rested on a pedestal that was raised in the center of a small pond built into a bed of rocks. Below them on a smooth slab of stone were the carved words:

> Every creature is a glittering
> glistening mirror of divinity.
> *Hildegard von Bingen*

Katherine's gaze instinctively fell upon the next image the angel's visitors were intended to see next — her own reflection in the pond below.

She heard the sound of a screen door opening and closing and turned to see the slight figure of a woman walking toward her from the house. The woman smiled at her. And then she stopped. Slowly she stepped again, intent on her visitor. As she drew closer, Katherine saw more of her features. Her hair was soft and white and swept up on her head, fine pieces fell around her face and neck. Her small blue eyes beamed. She too was studying every detail of the face in front of her as though she were looking into a mirror for the first time. She drew close to Katherine. Close enough to touch. There they stood, their eyes filled with one another.

It was a single movement that impelled her — her mother's hand involuntarily groping toward her daughter's hair. And all in a moment Katherine felt her body pressed against her mother's, her arms wrapped tightly around her body, her fingers kneading the flesh and bones of her back. Her own hair was being grasped in handfuls behind her, over and over in her mother's palms, as together they heaved in silent unison. They wept as they held in their arms the little girl, the young mother, the sister, the daughter, the strangers they had become, the years they would never recover.

And when their bodies had reached their final ebb, they looked again into one another's faces and beheld the women they had each become.

For a long moment they stood silently, holding tightly to one another's hands, absorbing every detail of one another's faces. And then her mother uttered the first words that were spoken between them. "My darling Katie," she said, her fingers again gravitating toward her daughter's hair.

Katherine was fixed on the crystal blue pools that were looking at her as though they had found their expressed purpose in this single moment. These were not the pale blue eyes she had looked into as a child. How vacant they had been. The woman she saw now in her mother's eyes had risen from life's threshing floor. She had found her way to a serenity that matched even Albert's portrayal of her. Perhaps Albert's impressions were true, she thought. What was certain was that the woman before her was as *present* as anyone she had ever known.

Standing there, looking into her mother's face, she felt another presence beside her. Mary Margaret had never been more present than she was in this moment. They had been three, she and her mother and her little sister. They had clung to one another for dear life. The same life that had ripped them apart and was now delivering them to one another, here, in this unearthly scene. Katherine could see that her mother too was filling her eyes with the two of them. Mary Margaret was there for her too.

As they sat together on the garden bench, Katherine's trepidation evaporated with her tears. Slowly she and her mother began to speak. And then they spoke as though they might never speak again, as though they would remain there in that very spot until every word had been spoken between them. They spoke of Albert and his letter and of the extraordinary connection Katherine had felt with him. They spoke of Agnes and her visit to Ann

Arbor and of how Agnes and Helen had hunted together for the Charlotte Brontë quote Katherine had cited for her aunt during her visit. They spoke of Katherine's family, Bill and Marion, and of the benevolent energy Helen had always felt from them. And before long they were sharing their stories of the yearning they had both felt for one another and of the constancy of Mary Margaret's presence in both of their lives. Helen's eyes glistened as she listened to every detail of Katherine's butterfly dream.

As Katherine watched her mother's expression and listened to her voice she experienced a deep sense of intimacy and familiarity. They knew one another's essence, she and the woman before her. They knew one another with a certainty that could not be diminished by time or circumstance. And now they were talking with one another as instinctively as childhood friends reunited after many years, retracing the lines of the life they once shared.

Helen squeezed Katherine's hands and continued to soak in the sight of her as she shared the rest of the story Albert had confided to Katherine. She told her of her many walks out onto the headlands at Chimney Rock when she would sit on the cliff overlooking the vastness and her senses would be filled with nothing but the sea.

"It was there on one of those days when the winds thrashed my body and I fell under the spell of the rhythm of the ocean that I heard Mary Margaret's voice. I felt her soothing my heart, assuring me that she was at peace." She squeezed Katherine's hand. "She told me I would see you again, that we would all be together again." She looked deeply into Katherine's eyes. "It's true, what Albert told you," she said. "I did speak to the man that day, the man who became my husband . . . But it was my heart that was rescued that day at the sea."

When her mother spoke of Mary Margaret, Katherine became fixed on the large oak tree, the one her mother said reminded her too of the one in their yard many years ago. She recalled how she and Mary Margaret had fled to the tree many times and waited there for their mother to come. There, they had pretended that they lived in an imaginary world with only the three of them and their special tree.

When Helen spoke of the Midwest to which she had never returned there was a longing in her voice. "The changing seasons keep one so at pace with life," she said. Yet she had found in her new home, she said, what she most needed from the natural world. When she spoke of the "California light," Katherine looked again at the luxurious array of color around them — the lush green of the periwinkle leaves, the deep fuchsias and blues of the primrose, the delicate yellows of glistening roses. She observed the pink hue of her mother's fair skin and the large brim hat that was draped on the bench cushion. Suddenly she was overcome.

"I feel like all my life I've been living part of my life," she said.

Helen squeezed her hands again. "We have both been living exactly the experience that would bring us to this precious moment," she said.

Katherine was intent on the oak tree where lifetimes of revelation were distilling before her.

"I've been working so hard all my life to grow away from my roots, you know?" She looked at her mother as she confessed, "Trying to deny them."

Helen's face filled with compassion. Then she too focused on the stately oak. "The integrity of every tree comes both from the passion with which it holds to its roots and the fervor with which it grows away from them."

Katherine looked into her mother's eyes. "It wasn't until today that I realized how much I have held to my roots."

Helen was holding her hands as though she were drenching her own in the feel of her daughter's skin. "You've grown so beautifully to this wonderful time in your life, your teaching and your writing, and people like Albert and Diana. Your faith in God and in life was so severely tested. But you did find your way."

Katherine's heart fell. How would she ever confess the struggle she had had all her life with God and with faith? "I'm still finding my way," she whispered.

It was only a moment before she recognized in her mother's eyes the one person on earth who possessed complete understanding of both the origins and the depths of her deepest conflict.

With deep affection Helen responded, "We're all finding our way."

Katherine was again struck by the equanimity she saw in her mother's eyes. It was the same quality she had seen in Albert from their first meeting. And this was the woman he praised as the powerful spiritual force in his life. How had she ever achieved such inner peace? How had she reconciled with a God that could ask her to endure such suffering?

And again as though she were reading her mind, Helen responded, "I too had a long battle with God for all that I felt had been taken from me. And yet look at what I have in this moment. When I believed I had been completely forsaken, could I ever have imagined such happiness."

Katherine was overcome by the same feelings she saw in her mother's face. And yet she could only speak the truth to her. "I wish I could tell you that I understand what you mean when you speak of God."

Helen looked at her emphatically. "From reading your book, I would say we think of God in the same way."

Katherine was struck by the same incredulity she had experienced in Cavanaugh's response to her book. She listened intently as her mother continued.

"To truly understand that the ultimate force behind the light in the universe is not something we can ever understand — that is as close as we can ever come to understanding God."

Katherine was moved by her mother's insight and by the way she had expressed it. She was equally stirred by the radical contrast with the ideas that had been forcibly imposed on her years earlier. Helen reached down and pulled a single daffodil and held it up in the sun before their eyes.

"That such a miracle could be," she said, "that is all I need to know of God." She handed the flower to Katherine. "I do believe in everything Jesus taught," she explained. "So much so that I embrace all of the other great teachers too, and all children of God, just as Jesus taught." Her smile brightened. "I always think of what Saint Francis said — "Teach Christ, always. But only as a last resort, use words.""

Katherine smiled. "Francis of Assisi?"

"He was almost here in the garden," Helen said as she nodded toward the angel sculpture. "We decided in the end we wanted an angel. She is one of Diana's creations. A gift from Albert and Diana."

"She's so beautiful," Katherine said. "The quote below her is lovely too."

Helen looked again into her daughter's eyes. "I believe in my heart that Jesus would be the first to encourage each of us on our own path of believing. What we saw in your father was not believing. It was his struggle to believe."

"I think I've always carried a deep loathing for that kind of believing," Katherine said. "The kind that could inflict such pain on others."

"It is never true believers that cause pain to others," Helen said. "If your father had truly believed that Mary Margaret would have been healed by prayer and prayer alone, she would have had the most powerful medicine there is. But that kind of energy can only come through in love."

As her mother spoke of Mary Margaret's passing, the tears that came to Katherine were the tears of a six year old girl. She drew the breath that would enable her to speak rather than weep.

"I think she died because she couldn't bear to see you hurt anymore." This time when Helen embraced her daughter, for the first time Katherine was able to feel the arms she had so longed for on that terrible night many years earlier. Her mother was able to hold her beloved daughter and to stroke her hair and speak to her tenderly. "She died because it was her time," she said. "As difficult as that is for us to understand . . . And she is still very much with us too. You know that, don't you, Katie."

When Katherine sat back to look at her mother, to tell her how much Mary Margaret was with her all the time, she was startled by a butterfly that fluttered near their faces and then flew to a nearby grouping of flowers. It flitted in and out of a cluster of deep blue and purple flowers.

"My butterfly friends," Helen said, as though she thought the butterflies too were listening. "That was the first garden I planted years ago. They've been keeping me company ever since." She looked at Katherine. "I suppose a scientist would find it silly to think that the butterflies have guided me? That they are the ones responsible for the garden?"

"No," Katherine said, "I would not find that silly at all."

"They've helped us both with our healing," she said as she looked again at her winged friend.

Katherine recalled the attentiveness with which her mother had listened to every detail of her butterfly dream. She had not been at all surprised at the image of Mary Margaret as a beautiful butterfly surrounded by light.

As she watched the butterfly dance in the California light Katherine again pored over the fragrant splendor that surrounded them. Helen responded to her silent reveling by taking her by the hand and walking with her through the garden and, one by one, as though each species was another member of the family, she introduced her to her flowers. She approached each long-stem beauty and ceremonially cut it with her knife until she held in her arms an enormous bouquet for Katherine to take with her to Albert and Diana's. Katherine watched her as she gathered her blossoms of lupine and Canterbury bells, Siberian iris and delphinium, hollyhocks and snapdragons and pride of Madeira.

Hours later, sitting at her mother's kitchen table and drinking her tea, Katherine was still assimilating the sight of the woman before her and the reality of their togetherness after so many years. She continually gravitated toward the warmth she experienced in her mother's penetrating gaze. She now understood her healing work in a way that could only have come from direct experience. She understood why people would come to her in their greatest hour of need, why even someone of Albert's strength of character would be fortified by the energy that flowed from the woman before her.

When the time drew near for Helen's departure, they both knew her next visit was one for which even theirs would step aside. Helen had explained that she was a woman who had struggled with breast cancer and had felt she was free of it. And now it was back with a vengeance and was taking over her body. She would be flying to Portland that evening and seeing her in the morning.

When the moment came, Katherine reached into her handbag and handed her mother a small gift package with a note for her Aunt Agnes.
"They're orange jellies," she said. "The ones she used to bring me when I was little."
Helen was deeply touched on behalf of her sister. "Thank you, dear. This will mean so much to her."
As they stood up they held tightly to one another's eyes and to

their intimate sense of shared understanding. They had found in one another a new beginning. One that could never be taken away. "I'll be back soon," Katherine said. "We'll see one another again soon."

Helen smiled with the same serenity that had held Katherine captive since the moment she arrived. "And in the meantime," she said, "you will continue to be with me every day."

They held one another in their arms for a long silent goodbye.

Leaving Inverness that day, driving along Tomales Bay, Katherine found a faithful friend in the part of the brain that operates an automobile with no conscious communication with its driver. The blissfulness with which she held the wheel and felt the wind in her hair was like the afterglow of her beautiful dream. And this was one she need not wake up from. The Katherine Ayers who had smelled the grass that morning in Ann Arbor would never be the same again. She had found a part of herself she had longed for all her life.

All the way to the ocean, along the winding forest roads, across the miles of pastoral countryside, she instinctively responded to the arrows pointing to the Point Reyes National Seashore. The large bouquet of flowers lay next to her on the seat, their fragrance flooding her senses with every gust of wind that swept across the landscape on its way from the sea. She followed the signs and parked the car and found herself walking the ascending path to the bluffs at Chimney Rock. All along the headlands long green grasses swirled like ribbons in the afternoon sun, drawing her up to the precipice. There she stood, high above the ocean, where the wind whipped her hair and the sound of the sea rose up to meet her. As far as she could see in every direction the panoramic splendor took her breath away.

She planted her feet in the grass and faced the ocean, her hair streaming in the wind. She closed her eyes and spread her arms wide and stretched her body long and strong. Her head fell back and she faced the sky. The butterfly, she thought, as the winds struck her body. The butterfly. Slowly she straightened and again beheld the scene.

The sky was as clear and blue as her mother's eyes. Its radiance reflected in the enormous waves that rolled from the horizon with sunlight glistening on every swell. And as the surf crashed against the rocks below, she felt herself responding to the very sensation her mother had described. It was as though her heart began to beat with the heart of the ocean, as though her heart had become one with the ocean's heart. It was there with the air and the sea and the sky that she understood for the first time what her sister had said to her in her dream. "It is all one. Here or there, it is all one life."

Suddenly, she was filled with a powerful sense of her singular human body standing there on the precipice. The narrow piece of earth that jetted out into the vastness was holding her there, suspended, surrounded by the grandeur of the sea and sky. The image was inescapable. She was standing on the very hand of God, she thought, observing his creation in all its glory. "Dear God," she whispered. "Dear God." She had struggled with him all her life only to find he was the very living presence she had passionately denied. "It's really true, isn't it?" she said to the sky as she recalled Cavanaugh's words. "We have no other way to think of you than in terms you have given us. Human terms," she said. Then she gazed intently at the distant reaches of the sea as she felt the wind blowing through her hair.

Twenty

She could hardly believe it when she opened her eyes to the clock at her bedside. It had been months since she had experienced such a long deep sleep. The beautiful guest room of Albert and Diana's Sea Cliff home was now bathed in sunlight. She drew the grand drapes wide to a stunning view of the ocean.

Albert and Diana had embraced her the previous evening with the warmth and understanding of cherished friends. Their intimate conversation had sent her to bed with the same peaceful feeling she now saw emanating from throughout their lovely home. The entire house in the light of day had an open airy feeling, with enormous windows all around and a breathtaking view of the San Francisco Bay. The dining table where they sat together for breakfast was situated as though on a glassed-in island overlooking the sea. The flowers her mother had given her now towered from their breakfast table in an elegant crystal vase.

"They are beautiful, aren't they?" she said to her hosts.

"I've never known flowers more exquisite than Helen's," Diana said.

Albert slid the dish of preserves toward Katherine's plate. "A friend of ours, one of the many she's helped over the years, says his healing began the moment he entered her garden."

Katherine looked at him emphatically. "I believe him," she said. Then she reached into the pocket of her sweater as she remembered something. "There is something I wanted to ask you about," she said as she opened up a piece of paper and handed it to Albert. "She said I might want to get this." She looked at Albert quizzically. "And then she said, 'If it ever occurred to me.'"

Albert looked at the piece of paper. "It's a homeopathic remedy," he said.

"I guess it won't surprise you that it was she who brought it up," Katherine said. "I have this problem with my neck. All my life, really. It tightens up whenever I'm under any kind of stress. And of course it was killing me by the time I arrived in Inverness yesterday. I didn't say a word about it but she was looking at it as though she could see the pain. Not in my face," Katherine stressed, "in my neck."

Albert smiled.

"She said if I take this I might find that it stopped seizing up altogether."

Albert read the words aloud, "Limenitis bredowii."

"I know so little about alternative medicines," Katherine said.

Albert smiled again. "Yes, in this culture we call it 'alternative' when it deals with the whole person instead of the symptoms."

Diana was already perusing the inside wall of the living room that from ceiling to floor supported an enormous library.

"Homeopathy is the principle of like cures like, right?" Katherine asked.

"Goes back as far as recorded history," Albert said as he stirred his tea. "Helen is open to all remedies, from the ancient to the modern allopathic. She just has a gift for zeroing in on what's needed. And I'm convinced that it's mostly her. It's her own energy that's the healer."

Katherine was struck by the word "energy." She was amazed at how her conception of energy had been affected by her experience with her mother. Once again she was reminded of ideas to which

Cavanaugh had introduced her.

"Here it is," Diana said, with her face in a homeopathy book. "It's a new one. They just did the proving on it a few years ago." She sat again at the table. "Limenitis bredowii," she read. "It's a butterfly."

"A *butterfly?*" Katherine said. "What do you mean?"

"It's from the California Sister Butterfly," Diana said.

Katherine was looking at Albert incredulously.

"Very interesting," he said.

Katherine was dumbfounded. "You mean it's actually made from a butterfly?"

"Each remedy is drawn from the properties of a particular plant or mineral or animal," Albert explained. "In this case, whatever substance is unique to this particular butterfly is the essence of the remedy. There are thousands of remedies, so the practitioner's knowledge makes an enormous difference in identifying the right one. I think it's as much art as science. And in Helen's case, I'm sure it's something else too."

"It's a regal butterfly," Diana read from the book, "with a dignified demeanor, found in canyons and hillsides where oak predominates." She continued scanning the page. "During their larval stage they extract an alkaloid from oak leaves that serves as a protective agent which they retain in their bodies throughout adulthood . . . A highly ritualized and graceful courtship dance. . . Their unique behavior," she announced with emphasis as she continued reading, "Unlike other species of butterfly eggs that are hidden and protected by the mother, the Limenitis bredowii lays its eggs out in the open and leaves them in a completely vulnerable state where they must fend for themselves to survive."

Diana laid the book down and observed Katherine's stunned expression. She reached over and stroked her hand. "I'll get us some more tea."

Albert too was observing Katherine's face. "The human body is an amazing thing," he said. "It has its own memory of everything that's happened to us. Everything we've ever felt."

Katherine sat motionless looking at him amazed.

"You know, the butterfly was considered by ancient cultures to be the one creature that contained within itself the promise of future generations."

Katherine was marveling at this entire scene. Though her four colleagues from Sundance were aware of her Initiative class and her deep involvement with butterflies, she could see that Albert and Diana were completely unaware.

"One thing is for sure," Albert said, "if Helen suggested it, it will be the exact one for you. In fact, you may even find that just being with her yesterday had the same effect."

"You mean, that the problem in my neck would . . ."

"Stop being a problem," Albert said with a smile. "Yes, that's what I mean."

"So you may be here more often now," Diana said hopefully.

"Yes." Katherine drew a deep breath as she again absorbed her new reality. "Yes. I'm sure I will."

"Yesterday was a lot to take in all at once," Diana said. "I'd be surprised if you're not exhausted."

"Yes," Albert followed. "We'll certainly understand if you want to postpone the Center for another time."

"Oh, no, I'm looking forward to it," Katherine said.

"It occurs to me now that our friend Michael was more tuned-in than he realized," Albert said.

"How do you mean?" Katherine attempted to disguise the full depth of the effect Cavanaugh's name had on her.

"It was Michael who felt so strongly that you belonged here."

"In San Francisco?"

"He was of course thinking about the Center," Albert said. "That was before we made any of these other connections. But it wouldn't be the first time Michael was more tuned-in than he knew, even with regard to you."

"How do you mean?" Katherine asked.

"It was Michael who first gave me your book and urged me to invite you to Sundance."

Katherine was thoroughly taken aback. She had never heard a word of this from Cavanaugh.

"He really wanted to pursue you for the Center too. Of course he knew he'd have to get you out for a visit first, see what we're doing." Albert smiled confidently. "I've seen a lot of serious scientists taken in by the work of the Center."

Katherine tried to cover her feelings. "Well, the truth is, Albert, he really hasn't pursued my visiting. Not since Sundance. You know how we all get tied-up with work. Even the emails dwindle after a while."

Albert looked at her. "And perhaps it was you he became reluctant about pursuing?"

She hesitated only a moment. "That was my sense of it, yes."

Albert exchanged an intimate look with Diana. "Yes, that was my sense of it too."

"We're certainly friends," Katherine said. "I have great admiration for him."

"And he you," Diana said.

"Yesterday, with my mother . . ." Katherine was startled by the ease with which she had said the word. "I still can't get over the sound of it."

Diana affectionately stroked her hand again.

"Some of the things she said reminded me of Cavanaugh."

"They're definitely kindred spirits," Albert said.

"You're all kindred spirits," Katherine exclaimed. "What does it mean that I'm suddenly colliding with all of you?"

She saw in Albert's face that he too found it a worthy question.

"And we're colliding with you," he said.

Katherine was having a hard time concealing her feelings about seeing Cavanaugh. "But you know, I've learned to trust people's instincts about not pursuing things. Especially when it comes to relationships."

Albert had picked up his teacup and was gently rolling the liquid inside in a circular motion.

"You know, the Tibetans have a wonderful thought on the subject of relationships," he ruminated. "They say that sometimes when a brilliant light appears it is too much for us and we instinctively gravitate back toward the faint soothing light, the one that is familiar. But in choosing the dimmer light, we remain within our old boundaries." He looked at Diana again. "I think that unfamiliar brilliance is frightening to all of us at first."

Katherine observed Albert and Diana, enamored of the way they looked at one another.

"It's funny how the very same thing some people are afraid of, others are afraid of being without," she said.

Diana immediately responded, "Oh, there is really only one fear. The one at the bottom of all the others." She looked at Katherine pointedly. "The fear of having it and then having to be without it again."

Katherine could feel both Albert and Diana's kind attention to her feelings. She looked again at her mother's flowers. "My mother and I talked about it a bit yesterday . . . this whole love thing. I can't believe the things we talked about."

"I'm sure," Albert said.

"I told her I didn't really understand why I had been alone most of my life, that it certainly wasn't that relationship was not a priority." She smiled as she recalled her mother's reply. "She said 'Oh no. You are alone *because* relationship is a priority.' "

Both Diana and Albert brightened.

"She said that we can't judge relationships in terms of how long they last or whether or not they feel like they work out. That what matters is how much they move us along. She said that with every relationship we're either being moved along on our own path or we're helping the other person along on theirs."

"Or both," Albert said.

"So even the ones that are painful or that make no sense at all — they have some value too."

Albert smiled. "Sometimes they're the ones that have the most value."

"She said that our ultimate relationship may be something very different from what we think we long for — that real "true love" is when we're devoted, not to one another, but to one another's paths."

Diana was admiring the bouquet that graced her table. "Yes, Helen believes that the real unifying force that holds the universe together is the same one that brings two people together. She says it is the daily work of the universe to bring each of us into a true union with another soul."

Albert grinned. "It's the ones who make the universe work the hardest who, when they do finally fall in love, love the most deeply."

Katherine relaxed into Albert's expression. "And is it my imagination," she said, "or is it kind of a general rule that the ones who make the universe work the hardest are usually men?"

Albert and Diana laughed. And with a full-on glimmer in Albert's eyes he looked into Katherine's. "Women do fall easier," he said, "but don't be fooled that men don't fall harder."

Katherine observed his expression again. And then Diana's. "Why do I have the feeling my visit is being sprung on Mr. Cavanaugh? He doesn't know I'm coming, does he?"

Albert became serious. "This trip was too important to have any expectations beyond your plans for yesterday."

"He'll be thrilled," Diana added.

"He's giving a talk on the new cosmology this afternoon," Albert said. "That'll give you a good sense of his work, which is really the heart of the Center. In the meantime I can show you around. You just have to let me know when I'm repeating what he's already told you."

"He's told me *nothing*," Katherine exclaimed. "And it's not for not asking, I assure you. He just kept saying that I needed to come and experience it."

"I'm not surprised," Albert said. "The Center is really Michael's genius, you see. It was something he said he knew 'in his bones' he had to do."

Katherine smiled at the familiar Cavanaugh expression.

"It was something Teilhard de Chardin said that really brought it into focus for him. I remember when it happened. From that moment on he wouldn't rest until the Center was built."

Katherine was only vaguely familiar with Teilhard de Chardin.

"Paleontologist?" she said.

Albert nodded. "And a Jesuit priest," he said. "He was quite a force. One of the great influences on Michael, though there have been many. Chardin said that humanity was being irresistibly led to create a new science, a science by means of and yet surpassing all of the other sciences. That's a pretty good description of the Center."

As Albert continued it was clear how much he delighted in talking about Michael and his work.

"He brings together brilliant minds," he said, "like those we had at Sundance, but from every discipline — scientists, philosophers, theologians, heads of state, tribal elders, authors, artists, healers – visionaries from every tradition. I sat in on a session last week where the most fascinating ideas came from a musicologist from South Africa. There are some amazing people involved. Just knowing they exist in the world kind of makes sense out of things for me.

And they connect at the Center in such profound ways. Together they look at the most recent findings of science right alongside classical and contemporary philosophies, the wisdom of spiritual traditions, the perspective of poets. And all with a concentrated focus on humanity's role in the evolving universe."

Albert cited a number of prominent scientists who had participated in programs at the Center. He talked about how closely scientists work with spiritual leaders from different faiths, embracing one another's ideas and learning from one another. "We're just beginning to see the powerful ways that the intuition of scientists can be informed by the spiritual traditions. And the ways science is illuminating the central truths the great traditions share. I don't think there's anywhere where that dialogue is more alive than at the Center."

Katherine and Diana listened intently as Albert went on.

"For instance, long before we ever discovered that atoms consist almost entirely of empty space, that our bodies and other things of material substance are in fact more nothingness than anything else — before we ever approached the enigma of the nothingness prior to the Big Bang — the Buddhists taught that nothingness was the source of all things." He sipped his tea. "There's been an on-going unified field theory group too, a fascinating group of physicists and visiting theorists, constantly collaborating with other disciplines. For Michael, the whole idea that the physical forces of the universe can be united in one mathematical scheme begs reexamination of ancient beliefs about the oneness of the universe."

Diana laid her hand down on the homeopathy book. "Medicine's another good example," she said. "There's been such incredible dialogue at the Center — gifted doctors and healers from so many traditions. And they all recognize that science is just beginning to understand things like meditation and yoga and other techniques that employ our own consciousness in our healing. And of course the mystics have told us for eons about the huge role our consciousness plays in our physical wellbeing."

"I understand Charles Lewis is a good friend of yours," Albert said. "The study of complexity is an important part of the Center's work too."

Katherine recalled Michael's comment at Sundance that Eastern philosophy has never perceived the world as anything but a complex system, that for centuries the 'unpredictability' of dynamic systems has been considered a fundamental and even sacred element in every system.

"I know Charles would be interested to know what you're doing," she said.

"Michael just mentioned Charles again the other day," Albert said. "I wouldn't be surprised if Charles hears from him."

"It's an exciting place, Katherine," Diana said. "Just pulsates with creative energy. And they're very deliberate about drawing ideas from every corner of the world and from all of time."

"And it's all about understanding our place in the universe," Albert said. "As Michael says, it's quite an adventure."

As Katherine listened to Albert speak of Michael a flood of emotion was rising inside her. She was sure her friends could plainly see how much she longed to see him again, how much she hoped he would be happy to see her. The truth was there had not been a single day since Sundance when he had not been her first thought when she opened her eyes in the morning and her last thought before she slept. She had felt his presence so strongly since the moment she arrived in San Francisco. He had been with her in her mother's garden when they talked about love, and when she stood above the ocean at Chimney Rock, and as she lay in her bed the night before knowing he was in the same city. Though she felt some ambivalence about appearing unannounced, somehow in the midst of this extraordinary visit, relaxing about surprising

Cavanaugh was something she could do.

The Center was a large triangular structure set in on a picturesque slope on the San Francisco side of the Golden Gate Bridge. To those familiar with its endeavors, its physical allure was attributable to the deliberate integration of a variety of woods, metals, stone and foliage from different parts of the world. Waving in the wind above the building was a large flag which it took Katherine a moment to recognize as an image of the globe. Not an American flag, she thought, an Earth flag. How Cavanaugh, she thought as she looked at Albert. He responded with a knowing grin.

On the lawn alongside the path leading up to the entrance was an enormous boulder that Albert said had remained undisturbed in its rightful place since long before the Center's conception. It had been carved by Diana's hand, in stalwart lettering, with the only words found on the exterior of the complex — "The Center."

Inside the main entrance she was again overcome by the sensation achieved by vast expansive windows on a sweeping ocean vista. When Albert apologetically withdrew to the office to take a call, she stood and absorbed the view. She meandered along the curved inside wall where a series of framed wall hangings lined the entire length of the lobby. Each frame contained a quote scrawled in elegant calligraphy and followed by attribution. The one closest to her was strikingly familiar. It was the heart of the Albert Schweitzer quote she had cited in her book.

"The deeper we look into nature, the more we recognize that we are united to all of life. From this knowledge comes our spiritual relationship with the universe."

She stepped to the next wall hanging which was a quote from Hegel. "Everything that from eternity has happened in heaven and Earth, the life of God and all the deeds of time, simply are the struggles for Spirit to know itself, to find itself, and finally to unite itself to itself."

Next was Ohiyesa, a Dakota Sioux. "The tree, the waterfall, the grizzly bear, each is an embodied Force, and as such an object of reverence."

Then Virgil. "Heaven and Earth, the watered plains, the moon's shining globe, the sun and stars, are all strengthened by Spirit working within them."

The next wall hanging contained a single Chinese symbol. Below it were three words, one on top of the other — "love," "benevolence," and "cosmic force."

Then Meister Eckhart. "God is in the innermost part of each and every thing. All creatures are the utterance of God."

The next name drew Katherine close to the wall. It was her second introduction to Hildegard von Bingen. "There is a living divine substance that glows in the beauty of the fields. It shines in the waters, and burns in the sun and the stars, and breathes in the verdure and in the flowers." She recalled Diana's beautiful angel in her mother's garden.

Next, on the wall beside the hallway that led to the "Conference Rooms" was a quote of Vaclav Havel. "It is not enough to invent new institutions. We must understand differently and more perfectly the true purpose of our existence on this Earth. The only option is a change in the sphere of the spirit, in the sphere of human conscience, in the actual attitude of humanity toward the world."

She continued along the corridor. When she came upon a Teilhard de Chardin quote she again drew close to the wall. "Every spark of life is equally sacred; for in the humblest atom and the most brilliant star, in the lowest insect and the finest intelligence, are the radiant smiles of the same Absolute."

"I'm sorry, Katherine," Albert said as he eagerly came up behind her. "Diana wants us to meet her at the restaurant. We want to go right in. Michael's just starting."

As they walked along another hallway which led to the auditorium Albert told her about the audience they would be joining. In addition to the current Center collaborators, he explained, there would be teachers, social workers, clergy, authors, even some corporate executives, he said — all of whom had signed on for this series of talks. As they stepped inside the intimate state-of-the-art auditorium, a couple hundred people were settling into their seats. They took two seats near the back of the hall just as the lights were dimming and Cavanaugh was arriving on the stage down in front. Katherine watched him as he stood silently for a moment and smiled at his audience. She recognized the thoughtful breath he inhaled before he spoke.

"What is the story of the universe?" he began. "Is it something that came into being with Western science a mere four hundred years ago? Or did it begin when the first humans stared in awe at the night sky? Primal peoples all had their own stories of how the world began. And each tribe's creation story was the essence of their spiritual identity. It was the foundation upon which they built their lives. The health of the tribe in fact depended upon the integrity of their story and the faithfulness with which they passed it along to each new generation.

"Today we are living with an empirical view of the story of the universe, of the birth of the cosmos and the stars and galaxies, of the evolution of life on Earth. We know that the emergence of human beings was a mere moment in a fifteen billion-year epic. And if we look closely we will see that the present phase of this evolution is utterly unique. It is the very first that will bear the marks of *conscious* evolution. Evolution which is now characterized not by biological, but cultural transformation. And it has accelerated to such a degree that dramatic social shifts now occur in mere decades.

"What is our story of the universe today? The story we will pass along to future generations? Will we integrate the amazing findings of science with the wisdom that has been passed down since our first ancestors stared in wonderment at the night sky? It has taken humanity thousands of generations to write this story. And if we were to pass it along in its entirety, the true *human* legacy, what a marvelous story there would be to tell.

"Every child could hear that the universe in which they live is one gigantic living organism, one they share with every rock and dandelion and sea otter and star in the entire world around them. They would learn that we are all composed of the same basic elements, and that we are all participants in the same unparalleled process that is the living universe. They would learn that since humans have been on Earth everything we have learned has pointed unmistakably to an unseen infinite power, a power that is the source of everything in the universe and is infused in every substance. It dwells in trees and in rivers and in dragonflies and grasshoppers and radiates from every living being.

"Every child could learn that they will make their own unique contribution to this evolving story. And that what they create may be just as astounding and as wondrous as the creation of stars. Or the emergence of oceans. Or the flight of the whippoorwill. For they carry in their cells the memory of the first explosions of light in the universe. And the very same power is alive in them. Whenever they are filled with the desire to hurl their truth into the world, they are filled with the same force that gave us Shakespeare, and Mozart, and sunsets, and daffodils. Whenever they show love and compassion, or care for a single one of Earth's creatures, they are reflecting the universe's highest quality, one that is now more essential to the future of life on our planet than any other cosmic force."

Katherine was riveted by the self-possession with which he

thrust his words into the auditorium. As she listened to his startling declarations she began to understand why she had been left with so many unanswered questions about his work. She recalled his evasive dance around her curiosity from their first moments at Sundance, and how he had avoided her questions ever since. He had known that her initiation to the Center would require some finessing. She now understood how perceptive he had been.

"The question of our significance in the vast trajectory of cosmic evolution is one that reaches beyond the means of any one tribe — of any one language. Yet science is indeed teaching us. The new science tells us that even when we reduce ourselves to mere matter, at rock bottom, among our most fundamental denominators — There are no things — There are only possibilities. Most important, it tells us that even the flapping of the butterfly's wings has effects beyond imagining. One person, one small network of people, can affect the world in ways we cannot at the present time begin to comprehend.

"If we have any doubt that we humans hold in our hands tremendous power, we need only observe our flaming imprint on the planet we inhabit, the only planet we know of that will support human life. We need only see the effect we are having on our atmosphere and our soil and our water, all over the globe. And what is the message that is before us? If we will only see it? The universe is revealing to us the next phase of our conscious evolution — the pathway that is the key to our own preservation. The first step is clear. We must come together. We must recognize that the fate of each of our children is inextricably linked with the fate of all children and with the fate of every one of Earth's creatures."

He focused intently on his audience. "It is not necessary that every person in the world cherishes life. It is only necessary that those who *do* cherish it enough for the whole world."

His gaze continued to sweep the room. "We have it in our power to become one tribe. One human community. A community rooted in our spiritual identity. A community that employs all of our ingenuity and inventiveness to actually care for one another, to provide for the future of our planet, and to teach every one of our children that they possess the power that gave birth to stars. We have it in our power to decide that this is what it means to be human."

Katherine sat motionless throughout his talk and all of the thoughtful dialogue with his audience that followed. So many things were falling into place in her mind, things he had said to their group at Sundance. She now understood the larger context from which they had come, the context that was uniquely Cavanaugh. She could not help asking herself if she had heard these words from any other physicist, would she not completely dismiss him? The same way Albert had been tempted to dismiss him when he first encountered Michael's "inexhaustible optimism," as he called it. And yet Albert had been drawn in too, hadn't he? Drawn in to the extent that he had built this entire Center around this man and his ideas. She remained transfixed as she watched him on the stage. A brilliant scientist whose ideas were antithetical to science. A man who subscribed to no religion and who was perhaps the most religious person she would ever know.

She and Albert sat silently while most of the audience cleared the hall. Then Albert laid his hand on her wrist and they looked at one another. As they walked down to the stage area where Michael was talking with a few remaining audience members, she felt her insides begin to tremble. When he turned and saw them approaching his expression was unmistakable. He was at first completely thrown and then completely thrilled at the sight of her. There were people to speak with and schedules to keep but she could see there were few things on his mind more important than speaking with her. When he asked about her plans for Sunday, she hesitated. She and Albert and Diana had talked about visiting Diana's studio and seeing her work.

"Which we can do tonight after dinner," Albert said eagerly. Michael was exuberant. He looked into Katherine's face with robust determination. "When was the last time you devoted yourself entirely to a day of spontaneous adventure?" he asked her.

"Well, let's see, I can tell you exactly. It was the last time I was in the company of the mad scientists."

Michael's laugh was bright. "Your four musketeers?"

"When she skied for the first time," Albert chimed in.

"Well, that's far too long ago," Michael asserted.

She basked in his familiar penetrating gaze.

Twenty One

"Spontaneous adventure" was exactly what one did with Cavanaugh. Or so Cavanaugh would have one think. He picked her up in the morning at Albert and Diana's declaring how deliberate he had been about making no plans. And from there, their perfect day unfolded just as he had planned. They drove across the Golden Gate Bridge and up into the Marin Headlands where they perched with the birds in the morning sun and viewed San Francisco from across the Bay. It was another gorgeous day. She admired the nation's fairest city, its mauve colored hues against the dark blue sea. She reveled again in the grand seascapes as they drove along the ocean highway toward Stinson Beach. There, they lunched on an outdoor patio at a funky little seaside grill — crab cakes and french fries drenched in sunshine and ocean breezes.

She looked at him across their tiny patio table. "I told Albert it took an auditorium full of people to extract more than a few words from you about what it is that you do."

He grinned. "I just thought you deserved a special introduction. Wish I'd known it was going to be yesterday."

"I see now that what you did say was pretty telling."

"What was that?"

"You said that when you realized what you really needed to do with your life you knew you had to leave academia."

"One of the more understated understatements, huh?"

Katherine commiserated. "Charles says one day we'll have a theory about complex organizations of humans too, especially the institutional variety."

"Yeah, I loved Charles' book," Michael said.

"He says one day we'll have finally identified the law of nature that dictates that inspired creative energy be pummeled into submission by politics and bureaucracy."

Michael chuckled. "It does seem to be a law of nature, doesn't it."

"I thought it was kind of amazing that two cosmologists could spend the time we spent together and not talk at all about our work. I realize now that what we did at Sundance was your work."

He smiled. "Albert did a great job of putting things into perspective, didn't he."

Katherine flicked a piece of her hair that had blown across her face. "So you think science is one seventh of the puzzle?"

"Whatever part, we know it's an important one," he said. "And we know it's in good company."

She squinted into his eyes. "You didn't think I was quite ready for all this, did you? Thought I was too much of a scientist. Or is it too much Midwesterner?"

His gaze slid circularly around her face and hairline. "I don't think you're too much of anything."

She could not resist smiling in response to his expression.

"Albert said you'd explain the name to me," she said.

Michael was amused. "He meant I'd explain why we never gave it a name. In the beginning," he explained, "when we talked about what we'd call the place, we joked about calling it 'The Center of the Universe' — which aside from the play on words was a good-natured jab at anthropocentrism. After a while we were so involved in what we were doing we never got around to the name again. And we'd been calling it 'The Center' so long it just kinda stuck. So one day Diana worked her magic on the stone and we had a little initiation ceremony, and that was it," he shrugged, "The Center."

"I think it's perfect," she said.

He looked at her pointedly. "I'm glad."

"Albert mentioned some of the people who've been here. I'm impressed."

"Some great heads have come through," he said. "And most with very little prodding. The place just has a way of attracting the right mix each time, whatever the project. And the ideas they generate always exceed our original vision. It's just a constant flow of affirmation that the mission's an important one."

"It's so fabulous that Albert makes all this possible."

"Oh, wow, Albert is the Center," he said.

"Funny. He says the same thing about you."

"He's an amazing human being."

"Funny. . . " She emphasized the word again as she grinned at him.

Walking along the beach, Michael talked from his heart about his work and the Center. After a while they found themselves sitting facing the ocean with their bare heels dug into the sand. There he told her about the book he was writing about the "new cosmology," as he called it. He confided to her that telling the truth he felt compelled to tell was one of the most difficult challenges he had ever faced.

"Can I ask you something?" She looked at him thoughtfully. "How is it that you know these things you speak of with such certitude?"

"You mean the things that make most physicists' hair stand on end?" He smiled admiringly as he examined her feet.

"Where does it come from? That intense knowing about things?"

"That can't be proven?" he said. "You know, every single person who's come through the Center is a product of the same system. We've all been taught all our lives, we even judge ourselves, not for how much truth we've seen but for what we can prove. And I'm not just talking about science. It's education generally. We've spent our lives documenting how we know what we know. It wasn't until I stopped and just listened, you know? — to what I knew in my bones. So many great minds have spoken the truth. It's there for the reading. And for the listening. And we all recognize it when we hear it. I've never been happier than I've been since I started just trusting that. If you can learn to stand tall in what you know to be true, you've learned a lot."

"Oh, but you do much more than that. You hurl your truth into the world," she said, underscoring his words from his speech. "That's not an easy thing to do."

"And speaking your truth out loud is one thing, isn't it. Seeing it on a page," he stressed, "for all of your Caltech and Stanford colleagues to see." He shook his head.

Katherine smiled an understanding smile.

"That's when you find out what you're really made of." He picked up a stone and heaved it. "That's what the visit with the Ute leader was really about for me. I mean, I learned a lot about their beliefs. It was one of the more profound experiences I've had with the tribes. But I also had a feeling about that particular trip that it had another purpose. Like whatever he would have to say would be something I needed to hear. I have a priest friend who says the only way God can speak to us is through other people. So when we really need an answer to a prayer, all we have to do is listen. I approached Ah Kah Nooch with every pore open, you know? And sure enough he just blew me away." Michael looked at her with deep humility. "He said he had a dream-vision in which he was told I was coming. I couldn't believe it. I was sitting with him in that sweat lodge — that dark little cell of a space." He shuddered a bit. "I'll tell you, your friend Charles is dead on, the sweats the Indians do on a regular basis — just one of them can fundamentally change a person. The only reason I made it through this one was

that I was completely hypnotized by Ah Kah Nooch's voice. He was drumming and singing — when all I could do was gasp for air, mind you. The sound reverberated right through me. And then suddenly he was speaking in English. He said 'Grandfather.' He calls the Great Spirit 'Grandfather.' He said, 'Grandfather, this man has come to us for a reason. It's about the Earth and all of its creatures.' And then he called on the eagle to give me wisdom. And on the buffalo to give me courage. When he said 'Give him the courage to tell the truth, Grandfather,' well, I just broke down."
Michael's face transformed. For the first time she was seeing the depth of his goodness. "That's what we all need, isn't it." He looked at her. "Just the courage to tell the truth."
Katherine was intent on his expression. "And have you felt like the experience with him made a difference?"
"I only hope I can live up to it," he said.
She smiled at him tenderly. "Well, I for one look forward to reading your book."
"And it'll mean a lot to have you read it," he said. He tossed another stone. "Ah Kah Nooch is sure right about one thing. It won't be for everyone."
"Only for people who are changing the world?" she said.
He turned to her with a look of sheer gratitude, just for the sight of her. He put his arm around her and squeezed.

As they drove again along the panoramic highway toward Muir Woods, Katherine was an unending font of questions about the Center. "So, can you give me an example of something you learned about the Ute beliefs, for instance, that you've examined alongside something from science?"
"Oh, there is so much there. In all the tribes," he said. "For instance, like Bucky Fuller said, the single most important physical fact we've learned so far is that no energy is ever created or lost, that the universe is eternally regenerative. The way my Ute friend

put it — with such serene assurance, he said, 'You know, the Creator never takes anything away that he doesn't replace with something.'" Michael looked at her from behind the wheel. "Their understanding of energy is so fundamental, the tribes. And they're very matter of fact about its source. When I told him about our unified field theory work at the Center he looked at me with those pacific eyes of his. He said, 'You know, if we were ever really able to break it all down we'd be face to face with spirit. He really got a kick out of it when I told him that the Center's collaborators believe that the ultimate theory is in the realm of spirit." He looked at her with the same eyes he had just described in his Ute friend.
"You two had a great connection," she said.
"We really did."
She watched him, with his hands on the wheel, his hair shining in the light from the sunroof, finessing the winding highway as though there were no tomorrow.

He knew exactly where to take her. It was the first time Katherine had seen Muir Woods. For a while she just gaped in silent awe as they walked the path through the majestic redwoods. Then they sat on a bench by a gentle stream in the middle of the historic national park. It was there that she told him about the purpose of her visit and about the extraordinary person and event she had experienced the day before. Michael was astonished to learn that Helen Dalton was Katherine's mother. He knew her well by her reputation and by Albert and Diana's relationship with her. Katherine watched the pristine water go by, amazed at the ease with which her story flowed from her. The story she had shared in her entire life only with Mary Claire. And now for the first time she knew the entire story. And it was a story she could bear to tell. It had found a happy ending, one that was still reverberating inside her. Each time she looked at Michael she was comforted by the intense sensitivity with which he listened.

"I can't explain the feeling. It's as though I've been hit by this enormous force, you know? And yet I'm feeling a wonderful sense of," she thought for a moment, "liberation . . . and peacefulness."

"I can see it," he said, watching her closely.

"You were so tuned into me at Sundance," she said. "I could hardly believe it. You even noticed my neck was bothering me when Franco was talking about his father."

Michael recalled the comment he had made which he now understood more fully.

"Franco wasn't alone with his struggle with religion," he said.

When Katherine looked at him this time she had relinquished all of her defensive cover. "Einstein has always been my protector, you know?"

He smiled at her lovingly. "Now there's a worthy suitor," he said. "At least in the brains department."

"I was thinking about something else Einstein said, listening to your talk yesterday." She observed his eager expression. "Great spirits have always encountered violent opposition from mediocre minds."

Michael was visibly gratified.

"And Einstein had his own ghosts, didn't he. Like all of us," she said.

"What was the line you quoted? – from *Motorcycle Maintenance*."

Michael was pleased she remembered his comment from one of their evening talks at Sundance. "Good ol' Bob Pirsig," he said. "He says 'We're all arrogant and conceited about running down other people's ghosts but just as ignorant, barbaric and superstitious about our own.' "

"It's so true," Katherine said.

Michael looked at her solemnly. "You had some very real ghosts, Katherine."

"Yes," she said. "Just as real as Franco's father's — whatever they are. You see, in my own way I've been disallowing other people's ideas about God just like he has. He, because he deemed them invalid — me, because I deemed them limited. There's no real difference, is there, especially in the way we can hurt people with our dismissal of their beliefs."

"I think it's healthy to reject tightly defined concepts of God," Michael said. "Especially the ones that are wielded with such fierce judgment attached to them."

"But as you said, whatever our God concepts are, humanizing them is the most natural thing in the world. The truth is, my God was just as human as everybody else's." She turned to him. "He was just someone I was ignoring."

"Trust me. The author of *The Relevance of Nature* was doing anything but ignoring God."

"But a truly expansive understanding of God, or of spirit, doesn't disallow anyone else's."

Michael was moved by her realization. He had been deeply affected by her story.

"From what Albert has told me about Helen, I knew she was one of those rare spirits walking about among us. I understand a lot better now. I'm really in awe of that kind of forgiveness and healing, the kind that can bring into being a spirit like hers."

"She said that for years she had unbearable memories of things that had happened, to all of us. And then she started replacing the memories each time with the image of my father in one of his heroic moments. She says we all have them. And then after a while, when she saw how the slightest shift in her own consciousness could make all the difference, she realized it was the same slight chemical fluctuation that distinguished a heroic personality from a troubled one. She says we are all equally susceptible, both to deep anguish and to heroism."

Michael was fixed on her face, trying to absorb what she had been through just the day before. She could feel the deep compassion that was visible in his eyes.

"And what about you?" she asked. "I never asked you about your upbringing for fear you'd ask about mine."

"Oh," he sighed. "I think the only fury in my childhood was in me."

She could not help laughing a little. "How do you mean?"

Michael stared at the stream as he reflected on his early years. "It was the deafening silence, I think, that affected me so much. I think I was even a little desperate to provoke fury, just to interrupt the silence. But nothing could move my parents to express anything, or to feel, it seemed, especially toward one another. I think being around all of that stifled emotion kind of tied me in knots inside. I guess that's why I've spent my whole life kind of unraveling into a wild man."

She took pleasure in his humor about his own intensity. "Well, you've certainly directed your unraveling in remarkable ways," she said.

"I guess on the outside I seemed like a pretty normal kid," he shrugged. "But I know I was filled with a lot of . . ." He was thinking about what word he would use.

"Turmoil?" she asked, remembering Mary Claire's comment.

"I was going to say 'chaos' but turmoil's a good word for it."

She smiled at him tenderly. Then she turned to the stream again and watched the water flowing over the rocks. "I'm kind of sorry I didn't take more advantage of our time at Sundance," she said. "Like Franco did."

"I think we were both holding back an awful lot at Sundance," he said.

She looked at him. He was indeed saying what she thought he was saying. She could see it in his eyes. He took her hand.

As they walked back on the path through Muir Woods and drove again along the winding roads, they talked away the hours as easily as the day flowed into night. And once again, "spontaneously" he claimed, their venue changed to another idyllic scene. The Pelican Inn was a little tavern restaurant embedded in the lush Muir Beach terrain. The thick ocean air was cool and wet as they walked in the moonlit darkness from the car. Michael put his arm around her. "Now, what do you suppose the chances are there'd be a moon like that tonight?" he said.

"Oh, I'm the wrong person to be asking about chances this trip," she said.

They sat at a table close to the fireplace, just as they had during their nights at Sundance. Katherine would later contemplate the perfection in it, the firelight flickering on his face as he bared his soul with the explanation she had longed for. The one she had been denied on their last night in December. When the time came, he drew one of his long familiar breaths and became deeply thoughtful.

"I do think there are some fundamental laws that have at least as much impact on our lives as the physical ones we've identified," he said. "And karma is definitely one of them. It's as inescapable as gravity. People associate it with Eastern ideas. It's actually a universal principle. It's been expressed in so many different ways. 'The love you take is equal to the love you make'— that's the one that hits home for me." He looked into her eyes. "The kind of relationship you represent, Katherine, I wasn't altogether sure I had it coming. And that's only part of the confession. It's true that I never gave my wife what she deserved all those years. God knows it's her absolute generosity that's enabled her to forgive me for that. The truth is that I married in the first place knowing it would be exactly what it was — a good marriage. We had two great kids. Now two incredible adults." He shrugged. "We had a good life. It was comfortable," he said, emphasizing the word. "*I* was comfortable," he added. "But once upon a time I'd have thought *comfort* was just about the worst fate imaginable. Didn't believe I'd ever give up on finding true love, however long it took. And then I fell in love. The kind of love that makes you feel like life has meaning, you know? It was before my marriage," he explained. "Someone that happened to me years earlier."

"Someone that happened to you," she said, appreciating the sentiment.

"I suppose some would say it was just first love, the way it affected me — that that's just the way first love works. But when it fell apart, I think that's when comfort started looking pretty good to me."

"What happened?" Katherine whispered.

"I don't know. Do you know anybody who had a great love that fell apart who can tell you what happened?"

She smiled at him tenderly. "Touché," she said.

He examined her face again. "I wondered when I met you if maybe I was being given a second chance, you know? To believe in it again. The truth is, I decided way back when that there were other things it made more sense to believe in than that kind of love." He let out a sigh of contrition. "That last night at Sundance, standing there with you . . ." He was studying the color of her eyes in the firelight. "It hit me all of a sudden what I knew was true. We can't ever expect to have what we don't believe in. It's one of those basic laws. Things come to us because we believe in them. And since there's nothing harder to believe in than true love — that's how we earn it."

Katherine watched the firelight on his face as she waited to hear what had changed since Sundance. He reached over and held her fingers in his. Then he looked at her with the certainty she had come to know in Cavanaugh. "There's another misconception about karma," he said — "that it's something we're powerless to change. I've come to believe that we're influencing our own karma every minute. And what we don't have coming to us we do have the power to earn." He looked deeply into her eyes. "When I saw you yesterday, God, it was like the answer to my own dream-vision. The moment I saw you, I knew I believed in love again."

Katherine was drinking in his every word, completely captive in his eyes. His hand felt sure and warm holding hers.

"My mother and I talked about it yesterday." She shook her head drowsily. "Or the day before, whenever it was, I don't know anything anymore."

Michael grasped her hand elated at the sight of her.

"She said that people who struggle the most with love are the ones who are the most deeply connected to their own souls. She said that the soul knows that love is its one true purpose." She looked at him as she stressed her mother's next words. "She said all we have to do is believe in it and eventually it will find us."

Michael's smile grew wide.

"She said it may appear in some unexpected form, or after a much longer wait than we expected, but we always know when it's arrived."

He held her hand tightly. "You asked me how I know the things I feel so strongly about. How do we know when we meet someone that they're going to change our life? Not just be another person in our life but fundamentally change it." His eyes blazed. "I just had to meet you. And when I did, I knew I was never going to be the same again."

They remained in the grip of one another's gaze.

As they pulled away from the Pelican Inn that night Michael's smile was the smile of a liberated spirit. "One more spontaneous adventure?" he said, gently drumming the dashboard with his palm. And once again they were on the winding Muir Beach roads that led back to the highway. Katherine felt a deep warm rapture as he caressed her hand in the dark. She looked over at him and confided something she was fully recognizing for the first time. "You know, there've been times when I've wished I had had more courage, writing my book."

"That's what's so amazing about the universe," he said. "When it's got something for us to say, it's going to come through. It's not even necessary that we recognize it ourselves."

"You really believe that what's coming through in all of the books and all of the emerging consciousness — that it's an actual phase in the universe's evolution."

"Absolutely," he said.

She looked out the window ahead. "I have to confess, I don't think I've ever identified so profoundly with the physicist in me as I did yesterday, listening to you talk about love and compassion being the most powerful force in the universe."

He smiled an understanding smile.

"It was just so shocking to hear you speak so publicly in such unquantifiable terms, you know? I found myself frantically reacting. Even imagined myself jumping up and challenging you about all of the other real forces in the universe."

Michael laughed, "That sure would have rocked my boat."

"And then I thought about it," she said as she looked at him again. "I mean, really thought about it, you know?"

Michael was intent, anticipating what she would say.

"I understood what you meant today when you said you have to stop and listen to what you know in your bones."

He watched her as she looked out the front window again and contemplated her thought.

"It occurred to me that human love and compassion is not the most powerful force in the universe. The most powerful force is believing it's the most powerful force."

In another moment she turned and looked at him. The reward he felt in her revelation was written all over his face.

"You made me wish I had the courage to believe," she said. "To believe that we could actually put all of our energy into relieving the suffering in the world . . . and into preserving our resources . . ." She was deeply thoughtful as she looked ahead at the approaching lights from the Golden Gate Bridge.

Michael had heard her every word.

"Chardin believed that at the center of the cosmos is a divine heart filled with love and compassion," he said, "and that it will gradually emerge and spread around the globe. He believed that we will eventually come together as a human family. Saw the greatest hope for it happening in the advancement of women around the world."

"Really?" she said.

"Oh yeah, have I got some books for you. Chardin saw the 'feminine' as the 'true unifying power.' " He glanced at her as he took great pleasure in his next words. "He also said that a woman brings complete self-revelation to the man who loves her." He squeezed her hand tightly. "I guess that's why we avoid intimacy so much, huh?"

She looked at him as he smiled at her brightly and squeezed her hand again.

Back in the city, she observed the rolling landscape now dimly lit by streetlights.

"John F. Kennedy Drive?" she said.

"I'm taking you to my special place."

"Golden Gate Park? — in the dark?"

"You wanted to know if I had any religious rituals."

"In the *park* in the *dark*?" she said.

His eyebrows bounded up and down. He was playing with her.

"You're not going to turn out to be an axe murderer, are you?" she asked.

His silent smirk persisted.

"You told me you breathe," she insisted, "like yoga breathing."

"That's part of it," he said.

Katherine looked out her window. "You said you run here?"

"Most every morning," he said. "If the truth be known, running's probably the only thing I'm really religious about. But this is a nighttime ritual," he added.

"*Cavanaugh!*"

He laughed as he took a curve in the road. "You'll see," he said.

"Moody Blues?" she exclaimed, examining a CD that had fallen to the floor. She recalled the hours in Cambridge many moons ago when she and Mary Claire had listened to the Moody Blues. The second CD she picked up gave her a similar thrill. Mozart's Twenty-Third Piano Concerto was one of her favorite pieces. She realized they had been so immersed in conversation they had not listened to any music. "Moody Blues and Mozart," she said.

"Moody Blues, Mozart and Milo. That's pretty much all a body needs," he said.

"Milo?"

"Milo's my cat. Do you like cats?"

"I do. I mean, not indiscriminately," she said.

Michael started to laugh.

"Well, cats have their own personalities too, don't they?"

"Absolutely!" He was delighted. "I have a Rinpoche friend who says cats are the most evolved of all the animals. They definitely have their own personalities."

"Is this the Rinpoche who said butterflies are not really Earthly creatures?"

"Yep."

She took pleasure in recalling his words — "That they're just 'winged souls passing through' ?"

"From one life to the next," Michael said. "I'll have to get you two together sometime just to talk butterflies."

"And he likes cats too, huh?"

Michael chuckled. "He'd definitely agree that they have their own personalities."

"It's true," Katherine said. "I've met cats I've immediately fallen in love with and others who wouldn't give me the time of day."

He laughed. "I've met a few of those myself. Milo can be a real snob too. He's just very discriminating," he said proudly. "He definitely knows people."

"I've sometimes thought if I were home enough I'd like to have a cat," she said. "I'd like a long-haired white cat, I think."

"And what would you name her?"

"I don't know. Maybe I'd call her 'Finally I'm Home Long Enough to Have a Cat.'"

Michael grinned as he put the car into park. "Milo's gonna love you," he said.

Quickly, he came around to her door. He pulled a jacket from the back seat, wrapped it around her, tucked a blanket under his arm, and then led her by the hand as they ran across the grass and stopped in what seemed to be a meadow.

"Where are we?" she pleaded. "I'm smelling flowers."

"Lots of them! It's the Conservatory of Flowers. Right up there, see?" He pointed up the hill. "There are gardens all around us. Anybody who loves flowers as much as you do should do this to the smell of flowers."

"Do *what?*" she laughed.

"Now," he said, lying on his back on the blanket, "I need you right here beside me."

Katherine lay down beside him. "How did you know I love flowers?" she said.

"You want a garden someday, remember?"

She was touched that he too recalled the details of their Sundance conversation.

"And anybody who'd seen your face when you were describing your mother's garden would want to waste no time getting you some flowers."

"Oh, wow," Katherine sighed, lying on her back and taking in the moonlit sky.

"I ordered it special, just for tonight," he said.

"This is your ritual?" she asked him looking at the moon.

"Oh, we're just getting started," he said. "You warm enough?"

"I'm fine."

"Okay, now the first thing you want to do is forget everything you know about the moon. Forget that it's two hundred and forty thousand miles away. Just trust your senses about where it is in relation to you . . ."

Katherine was aware of little else besides Cavanaugh lying next to her holding her hand.

"Everything you've ever learned about the moon, every theory you've ever let into your brain — just put it out of your mind. Every bit of it. Just concentrate on that amazing globe out there."

Her vision was now filled with the bright white moon and the star speckled sky.

"Now forget everything you know about gravity. Just feel the earth below you, holding you close. Just think, if the earth weren't holding us tight we'd be wandering off into space — just floating around like this globe we're resting on. And like the one out there that's hovering in the same space."

It was not long before she was feeling the very sensation he had described. They were indeed being held by the earth which was a spherical globe hovering in space, just like the moon before them which was now growing brighter.

"Just look at that amazing orb," he said fervently. "Imagine. It's influence on the tides may have been the single force responsible for bringing those first creatures out of the sea and starting this whole procession of life around us."

Katherine had never been more captivated by the lunar spell than she was in this moment. She could hear in Michael's voice that he was feeling the same thing. In another moment she began to notice the light from the moon radiating in distinct pulsations.

"Now if you keep your eyes directly on it," he said, "it'll take a little while, you'll see a white beam of light aiming directly for you."

In another minute she whispered, "Yes."

"Now, stay with the beam," he said. "Really concentrate on it."

She focused intently. She could feel the gravitational pull that was manifest in the light beaming toward her.

"Do you feel it?" he said.

She let out a sigh of amazement.

"Now breathe," Michael said.

Katherine drew in a deep breath.

Michael did the same and then he exhaled slowly.

"In the Upanishads," he said, "the 'prana,' the breath of life, is the thread that ties us to the entire universe."

"My yoga teacher says that's why she's always encouraging us to breathe," she said.

"You lie here long enough you'll know how true it is," he said. "When you breathe along with the moon, after a while you can feel it moving your breath, just like the tide. You can actually feel yourself breathing with the pulse of the universe."

Katherine was already experiencing the cadence he spoke of. She could feel her breath becoming synchronized to the pulsations of light that were emanating from the moon. "It's amazing," she said.

"When you asked me if I believed in any kind of religious ritual," he said, "I wanted to tell you how much I believe in prayer. But I wanted you to know what I meant."

"This is your prayer?" she asked him.

He lay there pondering. "I don't believe it matters one iota what

religion we are," he said. "What matters is that we believe in whatever it is that inspires us, in our highest and in our darkest moments, to pray. It's the one force in the world more powerful than love. Maybe it's the highest form of love. It's the only way we humans can consciously participate in the flow of divine energy that's constantly moving everything forward — this whole grand mess of life that's slowly, gradually righting itself. I always feel like I can do that best when I'm right here with just God and the moon."
Katherine lay silently absorbing the moment.
"And do you believe God responds to our prayers?" she asked.
"Absolutely," he said. "That's one of those things we just know."
"In our bones?" she whispered.
He rolled onto his side and propped himself on his elbow facing her. "God's responding right now," he said. Then he impishly lifted his ear toward the sky. "Don't you hear that voice?" he asked her. She laughed a little. Then in an exaggerated whisper he called out to the night, "Katherine! What on earth are you doing with that crazy Cavanaugh?"
Katherine's smile was radiant. "Well," she responded, still staring at the sky, "I believe Mister Cavanaugh is moving me along on a brand new path," she said. Then she turned her face toward him and fell into his eyes. And in one fluid movement his hand slid across her waist and his face moved steadily toward hers. The moonlight flickered as she closed her eyes. When his lips touched hers it was as though their mouths had known one another always, as though they would never be apart again. Lying there in the moonlit grass in Cavanaugh's arms, for the first time in her life she felt she was home.

Twenty Two

The weeks surrounding spring graduation were always a time of reflection for Katherine. The sense of passage was especially pronounced this year. It was as though she were part of some momentous shift, as though a kaleidoscope that had not been touched in years was in the hands of a child again. Inside were all the aspects of her life, rearranging themselves in a brand new scheme.

On the departmental front there had been one enormous blow from which she was still recovering. To no one's surprise the executive committee had decided against the department's continued involvement in the Initiative for Undergraduate Education. They had voted four-to-three to accept the new curriculum committee's recommendation "as written." It read like a declaration of support for the Initiative, emphasizing the department's continuing commitment to the enrichment of undergraduate education and citing its fundamental physics courses and innovative seminars. The justification for discouraging further involvement in the Initiative was couched in terms like "departmental needs" and "curricular priorities." Between the lines it was clearly stated that no physics faculty would be involved in any way in ridiculous puffery like this butterfly nonsense. The loss of her class was a difficult disappointment but it was easier to bear in light of all the extraordinary developments in her life and at the university.

The Initiative for Undergraduate Education was itself moving forward with the president of the university as its most vocal advocate. Delcourt's endorsement along with the response from students and from parents was making it impossible to deny the program a place in the larger curriculum. Mary Claire was now being consulted by other institutions, and favorable press was seeping into even the most conservative publications. Though there remained many hurdles ahead, the momentum was undeniable. The most powerful testimony was the jubilant bravado with which Mary Claire regularly spouted her favorite Robert Browning line —"God's in his Heaven – All's right with the world!"

Browning's sentiment was in fact an apt description of the general climate around campus. Charlotte Newberg, the director of the Humanities Institute, had been named the new dean of the College of Literature, Science and the Arts. Her appointment was part of a well-received new trend on campus, the increasing selection of some of Michigan's own for open deanships. Throughout the university there was a forward dynamism that was almost palpable. And to follow any one of its undulating waves to its source would have led one all the way to the top. As Mary Claire put it, Jonathan Delcourt was "the real article." He was an academician who had risen to the highest ranks without ever losing the spirit of a hands-on educator.

Katherine found it remarkable that her intimate friendships made her privy to such an inside perspective on the new president of the university. She had had little contact with previous administrations. She marveled at the current situation. She was the only one of Charles' colleagues who was aware of the extent to which he was in dialogue with Delcourt about the complexity program. And Charles and Delcourt were also having conversations with Albert Finn, and she knew well what promise there was in a relationship with the Finn Foundation. She was the only one who knew about the overture that had been made to Mary Claire about the LS&A deanship. After seeing Mary Claire in action with her exhaustive Undergraduate Initiative efforts, Delcourt and the provost had identified her as the best person for the job. Though Mary Claire had been deeply gratified by the acknowledgement, a deanship was not something she could ever consider. "I am a teacher," she had said to them, "That's who I am." Delcourt was not surprised. He and the provost had then made it clear that they placed the highest value on her recommendation. Mary Claire had not let on to anyone but Katherine the full depth of the pride she took in Charlotte Newberg's appointment to the post.

Though Mary Claire was confiding in Katherine about the extent to which Delcourt was involved in future plans for the Initiative, she had not shared her own secret hope that he would eventually weigh-in even on the physics department's decision to not participate. No one was more disappointed about the loss of Katherine's butterfly class than Mary Claire. And Mary Claire now had the ear of the president.

There was another momentous development in Katherine's life and in the life of the university that again afforded privileged insight to the president's character. David Maize was leaving the university. He would be spending the summer in Alaska with a group promoting local awareness of global issues surrounding the Arctic National Wildlife Refuge. From there he would be off to New York to his new studio in the Village. Life was indeed shifting to a brand new scheme. David had been with the art department for decades. The announcement of his departure had prompted Delcourt to ask him for a personal meeting. David had confided in Katherine about their evening together at the President's House and the visit he characterized as an "authentic connection." What surprised David most was the president's interest in what David had to tell him about the university. Delcourt had told him that he had been struck by something Doris Lessing had said, that it was the great misfortune of institutional leaders that they never made a point of consulting some of the most important people in the life of their institutions — the people who leave. Their intimate evening together had lasted until the early morning hours.

Of all the extraordinary events surrounding this new leader there was one from which Katherine was still reeling. Delcourt had asked her to give the commencement address at the LS&A graduation ceremonies. To an outside observer, of course, this would not have seemed an earth-shattering event. Katherine had been recognized by students for years as an outstanding teacher. Within the university power structure however this was a development of staggering significance. No faculty member had ever given the commencement address at Michigan. This was an honor bestowed upon famous alumni and international figures. Moreover, the selection process was considered sacrosanct — an elaborate, multi-layered committee process that deliberately engaged representation from all levels of the system. What had happened with this year's speaker was some kind of snafu that had come to light uncomfortably close to commencement. The selection committee had asked the president if in the interest of time he should not extend a personal invitation to one of the other candidates. It was Delcourt's decision to forego the other proposed candidates and to extend the invitation to one of the "extraordinary people who define the university today." When he phoned Katherine at her home one evening and asked her to give the address, he did so on one condition — that she understand she was not his second choice.

Once again Delcourt was creating tremors that were being felt on campus for the first time. And this time Katherine would have some hand in how his unprecedented decision was perceived.

She received a number of calls, from *The Ann Arbor News*, *The Michigan Daily* and several campus groups — How did she feel about the president's invitation? About the break with tradition? About being singled out among her colleagues? Of all the ways to incite the ever-present undercurrent in an academic environment, honoring a single faculty member was the ultimate lightning rod. Surprisingly, the feeling around campus was remarkably positive. *The Michigan Daily*, the student-run newspaper, generally the first to bring the undercurrent to the surface, instead went on record as favoring the president's decision. Katherine was delighted by the statement of hers that they chose to prominently display in their article: "I have learned a great deal from my students."

Inside the walls of the physics department the climate was different. Where Charles was thrilled almost speechless, Lloyd was simply speechless. He feigned no awareness of the situation whatsoever. Katherine knew he was incensed. And she knew he was not alone. At the executive committee meeting the week of the announcement the chill in the room was reminiscent of their now infamous butterfly debates. She could not have chosen a worse time to be proposing another "extra-curricular" item for the group's endorsement. She cringed when she saw it on the agenda in front of her. She and Charles were proffering a petition to the U.S. Administration, one that had been developed in concert with a number of peer institutions and national science organizations. The subject was global climate change. From the moment they entered the room, she knew what was coming. And she had a pretty good idea from whom it would come.

"Katherine, sometimes I think your fervor about the environment is second only to those students out on the Diag."

Coming from Lloyd, this was not a compliment. He had remarked at a previous meeting that he had just come across the Diag through another rally for "the latest fashionable cause." Another time he had groused about how tired he was of all the "ranting" about the environment.

"Didn't we go through this whole discussion with the Test Ban Treaty petition?" Nick Tullman asked as he looked at the document in front of him.

"Yes, but just because Washington ignores our concerns," Bob Gurzick said, "doesn't mean we shouldn't keep voicing them."

"I think Nick is referring to the fact that some of us believe petitions are not our business," Lloyd said dryly.

"I have some concerns about the science on this issue," Harold asserted. "As long as there's not a clear consensus, I don't think the department's name should be involved. I'm certainly not comfortable with it."

"What this petition is about, Harold," Bob Gurzick explained, "is making very public just exactly what the consensus is."

On environmental issues the group in the room was always divided. Katherine, Charles, and Bob Gurzick felt a responsibility to participate in the national dialogue as this was an issue for which physicists were among the minority conversant in the science. The rest of the group around table had no interest in environmental issues and regularly ignored circulated studies, even those generated by their own colleagues.

"And I return to my earlier statement," Lloyd remonstrated. "This is not the role of a physics department. We're not lobbyists."

Charles spoke up. "Lloyd, as a general rule, I agree with you. I think you'll recall, this has been my position even on nuclear issues. As strongly as I felt about the Test Ban Treaty, it was I who proposed we speak as individual scientists and not as a department. On this particular petition, however, I think it's critical that we step forward as an institution right along with our peer institutions."

His colleagues were taken aback. Charles had always been extremely protective of the university as a research institution. He believed that the special role universities play in society should be jealously guarded, that universities should be devoted to keeping inquiry alive and not be engaged as instruments of social change.

"First of all," Charles explained, "I think the environment has been sorely miscast as a controversial issue — and even worse, a political one. I personally find it incomprehensible that the two opposing forces could possibly be perceived as equivalents. As though profit-driven interests and environmental advocacy organizations — organizations that are about protecting our very sources of life" he stressed — "are at all the same species of *'special interests.'* " He looked around at his colleagues. "I know I am not alone in my knowledge of cases where the science has been tainted by the politics involved. Which is another reason why I think it's important for us to step forward — the entire scientific community. What we're asking for in this petition is for all of the science to be put on the table and examined openly by every reputable scientist who's spent their career studying the atmosphere. To have the entire situation, including proposed solutions, openly and aggressively debated, both for public information and for the development of a national policy." Charles looked at his colleague. "The bottom line here for me, Lloyd, is that this is all our responsibility. Both to see that it happens and to be up to speed on the science so we can participate in the discussion."

"I'm in agreement on this one too," Bob Gurzick said. "I think it does warrant our getting behind it as an institution. This national forum idea is long overdue. The international conferences have been unsuccessful because the real bottleneck is right here in the States. I think the most valuable thing that could come from it is that the American public would finally have a good hard look at the science — and with the politicians and the special interests out of the way."

Katherine could not hold back. "With regard to the students, Lloyd,

I'll be the first to admit that for some of them the environment is just another fiery cause, as you say. But many of these students *have* read the science. They're knowledgeable enough to understand that we really are talking about the future of the planet. Something that deserves every bit of passion we can all muster."

"And I think Charles is right, Lloyd," Bob Gurzick said. "I think this part of it is our responsibility."

Charles and Katherine had learned to recognize when enough had been said to the group on the other side of the table. They also knew that with or without the committee's endorsement the petition they had put forward would be going to Washington and with an unprecedented number of signatures from scientists from all over the country, including the majority of U-M's scientists. As Katherine observed Lloyd she realized that his temperament today was one she could take as personally as she had ever done before. This was not about the environment, or their appeal, or anything that would be openly discussed. This was about the president's invitation to her to speak at commencement.

The day of graduation was a day of flowers. There were red tulips from Mary Claire, bright yellow daffodils from Charles and Debra, and a large bouquet of wildflowers from David. The three bouquets sat together on her dining room table where she spent most of her morning reviewing her speech. Next to them was the pile of Teilhard de Chardin books she had been devouring since her time in California. She sat for a moment and stared at them as she recalled Mary Claire's saying, "It would be nice if your California people could be here." They were indeed, she thought. Their presence was profoundly felt. They had been with her all the while she prepared her speech and they would be with her when she delivered it.

The weather was just pleasant enough for ceremonies to

proceed in their traditional setting, outdoors in the Michigan Stadium. The one time Katherine was inside the football stadium the arena was completely transformed. Thousands of chairs had been placed on the field for the graduates and a large stage had been erected in front of them. All around the stadium the seats were filling up with guests.

A steady stream of dignitaries, colleagues and students greeted her near the stage. Among them was a special group of graduates who were eager to speak with her — Robert, Cynthia, Marisa and Tim, the four seniors from her butterfly class. The fact that they had come to commencement together was in itself immensely gratifying. The pride in their faces stirred her. She was not surprised to learn that Sir Robert would be returning to Michigan in the fall for graduate work with the School of Natural Resources. Cynthia Bruhn was off to New Haven where she would pursue a Yale Law degree. And Marisa Field was looking forward to the summer and then her graduate studies at Georgetown. The surprise news came from Tim. Tim McFadden had been on his way to becoming a third-generation Michigan dentist. He had said that from the time he was a boy he had never considered any other career. Yet the wheels were already in motion to change course toward his newfound passions. He would be working with a graduate studies committee on a degree combining psychology and philosophy. Katherine was thrilled to see each of them. The connection she felt with her butterfly students would be one of the most personal rewards of the day. They too had been in her mind as she prepared her speech.

When President Delcourt greeted her near the stage he was visibly buoyed by the festive mood. He smiled at her playfully. "I understand the real momentous first here is not that one of our own is giving the address but that we have you inside the stadium." Katherine smiled. "I'm embarrassed to tell you I just learned from

Charles that it's the largest in the country. I didn't know that."

"And for football games every one of those seats is filled," he said.

"It's quite an atmosphere."

It was difficult to imagine a more celebratory atmosphere than the one she had been asked to be part of on this day. The honor Delcourt had bestowed on her was immense, as was the task. "Thank you," she said to him as they held one another's hands in a heartfelt handshake.

The enormous audience began to still as the president approached the podium. From Katherine's seat on the platform she looked out into the sea of graduates and drew a deep breath. She marveled at the absolute whirl of it all. The events of this last year had turned her life upside down and around, and the exhilarating ride was not yet over. This is the way it happens, she thought. Without warning, change comes toppling down on us, rearranging us from the inside out, transforming us for the next stage of life — just like the butterfly.

There was a surreal quality to sitting there on the platform feeling the presence of the thousands in the stadium. As she watched Delcourt standing at the podium, it came to her that he too was one of the remarkable individuals who had entered her life during this amazing time. She thought about the people who were now in her life, the people who were her life. Michael's words resonated in her mind — "We're all finding one another. We're connecting with people who speak the same language, who know that it's time to decide what it is that we really value."

She listened to every word of Delcourt's opening remarks at the same time she was carrying on her own internal dialogue, preparing herself for what was to come.

". . . When I thought about how I would introduce Katherine Ayers today," he said, "it was important to me to say something about Professor Ayers as a teacher. It also seemed appropriate to consult someone I happen to know is one of her heroes. Albert Einstein, in addition to being a brilliant physicist, possessed a keen insight to a great many things. I was not surprised to find in his essays the precise sentiment I was looking for. Einstein said — 'Knowledge is dead. The school, however, is for the living.'

"Great thinkers have continually reminded us that real education is much more than an accumulation of knowledge. It is more than the generation of new knowledge. A real education is a living thing. At its best, it is a process that continues throughout our lives. Einstein's assertion is one we all understand. And yet, at every level of education, we have yet to reconcile this awareness with the standardized measures of accumulated knowledge to which we hold fast. And year after year, as young people reflect the evolving nature of our society and the same measurable results become more difficult to achieve, we are perplexed about solutions. Some propose that the answer is to ensure that our teachers possess the highest level of appropriate knowledge. Others suggest we test more rigorously and identify where students are failing to accumulate knowledge. And there are some who believe that the answers lie in more fundamental questions than those we are accustomed to asking — Are we providing an experience that is worthy of the energy we all bring to the process of learning? Are we helping young people to discover who they are and what it is that they value? Are we inspiring young people to learn? There are teachers who are asking these questions. And the rest of us need to pay attention. Because these educators represent real solutions for education. They represent the living process of learning.

"The University of Michigan has a long history of commitment to educational excellence. It is a commitment that reaches beyond high academic standards. And when our nation is in debate about the critical challenges facing education, we do not stand above that debate. We stand instead at the center. We speak not just to educational standards but also to educational values. The educational value I would most like to exhibit as an American institution of higher learning is the high value we place on great teachers."

As the students applauded and Katherine watched Delcourt standing at the podium, she was reminded again of the first word she drew from the pile at Sundance. "Leadership" was indeed a concept worthy of all the analysis it was being given at this critical time, she thought — for our nation, for education, for so many important global issues. She recalled her Sundance group's discussions about what it is that distinguishes a true leader. Watching Delcourt, it occurred to her suddenly that we all recognize a true leader when we see one. He is the person with whom, when he speaks about what he believes in, we find ourselves filled with pride at the thought of standing with him.

She was heartened by Delcourt's sincere acknowledgment of the faculty of the university, his fearless affirmation of the Initiative for Undergraduate Education, and the generous eloquence with which he introduced her. When she stood at the podium and sensed the enormity of the crowd, a surge of emotion welled up inside her. She held the edges of the podium in her hands and smiled at the audience. Then she drew a deep breath.

"President Delcourt, honored guests, fellow faculty, and especially members of the first graduating class of the new millennium."

The students cheered.

She looked at the written speech in front of her, the formal text LS&A had requested for publication. She had intended to deliver it verbatim but found she could not begin without expressing her response to the president's remarks.

"President Delcourt is right. Einstein has indeed been one of the heroes in my life. But as Einstein would remind us, all evolutionary phenomena are processes. The universe, humanity, education, human beings — each and every one of us — is a *process*. And part of the living nature of true learning is being open to new heroes in our lives.

"As I was thinking about what I wanted to say to you today it was another powerful thinker who came to mind. A man who was both an eminent scientist and a devout man of faith, Teilhard de Chardin. Like all heroes of human thought, Chardin was overcome all his life by a passionate desire to understand the world we live in. He also believed that our understanding of the world would one day include an understanding of humanity, an understanding of our true significance in the life of the universe. As I was contemplating your significance in the life of the universe, you who will soon be engaged in all kinds of endeavors that are shaping the world we live in, I could not imagine a more appropriate thought to share with you today than one of Teilhard de Chardin's.

"He said that we humans are not the center of the universe, we are actually something much more wonderful. We are the 'arrow pointing the way to the final unification of the world.' . . . It is difficult to imagine that Chardin, in the early part of the twentieth century, could have foreseen the special significance the word 'arrow' would assume during this past decade. Surely he never imagined the actual arrow that would be so much a part of our daily lives. An arrow we would see on a screen in front of us that we would move and direct and that would increasingly take us anywhere we wish to go in our pursuit of knowledge and information. And when he spoke of a 'unification of the world,' could he possibly have foreseen that by the end of his century we would all have a sense of our world as coalescing into a single global network?" She scanned the sea of caps and gowns. "A network that was unimaginable to generations before you. An increasingly global connectedness — in communication, in economics, in science, in medicine, in every area of our lives — that is dramatically changing our lives.

"What I would hope to impress upon you today is that this global web of connectivity is as yet far from global. It is far from inclusive, even here in the United States. More important, it is in and of itself devoid of meaning and value. It is a framework. A beginning. And you are the generation that will decide the meaning and the value this network will assume. It is you who will create the language and design the program for this emerging world connectivity. You have in your hands tremendous power. Power to create the culture in which this network will flourish. Power to affect the world in which you and your children will live.

"And in order to inspire your thinking, I ask you to imagine a 'unification of the world' that reaches beyond the technological connection of human beings around the globe. I ask you to imagine a world united in spirit. A world where all human beings look upon one another not as members of a particular race or religion or society or culture but as fellow inhabitants of the planet Earth. A world where all children learn above all to honor the dignity of every living creature, and to do everything in their power to ensure that the Earth and all of its creatures survive and flourish.

"I ask you to imagine that such priorities are not only possible but that future generations might find it incomprehensible that there once was an age when such priorities were associated with a particular ideology or spiritual belief, when they were not fundamental to all human beings.

"What I propose to you today, on behalf of Teilhard de Chardin, is that for one person to hold such a vision for the future of our world is more powerful than we can at the present time comprehend — and that the significance of each and every one of us in the life of the universe is as great as we *believe* it to be. I would also remind you that every single discovery, every cultural shift, every advance of civilization, began with what one person believed.

"How does one enter today's world of work, live in today's

society, and hold such a vision for the future of our world? I can only offer these few words of advice:

"Choose every experience in your life based on the people with whom you will be thrown into contact — and you will live a rich life. Because ultimately we judge the value of each of our experiences by the relationships those experiences brought into our lives.

"Whatever you decide to do with your lives, do it believing that the difference you will make in the world will truly make a difference — even if it is one you will see only in the faces of your children."

"Above all, trust what you believe and pursue what you love with the same devotion with which the stars burn in the night sky. For when we do this we are guided by a force far greater than ourselves.

She paused.

"President Delcourt has reminded me of another message that is important to share with you today." She looked out at the graduates. "Always be open to new heroes. Allow your heroes to be human. And never doubt the heroism in *humanness*. Remember that in the end our most treasured heroes will be ones we met in our kitchens and in our places of work and in the chance encounters of our chosen lives.

"And please, every time you see an arrow — whether it is the arrow on a computer screen you see in front of you every day, or any of the others you encounter on your chosen journeys — every time you see an arrow, just for a moment, remind yourself that you are the arrow pointing the way.

"I wish you Godspeed."

Twenty Three

"Hey, Katherine! How's this weather!"

"Larry! Haven't seen you in a while."

Katherine and Larry Lowenstein stopped on the Diag in the center of campus where students rambled in all directions. The freshly manicured grounds all around them were the venue for first-week classes that could not possibly have been contained indoors. There had been groups of students huddled with their professors on the lawn all morning. It was a day for savoring every moment with the uniquely September perspective that all good things must pass.

Larry's wild hair and carefree expression made her smile.

"What's going on over there in Randall?" he said. "You guys gonna get away with makin' sense outta things?"

"What do you mean?" she laughed.

"I'm not just decoration anymore!" he declared.

"Larry, you will always be decoration," she said.

"I'm gonna be doing some things out at the Finn building too. Pretty exciting stuff."

The major shift to which Larry referred was the impact Bob Gurzick was having as the new head of the physics department. The newly elected executive committee was making significant changes. Among them was the fact that Larry Lowenstein, the philosophy professor who had been called upon for years for committee duties for physics theses, no longer participated not understanding a single word. Doctoral candidates would now be discussing with Larry how their theses fit into the larger scheme of the history of thought.

The Herbert B. Finn Memorial Building, to which he referred, was the new facility going up on north campus, soon to be home to several innovative organizations including the "U-M Institute for the Study of Complexity." Delcourt had not only established the Institute as an autonomous interdisciplinary program with Charles as its director, with Albert Finn's assistance he was also providing the organization with a space of its own. The Institute had just announced the coming year's schedule of seminars that would bring together leading thinkers in a wide variety of disciplines. Charles was busy building alliances with complexity theorists all over the world.

Katherine and Larry remained intent on their destinations which were in opposite directions. "Tell Bob not to get too carried away!" he hollered to her. "Gotta have a few things left that make no sense at all!" He lifted up his arms with decided glee as he displayed his short sleeves. "Isn't this great!"

"September is the best," she called after him.

"See you at Mary Claire's!" he said.

There was much more than the weather at play in Katherine's lightness of heart. Larry's depiction was an excellent one — 'makin' sense outta things.' There were so many things in her life and in the life of the university that were evoking the same feeling in her.

Charles and Debra, Katherine and Mary Claire could not have chosen a better day for their time-honored tradition. For years they had stolen away during the first week of September classes for a picnic lunch in the Arboretum. The four of them sat with their lemonades and Mary Claire's chicken salad sandwiches on a hillside overlooking a meadow in the center of the Arb.

Mary Claire was intent on the scene before her. "It really is quite a place, isn't it."

Charles agreed. "We were here on Sunday with Avery." He perked up as he thought about the Avery story he was eager to share with the group. "What was it he said?" he asked Debra.

Debra recalled their five-year-old's words verbatim. "Do you think we're walking on God's brain?"

Charles let out a chortle chock-full of affection for his son. "We're just walking along, not thinking about much of anything . . ."

"And he asks if you're walking on God's brain?" Katherine marveled. "You do realize this child has a more profound sense of inquiry than most of the planet, right?"

Charles was still chuckling. "It took me a minute but then I looked around at what he was looking at and, you know, it made sense."

Mary Claire agreed as she took in the scene before her. "It's definitely good for the soul."

"Time to get into gear with him on the God and religion thing," Charles said.

"Just keep him away from the guy down at the river," Mary Claire exclaimed as she glanced at Katherine.

Katherine thought about the river man and his rock formation. "Oh, I don't know, I think he's a good one to expose him to — for just long enough to see his heart and hear about its message."

"Love and compassion, right?" Mary Claire asked.

"Love and compassion," Katherine said.

"You dig any deeper than that you get a little more than you bargained for, eh?" Charles lounged back on his elbows in the grass.

"So, what *are* you gonna tell Avery?" Mary Claire asked.

"We've actually been thinking about this for a while," Charles said. "Kind of looking forward to exploring right along with him."

"We thought we'd give him a lot of ideas to just explore for a while first," Debra said.

"She's got it all planned," Charles followed.

"We thought we'd start with the poets first," Debra said. "It'd be fun to get back into the poets with him. Wordsworth, Emerson, Rumi . . . Eventually we'll take him through all of the major religions. And all of the Eastern mysticism . . ."

Charles sniggered, "Save Einstein and company for a little later in the process."

"Then someday if he wants to make a choice," Debra said, "he'll have a real treasure trove to choose from."

"I know the Wordsworth you're thinking of," Mary Claire said, "from Tintern Abbey, right?"

"Isn't that a beautiful piece," Debra concurred.

Mary Claire looked up at the sky as she recited a passage with deep feeling:

". . . And I have felt
A presence that disturbs me with the joy
Of elevated thoughts; A sense sublime
Of something far more deeply interfused,
Whose dwelling is the light of setting suns,
And the round ocean, and the living air,
And the blue sky, and in the mind of man,
A motion and a spirit that impels
All thinking things, all objects of all thought,
And rolls through all things . . ."

"It's like music, isn't it," Katherine said.

"And what a great way to pull a child into 'the joy of elevated thoughts,' " Mary Claire said.

"So you'll do the poets first," Katherine said. "And then world religions and the mystics. And then 'work up to Einstein and company'." She looked at Charles as she repeated his phrase. "What a great way to put it."

"The great thinkers," Debra explained, "and the more abstract conceptions of God."

"Yeah, he'll be the youngest kid ever started on William James," Charles laughed as he patted his wife's thigh.

"Definitely his essay on Fechner," Debra said.

"Who's Fechner?" Mary Claire asked.

"Gustav Fechner was one of those geniuses like James who can only be described using all of the p's," Debra said — "philosopher, physicist, psychologist. The way James talks about him you'd want to learn German just to read him in his native language."

"This is stuff for Avery?" Katherine asked.

"Oh, it's great stuff for Avery," Debra said. "I get to tell a kid who asks if we're walking on God's brain that there was a very smart man, one of the first 'skologists,' as he calls them, who said that the whole earth and everything on it is one big mind."

"Fechner said that?" Katherine asked.

"He said that each one of us is a sense-organ of the earth's soul and that over time the earth absorbs all of the perceptions of human beings all over the world and the big mind grows." Debra's eyebrows bounded up and down.

Charles had lain back in the grass and was opening one eye to Mary Claire. "He says we only think the human brain is the most complex system there is, that someday we'll have figured out that our brains are all just little parts of a single mind."

"I thought you fell asleep before that part," Debra said to her husband.

"Me? Never."

"You two still read aloud to one another?" Mary Claire asked.

"Every night," Charles said contentedly.

"I read. He falls asleep," Debra said.

"Next thing we know," Charles snickered again, "Avery'll be praying to the Earth."

Katherine looked over at him "And how would you feel about that?" she asked him.

"Great," Charles said. "Prayer never hurt anybody."

No sooner had Charles uttered these words than he heard them in light of what he and Debra had recently learned about Katherine's history. He immediately looked over at her, conveying his sensitivity.

"No, I think you're right," she assured him. "Real prayer has never hurt anyone. And I imagine wherever it's directed it finds its way to the right place."

Mary Claire was lounging contentedly, fixed on the scene before her. "I actually think there's something to the idea that when you pray you put good energy into the atmosphere. I mean the kind of prayer Emerson talked about — 'the soliloquy of a beholding and jubilant soul.' "

Katherine smiled at Charles as they both noted the use of the term "energy." "Yes," she said, "I think that kind of prayer probably does put good energy into the atmosphere."

"I just want Avery to decide for himself," Debra said. "He's going to anyway. I think our job is to just keep feeding his incessant hunger."

"He always wants to know what all of his options are," Charles said proudly.

Debra smiled at Katherine. "We'll definitely be turning him onto some Teilhard de Chardin."

Charles perked up. "I'm still trying to figure out what's more amazing — that Professor Ayers actually quoted a priest at commencement, or that she skied."

He sheepishly waited, confident he had struck a chord with

everyone in the group. And then he chuckled at the emphatic sounds that came from his three cohorts.

Then Mary Claire spoke up. "Well, you know, we didn't actually see her ski," she said. "This may be pure fiction."

Katherine socked her leg.

"But then Chardin wasn't your everyday priest, was he?" Charles said in a more serious tone.

Katherine was emphatic. "No, he wasn't your everyday anybody."

"He'd be a great guy to have at the Institute," Charles said.

"And what do you think he'd say about complexity, Charles?" Mary Claire asked.

Charles reflected, "Well, he just saw the whole progression of complexification as an overall tendency toward that ultimate consciousness Fechner and so many others have talked about. He saw the universe as complexifying — from those first cosmic particles, to multi-cellular life, to civilized societies, and finally, to the integration of humanity with itself and with nature."

"He said all we had to do was increase our knowledge and our love," Debra said.

"Now there's a nice thought to share with Avery," Mary Claire said.

Katherine looked over at Charles again thoughtfully and asked, "And what will you tell him Einstein thought?"

"Yes, what *do* you think Einstein believed?" Mary Claire asked. "There are such conflicting opinions on that."

Charles was still lying in the grass and spoke up without moving an eye muscle as he invoked Einstein. "He believed a truly religious person is someone who has no doubt of the significance of things that neither require nor are capable of rational foundation, yet accepts that they exist with the same matter of factness as he himself exists. "

Katherine listened to Einstein with her arms wrapped around her knees, intent on the scene before her. After a moment she processed her thoughts out loud. "I wouldn't be surprised if Einstein had a real private change of heart at some time in his life — about God. And then it dawned on him that it didn't make a particle of difference, really, what his concept of God was. He realized that however his own ideas had changed, God never did . . . I think that's what made him a private and really quite reverent believer."

The group sat silently for a moment. Then Mary Claire piped up. "Avery's so far ahead of the rest of us he'll probably chomp right through all of the genius in the world and then land on something real simple like 'God is love and versa visa.' Who was it that said that anyway?"

A warm glow came over Katherine. "Pretty much sums it up, doesn't it."

Charles stirred in response to the expression on Katherine's face. "Speaking of fiction," he said. "You know, none of us has actually eyeballed this California cosmologist either."

"Yeah," Debra said. "Are you guys gonna carry on this entire love affair on the other side of the country?"

Katherine grinned at Mary Claire. "The wacky California cosmologist?" Her face glowed as she spoke of Cavanaugh. "He'd tell you the love affair is with his cat," she said. "Milo and I are pretty crazy about each other." Her smile became mischievous as she looked at Charles. "And actually, you are gonna get an eyeball full."

Mary Claire jumped in. "You think it's something that she skied — wait 'til you hear this one." She waited until Charles' and Debra's interest was sufficiently aroused and then she spouted, "She's actually going to a football game!"

"He's coming to Ann Arbor!" Debra cheered.

Katherine blushed. "The weekend of Mary Claire's party."

"I never thought I'd be grateful for Wolverine's disease," Mary Claire remarked.

"I actually think he's most interested in introducing me to the marching band," Katherine said.

"Look at her," Charles teased. "She's grinning like a school girl."

"So he's a marching band kinda guy, huh?" Debra asked.

"Mozart, Moody Blues and marching bands," Katherine said playfully.

"Well, Whaddaya know." Charles was delighted. "He's actually getting you to a game."

"It's about time he came," Debra groused. "He had you in California all summer."

"He's looking forward to the break," Katherine said. "He's finally nearing the end of his book." Her smile brightened. "Says Ann Arbor will be good for him."

Charles looked at her thoughtfully. "I look forward to reading his book," he said.

"Me too," she whispered.

In the midst of the momentary lull in conversation Katherine looked at Mary Claire with a nudge in her eyes. Mary Claire hesitated only a moment. "Charles and Debra, I have something to tell you too," she announced. "She drew in another dose of Katherine's bolstering smile. "I'm going to be adopting a child. I've started the process." She took another breath and then intuitively groped toward Debra for her response.

Debra immediately met her gaze with a determined smile. "I can't imagine a better mother," she said.

Mary Claire reached over and squeezed her hand. "I was hoping so much you would say that. I'd sure like to have the support of my friends."

"You've got it," Charles said.

Katherine's feelings now came bounding out. "Won't she just be the greatest mother?" she said.

Mary Claire was now breathing easily. "Yeah, well, I'm sure I'll be a terror too. But I'll give it my best."

"We'll be here for you, Mary Claire," Charles assured her.

"Thanks, Charles. And I want you to know, there was a time when I might have been doing this to fill in some kind of hole in my life. This feels different. I want a child who really needs a parent, you know? Someone other parents aren't eager to take. That's what it's about for me now. In fact, I'm glad I waited until I could feel this way about it."

"So what pushed you over the edge?" Debra asked her. She and Charles were aware that Mary Claire had been considering this move for some time.

It would be the first time Mary Claire had expressed it even to Katherine. "Actually, it happened the week Helen was here," she said. She looked at Katherine. "It was a moment when the two of you looked at each other, mother and daughter," she said. "That was when I knew for sure."

The visual connection that took place between Katherine and Mary Claire in this moment affected Debra to the point of becoming teary-eyed.

"You're gonna have some great support from all kinds of extended family," Charles said.

"I know," Mary Claire sighed. "And now that I've finally made the decision I can hardly wait for it to happen."

"It's so exciting," Debra remarked. "I can hardly wait too."

Mary Claire stretched back, propping herself on her elbows and fixing again on the trees on the other side of the meadow. In another moment she spoke up again. "You know, I don't ever look at a tree now that I don't think of what you said in your book." She glanced at Katherine. "About our connection to light. That if we knew how many light receptors there are on a single tree we'd be in absolute awe of them. What did you say they were? 'Veritable monuments to light'?"

"It's true," Katherine said.

Mary Claire was as happy as her friends had seen her. "It's amazing, isn't it?" she continued, "the way nature carves out a smooth green meadow in the middle of such dense foliage."

"An oak opening," Charles said. "That's what they first called Ann Arbor. It was a natural clearing in the trees where they could live and plant without tearing anything down."

"An oak opening," Mary Claire repeated the phrase, enjoying the sound of it.

"Legends say the tribes came from all around and gathered here for councils," he said.

"In Ann Arbor?" Debra asked.

"Before it was Ann Arbor," Charles said.

"And what do you suppose they talked about?" Mary Claire asked thoughtfully.

"Oh, I don't know. Probably the same thing we're still talking about." Charles stretched his arms as he sat up. "How we'll all live together." He began wrapping up their trash from lunch. "Great sandwiches, Mary Claire."

"Yeah? As good as Ali Baba, Charles?" she asked in fun.

"I swear he's gonna turn into a falafel sandwich one of these days," Debra said.

As they walked the winding path back through the Arb, Katherine and Mary Claire fell slightly behind Charles and Debra. They shared a covert grin as they observed the couple ahead of them.

"Together all these years and they still hold hands," Mary Claire said.

"The original 'virtual pair,' " Katherine said.

The "virtual pair" was one astrophysical metaphor with which Mary Claire was keenly familiar. "Avery really is from outer space, isn't he," she tittered.

Debra raised her voice as she called back to Katherine, "So, how is Lloyd's wife doing?"

"Much better," Katherine said. "He's sure doing better, knowing she's out of the woods."

"They've been together a long time," Debra said.

"I didn't tell you, Charles," Katherine spoke up. "He stopped in my office yesterday to thank me for the flowers. Made a point of telling me how much she appreciated that particular bouquet." Katherine's astonishment came through in her tone. "Felt like a real turning point."

"He knows you care," Debra said.

"Yeah, when it comes to family," Charles said, "that's when we know for sure we're all made of the same stuff."

"I sure saw it in his face," Katherine said.

"And have you heard from David?" Debra asked.

"Got an email yesterday," Katherine said. "He's really looking forward to Mary Claire's party. Said he planned his whole trip around it."

"And he has no idea, right?" Debra said, enjoying the conspiracy. "I can't believe the people you've invited, Mary Claire."

"Well, by the time you add the whole art department and all of his friends," Mary Claire emphasized. "We'll just have to be our cozy selves."

"And did he have a coronary when you told him you were going to a game?" Charles began expelling guttural sounds. "Can't believe you're actually going to a football game."

"He said he'd believe anything now," Katherine laughed. "He was actually pretty happy to hear all the news. He said, 'So virtual pairs really do happen!' "

Charles was amused. "Ol' Mr. Maize is talking astro-speak now, is he?"

"What's a virtual pair?" Debra asked.

As Charles explained virtual pairs to Debra, Katherine reveled in her own thoughts. She turned to Mary Claire. "Just one of the universe's small miracles," she said.
Mary Claire sighed. "Yeah, and who knows what others are in store." She put her arm around her friend as they continued walking. "Times they are a changin'," she sang out to the group.
"That's one thing we can count on for sure," Charles said.

Back in her office, Katherine scanned her roster of incoming emails while she sorted through the pile of mail on her desk. She noted a message from Nicholas Smuclovsky, her Stanford colleague — the latest installment in their spirited parley regarding their respective theories. As eager as she was to read it, it would have to wait. She had only a few minutes before she would have to leave for her class. She eagerly opened the package on her desk from Melbourne, Australia. Inside was a book from Russell Downie with a small scribbled note inside.

> *Katherine – How wonderful to have a friend I think of every time I see a butterfly! I thought you'd enjoy this description I came across from one of my favorite biologists.*
> *Love to you — and to Michael!" Russ*

It was a small worn paperback. The "95 cents" on the cover gave away its age. *The Biology of the Spirit* by Edmund W. Sinnott. Viking Press, 1955. The cover read: "An eminent modern scientist examines the biological evidence for the existence of the human spirit." She opened to the chapter Russell had marked — "The Metamorphosis of the Butterfly." Her gaze fell to one of the lines on the page:
" 'Here indeed is a miracle of transformation as amazing as any that was ever brought to pass by the waving of a fairy's wand or

a magician's incantation.' " She continued perusing on the next page. " 'Even in the body of the caterpillar there is present the so-called "imaginal bud," which simply bides its time until the hour arrives for it to take its part in the drama of regeneration.' "

She flipped to the title chapter, "The Biology of Spirit," and again allowed her gaze to fall on the page. " 'The man of science finds it hard to reconcile with the spiritual values so deeply planted in his heart. In the inevitable choice we all must make — between a belief in spirit as the supreme reality, and one that finds reality only in tangible, measurable things — our decision comes more often from unreasoned conviction than from rational argument.' "

She smiled at the thought of her Aussie friend. Then she placed the book in her bag along with the letter she had pulled from her pile of mail. It was a hand-addressed envelope from "M. Field" in Chicago. Marisa Field, from her butterfly class. She would be at Georgetown now, she thought. She must have been writing from her family's home in Chicago.

Before leaving her office she stood in the doorway and took in the sight of the sunflowers that towered from the vase on her desk. A warm glow came over her. She was immediately transported to the hills of Yosemite Park, the spot where Cavanaugh had said how much he looked forward to sending her flowers. And how perfect, she thought — Sunflowers. Standing tall in what they know to be true. She could not keep from smiling as she closed her office door.

On her way down the stairs, Bradley Jenkins, the department's star student was on his way up to the physics offices. "Professor Ayers!" he greeted her. Then he breathlessly grabbed a book from his bag and waved it at her. "I got Nicholas Smuclovsky's new book hot off the press," he said. "Have you seen it?"

"Bradley," she said, feigning surprise, "I didn't know you were interested in the Anthropic Principle." She took the book and looked at the title — *Why Are We Here?*

"It's a pretty good question, don't you think?" he asked her. His face betrayed the slightest trepidation as he waited for her response. She looked directly into his eyes. "I can't imagine a better one," she said. Then she smiled at him brightly and was on her way.

"See you later," he called to her.

"Bradley, if I know you, I'll see you sooner," she said.

She heard his laughter resonate in the stairwell.

Crossing the Diag on her way to Haven Hall she opened the letter from Marisa Field. She read as she walked, peripherally observing the bodies moving past her. Gradually she slowed to a stop in the center of campus.

Dear Professor Ayers,

I am writing this letter quickly because my parents have promised to mail it when they return to the States and they are leaving in the morning. I expected to be writing you from Georgetown, but in June I received word that I had been accepted for a Peace Corps assignment here in Togo and I decided to postpone my master's work until I return.

This experience was not an easy one at first. I am the only white person here in a community of about fifty thousand. That alone was a bit of a shock. Katherine pictured the beautiful blonde Marisa standing in front of the class in her butterfly wings. *To be honest, I didn't know if I was going to make it at first. The heat is so oppressive I almost fainted a couple of times. And when my parents saw the bugs I share my quarters with — the size of my fist! — I think my dad had to work hard at not picking me up in his arms and taking me home.*

It's hard to believe but I'm used to it now. And I can honestly say that I have never been happier. It's because of the people here. I've been working with women I have really come to love. They are beautiful people, Professor Ayers. Their faces remind me every day why I am here. I am doing everything I can to help them as they become self-sustaining. And it's funny, because I think I'm the one who is learning the most from this experience. More than anything it's taught me that people all over the world are so much more alike than we ever imagine. And we really do all share a language that has nothing to do with words.

I want you to know, Professor Ayers, how grateful I am to have had you as a teacher. Knowing you has convinced me that teaching is the most important work there is. I hope to see you again one day when I visit U-M. I will always be grateful for my experience there. (I actually saw a guy with a Michigan cap the day I arrived here in Togo. I hollered "Go Blue!" to him and he lit up and said it back.) I wish you all the best with your work, and with your classes this year, and with everything, Professor Ayers. You deserve all the happiness in the world.
Sincerely, Marisa Field.

Katherine wiped a tear from her cheek before she entered the lecture hall. The flock of students were all taking their seats. She put down her things, settled on the edge of the desk and smiled as she began perusing their faces. Their guileless inspection of her was unaffected by her direct observation of them. Soon they were all sitting silently waiting for her to speak. She deliberately waited another moment.

"So, why study butterflies?" she asked them.

The students looked at her, their eyes searching.

*Other books by
Christine Mary McGinley*

The Words of a Woman:
A Literary Mosaic

Detecting the Gleam of Light:
Thoughts for the
Aspiring Creative Writer

The Understanding of Good: Thoughts
on Some of Life's Higher Issues
By Jeanne de Vietinghoff
Translated by Ethel Ireland Helleman
Edited and Introduced by
Christine Mary McGinley

For more information:
GleamOfLightPress.com

Book design by Joanne Morgan